I0732651

Summer People

Summer People

ELENA GRAF

PURPLE HAND PRESS

Purple Hand Press
www.purplehandpress.com

This is a work of fiction. Names, characters, places and incidents are the product of the author's imagination or used fictitiously, and any resemblance to actual persons, living or dead, businesses, institutions, companies, events, or locales is entirely coincidental.

Trade Paperback Edition
ISBN-13 978-1-953195-09-8
Kindle Edition
ISBN-13 978-1-953195-10-4
ePub Edition
ISBN-13 978-1-953195-11-1

Cover photo by Aleksandar Georgiev
Editor: Elaine Mattern

08.26.2023

*In the midst of winter, I found there was,
within me, an invincible summer.*
—Albert Camus

1

Kneeling on the deck, Liz Stolz carefully planed the beveled edge. Her boat had been out of winter storage for months, but she was only now getting to the work it needed. Since March, she'd spent every free weekend giving COVID shots in an old racetrack converted into a mass-vaccination clinic. When the call went out to the medical community, Liz had been one of the first to volunteer. She never minded giving up her free time for a cause she supported, and she was glad to be away from home while her ex-wife finished packing her things.

The divorce had been settled quickly, but it seemed to take forever for Maggie to locate the possessions accumulated over their seven-year marriage and the six-decade lifetime that had preceded it. Maggie kept things because she needed physical anchors for her memories—watercolor paintings of Acadia National Park, her daughters' report cards, playbills from long-ago productions, jars of sea glass and pretty shells.

Liz had let Maggie take everything she wanted rather than haggle, but she'd asked for time to scan the photographs from their college days. Liz had burned all her mementos from that time. Maggie had kept hers in a lidded box, transported from home to home, carefully stored wherever she'd landed. Among its treasures was the perfect pink rose that young Liz had given Maggie after an argument. When Liz tried to lift the dried flower out of the box, its fragile petals crumbled.

You can't go back, only forward.

While she'd been thinking about Maggie, Liz had removed too much wood from the back of the board. The gap annoyed her. She liked precision in everything she did, but the hatch cover only needed to be tight enough to keep out a downpour or a direct hit by a wave.

"Am I the first one here?" asked a familiar voice. Whether she was speaking or singing, Lucy Bartlett's soprano was distinctive. "Where is everyone?" she asked, clutching her sundress for modesty while she climbed aboard.

"They're coming later. I wanted some time alone with you." Liz put down her plane and brushed the fine shavings off her jeans.

"Don't get up," Lucy said, leaning on Liz's shoulder. "I can see you're busy." She held onto the wide brim of her sun hat as she bent for a kiss. To Liz's surprise, Lucy's lips landed on hers. Since that kiss last summer, they'd mostly avoided kissing on the mouth. Liz wondered what had changed while Lucy was in New York.

"What are you making?" asked Lucy, taking off her sunglasses to see better. "That wood is beautiful."

"It's mahogany left over from that armoire Sam and I built for Olivia. It resists decay, so it's good for boat parts. I'm making a new hatch cover." Liz held the boards together to show the fit. "The boards are beveled on the edges to fit snugly and keep out the rain." Lucy ran her finger along the glass-smooth edge. "Careful, it's sharp!"

Lucy picked up the tool Liz had been using. "What is this thing?"

"A block plane, one of many I have in my tool chest. I have literally thousands of dollars invested in tools I will never use."

"Looks like you're using it now, or am I missing something?"

"Such a smart ass."

"Hey, is that any way to talk to someone you haven't seen for weeks?"

"No, it's not," Liz admitted. "I really missed you."

Lucy trailed her fingertips down Liz's cheek. "I missed you too." She planted another soft kiss on Liz's lips.

When Liz stopped smiling like a fool, she asked, "Is it official now?"

"Yes! The dissertation committee approved my proposal, and Spangler will be my advisor. My comps are scheduled for next month, and they accepted all my theology credits from my master's program. That could end up saving me almost a year of coursework." Lucy combed her fingers through her red hair before repositioning her hat and tightening the cinch cord to secure it against the wind. "I never knew it would be this hard when I signed up, but Erika kept saying I should."

"And she was right."

"I really want to write this book, and having those extra letters after my name will give it more credibility."

"Well, maybe. How often will you have to go down to the city?" Liz, who'd grown up in the nearby suburbs, still called New York, "the city," as if it were the only one. Lucy understood, having lived in Manhattan when she'd studied at Juilliard and during her opera career.

"It depends on the class," Lucy explained. "Some classes will be completely remote. I'll probably have to appear in person at least one week every semester, maybe more. I have to go back at the end of June to turn in all my papers and sit for orals. Until then, I need to study like a fiend."

"Not like you don't have anything else to do," said Liz, getting up to open a sling chair, so Lucy could sit down. "It's a good thing you have Tom as backup."

"It's a good thing I have Tom, period. Without an associate rector with his experience, I never would have considered going back to school." Lucy took a tube of sunscreen out of her canvas tote bag and squirted a thick, white snake down each arm.

"Good girl," said Liz, watching Lucy rub in the cream. "I don't want to remove any more pre-cancerous lesions from your skin. Put some on your face too."

"My makeup has the highest-level sunblock they make, and it covers my freckles too. What more could I ask for?"

"Someone to do a full-body inspection on a regular basis."

"My doctor does that now."

"She would do it more often if you'd let her." Liz wiggled her eyebrows to emphasize the lewd suggestion.

The smile in Lucy's green eyes went flat, instantly wilting Liz's grin. "And you were being so good," Lucy said in a disappointed tone.

"Old habits are hard to break."

"Liz, my love for you is not a joke," said Lucy sternly. "I take it very seriously, and I hope you do too."

"Of course, I do!"

Lucy reached out to touch her shoulder. "Oh, Liz. I hate to be a scold. I hate it as a priest. I hate it as a mother, and you can be darn sure, I hate it in my love life! Please, don't put me in that position."

Lucy's continued stare made Liz uncomfortable, so she picked up another board and inspected the edge. "If you love me, why are you making me wait?" she mumbled.

"I'm not *making* you, Liz. We talked about it, and you agreed…willingly, I might add. We're *both* waiting, and you know why. It's only been five months since Erika died. You don't just snap back from losing a spouse. Grief takes time."

"How much time?" Liz asked, knowing Lucy's answer would be vague.

"Everyone's different. Some people in my bereavement group still show up years after the death of a spouse."

"They're probably lonely and come for the social interaction."

"I try to weed those people out and ask them to move on. Otherwise, the group gets too big. If they stay more than a year, I usually send them for individual therapy."

"And what about you?"

"I've been seeing Gloria Parrish."

"That shrink who talked Maggie into leaving me?"

"Please don't call her a 'shrink,' Liz. It's disrespectful. And, yes, she's the same therapist Maggie was seeing, but we don't talk anyone into doing anything. We listen and ask questions and help people decide for themselves." Lucy sighed. "You're mourning your own losses—your marriage, your mother's death, losing your best friend. You'd probably benefit from seeing someone."

"No," replied Liz bluntly. "*No* shrinks." She could read Lucy's frustration in her eyes and the furrow between her auburn brows. The permanent frown lines were the only wrinkles in her otherwise youthful face. They'd grown noticeably deeper since her wife's death.

"Liz, you play the stock market," said Lucy. "Think of waiting as an investment. If we rush things now, before we're ready, it could ruin our future. Look what happened when you rushed into marrying Maggie."

"You should talk. You rushed into marrying Erika."

Lucy gazed into the harbor. "Good thing too. Turns out we had no time to lose."

"You didn't know about the aneurysm when you married her. You thought you'd spend the rest of your lives together."

"And we did…. The rest of Erika's life. Our time together was a gift."

"I guess it helps to be religious and think everything happens for a reason."

Lucy stared at her. "You know that's not what I think. Liz, what's with you today? You sound out of sorts."

While Liz thought about the question, she made a big show of taking apart the plane to blow out the swarf and reset the blade.

"Liz?" Lucy prodded. She reached out and lifted Liz's face by the chin. "Look at me."

"It's not fair. Erika was only sixty-two. She was a decent, generous person. She didn't have an easy start in life growing up in East Germany, but she worked her way up to be the best in her field. Her students loved her. Her friends loved her…I loved her. She didn't deserve to die so young."

"It has nothing to do with what we deserve, Liz. You're a doctor. You know better. It wasn't punishment. It's just what happened."

"Don't you get angry with God? I would…if I believed in Him."

"Her," Lucy corrected.

"Whatever," said Liz in a sullen tone. She felt Lucy's eyes on her, so she deflected. "Put sunscreen on your legs and feet too."

"I did already," said Lucy. "You weren't paying attention. Why are you so cranky today?"

Liz looked up. "I'm sorry. Do I seem cranky?"

"Yes."

Liz thought about it for a moment. "I'm frustrated. I missed you so much while you were away. I couldn't wait for you to come back. I wanted to call every day, but you'd asked me not to."

Lucy sighed. "I know, Liz. But you need to give me time. Please. I love you. Please be patient." She reached out her hand. Liz eyed it for a moment before taking it. "Let's enjoy this beautiful day with our friends," said Lucy. "All right?"

"Yes, fine," Liz agreed, but her tone was still surly. She wondered why she allowed Lucy to win every argument when she would debate anyone else to the death. That was the definition of a compelling argument, as Erika had frequently reminded her. "An argument so powerful and well-reasoned that one either believes it or drops dead. Of course, that's not original to me. Rorty said it first. People were always saying outrageous things in those days." Liz smiled. Sometimes, she heard Erika's voice in her head as if she were sitting right beside her instead of lying in the churchyard at St. Margaret's.

And you were one of those people saying outrageous things, Liz thought. *Remember the time you told off Peter Unger? That was priceless!*

And very satisfying, to be sure!

"Liz, is there anything I can do to help you get ready?" Lucy asked, interrupting Liz's mental conversation with Erika.

"Not really. I staged the drinks and snacks in the cabin. It's too windy up here. If you want wine, there's an open bottle of sauvignon blanc in the fridge downstairs."

"I'll wait for the others. Who's coming?"

"Olivia and Sam. Tom and Jeff. Cherie and Brenda are going hiking today. They discovered a new trail that's supposedly Hobbs' best kept secret." Liz added in a dramatic Greta Garbo imitation: "They want to be alone."

"Well, they're newlyweds. What do you expect?"

"It's black-bear season. I hope they don't get a surprise while they're humping in the woods…or come back full of ticks I have to extract."

Lucy laughed. "I doubt the Hobbs police chief is so desperate she needs to have sex in the woods."

"Sometimes it's fun to have a change of venue."

Lucy nudged Liz with her sandaled foot, her bright-red toenails instantly getting Liz's attention. "I'll have to remember you said that." Liz didn't respond, so Lucy nudged her again.

"Cut it out, Lucy. I'm trying to behave, so I don't get yelled at again."

"Who's yelling? What did I miss?" said a hearty male voice. Tom Simmons' gray head popped up over the deck rail. He climbed into the boat, followed by a tall, slender man with a shaved head. Tom was wearing sandals and shorts, despite the cool temperature. Jeff White, Tom's partner, was more sensibly dressed in jeans and a windbreaker.

"Aren't you pushing it a little, Thomas?" asked Liz, glancing at his sturdy legs covered with wiry, white hair. "It's not even Memorial Day, and you're in shorts already?"

Tom glanced down at his shorts and wiggled his toes in his sandals. "Liz, you're the one who told me the men up here wear shorts all year."

"They do. That doesn't mean you need to be as stupid as the rest of them. It's going to be cold out on the water today. There's quite a wind."

Tom held a canvas bag aloft. "A change of clothes."

"Stow your bags below and help yourself to drinks while you're at it."

"No COVID shots today?" Tom asked, setting down his bag.

"Demand is slowing, so they asked most of the volunteers to stop coming. Rumor has it they'll close down the clinic soon." Liz slipped her plane into its leather case and put it into her tool bag. "I think this project will have to wait for another time."

Jeff stuck his head out of the cabin. "Can I bring up drinks for anyone? There's an open bottle of sauvignon blanc on the door. Is that for something special?"

"That's Lucy's wine," said Liz.

"Oh, Mother Lucy," said Tom, bowing, his hands prayerfully pressed together, "may I have a glass too?"

"Of course. It's not my personal wine. Anyone can have it. Right, Liz?"

"Right, and there's more where that came from. If someone wants to be helpful, he can open another bottle and put it in the fridge." Liz swept up where she'd been working and threw the shavings over the side.

"You throw your dirt into the harbor?" scolded Tom.

"It's just wood shavings. Biodegradable." Liz stowed the broom and dust pan. "It's time to get this party underway. The boat, too, if Sam and Olivia will ever get here. I told them I'm leaving at two, with or without them."

Tom pulled his phone out of his pocket. "They have five minutes to spare. Give them time."

"They're probably home in bed fucking their brains out," said Liz.

"Liz!" said Lucy, raising a brow.

"Oh, Lucy, it's a losing battle," Tom said. "I've known Liz for over forty years. She's always had a potty mouth. You'll never reform her. Believe me. Everyone's tried."

Liz turned to Tom's partner for sympathy. "Jeff, please remind me never to invite these priests aboard *The Wet Lady* again."

Jeff laughed. "Tom is my ticket, so I guess you'll have to invite him if you want me to come along."

"But I don't have to invite the redhead. She's nothing but trouble." Lucy offered a radiant smile in response, which Liz ignored. "I should warm up the engine. It's probably still a little sluggish after all those months in storage." She made a little bow. "Thank you all for coming out on *The Wet Lady's* maiden voyage of the season. Hopefully, we don't get stuck out there."

"You're not really worried, are you?" asked Tom anxiously.

"Nah. They gave it a tune-up and replaced the plugs." The engine put out a little smoke but turned over on the first try. The entire deck rumbled briefly before the engine fell into its rhythm and idled smoothly.

"Don't leave without us!" Olivia called dramatically as she climbed up the ladder. "I brought food and wine!" Tom reached down to help her with her bags. "There's more," said Olivia. "Samantha is right behind me."

Jeff reached down and brought up more bags. "Whatever you have in here, it smells good…really good."

"That's my chicken satay. I hope you like it, Jeff."

"Peanut sauce?"

"You bet."

A tall woman with short brown hair put her long legs over the rail. She waved to the others.

"Sam, about time you got here," said Liz. "Can you help me cast off?"

"Sure thing. I'll take the back."

"You mean, the stern."

"Yes, the stern. You can always tell new boaters," Sam said, rolling her eyes. "They have to show off to impress people."

"Thanks, Sam. I thought you were my friend."

"I am your friend," Sam said with a grin. "Liz, it's your day off. Relax." She patted the air for emphasis.

2

In her mind, Lucy heard Liz's lectures on protecting electronics as she crawled under the desk to look for an open slot in the power strip. "The weather in Maine is crazy. You don't want to fry all your hard work." Her favorite tech head had also given her a portable hard drive, but Lucy didn't need anyone to tell her that she needed to back up her files. She had all her sermons on her laptop, not that she'd ever think of reusing them, but sometimes they were useful for inspiration. Now, she also had her doctoral dissertation on the computer, so she needed to be more careful.

Moving into Erika's office was much harder than she'd expected. Lucy hadn't changed a thing since her wife had died. When Ellie, the housekeeper, dusted and cleaned, Lucy insisted that everything be returned to exactly where she'd found it. Raised in the spartan environment of the impoverished GDR, Erika had never been one for clutter. There was a picture of Erika's parents on the desk along with a wedding picture showing Erika and Lucy in their white bridal gowns. Beside it, was a framed photo of Erika and Liz on vacation in Italy almost forty years ago.

Otherwise, the desk was bare except for a lamp with compartments for writing implements, paperclips, and a note pad. Lucy took out the pad to look at Erika's familiar handwriting with its strong, decisive letters, uniform in shape—the square penmanship they'd taught in German schools after the war. The note Erika had written was a reminder to pick up pearl barley for soup. It was the last meal she'd ever cooked.

When Lucy had come up to bed that night and found Erika unresponsive, she'd called Liz even before dialing 911. Brenda had arrived minutes later, responding to the call over her police scanner. They'd stayed with Lucy while she'd helplessly watched the EMTs strap her wife's motionless body onto a stretcher and carry her away. Because of the COVID restrictions, Lucy couldn't ride in the ambulance, so Liz had driven her to the hospital—too fast, as usual. During the winter surge, the emergency department had banned visitors. Bundled together in an old quilt Liz kept in her truck for winter breakdowns, they'd waited in the January cold for news of Erika's condition. When it came, it was devastating.

Lucy's heart ached as she sat down behind the desk where Erika had sat to write her last book. Liz had read the nearly complete draft and suggested sending it to Colby, where Erika had taught. "I'm no expert on Hegel, and neither was Erika, but this is an interesting take on his political thinking. Maybe someone in the philosophy department can edit the manuscript for publication." That was something else Lucy meant to get around to doing, but there was so much involved in settling the estate. Fortunately, Liz, the executor, had been handling most of the details.

The mesh seat of the desk chair was too high. Erika had been a head taller than her diminutive wife. Lucy let a little air out of the pneumatic lift so that her feet could rest flat on the floor. Before she opened her laptop, she gazed at the bookshelves lining the walls. This was the library of the world's greatest Habermas scholar. Like most philosophical specialties, it was an esoteric niche. "A much needed lacuna in the literature," Erika had often said, quoting the old joke that made sense only to graduate students and academics. Lucy had once tried to read one of Erika's books but had found it impenetrable. Admittedly, theoretical subjects weren't Lucy's strength. No wonder Professor Spangler looked so surprised when Lucy appeared at his door and said she wanted to do a PhD in theology.

"You always seemed less interested in theory than practice, Lucy. I assumed if you went on for a doctorate it would be in pastoral counseling."

"I already have a license in psychotherapy, so I don't need it."

"But, Lucy, is this your strong suit?" Spangler asked, sitting back in his chair. His calm, gray eyes probed Lucy's until she wanted to squirm. Not that he ever did anything to intimidate her, but he was a world-famous theologian. Lucy had looked up to him since divinity school.

"I've developed a deeper appreciation for theory from my wife."

"If anyone knows how to make theory accessible, it's Professor Bultmann. Her PBS interviews on the political situation are brilliant." Erika was still alive then, at the center of conversations about how political discourse had been degraded. The attention she was getting from the media made many academics jealous, but Lucy detected no envy in Spangler's voice. He smiled and got down to business. "As I wrote in my email, your ideas are very original, but any book about sex is going to be controversial. You'll probably be incinerated in the reviews. Are you sure you're ready for this, Lucy?"

"Who better to talk about physical love as an expression of God's love than a survivor of rape?"

Spangler's eyes widened at the mention of the word. "I'm so sorry, Lucy. I didn't know."

"Not many people do, and if it weren't for a special person, someone who thought I was worth saving, I might not be sitting here wearing this collar. In fact, I'm not sure I'd be sitting anywhere."

"Was it that bad?" he asked, his eyes clouding with concern.

"It was a very difficult recovery. There were times when I didn't think I'd make it. But I was pregnant, and if I took my life, I'd take two. I couldn't do that any more than I could have an abortion."

"Can you tell me about it?" he asked gently. When Lucy hesitated, he added, "I understand it's difficult. You certainly don't have to tell me."

"My testimony about the rape will be part of this book, but I'll tell you the short version."

Spangler assumed what Lucy had come to know as his pastoral face— open, interested, and patient.

Lucy took a deep breath before she began. "I was at the height of my career as a singer with engagements all over the world. My agent was embezzling from me, small amounts at first, but then he got bold. To cover his tracks, he stopped paying my taxes."

"That's terrible, but I've heard of it happening to other performers."

"It's actually more common than people think. I had to sue him to get my money back. Someone at the Met, a high-profile director and producer, offered to help me, but he had an ulterior motive. He wanted a sexual relationship. I wasn't interested, so he forced himself on me. I complained to the Met management, but they took his side, although my complaint against him wasn't the first. He tried to pay me off to shut me up. When I found out I was pregnant, I used the money to get away from New York. I didn't want him to know I'd conceived a child from the rape and get involved. I went to a remote village upstate, where I gave birth to a daughter and put her up for adoption. It was selfish, I know, but I'd been preparing for an operatic career my entire life, and I wasn't ready to give it up."

While she'd been speaking, Spangler had maintained a mostly dispassionate expression, but his eyes had widened with each sordid revelation. "But you did give it up."

"Not voluntarily. I tried to make a comeback, but my rapist had me blacklisted at the Met. I went to Europe and sang in the big houses. The City Opera offered me parts, but never the Met. As my career sputtered, I became progressively more depressed. I let my voice go. Then I couldn't get engagements anywhere. People wrote it off to early burn-out, another promising singer who'd peaked too early. When I was at my lowest point, a friend from Juilliard called to ask me if I would sing with her. The gig was an ordination at St. John the Divine. That's how I met someone who helped me get my life back." Lucy wondered if he would make the connection with Susan Gedney. They'd taken his class together. He knew they were close friends. "Professor, do you believe that people come into our lives for a reason?"

"I don't believe in direct intervention. I believe God created the world and handed it over to his creation to manage…for good or ill." Spangler smiled. "You know what I believe, Lucy. I spent a whole semester lecturing on this subject."

"I remember it well."

"Lucy, I admire your bravery, but this is a very personal story. Are you sure you want to expose yourself in your book?"

"I'm sure. Telling our painful stories can help others heal. Sometimes, it can help *us* heal."

Spangler gave her a long, thoughtful look. "Lucy, I have to admit that when you were in my class, I wondered about you—a retired opera star who wants to be a priest? I didn't always take you seriously, but I do now."

"I'm going to need a lot of support to be worthy of your confidence, Professor."

"Jerry," he said warmly, "Call me Jerry."

Lost in her memory of the conversation, Lucy hadn't noticed her phone flashing. She'd put the ringer on mute during her afternoon counseling sessions and forgotten to turn it back on. The photo on the screen showed a handsome, gray-haired woman caught in a rare, full smile. Lucy swiped open the call. "Hello, Dr. Stolz."

"Johnston's has seared scallops on special." Liz never said, hello, as if a greeting would waste too much time.

"Liz, I have to study for my class tomorrow, and I've barely written half a chapter since I got back from New York."

"I can pick up dinner and bring it over to you," said Liz in a tantalizing tone.

Lucy sighed because the offer sounded so appealing. "No, if you're here, it will be too much distraction."

"Distraction?" Liz was grinning. Lucy could hear it in her voice.

"I meant temptation."

"Does that mean we can never be alone together?" asked Liz anxiously.

"No, it means I'm feeling a little weepy today, so I'm more vulnerable to someone with strong arms and a soothing voice."

"Hmm. That's the first time someone's called my voice soothing, but I'm always happy to give you a shoulder to cry on."

"Never mind. It might be good for me to get out of here. I'm using Erika's office for the first time. It's hard."

There was a long silence. "I'm sure it is."

"How about I meet you there?" Lucy proposed. "Six thirty?"
"Perfect."

As usual, Liz hung up without saying goodbye. Lucy put down her phone and realized that Liz had called instead of texting. The change in behavior began during the bad patch last winter, when Lucy had let the messages pile up in her inbox. People had started calling because it was the only way to get her attention. *Good*, she thought, *it's nice to hear a human voice instead of reading words in a little blue bubble.* As a therapist, she always preferred to hear the caller's voice because it told her so much about their mental state.

Lucy thought about what to wear, reluctant to change out of her yoga pants and the worn T-shirt Erika had given her to wear to bed. Going out also meant putting on a bra. Lucy was too big to ever go braless in public. Besides, that would encourage too much attention from Liz, who never seemed to get enough of looking at that part of her anatomy. Lucy checked the weather app on her phone to see if it was warm enough for a sundress.

She managed to write a few more pages before she had to leave. Fortunately, she was driving away from traffic because the summer people, desperate to escape the cities after a year of confinement, were already arriving in Hobbs. Johnston's was on the other side of town. It was an old-style, family restaurant only the locals knew. When Lucy had first arrived in Hobbs, Liz's wife, a trained chef, had shown her all the best out-of-the-way eateries where authentic, local food was served.

Lucy had been genuinely sad when Maggie and Liz split up, but as a marriage counselor, she knew that even the strongest marriages could fail when the partners changed and grew apart. Sometimes, it was better for spouses to part amicably than grow to hate one another. Talking to Tom and Gloria Parrish had helped Lucy deal with her part in the end of the marriage. She dearly hoped that Liz could one day forgive Maggie for cheating on her with a man. That was the one thing that Liz claimed she could never forgive, but her love for Maggie ran deep, and they had such a long history. Lucy said a silent prayer for them to heal.

She changed and headed to Johnston's. The restaurant parking lot was full when Lucy arrived, but someone pulled out of a spot right in front. Liz, who was already seated at a picnic table, beamed when Lucy pulled in to park. Liz's expression was so natural in those moments, such a departure from the deliberately calm 'doctor face' she usually wore. It gave Lucy a glimpse into what Liz might have been like when she was young, before her medical training had ground her into a high-performance surgical machine.

Lucy knew how hard Liz had been working to unlearn those negative behaviors—the otherworldly calm that sometimes made her seem indifferent and the confidence that many mistook for arrogance. Liz had been modifying her behavior with exaggerated informality in the office, insisting that people call her by her first name, and wearing hiking clothes in the summer as if she couldn't wait to get out of the office and hit the trail.

"Thank you for coming," Liz said, moving to the center of her bench to balance the weight as Lucy sat down. "I'm hoping we do this more regularly."

"Eat here?"

"It doesn't have to be here. We can eat anywhere you like. Maybe you'll come over and let me cook for you. I am trustworthy, you know. You don't need a chaperone."

"I know, Liz, and I want to spend more time with you, but I need to study…and I still have a day job. Which reminds me, I have to write my sermon tomorrow, and I haven't even looked at the readings." Lucy opened the menu. The scallops sounded good, but she wanted to see what else they were offering.

"I'm coming to church on Sunday," Liz volunteered, which made Lucy look up.

"What brought that on?"

Liz shrugged. "I would have been coming all along. I only stayed away because of Maggie's stupid suspicions."

"Well, they weren't completely stupid. They had some basis in reality, but I thought you only came to hear her sing."

"I only said that so you wouldn't think you could convert me. I came to support you too."

"That's kind, Liz, but I'm the rector, and I've been doing this for a while. I appreciate your good intentions, but I don't need support."

Liz compressed her lips in frustration. "Now, you don't want me to come. When we first met, you kept inviting me even though you knew I'm an atheist."

"That was before I knew how stubborn you are. Now, I know better." Lucy returned to the menu. "If you're coming on Sunday, make sure you make reservations online. Space is limited by the COVID restrictions."

"I really come to watch you do your priest thing."

Lucy looked up and studied Liz's face. In the earnest blue eyes, she saw a veiled emotion she couldn't quite interpret. *What's going on in there?* Lucy wondered.

"My priesthood intrigues you, doesn't it?"

"That's why I come to watch." Liz's grin was the nervous kind meant to cover discomfort.

"I'd be delighted if you came, Liz, but don't do it for me. Do it because you want to."

"I never do anything unless I want to."

3

Liz watched Harriet Keene while she reviewed the trust proposal. After decades as a physician, Liz could read people fairly well. Harriet was trying to be respectful, but she wasn't enthused about the plan.

"I've looked over your proposal and the spreadsheet," Harriet finally said, "but honestly, Liz, all this effort to flip the bird at big medicine? I mean, *really*?"

"Believe me," said Liz, sitting back in her chair. "*Nothing* would give me more pleasure."

"I heard Southern Med is offering you a lot of money."

"Doesn't matter."

Harriet turned to Olivia. "What do you think of this scheme, Ms. Enright?"

"Please, call me Olivia," said Olivia, smoothly slipping into her boardroom persona. "May I call you Harriet?"

"Of course." Harriet seemed charmed by Olivia's practiced smile. Liz wanted to roll her eyes.

"As Liz's financial advisor, I think it ties up too much of her cash in her business. That said, preserving the independence of Hobbs Family Practice is important to her personally as well as to the community. She runs her business efficiently. The economies of scale offered by corporate medicine don't really apply. If the market keeps on this trajectory, the profits from the trust can eventually pay off the loan she's made to the practice and the mortgage on the property. Her partners won't need to worry about buying her out when she retires or be forced to sell to Southern Med. In short, it achieves her objectives."

"I'll be honest," Harriet said, flipping through the paperwork again. "Complicated trusts like this are out of my wheelhouse. I think you need an attorney who specializes in this kind of thing."

"But, Harriet, you've been my lawyer since I moved to Maine," Liz protested.

"That was for real estate transactions and business permits, not complicated trusts like this."

"You handled my divorce."

"A first-year law student could have handled your divorce. That pre-nup divided everything into hers and yours. There was nothing to do except make sure Maggie had the title to her car."

"The pre-nup was your idea," Liz pointed out. "I know I was against it at first, but I'm glad you talked me into it."

"I always advise older people with money that love isn't everything, especially when there are multiple heirs involved." Harriet pursed her lips. "Liz, I hate to disappoint you, but I'm out of my depth here. I think you should talk to Melissa Morgenstern. She specializes in trusts."

"Sounds expensive," said Liz, frowning.

"Maybe, but it's worth it if she gives you good advice. She's out of Boston, but she's visiting her mother for the summer. I helped her parents when they wanted to build a house in the salt marsh. The environmentalists lost their minds."

"I don't blame them," said Liz. "People shouldn't be building in the marsh."

"The town wants more development to help business," Harriet explained, as if Liz, who was president of the chamber of commerce, didn't already know. "After her husband died, Mrs. Morgenstern hired me to deal with the permits, but the town was still giving them trouble. Her daughter wanted to help, so she got herself admitted to the bar in Maine."

"What do you think, Liv?" She glanced in her direction.

Olivia shrugged. "Why not talk to her?"

"She's sharp," Harriet said. "Radcliffe summa cum laude and Harvard law with honors. Smart girl."

"Girl?" Liz repeated with a frown.

"Fortyish."

Olivia nudged Liz's elbow. The silent communication meant, "that's irrelevant. Stay on task."

"All right, Harriet, I'll meet with her, but I still want you to handle it."

"Let me call her and see if we can set something up for this week. Can you wait? I'll call her now."

Liz turned to Olivia while Harriet waited for her call to be answered. "Why is this so complicated? You told me it would be simple."

"It is simple from a financial point of view," Olivia said. "Basically, you're creating an endowment, like I did for St. Margaret's, but Hobbs Family Practice was set up as a for-profit entity."

"Can't I just change it?"

"Maybe, but it's not that simple. For a non-profit, you'll probably need a board of directors. I doubt you want that kind of interference into your practice any more than you want intrusion from big medicine. Besides, why should you limit your profits? You like to make money, don't you?"

Liz slunk down in her seat and crossed her legs. "Whatever happened to being an old-fashioned country doctor?"

Olivia laughed. "You know what happened. Insurance companies. Big pharma. Corporate medicine."

"If I had known, I would have switched professions."

Olivia gave her a skeptical look. "No, you wouldn't. Being a doctor is who you are."

During the sidebar conversation, Harriet's persistent smile led Liz to assume a social connection with the young lawyer beyond professional acquaintance. "Melissa says she's out for a run," Harriet explained, muting the call. "She can stop by now if you can wait."

Liz shrugged. "Sure, why not? It's my day off. How about you, Liv?"

"I took the morning off, anticipating this meeting could run long. No problem."

Finally, Harriet ended the call. "She'll be here in five minutes. She apologizes for being sweaty."

Liz smiled but resisted the impulse to say she didn't mind sweaty women. Since she'd been seeing Lucy, she'd been making a concerted effort to rein in the sexual innuendos. The woman they were about to meet was Gen-X and would probably find suggestive comments offensive. Liz might grumble about needing to reform, but she admired the younger generation for pushing back on sexist remarks and unwelcome overtures. When Liz was coming up through the ranks, women were told to shut up and ignore them.

While they waited for the lawyer to appear, Liz tuned out the conversation Olivia and Harriet were having about the ownership of the beach property. One reason Liz had never bought waterfront property was the entitled attitude of the homeowners.

In case she needed to explain her rationale to the trust lawyer, Liz reflected on how she'd gotten here. She had done all the right things in her career. After med school at Columbia, she'd worked her way up the surgical hierarchy at Yale to become chief and head of the department. Just when she thought she'd finally arrived, the hospital was reorganized under professional 'administrators.'

Then came the malpractice suit. Liz performed a routine lumpectomy on a fading movie star. The woman didn't want to lose her hair, so she refused the chemo and radiation Liz had recommended. When the cancer recurred, she sued. Her celebrity lawyer turned the suit into a publicity stunt, and the story hit the papers, even the tabloids. Months later, the ruling from the medical board made the case too shaky to pursue, but by that point, Liz was disgusted.

She took early retirement from Yale. Jenny, her partner, suggested she open a private surgical practice, but the malpractice insurance premiums turned out to be exorbitant. She was too young to retire, although many high performing surgeons burned out in their fifties and retired to golf resorts. Liz didn't play golf, so that wasn't an option. In a cloud of discouragement, she retreated to Maine, where she'd vacationed for years.

She'd met Tony Roselli, the director of the Webhanet Playhouse, when she'd responded to a "is there a doctor in the house?" request. Over lunch one afternoon, he asked her advice about finding a new doctor. The family practice in Hobbs was shutting down because the retiring doctor couldn't find anyone to replace him.

"Why not?" Liz asked.

Tony rubbed his fingers together. That was the exact moment when Liz decided to move to Maine. Leaving Connecticut meant ending her twenty-year-plus relationship with Jenny and moving out of their enormous, showcase house on Long Island Sound. It also meant spending her free time in special training so she could learn how to treat patients without cutting them open.

"Liz, can you believe it?" Olivia asked, interrupting Liz's retrospective. "The trust lawyer's mother is my neighbor."

"No kidding," Liz said absently.

"Yes, you know that big, gray house down the street."

"That will be Melissa," said Harriet, responding to the knock on the door. She opened it to a tall, willowy woman with long, dark hair and the kind of figure only the young enjoy. Her voltaic blue eyes scrutinized the two women sitting in the visitors' chairs.

Liz got up to shake the newcomer's hand. "Hello, I'm Liz Stolz, Hobbs Family Practice. I'm the one causing trouble here."

The woman laughed. "Creating a trust to preserve your independence isn't trouble. It's smart."

Harriet pulled another visitors' chair out of the corner. The young attorney sat down and crossed her long legs. Liz guessed that she and Melissa were probably about the same height, close to six feet.

"What you see here is two-thirds of the triumvirate that runs Hobbs," Harriet explained to Melissa. "Olivia Enright is the town manager. Dr. Stolz is the managing partner of Hobbs Family Practice."

"Where is the other third?" the young woman asked, looking around.

"That would be the Episcopal rector, Lucy Bartlett," Harriet said. "There's a board of selectmen who think they run things in Hobbs, but it's really these ladies. They pull all the strings behind the scenes. If you want anything done in this town, go to them."

"I see," said Melissa continuing her inspection of Olivia and Liz with shrewd eyes. "Good to know. I'm just one of the summer people, so I try to stay out of local politics."

"But you ran interference when your parents wanted to build that big house in the salt marsh, so you do get involved," said Liz. She smiled but there was a challenge in her tone.

"I'm your neighbor two doors down." Olivia extended her hand. "When my son built the house, he had to throw some money to the planning board. Supposedly, it went to wetlands purchase for the estuarine preserve, but sometimes, I wonder."

Melissa coolly listened to what might be considered hostile comments without a hint of what she thought about them. *She's good,* thought Liz.

"My parents did it by the books and paid for the environmental study before they built. I only got involved because I thought I could help, but I'm keeping my Maine license because someday, I might move up here."

"Really?" asked Harriet, perking up. "But I thought you're a partner in that firm in Boston."

"I am, but the kind of work I do can mostly be done online. I'm hoping we can continue to work remotely once the pandemic ends. I'm going to see how it goes this summer. It's an experiment."

"Well, I hope it works out for you," said Harriet. "I moved here twenty-five years ago and never looked back."

"I'll need the paperwork to review to see how I can help Dr. Stolz," said Melissa.

"I can give it to you now."

Melissa shook her head. "I'm still out on my run. I'll pick it up later, if that's all right."

Harriet smiled. "Of course, dear. Ring the office to make sure I'm here. I can't seem to find a new admin. There's such a labor shortage now."

"It's that extended unemployment," Olivia said, shaking her head. "Who wants to go back to work when you can collect more money staying home?"

"Careful, Olivia. You're showing your Republican stripes." Liz nudged her with her elbow.

"I'm still a Republican," replied Olivia indignantly. "Just not *that kind* of Republican."

Liz could see that the newcomer was uncomfortable with the political banter. "Thanks for interrupting your run. When you've had a chance to review the paperwork, we can set up a time to talk. Meanwhile, I'm sure Olivia can answer any questions you might have about the financials." Olivia nodded agreeably.

"Sounds great," said the young woman, getting up. "Nice meeting you both."

After she left, Olivia got up and tugged Liz's arm. "Come on. Let's let Harriet get back to work."

Harriet collected Liz's copy of the papers into a folder and handed it over with a smile. Obviously, she could hardly wait to get it off her desk.

Liz followed Olivia out to the parking lot. "Nice girl," Liz said, clicking open the doors to her truck.

"Liz, who are you trying to kid?" Olivia said in a sharp tone that made Liz spin around.

"What do you mean?"

"Your eyes practically jumped out of your head when you saw that woman."

"She's very attractive. Don't you admire a pretty woman when you see one?"

"Of course, I do, but I don't drool over her. Liz, you're old enough to be her mother!"

Liz flinched. Usually, Olivia was more tactful. "I'm not interested in the young ones. They're boring."

"That's not how it looked to me."

"Olivia, what are you trying to say?" Liz stood at her full height, which dwarfed the petite woman.

"Don't you *dare* hurt Lucy," Olivia said, wagging her finger under Liz's nose. "If you do, you'll have me to answer to."

Liz's face was flaming. Good thing she had a tan from being on the boat, which would partially hide the blush. "Olivia, I don't appreciate unsolicited advice, but if you feel obliged to offer it, know this. I would *never* hurt Lucy."

"Good. Remember that," Olivia said with a warning look and got into her car.

Liz watched the Lexus drive out of the lot. *Damn*, she thought, *are we that obvious?*

4

Lucy waited to see what Liz would do. Some people waited until the last minute, so Lucy always lingered at the altar rail, trying not to look too eager. She never wanted anyone to feel pressured to come to God's table.

Liz was always a little standoffish when Lucy was in her role as a priest. Erika had been the same way, but she was an agnostic, whereas Liz proudly called herself an atheist. She could go on for hours about Christianity's oppression of women and LGBTQ. The pedophilia scandal, and the racism of the "Christian Wrong," as she called right-wing evangelicals, made her furious. Now, she had the graves of indigenous children in religious schools to rant about. Yet, despite her outspoken views of religion, she kept coming back.

According to Erika, Liz's interest in religion went back to her college days. She'd studied theology before switching her minor to philosophy. Apparently, it was more than youthful curiosity because Liz could knowledgeably argue the fine points of contemporary theology. That didn't surprise Lucy. Liz, a self-described encyclopedia of "useless information," always did a deep dive into any topic that interested her.

Lucy regretted her indifference when Liz said she planned to come to church. Clearly, she had been looking for encouragement, but showing too much interest would only have scared her away. Dealing with her complex personality was a balancing act, but Lucy never doubted her good faith. She'd learned that the most diehard deniers were often the sincerest seekers. Lucy would much rather have an honest atheist in her pews than a bigoted, faux Christian.

Lucy glanced down at the paten holding consecrated hosts and quickly said a prayer for forgiveness. God had commanded her to love her enemies, even when it was hard—especially when it was hard. She looked up and saw a tall figure approaching. As Liz reached out her cupped hands, her blue eyes boldly held Lucy's gaze. Lucy tried to interpret the silent communication. *Was it a challenge? An entreaty? A dare?*

After the liturgy, Lucy was glad that the outdoor fellowship was brief. Although she usually enjoyed catching up with her congregation, it still felt so strained with the need for masks and shouting at people from six feet away. She went into the chapel to hang up her vestments. A voice behind her said, "I promise I'm not spying on you while you undress." Lucy turned around to see Liz, leaning rakishly in the doorway.

Lucy closed the vestment closet. "Good morning, Liz. I see you made it." She reached up for a hug. Liz scooped her into her arms and held her close.

"I stopped by to see if you're joining us on the boat today," said Liz, finally letting her go.

"I'd love to go, Liz, but I really need to study."

Liz's little-girl pout was fetching. "But you're my excuse for Brenda to invite Cherie, and for Sam to invite Olivia."

"Why do they need an excuse to invite their partners?"

"We prefer to hang out while we fish. Partners get in the way."

"In the way of what?" asked Lucy.

Liz looked flustered by the question. "Fishing…among other things."

"Olivia told me she loves to fish, but she stays away, so you and Brenda and Sam can do your butch thing."

Liz made a face. "That's so old-school, but there are certain things that Sam and Brenda and I like to do separately from our lady friends."

"Drinking beer, for example?"

"Well, Brenda has to limit her alcohol intake because of heart meds, so not much beer these days," said Liz, reaching for Lucy's bag. "We've all cut back to support her."

"That's big of you," said Lucy. It sounded too sarcastic. She took Liz's offered arm to make amends.

"I invited someone else too. The new lawyer who's helping me with the Hobbs Family Practice Trust."

"Aren't you worried she'll feel out of place with all the partnered ladies?"

"You're not partnered," said Liz. "Neither am I."

"No, but everyone presumes we will be."

"I'm more worried that she'll feel out of place with all the old ladies, but we need young blood in Hobbs. She says she's thinking of moving up here."

"We certainly need young people in Maine. Too many are moving away."

"Maybe that will change with broadband coming into the northern part of the state. Working remotely is changing everything." Liz handed over Lucy's bag when they reached her car. "Please say you'll come out with us."

"If you promise to bring me home at a reasonable hour. I really have to study."

Liz opened Lucy's car door. "I promise, but I was hoping you'd come over for dinner. I'm making grilled pizza."

Lucy put her bag on the passenger seat and started the engine. "I'd love to, Liz, but what don't you understand about 'I have to study'?"

"I heard you, and I do understand, but I have to catch up on my reading. After dinner, you can study, and I can read. A little dress rehearsal for what life with me might be like."

"All right," said Lucy reluctantly, "if you promise to let me study."

Liz raised her hand. "You have my word."

When Lucy got home, she changed into jeans and a long-sleeved shirt. Covering up meant she would need less sunscreen. If need be, her old jeans could go through the washer on hot water. She'd always found fishing to be a messy activity.

She had an hour before she needed to leave, so she tried to squeeze in some studying. When she finally glanced at the time, she already knew she'd be late.

"Come on, Lucy! We're all waiting on you," Liz called irritably as Lucy raced down the dock. The engine was running. Sam and Brenda were positioned to cast off the lines. Olivia reached down to grab Lucy's canvas bag.

She offered her hand again, and Lucy was surprised to feel herself being lifted up. Olivia's slim build belied a strength no one would ever suspect.

Lucy tried to find her sea legs as the boat started to move. She grabbed the side to avoid losing her balance.

"Whoa there. Need help?" Lucy looked up into brilliant blue eyes.

"Thank you so much," said Lucy. "The skipper is a cowboy."

"So, I see," said the woman. She smiled and offered her hand. "We haven't met. I'm Melissa."

"You're the lawyer who's helping Liz."

The woman smiled as if that amused her. "And you're the parson. Also known as the other third of the triumvirate that runs Hobbs."

"I don't know about that," said Lucy modestly, "but I am the rector of St. Margaret's."

"I know. Your name sounded familiar, so I looked you up on Facebook and found out I was already following you. We're friends through my sister, the reformed rabbi. You worked together on the LGBTQ youth project."

"Oh, my word! You're Rebecca's sister?"

Liz's voice shouted from the pilot house. "Will you two sit *down*, please!"

"I think she wants us to sit down," said Melissa, offering her hand. "Here, let me help you." *She's being attentive because I'm older*, realized Lucy with surprise. Sometimes, people were deferential because she was a priest, especially when she was wearing her collar, but never because they thought she was elderly. The thought was so unnerving Lucy almost didn't hear Melissa's question: "Do you like to fish?"

"I do."

"I don't fish, but I'll use any excuse to be out on the water." Melissa's smile showed almost childlike delight. "It pays to know people with boats."

"It does," Lucy agreed, glancing toward the pilot house, where Liz was talking to Sam and Brenda.

"I also wanted to meet Liz's friends. I always knew there were plenty of gay women in Hobbs, but we're everywhere!"

"There aren't really that many, but we've managed to find one another."

"Hobbs is looking more attractive all the time."

"Are you thinking of moving here?" asked Lucy, even though Liz had already told her.

"Maybe. It depends on whether the firm will agree to let me continue to work remotely."

Liz came down from the pilot house and sat next to them.

"Who's driving the boat?" asked Lucy anxiously.

"Brenda."

"And you trust her to drive your precious *Wet Lady*?"

"Sure. She pilots the police launch all the time." Liz gave Melissa a frankly admiring look. "I see you already met the rector. Be careful. She can make anyone do anything. You'll soon be giving her free legal advice in exchange for her smile. Isn't that right, Mother Lucy?"

"Is this true, Rev. Bartlett?" asked Melissa curiously.

"No, she's just teasing. Liz is a terrible tease."

Liz winked at Melissa, who was indeed a beautiful woman with clear skin devoid of wrinkles, not even fine lines around her eyes. Her bare legs were long and shapely. Her neck was smooth, hardly a crease. Lucy found herself involuntarily touching her own throat. Lately, she'd been using expensive creams guaranteed to turn back time, but she knew there was a tipping point. One day, a woman still looked young. The next, the wrinkles appeared, and the jowls drooped, no matter how many jaw exercises you did or miracle moisturizers you applied.

Lost in her meditation on aging, Lucy hadn't heard a word of the pleasant conversation Melissa and her host were having, but she could tell Liz was enjoying the view. She was a shameless flirt. Fortunately, Brenda called Liz back to the pilot house because she wanted to fish.

Sam and Brenda caught nice sized stripers. Olivia had one on the line, but it got away. By the time, they returned to the harbor, Lucy was sleepy from the ocean wind in her face all afternoon. She wished she hadn't promised Liz she'd come for dinner, but she always tried to keep her word.

"I'll meet you at your house," said Lucy after Liz's guests had left. "I want to go home and take a shower first."

Lucy sat inside the open door of her SUV watching Liz walk to her truck. The lead weights on the fishing line danced in time with her step. She was whistling a tune that sounded faintly Celtic. Lucy took her cheerfulness to mean she was looking forward to their evening together.

Lucy headed to Liz's with an appetite. Liz was known for her grilled pizzas. Erika had tried to replicate them but had never succeeded. "You can't top perfection," Liz had once told her friend with good-natured arrogance as she'd demonstrated once again how to brown the bottom without scorching it.

"I'm hungry as a wolf," Lucy declared when she arrived.

"Sorry to disappoint you, but you're too small to be a wolf. A fox, maybe. Goes with the red hair and your *foxy* looks," said Liz, pouring her a glass of wine. "Come out and keep me company while I grill."

The good smells made Lucy hungry, and a short time later, Liz shoveled colorful pizzas onto their plates. While Lucy ate, she remembered how much she'd enjoyed visiting with Maggie and Liz on that deck when they'd first become friends. Their company had kept Lucy from being lonely during her first winter in Hobbs. She thought sadly of how much she missed Maggie. That fateful kiss had not only destroyed Liz's marriage. It had also deprived Lucy of her best friend and favorite shopping companion.

Lucy thought back to Liz's flirtatious behavior on the boat while she watched her innocently eating her pizza. "Liz, can you be faithful to one person?"

"What?" asked Liz with her mouth full. She finished chewing and swallowed. "Where the hell did that come from?"

"You were flirting with Melissa Morgenstern on the boat."

"I was not!" Liz protested in a righteous voice.

"Yes, you were. You do it so much you probably don't even realize it."

Liz scowled. "What's wrong with looking at an attractive woman? It doesn't mean I have to fuck her. Besides, Melissa is a child. I don't do children."

"She's not a child, Liz. She's at least forty."

"Lucy, what's the real question? Are you asking if I can be faithful to you?"

"Yes, I guess I am."

"Stop worrying. If you and I get together…maybe, I should say, when you and I get together, I will be faithful to you."

Lucy took a sip of wine and studied Liz, who by now had demolished her pizza and sat patiently waiting for Lucy to do the same.

"I'm surprised to hear you say that."

Liz looked mildly insulted. "Why? I know they say you can't trust a cheater. I know that coming on to you while I was married didn't set a good precedent. But if you hadn't stopped me, I would have stopped myself. I keep my word. If I say I will be monogamous, I will be."

"There's more to cheating than having sex."

"I am aware of that. I admit to coveting my neighbor's wife, but I did not commit adultery."

"You're splitting hairs."

"Isn't that what you theologians do?" Liz's eyes were so blue in her tanned face they seemed to twinkle. "Don't they argue about how many angels can dance on the head of a pin?"

Frustrated, Lucy crossed her arms on her chest. "There's such a thing as being emotionally unfaithful."

"If that's the case, every sexual fantasy, even reading a steamy novel or watching porn could be construed as adultery."

"Liz, you have an answer for everything. Sometimes you're too smart for your own good."

"But I am honorable. Remember? I'm your pledged knight."

Lucy reached out and patted Liz's much larger hand. "Yes, you are." Lucy sighed. "Sometimes, I just don't know what to do with you."

Liz insisted on doing the dishes and sent Lucy to study in the living room. Lucy, who'd lived in that house during the lockdown, felt completely at home. Curled up on the sofa with her book, she listened to the sound of dishes clattering in the kitchen. The comforting domesticity reminded her of married life with Erika. She smiled and opened her tablet. Soon, she was deeply into her book.

Liz startled her when she flopped onto the sofa beside her. She flipped open her iPad and got right down to work.

"Maggie told me you read two hours a day for your job," Lucy said.

"Two hours is an exaggeration. I try to read while I'm doing other things, like drinking my coffee in the morning. I listen to audio versions while I walk, but I can't see data and charts, so it's not ideal." She nodded toward Lucy's book. "Get to work. You're supposed to be studying."

The summary of recent Anglican theology was helpful but dry. Watching Liz read was much more interesting. Liz's finger flicked across the screen, turning pages at an amazing rate.

"I wish I could read that fast," said Lucy. "What are you reading?"

"An article about clots in COVID patients who have recovered. What are you reading?"

"I'm reading Katherine Sonderegger. She's a systemic theologian, who believes the unity of God is more important than the concept of the Trinity."

Liz shrugged. "The Trinity is an obvious rip-off of Plotinus. Shameless plagiarism."

"Liz, I know you're not a believer, but please try to be respectful."

"I am being respectful. I'm simply stating a fact."

Lucy remembered Liz's strange expression that morning. "What was going on with you during communion? You looked so strange, almost like you were afraid of me."

Liz compressed her lips as she thought about Lucy's question. "I still can't figure out how I feel about the priest thing. It's weird, and it does scare me a little."

"Why?" Lucy put down her book, so she could pay attention.

"I'm afraid you'll touch me with your priest's hands and I'll become…a flesh-eating zombie!" Liz's serious expression gave way to a grin.

"Liz!"

Liz's grin faded. "I don't understand, and I'm not usually frightened by what I don't understand. Instead, I research it and think about it until it makes sense to me. But no matter how hard I think about you and your faith, I just don't get it. That gives you power over me, which is scary."

Lucy frowned, trying to discern the implications of Liz's words. "You're frightened by my faith, but you still find it attractive?"

"Drawn to it like moth to flame, but I'm trying to avoid being incinerated."

Lucy studied Liz's face and realized she wasn't joking or being ironic. She was articulating something she felt deeply.

Liz moved closer and pulled Lucy's bare feet into her lap. "You're supposed to be studying. I don't want to get blamed for distracting you, or you won't come back. Here, this should relax you." She began to massage the ball of Lucy's foot.

"Oh, that feels so good. Now, I'll never be able to concentrate."

"Ignore me and enjoy it," said Liz. She picked up Lucy's book and handed it back to her. "Read," she ordered.

Lucy couldn't ignore Liz's strong fingers kneading the muscles in her foot. After Liz finished one foot, she moved to the other. It felt so good that Lucy was mesmerized with pleasure. Then Liz's finger insinuated itself between her big toe and its neighbor and moved back and forth suggestively.

Lucy snatched her foot back. "Liz!"

Liz laughed. "Hey, no sex. I have to get my feels some way."

"You're so bad."

"That's why you love me. You're attracted to bad girls."

"No, I love you because you're good. You're loving, and kind, and generous..."

"Lucy, you're blowing my cover." Liz hid her face with her hands and peeked through her fingers.

Lucy tickled Liz's armpit with her toes. "You *want* your cover blown. You want someone to see you, the *real* you."

Liz caught Lucy's foot and held it tightly. "Stop. I'm ticklish."

"Hey, no sex. I have to get my feels some way."

Liz's warm hand, holding her foot, felt good and sexy, but also reassuring. "Liz, will you hold me? Hold me…like you held me in your truck while we were waiting to hear about Erika."

Liz made a face. "Why would you want to go back to that awful night?"

"I don't. I just miss being held. Don't you?"

"Yes," Liz admitted with a faraway look in her eyes. "I do."

Liz nudged her to sit up and put her arm around her. Lucy nuzzled against Liz's breast. Below the perfumy laundry soap, she could smell Liz's scent. It was different from Erika's, more solid somehow because the business of Liz's life put her squarely in the physical world. She smelled so real.

5

Melissa watched her mother methodically prepare her coffee as she did every morning, adding two sugars and a splash of half-and-half. Ruth brought her cup to the sunroom to enjoy the panoramic view of the salt marsh. She had fallen in love with the picturesque location on a vacation in Maine, and her husband, who'd adored her, had fought with the town for the right to build there for almost five years. Unfortunately, he hadn't lived to enjoy it.

After he'd died, his wife had aged dramatically, growing grayer and more stooped by the day. Ruth was only a year older than Liz Stolz, and Melissa couldn't help but compare them. The town doctor could jump up and down the levels of her boat deck like a woman half her age. She radiated energy, whereas Ruth lacked interest in anything but sitting on the beach or shopping at the Kittery outlets. Of course, she'd been lonely since losing her husband, but the isolation of the pandemic had turned her grief into soul-stealing depression. Melissa had hoped that spending the summer with her mother would help lift her spirits. So far, it wasn't working.

"You're up early this morning," Ruth said as Melissa brought her coffee to the table.

"I have a meeting with Liz Stolz at seven," Melissa explained, gazing out the window. Like the sea that fed it, the marsh looked different every day. In the morning sun, the sea grass was multiple shades of green. A crane high-stepped through the tall grass like a dressage horse.

"How was the boat trip?" Ruth asked.

"It was fun. I met most of the movers and shakers in town, the 'town mothers' I guess you could call them. I met your neighbor, Olivia Enright. She's the town manager, you know."

"I don't bother with local politics," her mother said with a dismissive wave. "It's so petty."

"Did you know your neighbor runs this town?" asked Melissa, as much to check her mother's mental state as to make conversation.

"I know she's a crook. She was involved in that insider-trading scheme."

"Her son did the illegal trading."

"But they investigated her too."

"Yes, because it was her company. She sold her interest in the company and stepped down as CEO to avoid any suggestion of fiduciary malfeasance."

"It proves she's guilty."

"It proves she's a smart woman, who does the right thing. Unfortunately, she got punished for it. A man probably would have gotten away with it."

"Stop with the feminist silliness. You and your sister," Ruth complained. "I knew your father shouldn't have talked to you about politics so much."

"I loved when Daddy talked to me about politics. I learned so much from him. So did Becca."

Ruth made a sour face.

"I should introduce you to Olivia and the others," said Melissa. "I bet you'd like them."

"What do I want with a bunch of old dykes?" When she'd returned from the boat trip, Melissa had referred to the women she'd met as "an interesting bunch of old dykes." She'd meant it as a back-handed compliment, but now, her mother had twisted it into an insult. "I have two children. Both are gay. How can this be?" said Ruth, shaking her head.

Melissa sighed. This was old ground, so she sipped her coffee and kept her mouth shut.

Ruth got up and glanced toward the kitchen. "You want a bagel? Your sister brought all that lox from Zabar's."

"We should freeze some of it."

"If you'd eat more, we wouldn't have to."

"I can't this morning. I'm seeing Liz Stolz."

"Why? Are you sick?"

"No, it's legal business. All the small family practices are being gobbled up by big health networks. Dr. Stolz is trying to keep her practice independent."

"That's good. It's nice to get an appointment when I'm sick. Imagine that? I see her partner, Dr. Pelletier, but I hear that Stolz is a good doctor. I heard she was famous before she came to Maine."

"She was chief of surgery at Yale New Haven. Her book on breast cancer made her a celebrity."

"So, why is she practicing medicine in a little town in Maine?"

"Obviously, because she loves it." Melissa pulled her phone out of her pocket to check the time. "Gotta go, Mom." Melissa bent to kiss her mother on the cheek. "See you later."

The trust proposal, sitting in a manila envelope on the passenger seat, was very much on Melissa's mind while she sat in the bumper-to-bumper traffic on Route 1. Dr. Stolz's cover letter was so logical and succinct it could have been written by an attorney, but Melissa was particularly impressed by the closing argument, which was full of passion for community medical practice. At a time when medicine had become a faceless, corporate machine, this was a project she could get behind.

She was surprised when the doctor had said she wanted to meet at the Hobbs Diner. Melissa had always dismissed the place as a tourist trap. When she arrived, the line of waiting customers snaked out the door into the parking lot. Melissa elbowed her way inside to see if there was a waiting list. Her phone vibrated in her pocket.

"Don't worry about the line," said the voice when she answered. Melissa realized it was Liz Stolz's voice. "Paula will show you where to go."

"Who's Paula?"

"The counter waitress. She has bright red hair like the Queen of Hearts in *Alice in Wonderland*. Can't miss her."

The call clicked off. Melissa pushed through the crowd to the counter. The red-haired waitress, who was slapping down paper placemats as new diners sat down, tilted her head to show the direction. "Doc's back there. Turn right after you step down."

Melissa walked through the dining room, amazed to see how things had instantly snapped back to normal since the restrictions had been relaxed.

The restaurant was as jammed as it would be on any weekday during the season, proof that the summer people had returned in full force. Everyone was so tired of the pandemic, so tired of staying away from their friends, so tired of eating at home instead of in their favorite restaurants.

"Thanks for coming," said Dr. Stolz as Melissa pulled out a tubular metal chair like those in her grandmother's old kitchen in Floral Park. "I hope you don't mind the casual atmosphere."

"It's an unusual choice for a business meeting," Melissa replied honestly. When Dr. Stolz narrowed her eyes, Melissa realized the invitation had been a test and quickly added, "but I hear the food is good."

"Our diner is not for everyone, but we like it." The doctor glanced around. "I don't usually eat here during the season. Too crowded. I only invite people I like to eat here with me."

"Thanks, Dr. Stolz. I'm flattered."

"Call me Liz." It was an order, not an invitation.

Melissa felt the doctor giving her a quick once-over. She smiled to chase away any impression that the inspection made her feel uncomfortable, but she did feel overdressed. Everyone else was wearing shorts and bright colors, including the doctor. Melissa wore a beige linen pants suit and heeled sandals, casual by city standards, but grossly out of place here.

"You didn't have to get dressed up for me."

"I like to look professional when I meet with a potential client."

"Dress for success, they used to say. And I say, never again!" Liz raised her pointed finger for emphasis. "I love retirement."

"But you're not retired. You seem very busy."

"If you think I'm busy now, you should have seen me in the day. I never even got a chance to eat, but I do now. Can't you tell?" Liz patted her little tummy and pushed the menu in Melissa's direction. "I always eat the same thing, but you might want to look at the menu. I recommend the blueberry pancakes. The lobster Benedict is also good."

"I've had it. Delicious, but too rich for me."

A waitress came to fill their coffee cups. Liz looked up and smiled at her. "Thanks, Lois."

The waitress pulled her pad out of her pocket. "An egg-white spinach omelet for me, please," said Melissa.

The waitress scribbled on her pad and dashed a handful of individual creamers out of her apron pocket.

"Unfortunately, I have another meeting after this one," Liz said, dumping cream into her coffee. She peeled open two more. Melissa hoped she saved some for her.

"What I have to say won't take long," said Melissa. She glanced around the booth. One side was against the window; the other backed up to the common coffee counter. "When you said to meet here I worried that we wouldn't have privacy."

"This is my office away from the office. As you can see, no one can overhear our conversation." Liz took a sip of coffee. "Yes! Strong enough to take the shellac off a violin." She smiled at her own joke, then assumed an unnervingly blank expression. "So, what did you think of my proposal?"

At this point, Melissa would usually set her watch to get the meter running, but she didn't. She'd already decided to do the work pro bono. She took a sip of coffee to encourage her thoughts and instantly visualized shellac melting off a violin.

"Ms. Enright's financial plan is brilliant as you might expect from a financial analyst of her caliber. The way you've laid it out will work, of course. Kudos to you, not being an attorney."

"But…" said Liz, cupping her hand to her ear. "I hear the but coming in loud and clear."

Melissa smiled at Liz's folksy antics, but she had no doubt she was dealing with a sharp businesswoman. "But there are simpler ways to accomplish your goals that will save you more in taxes."

"What's wrong with my way?" asked Liz, narrowing her eyes.

"You're tying your partners' hands, which will ultimately cause resentment. You're better off creating a limited corporation and making yourself and your partners employees. You can continue to hold the controlling interest. They can purchase shares to work off the debt and eventually buy you out. You remain in charge until you're ready to retire. Afterward too, if you set it up that way. Make the building an asset of the corporation, charge the practice rent–"

"Okay. I get the idea. You're suggesting a more conventional solution." The doctor's quick assessment impressed Melissa. She'd worked with medical professionals on trusts. They weren't usually so astute.

"I believe in keeping things simple when you can," said Melissa.

Liz sat back as the waitress slid a plate of fried over-easy eggs, bacon, and whole-wheat toast in front of her. "Sounds like you've got everything figured out."

"Not everything," said Melissa modestly. "There are some details I still have to think about. The succession plan will take some creative thinking." When the waitress put the pale omelet in front of her, Melissa wished she'd remembered to ask her to skip the fried potatoes. She looked up and saw Dr. Stolz eyeing her plate and felt her judgment. "This is about as much cholesterol as I'm willing to tolerate," Melissa explained.

"That's been a misconception for years. In fact, you absorb very little cholesterol from food. That doesn't mean you should go crazy, but a few eggs aren't going to hurt you."

"I like your common-sense approach."

"I believe in keeping it simple too," said Dr. Stolz with a wink. She dipped the corner of her toast into a perfect over-easy egg yolk. "So where do I go from here?"

"I'll draw up the outline of the steps to take. Harriet should be able to handle setting things up, and if she has questions, I'll be happy to help her."

"So, will she bill me, or you?"

"My part in it is gratis."

Liz looked up with surprise. "There's no need for that. I can afford to pay you."

"I know, but the time I've spent on this isn't even worth opening a billing account for you. Maybe I'll ask you to return the favor sometime."

"If I can, and it's not illegal. Just don't ask for opioids or psychotropics. I'm not a pusher." Liz smiled and raised a brow, but Melissa heard the clear warning. "Sometimes when I do business in here, I feel like I'm in a mafia movie."

"I don't think the mafia is big in Maine," Melissa replied dryly.

"No, probably not," Liz agreed. She bit into her toast. "What kind of barter did you have in mind?"

"Maybe you know a nice guy for my mother. She's had trouble meeting people in Maine. You know how it is. The summer people come and go and never make any real friends."

"The summer people don't even know there's something on the other side of the turnpike. When I first started coming up here, I didn't either." Liz signaled to the waitress and pointed to her coffee cup. "Is your mother divorced or a widow?"

"Dad died two years ago. Lung cancer. He smoked a long time before he quit."

"I'm sorry."

"Mom tried on-line dating for a while but only met one loser after another. If you're a widow with some money, the vultures are at your door, and they all want sex by the second date."

"Viagra, the curse of older women. I have patients who ask if I can prescribe a placebo for their husbands."

"Do you?"

Liz laughed. "No, of course not, but when I can, I counsel their husbands to be more sensitive."

"I worried about Mom when she was in Florida. The happy hour lasts twenty-four-seven. Everyone is always tanked."

"And STDs are rampant." Liz looked thoughtful as she chewed her toast. "You could also ask Lucy Bartlett. She might have someone who's graduated from her bereavement group."

"The Episcopal rector gets Jews in her group?"

"Her group is sponsored by the county department of human services. It's non-denominational." Liz glanced at her watch, drawing Melissa's attention to it. *Who wears watches anymore, especially a fancy gold chronometer with shorts and a T-shirt? I wonder if the casual look is just for show.*

"I'm afraid I have a hard stop at eight-thirty," Liz said, tapping her watch. "The new assistant principal of the elementary school is being introduced to the town council. I'm on the advisory board, so I'm supposed to show up. Olivia thinks the new principal goes to our church."

"You mean St. Margaret's?"

"No, I mean she's gay. Sorry. That expression is probably before your time."

"Actually, I've heard it before. I'm not that much younger, you know."

Liz shrugged dismissively. "If you're really thinking of moving up here, you should come with me to see how the town really works…or doesn't. It's a public meeting."

Melissa didn't have any particular plans for the day, but she didn't look forward to going home and looking at her mother's sad face. Besides, she was already dressed for a meeting.

"Sure. Why not?"

"Finish your breakfast, and we'll head over."

Melissa felt self-conscious about being overdressed standing among the people gathered for the meeting. The other attendees were wearing shorts and sandals, but she mustered the confidence she used in C-suites and ignored the stares. The people who greeted the doctor were friendly but respectful, demonstrating her influence in the town.

When they had a moment alone, Liz leaned over to speak confidentially. "That's the new assistant principal speaking to Olivia. She's kind of cute, don't you think?"

Melissa followed Dr. Stolz's line of sight and saw a pretty woman with long, blond hair. As if she'd sensed someone looking at her, the woman gazed in their direction. Across the room, her warm brown eyes met Melissa's, and she smiled.

"Melissa?" asked Liz, nudging her gently with her elbow. "Melissa, did you hear what I said?"

6

Courtney Barnes tried not to feel overwhelmed by the onslaught of well-wishers after the meeting. She wasn't naturally good at remembering names. When she'd been a classroom teacher, she could assign students to desks and learn their names by their location. Now that she was in administration, she'd need other tricks to help remember. Connecting an individual's appearance helped, such as Olivia Enright's piercing blue eyes or Rev. Bartlett's collar and red hair. She could identify the tallest woman in the room by her height. That was Dr. Stolz, the head doctor at Hobbs Family Practice. She also had a connection to the school board that Courtney struggled to remember.

Because it was a school day, the town manager had made the introductions instead of the principal. Before Courtney headed to the council meeting, Barbara Henderson advised her to pay attention to the subtle, behind-the-scenes power structure in Hobbs. "There is a group of powerful women who pretty much run everything. Make sure to stay on their good side." Courtney wondered how the sweet-faced, white-haired woman could have possibly run afoul of anyone. Rumor had it she would be retiring soon, which meant Courtney would be in line to succeed her. Being principal in a school district like Hobbs would definitely be good for her career. More importantly, she desperately needed the boost in salary.

As Courtney reviewed the names of the key players, she assessed each for potential risks to her success. Olivia Enright seemed calculating. Lucy Bartlett, the petite rector of the Episcopal church, had the warmest smile, so she probably wouldn't be any trouble. Courtney didn't know what to think of the town doctor, who stood in the back, watching everyone with a little frown. Dr. Stolz had introduced her to a woman wearing a tailored linen suit that made her stick out in the crowd. Courtney was glad she'd been advised to dress casually for the meeting.

The woman, who otherwise looked so confident, had practically stuttered when she'd repeated her name and offered her hand. "Melissa Morgenstern. I'd like to talk to you, but I can wait until you're done here." Courtney was too busy shaking hands and smiling at people to think about how odd the request was. In fact, she almost forgot about the tall woman until she turned around and saw her chatting in the back with the doctor.

"Hi, thanks for waiting," Courtney said, interrupting their conversation. The woman in the linen suit beamed with pleasure. "You don't really know me, but I wonder if you have time for a cup of coffee?"

The invitation took Courtney completely by surprise. Unfortunately, it didn't matter because she was due back at school. "I'm afraid I don't right now, but maybe another time?"

"How about this afternoon? When do you get out of school?"

Courtney laughed. This woman was certainly persistent. "I usually leave by four."

"That works for me. We could meet somewhere." Then she looked baffled. "Except, I don't know anywhere to go. Liz, can you recommend a place to have coffee? I mean, other than Awakened Brews. It's closed in the afternoon."

Courtney noticed the amused look on the doctor's face accompanied by a raised brow. *What am I missing here?*

"Well, you could go to the diner. They're known for their blueberry pie, but it will probably be jammed today, now that the tourists are here. You could try House 145. They bake their own cakes and muffins. You know where it is?"

"No, but I'm sure I can find it, if it's on Route 1."

"There's only one thing," Courtney said, interrupting, "I have to pick my daughter up from baseball practice at five-thirty." The woman's smile faded slightly at the mention of the word 'daughter.' Courtney wondered what that was about. "If you don't mind a short date, I can meet you there by four-fifteen." At the word 'date,' the smile returned to the woman's face.

"I look forward to it."

One of the selectmen returned to introduce himself. When Courtney was done talking to him, she looked around for the woman and the doctor, but they were gone.

Courtney almost forgot she'd agreed to have coffee with the woman from the morning's meeting. After school, she was still thinking about the third-grade class she'd observed. The term still had a few more weeks to run, and they would be critical because the students had been in and out of the classroom during the pandemic. They seemed as dazed as in the beginning of a school year. The staff seemed equally confused, and not everyone had returned when school had reopened. The position at Hobbs Elementary had appeared at the last minute because the previous assistant principal was a COVID long hauler who'd gone out on disability.

As a May graduate, Courtney had been applying for fall openings. The sudden end-of-the year vacancy had taken her completely by surprise. She'd had to move herself and her daughter with no preparation. The summer tourist season had already begun, which meant rentals were scarce and she had to take the first place she could afford. Everything since the divorce seemed so haphazard and impermanent. She felt like she was being swept along in a raging river. Trying to avoid the rocks on the way down was the best she could manage.

Courtney's brain was programmed to turn left out of the school parking lot. When she remembered her date, she had to make a U-turn at the convenience store. She headed down Route 1, looking for the bakery. The GPS suddenly demanded that she turn right. When she saw the tiny, easily missed sign, she realized why the annoying voice was so insistent. There was only one car in the parking lot—a high-end BMW. Embarrassed by the fancy company, Courtney parked her old Subaru at the end of the row.

The bright sunlight outside left Courtney temporarily blind when she stepped into the old, repurposed barn. She gave her eyes a minute to adjust before scanning the interior. A tall woman got up from a table with an old barrel for a base and waved. As Courtney approached, she was relieved to see that Melissa had changed into jeans and a striped, boat-neck top that gave her a jaunty, nautical look. Her dark, curly hair was tied back. She looked much friendlier without the suit.

"I was afraid I couldn't find the place, so I came early," Melissa confessed, getting up as Courtney sat down. "While I was waiting, I drank too much coffee, but I didn't want to hit the ladies' room and chance missing you."

"Go pee, while I'll figure out what to order."

"The blueberry muffins look awesome, but they're big enough for three people."

"Let me take a look. Maybe we can split one."

Melissa headed halfway to the bathroom door before walking backwards to say, "The salt-caramel latte is to die for."

As Courtney approached the counter to order, a pleasant, middle-aged woman came to greet her. "Are you the baker?" Courtney asked.

"The baker, the barista, the waitress. You name it, I do it."

The blueberry muffin did look scrumptious, but as Melissa had said, it was enormous. Courtney ordered one and two plates. "My friend recommends the salt-caramel latte."

"It's our most popular drink. Would you like one?" Courtney nodded and dug into her purse for her wallet. "No, it's already paid for. Your friend opened a tab."

"I've never heard of running a tab in a coffee shop."

"Some customers like to sit here while they work. When you stay for most of the day, it's easier to run a tab."

When Melissa returned to the barrel table, Courtney scolded, "You didn't have to pay for both of us."

Melissa shrugged. "I invited you. Next time you can pay."

The barista brought their order to their table. The enormous muffin was as delicious as it looked, but even half was too much.

"I'm sorry I have such a short time to spend with you," Courtney apologized. "It's not easy with kids. They reach a certain age and they're into everything—school clubs, sports, Scouts…"

"Can't the other parent help with transportation?" Melissa asked casually, tapping up the last crumbs of muffin with her fingertip.

Courtney narrowed her eyes, recognizing the real purpose of this question. "No, I'm divorced." *A strange woman picks me up at a meeting and thinks she's going to interview me? No way.* "Tell me about you, Melissa. Do you live in Hobbs?"

"No, I'm just visiting for the summer. My mother has a house near the beach."

"How lucky to have someone with a beach house. I'm renting until I can find something more permanent. The rents here aren't cheap."

"I bet they're not. But they do have something called 'winter rentals,' and they're dirt cheap. Works well for students and college faculty. Where are you staying?"

"On the other side of the highway. I found an old trailer with enough space for me and my daughter. It's pretty run down, and I don't think it's well insulated. I really need to get out of there before winter."

"I hear the winters up here can be brutal."

"I've heard that too, but our winters in Connecticut could be just as bad."

"Someone I know in town is a real estate lawyer. Well, really a general practice lawyer, everything from wills to divorces, but most of her work is in real estate. She might know of rentals. If you give me your number, I can pass it along to her."

What a smooth way to get someone's phone number, thought Courtney, but Melissa seemed solid. After all, hadn't she come to the town council meeting with the doctor? That, in itself, was a recommendation.

"What kind of work do you do?" Courtney asked.

Melissa got to the bottom of her latte with a gurgle. "Pardon me," she said with a quick smile. "It was so good I had to slurp at the end. But those sugary coffee drinks can pack on the pounds." She patted her enviably flat tummy. "But one now and then is fun. What do you do for fun, Courtney?"

Back to interviewing me again, thought Courtney. *No, you don't.*

"Me, first. I asked what you do for a living, and you…didn't tell me."

"I'm an attorney."

"Really? What kind? Real estate, like your friend?"

"No. I'm a trust lawyer."

"Oh." Courtney had never heard of a trust lawyer. It sounded like an unusual specialty, one that Hobbs wouldn't have much call for. "Where do you practice?"

"I've been working in Boston, but I'm originally a New Yorker." Melissa frowned. "Your expression told me that's not necessarily a positive."

Courtney smiled to dispel the idea that she didn't approve. "I didn't mean anything by it. I was really thinking you're a long way from home."

"My sister brings us supplies. She lives on the Upper West Side with her wife."

Melissa had announced her sister's sexual preference casually, but Courtney could feel her reaction being scrutinized. She wondered how much to reveal. Her experience of coming out to strangers had been mostly negative. "Do I read?" she asked.

"Read as what?" Melissa asked, stealing a crumb of leftover muffin from Courtney's plate.

"You know. As a woman who prefers women."

Melissa shrugged. "Not particularly."

Courtney weighed how much to say, but Melissa was waiting patiently for an answer. Courtney decided that if she put it out there, at least, she'd know where she stood. "I'm bi," she announced and braced herself. Melissa continued to smile pleasantly. Being an attorney, she'd probably learned to keep her feelings to herself. "I'm cautious about telling people," Courtney explained. "Some gay women won't go near a bi woman."

Melissa looked thoughtful. "Why is that?"

"They think that bi women can't make up their minds. That saying you're bi implies permission to cheat, a lack of commitment to one person."

"Well, you divorced your husband," said Melissa staring into her latte cup, obviously looking for more.

"Yes, but not for any reason related to being bi. We had problems in our marriage unrelated to my sexuality. He wanted to move to the West Coast. I wanted to stay in New England. But things hadn't been good long before that."

"Thank you for sharing that," said Melissa. "You don't really know me. You say other people have misconceptions. What does bi mean to you?"

"It means I fall in love with a person, not a gender. What does it mean to you?"

Melissa frowned. "I don't know. I guess, like other gay women, I've wondered why bi people can't make up their minds."

"It's not that simple. People can be attracted to one sex or another at different times in their lives. Some women marry to have children. Sometimes, you just fall in love, and the person's gender doesn't matter. We've forced people to take a position for political reasons. Choose: gay or straight. If you're bi, you're just confused, but that's not necessarily true."

"That's an interesting point of view," Melissa said neutrally. "And you're an interesting woman, Courtney Barnes. I'd love to sit and talk to you all afternoon, but you have exactly five minutes to finish your latte." She pointed over Courtney's shoulder. Courtney turned around. She saw the time on the antique clock and realized Melissa was right.

<h1 style="text-align:center">7</h1>

Lucy rifled through the resumes in the folder, looking for the one sent by the person waiting outside her office. Cramming for her exams had put her behind in her parish duties, including hiring a new music director to replace Maggie Fitzgerald.

The resume she'd been searching for turned up in the middle of the pile. Once she began to scan it, the essential details came back to her. The candidate had graduated from the Yale School of Music with a concentration in voice. She'd done a minor at the divinity school in sacred music. On paper, she sounded perfect, but Tom had only ranked her number three of the top candidates. *What was that about?* Lucy wondered.

After working in the classical music world for years, she knew how to hunt down another singer. She started with the obvious. She Googled her. There were no hits for Denise Chantal, but there were a few for a counter-tenor by the name of Dennis Chantal. Lucy's search got no further before Jodi, her admin, knocked on her door. "Mother Lucy, the candidate is here for the interview."

"Jodi, you don't have to get up and come in. You could use the intercom on the phone."

"I know, but I read that sitting too long isn't supposed to be good for you."

"Walking ten feet into my office isn't much exercise," replied Lucy dryly.

Jodi shrugged. "Better than nothing."

The first thing Lucy noticed about the candidate was how tall she was. Ms. Chantal wore a beautiful blue dress with a coordinating scarf and dressy flats. Being tall, she probably didn't want to emphasize her height. When she extended her hand, Lucy noticed the size of her wrists. The Dennis-Denise discrepancy finally made sense.

"Thank you so much for taking the time to see me, Rev. Bartlett." The voice was feminine and perfectly modulated.

Lucy gestured to a visitors' chair. "Thank you for coming in today. I apologize for not reading your resume more carefully. I'm hoping our conversation can fill in the gaps."

"I'm sure you've been inundated with applications. No one can get any work with all the concert halls and opera houses shut down. You must have gotten millions of resumes."

Lucy smiled at the exaggeration. "Hundreds. We're not paying that much for the position."

"Any paying job is better than no work at all."

"Of course, it is. Those lean times can be frightening. I used to be in the arts myself."

"I know. You are the great soprano, Lucille Bartlett. I'm one of your biggest fans."

Lucy studied Ms. Chantal's face to evaluate the remark. She never minded sincere praise, but she hated flattery. "Nowadays, I only sing in church, for my friends, and, occasionally, for charity."

"Such a shame your career ended so early. I have every one of your recordings. In fact, you're the main reason I applied."

"So, you're not serious about the position?"

"Of course, I'm serious. I am absolutely serious. But working for you would be such an honor."

"You would be working with me, not for me. And I don't have the last word on hiring. The vestry makes personnel decisions based on my recommendations and those of Rev. Simmons. You'll need to come back for another interview if we decide you are among the final candidates. Do you understand?"

"Yes, Rev. Bartlett. Perfectly clear."

"Good. Now, from what I gather from your resume, you've had excellent vocal training. We have several fine organists in the congregation, but could you play the organ if necessary?"

"I've been trained to play keyboard music. I admit I'm a little rusty on organ pedals and the stops, but I could brush up."

"St. Margaret's has a historic organ, built in the early 1900s. The sound is magnificent."

"I look forward to playing it."

"Is this your first time at St. Margaret's?"

Denise made a sad face. "Unfortunately, your church has been closed since I came back to Maine."

"A great hardship to us all, but we'll be opening the outdoor chapel soon. Are you a Mainer?"

"Yes, I was born and raised in Thomaston, but I haven't been back since I left for college. I was in Munich when the pandemic hit and felt lucky to get home. My friend had a cheap winter rental in Webhanet, which is how I landed here."

Lucy picked up the resume and scanned it again. "I see you've had some training in choral direction. For obvious reasons, that's very important in this role."

"I love to sing in a choir but also to conduct."

"You don't mind that you won't sing solo very often?"

"Actually, I'd be reluctant to sing solo. I'm trying to retrain my voice."

"From countertenor?"

"Yes." She eyed Lucy cautiously. "So, you did research me."

"Very briefly. Only to see if you'd been successful in your singing career."

"I was getting there."

"As you probably know, it's against state law to ask questions regarding gender identity or sexual preference in a job interview. That said, I'll listen sympathetically to anything you'd like to tell me. It won't leave this room unless you give me permission to share it."

"You're a priest, so I suppose I can trust you," the woman said, but a shadow of concern passed in her eyes. "How did you guess I'm trans?"

"Without the hint from researching you, I probably wouldn't have figured it out. Tell me how a promising countertenor makes the choice you did."

As the woman searched her face, Lucy saw the exact moment when she decided it was worth the risk. "I was getting plenty of gigs—concerts, here and in Europe. I was invited to do a number of recordings. After I made my debut at the summer festival in Aix, I joined the Munich opera. I'd known for years that I was living in the wrong body, but the gender dysphoria kept getting worse until I had to do something about it. I didn't realize it would end my singing career."

"Because of the prejudice?"

Denise smiled sadly. "No, because of the competition. A talented countertenor is in higher demand than a mediocre female alto."

"That's a high price to pay."

"It is, and when I have my bottom surgery, it's irreversible. I'll be a *castrato* like the famed singers of the Renaissance. Well, not really. They were castrated before they matured."

Lucy folded her hands in her lap and studied the young woman. "Thank you for being candid, Ms. Chantal. I can imagine it's been difficult for you to find work."

"Please call me Denise, and it's easy to be honest with you, Rev. Bartlett. For one thing, you're so kind. For another, you're a singer, and you know what I'm talking about. Hardly anyone else does. My friends think I'm crazy. Many of them can't get any work, and here I am blowing my career to become a woman."

"You say you're retraining?"

"Once I have the body of a woman, I want to become a true alto. Except I can barely afford the rent, never mind a voice teacher."

"Will you sing for me now?"

"What?" Denise flushed. "I didn't prepare anything. I didn't expect to audition for this role."

"It's nothing formal. I just want to hear your voice to see if I have any suggestions."

Denise stared at the floor and swallowed hard. Lucy realized she was trying to hide tears. "I'm sorry. You don't need to sing if it makes you uncomfortable."

"No, it's not that. I'm moved that you would care enough to try to help me."

"I'm a priest. It's my job to help people," Lucy said, smiling to lighten the atmosphere.

Denise gave her a firm look. "It's not your job to rehabilitate trans countertenors."

"No, but as one singer to another, I will say, never give up singing. I almost did, and I've always regretted it because I nearly wrecked my voice. And even though I no longer sing on the stage, I sing because God gave me this gift and wants me to use it."

"It is a gift from God," Denise agreed. "Your voice, especially."

"Won't you sing for me? Just a few bars?"

"As a countertenor?"

"Lead with your strength," said Lucy, sitting back to show she was ready to listen.

"I don't have any accompaniment."

"No problem. I subscribe to a service. What would you like to sing?"

"Vivaldi's '*Vedro con mio diletto*.'"

Lucy found the accompaniment on her phone and turned up her speaker to high. Denise stood and Lucy could see she had excellent posture for a singer. The introduction played through, but Denise didn't sing on cue. "Again?" asked Lucy. The woman nodded, so Lucy restarted the track. This time, a sublime tone, perfectly in the high register and exquisitely pure, came from Denise's throat. The magnificent but eerie sound gave Lucy chills. When the piece concluded, she didn't know what to say, so she merely applauded.

"Thank you," Denise said, tapping her clasped hands over her heart.

"You are truly gifted."

"From you, that is the highest praise."

"Will you sing something using your chest voice in the alto range?"

"Can you stand to hear it?"

Lucy smiled warmly. "Believe me when I say, I've heard everything."

"I bet you have."

Denise chose Bach's cantata *"Vergnügte Ruh."* Lucy listened carefully. She could hear the effort Denise was making to keep her chest voice on key, but she kept smiling to encourage her. When Denise finished, Lucy said, "I could hear you cheating and slipping back into your head voice, but it was beautiful and very brave."

"Thank you, Rev. Bartlett," said Denise, sinking down in her chair. She looked so defeated. "You're being kind. I really struggle in the lower register."

"I can hear it."

"I know. It's so discouraging."

"Don't be discouraged. Just keep working on it. Maybe I can give you some pointers."

"You would do that?"

Lucy nodded.

Denise studied her face. "I think you might be willing to give me a shot. Am I right?"

Lucy gave herself a moment to consider what to say. "I admit that I haven't studied all the resumes as carefully as I could, but yours is impressive. Your talents would be a wonderful addition to our music program, especially with your background in sacred music. I love the old hymns, don't get me wrong, but we have a sophisticated congregation here in Hobbs." Lucy wouldn't mind introducing more serious music into the liturgy, but that turned worshipers into an audience. She hadn't yet figured out what to do about that.

Lucy knew she'd been lost in her own thoughts too long when Denise asked, "What can I do to convince you, Rev. Bartlett?"

"I'm convinced. But you need to convince the vestry."

"Forgot about them."

Lucy laughed. "I never do, and they never let me. I'll recommend that they call you for an interview. I won't say a word about your gender status. You can tell them if you want to. Do you have any questions?"

Denise looked at Lucy for a long time before blurting out, "Do you have health insurance?"

Lucy was startled by the direct question. "We do, but it's not the greatest. Are you worried about having your surgery covered?"

"No, I've already saved up for that. I just want to make sure this job has benefits. I know you're not supposed to ask that question on a first interview, but I'm desperate."

"We do have benefits. They're pretty basic, but we do take care of our people." Lucy rose and extended her hand. "We'll be calling candidates back next week. Are you available?"

"I'll make sure to be available!" Denise jumped up from her seat. "Oh, thank you, Rev. Bartlett! I wish I could hug you. Don't worry. I've had my shots."

"I'm a hugger too, but let's wait. Okay?" Denise looked disappointed, so Lucy added, "It's good to be cautious until we know it's safe."

After Denise left, Lucy leaned against the door and wondered what she'd gotten herself into. When she returned to her desk, she picked up her phone and called Liz.

"Lucy! To what do I owe the pleasure?" said the cheerful voice on the other end of the line.

"I need to talk to you, so I'm inviting myself for dinner."

Liz laughed. "Good thing I always cook extra."

8

"Hello! I'm here," Lucy announced, calling through the house.

"In the kitchen," Liz called back.

Lucy found Liz was skewering pieces of swordfish to make fish kabobs.

"Thank you for leaving the door open for me."

"That glass is for you." Liz nodded to a glass of white wine, while she washed her hands in the kitchen sink.

"Such good service. The door is open, my wine is poured, my dinner is being prepared. I could get used to this." Lucy rubbed the small of Liz's back. "Thank you so much for letting me come over. I really need to talk to you." Lucy glanced around the counters, where the ingredients and serving dishes were lined up with their usual precision. "What can I do to help?"

"You could give me a kiss," Liz said, bending so that their faces aligned. Lucy gave her a deep, soulful kiss. When she withdrew, her eyes were full of mischief. "More," said Liz with a dreamy smile.

Lucy gave her a quick peck on the lips. "More later. You're busy now, and I'm starving."

"Come out to the deck while I grill the fish," said Liz. She gave Lucy a quick once-over, relieved to see she had changed into a pretty sundress and left her clerical blouse and collar at home. When Lucy was on Liz's time, she much preferred the woman to the priest. "Bring your wine…and mine." Liz nodded to the location of her glass.

Liz carefully laid out the kabobs on the grill.

"You have a cute ass," said Lucy.

"What?" asked Liz, turning around. "You're looking at my ass?"

"You're busy and not watching, so I can."

Liz closed the grill cover and took the Adirondack chair next to Lucy's. "Let me get this straight. *I'm* supposed to be on good behavior, but you can say whatever comes into your head."

"That's right. My rules."

"What if I don't accept them?"

"Too bad. That's how it goes," said Lucy, smiling. "Besides, you should learn how it feels to be a sex object."

"Why?"

"So you learn to treat women more respectfully."

Liz released her breath slowly, imagining steam coming out of her ears. "I don't know about that. How about we make the rules together?"

"All right, I can agree to that." Lucy raised her glass before taking a sip of wine. "Thank you for having me tonight. I need a smart person to help me figure something out. Erika was always good at that."

"Is this going to be a long one? Because the fish kabobs only take a few minutes."

"Yes, a long one. Maybe we should wait until we sit down to eat." Lucy rubbed her bare arms. "I should have worn a jacket. It's really chilly out here!"

"We're going in soon, but there's a hoodie hanging on the hook in the hall closet. You know where it is."

Lucy headed in for the sweatshirt while Liz collected the kabobs off the grill.

"This is why I loved to borrow Erika's clothes," said Lucy, holding the door for Liz on her return. "Her hoodie was like a coat on me."

"If you're cold, switch on the propane stove while I get the rest of the food from the kitchen."

Before Liz sat down, she took a small box of matches out of her pocket and lit the candle on the table. "A little atmosphere would be nice. Help yourself, Lucy. Don't let the food get cold."

Lucy put a skewer of fish on her plate. "I always feel so at home in this house. I really enjoyed it when we were all living here during the pandemic and had those noisy, communal meals. You probably thought it was awful."

"No, I enjoyed it. I like company...on my terms. It's too quiet being alone in this big house."

"I know what you mean," said Lucy with a sigh, "but Emily will be home in a few weeks."

Liz reached for the platter to serve herself. "So, what's on your mind, Rev. Bartlett?"

"You know I've been interviewing candidates to replace Maggie as music director. I think I've found someone."

"That's good," Liz said idly as she spooned rice onto her plate.

"She's trans."

"What?" Liz asked, the serving spoon poised in mid-air. She raised a brow to indicate her surprise but continued serving herself. "Since you're using she/her pronouns, I'm assuming we're talking about a male to female transsexual."

"Yes, exactly. She was a countertenor, an amazing one. What clarity of tone! Like pure, sweet cream. Mmm. Delicious."

"You like her voice, so you're hiring her?"

"No, I like her courage and her honesty. We had a good talk. For the first time, I understood how critical it is for a trans person to embrace the physical changes. This woman is willing to give up a promising career and a spectacular voice to be in the right body because it's essential to her personality."

Liz could think of multiple objections to this series of statements, but she recognized that Lucy was on a roll, and interrupting her would not be a good idea.

"A singer's voice is about the body," Lucy continued. "Female bodies naturally sing treble. Male bodies, with their longer vocal cords naturally sing the notes on the bass clef. It's as if God designed us like a musical instrument or an orchestra. Countertenors sing in the head voice to emulate a female, but they can't ever truly achieve it. This woman wants to learn to sing as a female in a trans body. That's very ambitious."

"I'm no expert on singing or gender reassignment, but I do know one thing. No matter how many hormones this person takes, those vocal cords aren't going to get any shorter." Liz watched the pucker grow between Lucy's auburn brows. "I'm sorry, but those are the facts."

"You and your blunt medical talk. You could try to be more sensitive!"

"Probably, but I can't understand why people would deliberately mutilate their bodies."

Lucy was obviously so shocked her mouth opened. "Liz, that's harsh! I can't believe you said that!"

"Hear me out. When I was a breast surgeon, I removed women's breasts because they had cancer. It was a desperate measure to save their lives and a horror for them to lose a part of their body, something associated with feminine beauty. The idea that someone would voluntarily have 'top surgery' makes *no* sense to me."

"It doesn't make sense to me either, but it doesn't have to make sense to us. Our opinions don't matter. We don't need to understand. This is someone's existence we're talking about. We don't debate existential threats to another human being."

Liz crossed her arms on her chest. "Well, if you have it all figured out, why are you asking me?"

"Because I think out loud. Erika used to say I'm a lateral thinker."

"You think like this." Liz held out her arms, and drew circles in the air. "Erika was right. I'm sure she's listening now."

"I'm sure she is and shaking her head like you are, but she was more tactful when she disagreed with me." Lucy accepted the offered salad bowl. "I admit I've had my doubts about trans. I especially worry about the rush of young masculine women to transition before they learn they're perfectly valid the way they are. Liz, when you were growing up with your brothers and doing all those boy things like hunting and riding motorcycles, did you ever wish you were male?"

"I used to get annoyed when I had to do the dishes while my brothers got to do fun chores like mowing with the lawn tractor. I resented getting stuck with women's work like folding my youngest brother's diapers. Don't look at me like that. We still used cloth diapers in those days, and we should again instead of sending all that shit to the landfill."

"Liz, I'm eating."

Liz frowned in Lucy's direction. "Get used to it. Living with a doctor means talking about bodily processes."

Lucy put a forkful of fish into her mouth and chewed thoughtfully. "What do you think about the proposal in Augusta banning trans women from women's sports?"

"I don't know what to think," said Liz. "Supposedly, after transitioning and hormone treatment, trans women are no better at sports than any other women. I don't know if those studies are worth anything. It's counterintuitive. Once puberty starts, male bodies change dramatically. Some things can't be reversed. Like your candidate's vocal cords."

"But we need to be fair," Lucy said. "Don't we?"

"Yes, we need to be fair, but what's fair? Some people are born with longer legs or arms. Look at Michael Phelps. He has abnormally long arms for a human being, which makes him an ideal swimmer. A gymnast with an especially short, light body has a natural advantage. All people are not created equal."

Lucy speared a cherry tomato with her fork and popped it into her mouth. "I need you to lobby Olivia in Denise's favor."

Liz looked up to stare at her. "Do I have a choice?"

"No." Lucy smiled one of her radiant smiles. "Of course, you have a choice, Liz, but I could really use your help here. If you can convince Olivia, and she goes along with it, everyone else will."

"Lucy, let me get this straight. You want me to help you rig the decision?"

"All decisions are rigged, Liz. That's what Erika told me. Our likes and dislikes, early upbringing, even where we grew up, influence how we make decisions. I'm trying to figure out how to offset the prejudice against trans people, so Denise has a fair chance."

"Then you need to give me more ammunition than 'Lucy wants your vote.' That's not going to cut it."

Lucy frowned as she thought. "I'm going to invite Denise to sing this Sunday. When people hear her sing, they'll understand. She has all the right training, but it's her love for music, especially sacred music, that makes her right for the job."

"When I was at Yale, I had to make a lot of personnel decisions. I never hired surgeons because they loved operating."

"My instincts say this is the right decision."

"Well, Lucy, your instincts are usually pretty good." Liz got up and stacked the dishes. "I'll do the dishes."

"Let's do the dishes together, and then I need to study."

"Are you going home?" asked Liz, trying to hide her disappointment.

"No, I thought I'd study here. You don't mind?"

"Of course not, but I'll do the dishes, so you can get to work."

After tidying the kitchen, Liz came out to the living room to find Lucy intently focused on what she was reading. She didn't want to disturb her, so she stretched out on the neighboring sofa and opened her tablet. She was just settling in when she felt Lucy's eyes on her. "Something wrong?"

"You could sit closer, you know."

"There's not enough room for both of us. I like to stretch out when I read."

Lucy patted her thigh and smiled.

"You want me to sit on your lap? I think I might crush you."

Lucy rolled her eyes. "No, Liz. I'm inviting you to put your head in my lap. Being physically close is part of courtship."

Liz moved to the other sofa. Lucy lifted her tablet so Liz could lay her head on her thigh. "See? Now, isn't that cozy?"

"I thought you were studying," Liz mumbled. "I don't want the blame if you fail your exams."

"I try not to blame others for my failings." Lucy slightly adjusted her position. "Your head is heavy. Must be that big brain inside." She stroked Liz's hair. As Lucy continued to pet her, which was mesmerizing, the image of a pampered puppy formed in Liz's mind. She had no tail to wag, but she considered wiggling her rear end to show her appreciation. Eventually, the petting stopped, allowing Liz to go back to her book.

She jumped when Lucy suddenly said, "Liz! What are you reading? That's not medical stuff!" A hand appeared overhead and tried to snatch away Liz's iPad. After a brief tug-o-war, Liz gave in and let go. She tried to relax while waiting for Lucy's reaction. "*The Anglican Communion at a*

Crossroads: The Crises of a Global Church," Lucy read aloud. Liz reached for her tablet, but Lucy held it out of reach. "Liz, why are you reading this?"

"You said you used to talk to Erika about your ideas. This book seemed like a good place to catch up on what's going on in your Church."

Liz reached her hand up, expecting her tablet to be returned, but she heard it being set down on the coffee table. Lucy nudged her. "Liz, sit up."

Liz sighed, but she obeyed. The serious look on Lucy's face made her anxious. "Oh, no. Have I done something wrong again?"

"No, you've done something right." Lucy pulled her face to hers and kissed her. She tried to open Lucy's lips with her tongue, but she lightly pushed her away.

"That was only a thank-you kiss. If we continue, I'll get all aroused and I won't study." Lucy gently squeezed Liz's cheeks. "Be patient. We'll get there." She patted her lap, and Liz recognized the invitation to return. She tried not to look disappointed when Lucy handed back her tablet.

9

Melissa had to ask three times before she found the right baseball diamond. The town park had multiple games going on simultaneously, and the place was swarming with pre-teen girls in colorful uniforms. Unfortunately, Melissa had forgotten to ask Courtney the school colors. She ought to know them by now. She'd seen enough signs around town for car-wash fundraisers, banners congratulating graduates, and the school band marching in parades. As one of the summer people, she'd never paid much attention, but if she wanted more than a summer fling with the assistant principal, she probably should.

Aren't you getting ahead of yourself? You spend a half hour drinking coffee with a woman, and you're already thinking of a possible relationship? Slow down!

Some of her hurry came from her lack of opportunities for sex. She'd broken up with her girlfriend, a pediatric surgeon at Dana Farber, right before Hanukkah. Her friends in Boston attempted to play matchmaker, and she'd tried online dating, but what was the point if you couldn't get together with your prospective dates?

Melissa finally found the home team. She'd read in the local paper that the Hobbs Hawks had recently changed their name because their former moniker, Hobbs Tomahawks, disrespected Native Americans. Now, instead of an Indian hatchet, the team logo was a hawk in flight. The graphic was an improvement, but Melissa hated to side with conservatives, who objected because "it's always been that way."

She spotted Courtney across the field. She waved to her and she waved back. A ball whizzed past Melissa's ear, reminding her that she should have taken the long way. When Melissa was in school, girls only played softball. Now, they played baseball too. Being hit by one of those could be painful.

Although Courtney had the entire top bleacher to herself, she moved over to make room for the new arrival.

"Hey, Melissa. I wasn't sure you'd make it. Thank you for coming."

"I came to root on the home team." Melissa's guarded message, her way of trying not to seem too eager, fell flat. She tried again. "I want to watch the soccer moms supporting their daughters."

"It's a baseball game," Courtney pointed out dryly.

"I see that. I'm no expert when it comes to sports, but that much, I know."

"I'm not athletic either, but Kaylee's dad is a phys ed teacher. He coached the girls' team in her school. Of course, she had to be on it." Courtney pointed to a slim girl in the outfield. "That's my daughter, number fourteen in the outfield. She's athletic, unlike her mother, who can't catch to save her life."

"Don't feel bad. I can't catch either."

Courtney smiled, seemingly pleased to learn that they shared this deficit.

"Baseball is such a slow game," complained Melissa, stretching out her long legs. "I've never understood what people see in it."

"Me neither." Courtney moved closer. "I was afraid I'd scared you off." When Melissa gave her a quizzical look, she added, "When I told you about being bi."

"Honestly, I'm not sure what bi means, and I may have acquired some bad attitudes. I'm willing to be educated."

Courtney smiled. "Since I'm in the education business, you came to the right place. It's not a deal breaker, is it?" Courtney's anxious expression was touching. Melissa patted her thigh reassuringly.

"I like to think I'm open minded, but my mother will probably object to you because you're not Jewish."

"You're Jewish?"

"Come on! You didn't know? With a name like Morgenstern?"

"Sorry. There weren't many Jewish people where I grew up."

"Then hopefully you don't know about all the stereotypes."

"I'm afraid I don't." Melissa studied Courtney to make sure this wasn't a joke. The woman couldn't really be that sheltered, but apparently, she was.

"People say we're too aggressive, too clannish, too entitled…"

"Is it true?"

"Like all ethnic prejudices, there's probably the tiniest grain of truth, cultural traits that are exaggerated in some women, more in my mother's generation than in ours."

"I've never dated a Jewish woman before," Courtney admitted.

"So, we're both in for a new experience."

"I'm looking forward to it," said Courtney with a warm smile like the one that had turned Melissa's head when they'd first met.

There was a loud cheer from the ball field, but they didn't turn to look. "I think we're missing something," Courtney said, finally releasing Melissa's gaze.

Melissa saw girls scrambling on the ball field, and the ball zinging from one base to another, but what had happened beforehand wasn't immediately clear. The people on the bleachers on the other side of the field began cheering and jumping up and down, so she assumed the development wasn't good for the home team. She glanced at the scoreboard. Another run was posted to the visitors.

Melissa scrutinized the behavior of the girls on the field. There was nothing "girly" about them. They meant business. What a change from when she was growing up! There were always the "jock girls," even in her mostly Jewish school in New York, where academics were far more important than sports. The coach of the girl's basketball team had encouraged Melissa to try out because she was so tall. She made the team, but she was uncoordinated and sat on the bench for most of the games. She'd only stuck out the season because her father hated "quitters."

"I'm glad you came." Courtney gently patted Melissa's knee.

"Me too."

"Maybe you can come over for pizza after the game?"

"You found a place in Hobbs that makes good pizza?" Melissa asked with exaggerated surprise.

Courtney laughed. "It's better than most places up here. You'd think a resort town would have a dozen good pizzerias."

"Nothing like New York pizza."

"I beg to differ," said Courtney. "Pepe's in New Haven makes the best pizza in the world."

"You lived there?"

"Nearby. In Branford. I got my administration degree from Quinnipiac."

"The place that does all the polls?"

"Among other things."

"What made you want to be a principal?"

"The Connecticut public schools pay well, but the real money is in administration. That wasn't the only reason, of course. I love teaching., and I love kids. The superintendent liked me and encouraged me to go for an advanced degree."

Melissa listened carefully, storing away the information. One thing she'd learned in legal practice was to collect details that might be useful later.

"Where did you go to college?" asked Courtney.

"Radcliffe. My father really pushed me to get into one of the Seven Sisters. He went to Harvard Law. So did I."

Courtney gave her a look between admiration and disapproval. "Rich girl, huh?"

"Not really. Dad worked hard to get into Harvard Law. He didn't come from big money. His father was a rabbi."

"I shouldn't make assumptions about people," said Courtney, patting her hand. "Sorry." Melissa's hand tingled at the touch of Courtney's.

Shouts from the ball field made Courtney suddenly jump up and cheer. "Nice play, Kaylee! Way to go!" She turned to Melissa with a grin. "You can always tell the sports mamas."

"I like the way you encourage your daughter."

"Thank you," said Courtney, looking pleased. When she sat down again, she sat close enough for their hips to touch. After that, Melissa's mind wasn't on the game. She took her cues from Courtney and the others on the home team bleachers about when to groan or cheer.

When the game was over, there was a brief meeting of the team with the coaches before the girls streamed off the field with their bats and gloves. The slim girl Courtney had pointed out headed to where they sat.

"Come meet my daughter," said Courtney, stepping down the bleacher.

Melissa felt the girl's eyes taking her in. They were the same warm brown with gold flecks as her mother's. She was a blonde too.

"Kaylee," Courtney said, "I want you to meet Melissa Morgenstern."

"Hello, Ms. Morgenstern."

"Hello, Kaylee. You can call me Melissa." The girl turned to her mother, who nodded permission.

"I'm in the school system, so she's been encouraged to be more formal with adults."

"A little formality is good." Melissa reached out her hand to Kaylee. The girl's felt a little sweaty, but she had a good grip. *Good for you,* Melissa thought. *It's never too early to learn the value of a firm handshake.*

"The pizza place is on the way home. It's a little hole-in-the-wall general store that caters to fishermen. We live near the brook that feeds Jimson Pond."

"I hear it's nice out there, although I hardly ever venture over the highway to the other side of Hobbs," Melissa admitted.

"Maybe you'll have an excuse now." The little suggestive twitch of Courtney's brow surprised Melissa. She wasn't sure what to do with it, especially because she preferred to be the one who made the first move. Her solution, as usual, was to take charge.

"If you tell me the address and what you like on your pizza, I can pick it up and bring it over."

"No, this one's on me. You paid last time, and you promised. Besides, Kaylee likes to come in and choose her sodas. The brewery in Portland makes craft sodas, and this place has a fill-your-own-six-pack deal. She thinks that's the coolest thing."

Melissa decided not to argue about who would pay. Hopefully, there would be other occasions to fight this battle. Obviously, she had more resources than Courtney, but creative socialism could wait until they knew one another better. She browsed the store while they waited for the pizza to bake.

Like many general stores in Maine, this one had a wide variety of items—everything from Band-aids to potato chips. There was an old-fashioned refrigerator full of snap-lid paper containers of night crawlers and mealworms, but right next to it was a display of craft beers from all over New England. Beside the shelf of white bread and split-top hot dog rolls was an impressive selection of wine. Melissa chose a pinot she'd tasted and enjoyed. It was a few dollars more expensive than she'd pay in town, but she didn't mind giving a little extra to a small business.

"You ready?" asked Courtney, locating her in the wine aisle.

"Just let me pay for this, and I'll be right with you."

"That's a lot of money for a bottle of wine," said Courtney, looking at the price on the shelf.

"But it's worth it. You'll see."

Melissa followed Courtney down the country roads. Good thing the satellite signal was strong in most of Hobbs because she doubted that she could ever find her way out of the maze of back roads. In this rural part of town, there were only signs at major intersections. It would be easy to get lost, especially in the dark. Was that hopeful thinking? That it would be dark when she left? The days were longer now that summer was approaching.

They arrived at one of the neglected trailers common in the back country, but the interior was clean and tidy. "You led me to expect a dump," she said as she followed Courtney into the house. "This is actually a sweet, little place."

"I like to set expectations low and exceed them," Courtney said, dropping her school bags on a bench with a gingham cushion. "It's much too expensive for what it is, but I found out about the job just as the summer tourist season was getting started, so I couldn't be too choosy." She called down the hall in the direction Kaylee had disappeared. "Take a shower, honey. Then we can eat."

"It must be hard to be a single parent," Melissa observed as Courtney put the pizza in the oven to stay warm.

"It wasn't much easier when Doug was in the picture. He coached every sport possible for the extra money. He was busier after school than I was." She took a corkscrew out of a drawer and put it on the counter. "Will you please open the wine?"

Melissa was pleased to have something to do while Courtney raced around the kitchen, bringing plates to the table and folding paper towels to use for napkins. "I suppose we could use some glasses. Do you mind not using the wine glasses? They're delicate and need special care. I've already broken most of them."

"Of course. Anything that holds wine is good with me."

Courtney took out three sturdy juice glasses. Melissa filled two of them, handed one to Courtney, and they clicked. "Welcome to my humble abode."

Kaylee returned with wet hair. Melissa noticed her toenails were painted bright green with sparkles. She took the remaining juice glass and popped the lid off a brown bottle. "I love blueberry soda," she confided, pouring the pale-violet liquid into the glass. "It's my favorite."

"Everything is blueberry up here," Melissa said, "but that looks good."

"Want a taste?"

Melissa hesitated. "Sure," she finally said and took the glass Kaylee was offering. "It is good." She felt Courtney studying her as she spoke to her daughter and realized she was making subtle assessments. She hoped she'd passed the test.

They were silent while they ate, sitting at the tiny table in the dining room. The pizza was a New-York style, thin crust type, and a passably good imitation of the real thing, well seasoned and not overly greasy.

"My sister has two girls your age, Kaylee. They're coming up to visit this weekend. Would you like to meet them?"

Courtney was watching the interaction cautiously. Maybe she didn't like the idea that Melissa was negotiating directly with her daughter.

"They're the same age?" asked Courtney. "Are they twins?"

"Yes, but not in the usual sense. My sister and her partner did in vitro fertilization. They had the same sperm donor. Each carried her partner's fertilized egg. Instant family."

"Oh," said Courtney. Melissa listened for hints of judgment, but she didn't hear any.

"Becca was invited to give a guest sermon at St. Mary's by the Sea because June is Pride Month. Apparently, the opening of the Episcopal summer chapel is a big event in Hobbs. Would you like to come along?"

Courtney's eyes widened. "I'm not religious," she said quickly and downed the rest of her wine.

"I'm not either, but with a sister who's a rabbi, I need to show up…to support family, of course. And it's a beautiful setting. There's an outdoor chapel with the altar overlooking the ocean. You've met Lucy Bartlett, the rector, at your 'coming out' meeting the other day."

Either Courtney didn't get the double meaning or was deliberately ignoring it for Kaylee's sake. "Yes, I remember her, the woman with the red hair and the beautiful smile."

"That's the one."

Melissa waited patiently while Courtney chewed her pizza, evidently considering the invitation. "Will your mother be there too?"

"Of course. She's one of Becca's biggest fans."

"What do you think, honey?" asked Courtney, turning to her daughter.

"Sure, Mom. If you want to."

"Okay, then," Courtney concluded with a nod. "I guess we're going."

10

Courtney had barely managed to hide her panic when Melissa had invited her to a church service. Since her mother had joined a Pentecostal church and was "born again," the idea of attending a church service completely turned her off.

Before her conversion, her mother was an ordinary, decent woman who called herself a Methodist and volunteered at the food pantry. Afterwards, she watched nothing but Fox News and railed against "libruls." If her mother's church friends knew Courtney was seeing a woman, they might even picket her house. That is, if they knew where she lived, but she hadn't said a word to her mother about going back to school, the divorce, or moving to Maine. Her relationship with her mother had become so toxic she'd been tempted to cut her off completely. She still telephoned her mother on her birthday, Mother's Day, and holidays. Despite turning into a raging religious fanatic, she was still her mother.

Of course, it was too early to say Courtney was "seeing" Melissa. Two hurried meetings in public places and a take-out pizza could hardly be called "dates." Courtney kept reminding herself to be cautious. She was now the assistant principal in a small town. People could have funny ideas about LBGTQ people, no matter how many rainbow flags flew outside Hobbs' tourist establishments. She really needed this job now that Doug was God knows where. Until she felt more secure in her role and got to know the townspeople better, she'd better keep a low profile.

Courtney opened the door partway and called into the bathroom, "Are you almost finished in there?" Clouds of steam billowed out. A fine mist of vapor frosted the mirror over the sink. "How about leaving some hot water for your mother?"

The faucet cut off with a loud thump. In response, the pipes vibrated in the walls like a backup percussion section. The place was built like a tin can.

"I'm done, Mom. You can have all the hot water you want." It sounded generous, but it would take at least fifteen minutes for the heater to come up to temperature again.

Courtney wasn't about to waste time arguing. As a teen, she'd been equally guilty of hogging the bathroom. What was it about teenagers and bathrooms? Preening for dates didn't completely explain it. Maybe it was the solitude. The shower was a safe space to be naked without someone laughing at your flat chest or the zits on your butt. Despite reaching back to her own adolescence to find compassion, Courtney was glad she'd chosen elementary rather than secondary education. Younger children were so much easier to figure out. Teenagers couldn't even figure out themselves.

Kaylee walked by in her bathrobe with her hair wrapped in a towel. "I can't believe you're making us go to church. I thought you hated church because of Grandma."

"I don't hate church. I just hate fake Christians who judge everyone."

"But aren't you judging them?" asked Kaylee, hands on hips, mocking her mother's stern expression.

Her mother opened her mouth to speak before realizing that Kaylee was right. She *was* judging them. That kid was way too smart for her own good. Too bad Hobbs didn't have a gifted and talented program, but that was too much to ask of a small school district.

"*They're* intolerant," protested Courtney. "Being tolerant doesn't mean I have to tolerate intolerance."

Kaylee gave her an indulgent smile as if she were the parent and Courtney the bratty adolescent. "Who says you do?" Kaylee said, cocking her head. She headed to her room and closed the door more forcefully than necessary. Courtney stared down the hall, wondering how long this period of her daughter's development would last.

While Courtney waited for the water heater to come up to temperature, she reviewed the possible selections to wear. She eliminated the dress with the super-short hemline as inappropriate for church and certainly not the best choice to meet someone's family. Courtney wanted Melissa's mother to think she was a respectable woman. Besides Melissa's family, half of Hobbs would be attending this event, which meant seeing her students and their parents.

Kaylee came into the bathroom while Courtney was putting on her makeup. She surveyed her daughter out of the corner of her eye. "Put on real shoes. You're not wearing flip-flops to church."

"Mom!"

"You heard me."

Kaylee returned wearing neon-colored running shoes that clashed with her top and skirt. "Come on, Kaylee. Give your mother a break." Kaylee rolled her eyes and sighed but returned wearing violet flats that more or less coordinated with her outfit. "Thank you," murmured Courtney, grateful that her daughter was mostly cooperative. At Kaylee's age, Courtney had given her mother hell.

Courtney knew she'd come to the right place when she saw the white, red, and pale blue flag flying below the Stars and Stripes. Below the Episcopal flag flew the rainbow pride flag. *Well, that's different*, thought Courtney. She stopped to read the sign:

St. Mary's by the Sea
A Welcoming and Affirming Episcopal Church
The Rev. Lucille Bartlett, Rector
The Rev. Dr. Thomas Simmons, Associate Rector.

"Is this going to be long?" Kaylee asked, slouching her way along the gravel path to the outdoor chapel.

"I don't really know. I've never been to an Episcopal service before." Courtney patted her daughter's back. "Stand up straight, honey. You'll get round shouldered." As she said it, Courtney remembered her own mother saying the same thing when she was an adolescent. Kaylee gave Courtney an angry side eye, but she adjusted her posture.

People were already seated six feet apart on the park benches that served as outdoor pews. Other people sat in sling chairs and beach chairs. No one had said anything about bringing a chair, but, like most people in

Hobbs, Courtney kept folding chairs in the back of her car for impromptu visits to the beach. She was wondering if she should go back to get them when she noticed Melissa waving to her. She was the tallest woman in sight, but beside her was a woman nearly as tall. She had the same dark, curly hair and closely resembled Melissa. Courtney surmised she must be her sister, the guest preacher.

Courtney approached, feeling the eyes of the women with Melissa giving her careful scrutiny, the older woman particularly. Courtney knew exactly what to do in this kind of situation. She smiled broadly and said, "Hi, I'm Courtney Barnes. And this is my daughter, Kaylee." She nudged Kaylee forward like an offering to angry goddesses. Few women can turn away an attractive child.

Melissa's sister, who was wearing a dark suit but no other sign that she was clergy, extended her hand. "Hi, I'm Rebecca Morgenstern. We've heard so much about you," she said with a glowing smile. "And this is my mother, Ruth, my wife, Judith, and our daughters, Naomi and Sarah."

"Leave it to my bossy sister to take over the introductions," Melissa said, moving in protectively. "Can you tell she's the oldest?"

"Well, technically, I'm the older, since there are only two of us."

"And the grammarian," said Melissa, rolling her eyes. Despite the competitiveness, Courtney sensed that the two sisters were fond of one another, and Rebecca's close resemblance to her sister made Courtney instantly like her. She felt herself relaxing by degrees.

Once the Morgenstern women had satisfied their curiosity about the newcomer, they returned to their earlier conversation. Kaylee was busy getting to know Rebecca's daughters. Now that no one was watching, Courtney dared to reach for Melissa's hand and give it a squeeze. "Thanks for inviting me," she whispered.

Melissa responded with a warm smile. "Thanks for coming. Not everyone would accept a date to a church service."

"I almost didn't."

"Oh?"

"There's history."

"You'll have to tell me."

"I will sometime, but not here. It's a long story."

"Okay. I look forward to hearing it another time because that means I'll see you again." Melissa took Courtney's arm. "Why don't we take a look at the ocean?"

"But Kaylee…"

"Don't worry. My sister-in-law will keep an eye on her. She's a teacher too. She watches all kids like a hawk." She lowered her voice. "I need to speak to you privately." That sounded ominous. Courtney's eyes widened. "Don't worry. I just want to ask you something without all their ears cocked in our direction."

They stood at the seawall, but instead of looking at the ocean below, Courtney kept her eyes carefully trained on Kaylee. There was no need, of course. Kaylee looked perfectly happy chatting with Melissa's nieces, and Melissa's sister-in-law was indeed watching them all like a hawk.

"I apologize. I hadn't expected that to be so awkward," said Melissa. "As you saw, my sister takes over. She can be intimidating."

"She comes on pretty strong, but she has a kind face, and she's almost as pretty as her sister."

The compliment made Melissa smile. "You always look at the bright side, don't you? I like that about you. I know we've just met, but will you come to dinner tonight? My sister doesn't visit often, and I'd like you to get to know my family."

Courtney's caution brakes slammed on, and she backed up a step. She didn't want to discourage Melissa by saying it was too soon for that. Instead, she said, "I don't want to intrude."

"Impossible. Dad used to invite strangers off the beach. Mom didn't always like that, but she welcomed them. She became so used to him bringing home new people she's forgotten how to make friends on her own."

"That's sad. So many widows are lost without their husbands."

"She's lost all right," Melissa said, gazing in her mother's direction. "Please say you'll come. Judith grew up in Israel, and she's making a Middle Eastern feast called a Meze. It has falafel, and hummus, stuffed grape leaves, tabouli, and all kinds of tasty things. I'm sure Kaylee will find it educational."

Courtney admired Melissa's cleverness. Obviously, she knew an educator couldn't resist that argument. She looked over to where her daughter stood laughing with the twins. "She seems to be having a good time with your nieces. She hasn't had a chance to make many friends in Hobbs."

Melissa reached for her hand. "Please say you'll come for dinner." Her blue eyes were mesmerizing.

"Hello, Courtney." Courtney dropped Melissa's hand like it was on fire and spun around. She was relieved to see Lucy Bartlett standing behind her. The green vestments she wore fluttered in the gentle breeze from the ocean. Her red hair was pinned up in two circular braids at the back of her head. She smiled at Melissa. "I'm glad your sister talked you into coming today."

Melissa laughed. "You think I could get away with *not* coming?"

"You're wearing your Princess-Leia hairstyle today," said another voice, approaching from behind. Liz Stolz, looking sharp in a navy pants suit, nodded greetings to Melissa and Courtney before bending to touch her cheek to the priest's. "Good morning, Lucy. Are you expecting an attack by the Empire?"

"No, but just in case, I've called in reinforcements from the Republic. Melissa's sister is giving the sermon this morning."

Dr. Stolz smiled in Melissa's direction. "I look forward to hearing her preach." She nodded to Courtney and Melissa in turn. "Thanks for supporting our Mother Lucy. She needs all the support she can get."

"Stop, Liz," said Rev. Bartlett, lightly elbowing her. "They don't know you're kidding." She patted Courtney's arm and turned to Melissa. "Great to see you, both."

Courtney's eyes followed the two women as they walked away, noting the doctor's hand at the small of Rev. Bartlett's back.

"Do you see what I see?" Melissa said, watching too.

"I sure do. They're in love."

"Crazy in love," said Melissa, scrutinizing them. She glanced back to where her family was sitting. "I see my sister putting on her tallit. They're getting ready to start the service. We should get back to our seats."

A recorder began to play. A procession led by Rabbi Morgenstern came down the center aisle. "That's different, letting a guest preacher lead in her church," whispered Melissa near Courtney's ear. "That Rev. Bartlett is quite an iconoclast. No wonder Becca loves her. Birds of a feather…"

Bringing up the rear of the procession was a tall, elegantly dressed young woman leading the hymn. Melissa nudged Courtney with her elbow and showed her a paper with the words for the hymn. "We can share," Melissa said. "I like to sing. It doesn't matter what."

After the hymn, Rev. Bartlett addressed the congregation. "Good morning and welcome to our outdoor chapel on this gorgeous second Sunday after Pentecost. St. Mary's by the Sea is privileged to welcome two special guests. To celebrate Pride Month, we are offering special prayers for the LGBTQ community which, despite great strides in legal rights and acceptance, remains under siege. God created every one of us in their image. Diversity is God's imagination on display. This morning, my dear friend, Rabbi Rebecca Morgenstern of Temple Beth Shalom in New York will give the sermon. Rabbi Morgenstern is a tireless advocate for LGBTQ youth. Our other special guest is Denise Chantal, who is a candidate for music director of our parish. Before we begin today's liturgy, Ms. Chantal will sing something to inspire us on this beautiful, summer morning."

Rev. Bartlett took a seat next to Melissa's sister. She reached for her hand, and they exchanged a warm smile. There were a few coughs and sneezes as the congregation waited, but otherwise, the only sound was the waves crashing on the rocks below. The extraordinarily tall woman stepped to the center of the flagstone patio in front of the altar. She folded her hands in the traditional singing position and smiled in Rev. Bartlett's direction. The priest took out her phone and made a few taps. Pre-recorded music flowed through the speakers. After an anxious smile toward Mother Lucy, the singer began. The pure sound that came from the woman's throat sounded almost otherworldly. It was sublimely beautiful, but oddly androgynous.

Melissa leaned over and whispered into Courtney's ear, "Is that a trans woman?"

Courtney had never met a trans woman before, so she couldn't say. She corrected herself. At least, she didn't *know* she'd met any. She studied the singer more carefully. Apart from her height, she looked as feminine as any woman, even more so than some. Courtney glanced around at the others in the congregation and saw that everyone was as fascinated as she was. They were hanging on every note.

11

"I thought Denise did a wonderful job of leading the music at Sunday's worship. Does anyone disagree?" Lucy looked down the conference table at the long faces. The vestry members stared at the tabletop, their hands, their phones, anything but their rector. Lucy glanced across the table for a sign of support from Tom, but he wouldn't even give her eye contact. "Well? Someone say something!" She stared at Tom until he raised his eyes.

"Lucy, we all agree that Denise is exceptionally well qualified and very talented."

"But?" Lucy demanded. She glanced at Olivia, hoping to find some support, but Olivia suddenly found her pen enthralling.

"Legally, we can't discuss it," said Abbie, the senior warden. "In our state, we can't discriminate on the basis of gender or sexual identity."

"That's right," said Lucy, trying to keep the impatience out of her voice. Tom was staring at her, looking worried. He was the only one in the room who had ever seen her in a full-blown temper. She smiled to reassure him. "And there's a good reason for that law," she said, still holding Tom's gaze. "People have crazy ideas about trans people. They worry about them in bathrooms. I'm gay. Do you worry about me being in the ladies' room with your daughters?"

That got their attention. Suddenly, everyone was looking at her. "Lucy, we know you're a woman," said Olivia. "For goodness' sake, you're a priest!"

"Look at the Roman Catholics to see how that protected them."

Olivia's face, usually so controlled, showed her frustration. "Lucy, we all know you to be an upstanding, moral person. *That's* why we trust you with our children."

"So we distrust someone simply because she's trans? Why can't we give her the benefit of the doubt?"

Abbie stared at her. She was the only person besides Tom and Olivia who would dare to confront her in a vestry meeting. "Mother Lucy, it sounds like you want to hire Denise *because* she's trans. To prove a point."

"No, I want to hire her because she's the most qualified. No one even comes close." Lucy looked around at the frowning faces. "Let's be honest. The only reason we haven't already offered her the job is she's trans. I'm leaving for New York tomorrow, and this needs to be settled. We said we would get back to these people last week."

"Mother Lucy," began Jim Duggins, the verger, "we are a welcoming parish. We turn no one away. When you came out, we all supported you. Why do we have to keep proving how tolerant we are?"

"We're not trying to prove anything," Lucy said. "It's about hiring the most qualified candidate, and not turning her down because we don't understand her gender choice."

"Gender is not a choice," said Pete Cote, the oldest member of the vestry. "God makes us male or female. It says so in Genesis."

"It's not that simple, Pete," Olivia said quietly. Lucy was pleased to hear the patience in her voice, even though it was a little forced. Not long ago, Olivia would have run over the man to assert her opinion.

"I hope she doesn't expect us to pay for her treatments," said Abbie, folding her arms under her significant breasts. In a former life, she had run a large division of a major corporation. Like any good company woman, she was always scanning for risks that threatened the bottom line. "I've heard that surgery can be very expensive, which will make our premiums go up. We can barely afford them now."

"That's my fault," said Lucy, "I was on Erika's insurance while she was alive. Now, I'm back on the church's plan."

Olivia shot a disapproving look in Abbie's direction. "Lucy, don't blame yourself for losing your health insurance because your spouse died. Denise assured me that she will cover all the costs directly related to her transition with her own funds. She expects nothing from us other than the same basic coverage all church employees get."

Tom looked sheepish. "Lucy, you are the rector, but it is the duty of the vestry to hire staff."

"Yes, and I would never try to force a decision on you." Lucy sighed in resignation, certain she'd already lost the argument. "I have my own reservations."

"Will you share them?" Olivia asked.

"There are many conservative people in our parish. They've barely gotten used to me being gay. Maybe asking them to accept a trans music director is a bridge too far. But I feel it would be an injustice to turn away the most qualified candidate for the sake of keeping the peace."

"People had nothing but good things to say about Denise's performance at the outdoor worship service," Olivia said. "She is exceptionally good at passing. Maybe some people won't perceive that she's not a genetic female."

"But if it gets out, it could precipitate a crisis in the parish, which could be worse," Abbie said in a practical voice. "People might accuse us of trying to hide something."

"Certainly, we're not going to make a grand announcement," countered Olivia. "Oh, by the way, we've hired a trans music director…No, it has to be her choice to come out as trans, but if we decide to hire her, we must all agree that we will support her. And we can't deny that we knew."

"I suggest we take a vote," said Tom. "All those who support the candidacy of Denise Chantal, please raise your hands."

Lucy raised her hand and saw that five of the seven members of the vestry were in favor. Tom and Pete were opposed.

"The ayes have it," said Tom. "We will offer the position to Ms. Chantal. Now, we should discuss how to handle the fallout from the decision."

Lucy patiently listened to the debate before weighing in. "It's not our business to tell anyone about Denise's gender status. But I agree with Olivia, we must be unified in our support of her when it comes out, and we know it will. Is there anyone in this group who cannot agree to this?" She looked up and down the table. Everyone was shaking their heads. "Let me state it more positively. Can I have a show of hands to pledge support for Denise?"

This time, they all raised their hands.

"Thank you," said Lucy. "Abbie, I'll leave it to you to draft a letter offering the position. In my absence, Father Tom can sign it."

After the meeting, Lucy gathered her papers into her bag. Although she was exhausted, she was pleased with the result and relieved the meeting was over. She'd been through some tough vestry meetings at St. Margaret's, but this counted as the worst.

As she turned to head to the door, she noticed Tom waiting for her.

"I want you to know that even though I voted against Denise," he said, "I think she will be a good music director."

Lucy searched his face for clues to why he felt it necessary to make such a statement. "So, why did you vote against her?"

Tom let out a long sigh. "I wish I knew, but I can't put my finger on it. I can tell you it has something to do with me, and not with her. She is very qualified and professional. When I figure it out, I'll let you know."

"Please do because I'm still trying to figure it out myself. But one thing I know, I don't need to understand why someone is trans. I only need to accept them and love them like anyone else."

"I wish we could all love as generously as you do, Lucy." Tom walked her out to the car, reviewing the things that might come up during the two weeks she would be away. "Good luck in New York," he said, holding open the car door for her. "I know you'll ace your exams."

"Thanks, Tom. Call me if you need anything."

When Lucy saw the time on the dashboard, she flew into a panic. Liz would be waiting for her and getting impatient. Lucy took the back road through the supermarket parking lot to get to Beach Road. She resisted the urge to speed, especially because there were so many pedestrians on their way to the beach.

The familiar Audi was parked in the driveway when she got home. Lucy smiled when she saw that it had been carefully positioned to keep the garage doors clear, which would enable her to pull her car inside. Liz was always so practical.

When Lucy emerged from the garage, the sound of opera playing through the car speakers was so loud she could hear it through the closed windows. Liz had reclined the seat, and her eyes closed. With that noise, she couldn't possibly be asleep. Lucy tapped gently on the window. Liz sat up, looking startled and rolled down the window. "I didn't even hear you drive in," she said, lowering the volume.

"How could you? I'm surprised you're not deaf." Lucy listened more carefully and identified the track playing through the Audi's super-premium sound system. "Listening to me again?"

"I can never get enough of hearing you. I wish you'd made more recordings."

"I have some you've never heard."

"You do?" Liz's eyes instantly widened with excited anticipation.

"I'll even let you rip the CDs, but I'm not sure how I feel about you fetishizing my voice."

"I am not!" protested Liz indignantly.

"Yes, you are. Don't lie to me." Lucy leaned through the open window to kiss her. "You're all dressed up. I guess we're going to a nice place tonight."

"It's your last night before you leave. I want it to be special."

"So, you're celebrating because I'm going away?"

"No!" Liz protested.

Lucy lightly pinched her arm. "Liz, you're so literal. Just like Erika. Must be a German trait. Come in while I get changed."

Liz turned off the music and got out of the car. She reached for Lucy's bag to carry it to the door.

"I'm really sorry I'm late." Lucy unlocked the door and shoved it open with her shoulder. "Denise's candidacy was even more controversial than I expected."

"People have come a long way in accepting gays and lesbians, but trans is another story. The other side has made trans the new front in the culture wars," said Liz, handing Lucy her bag. Liz was a stickler for order, so Lucy put it neatly inside her office door rather than dropping it on the sofa as usual.

"Thank you for driving the Audi tonight instead of your truck. It's hard to get in and out of a truck in a dress."

"That's only because you're so tiny. Normal people do just fine. I'll teach you sometime."

"You mean you'll wear a skirt?"

"For the purposes of instruction only."

"I've seen you in a skirt."

Liz frowned. "I must have been in drag."

"At a funeral? I don't think so. And you wore a dress to Brenda's wedding."

"Busted!" Liz kissed the top of Lucy's head and gave her a gentle nudge. "Go change. I'm hungry."

When Lucy came down the stairs wearing her favorite red dress, the one that clung to her backside, the frank admiration in Liz's eyes made her smile. Lucy was used to being admired by men, and occasionally by women, but it was nothing compared to the way Liz looked at her. Lucy could be wearing rags, and Liz would have that same adoring expression on her face.

They headed into town. While Liz's eyes were on the road, Lucy took the opportunity to check out her outfit. Liz was wearing dress slacks and an arty, loose blouse with a variety of necklaces that vaguely matched in color but not in shape, which created a kind of modern sculpture at her throat. She seldom wore earrings but tonight, she did.

"I like your style, Liz," Lucy said. "It's unconventional, but creative."

"People say I clean up well. I learned from Erika's ex how to use colors and shapes to make simple things look dressy. She was an artist, but you knew that."

"Were you close to Jeanine?" Lucy asked. She actually knew very little about her wife's former partner, feminist artist Jeanine Sanders, who'd died suddenly of a heart attack before Lucy had met Erika.

Liz looked pensive. "I'm not sure I could say we were close. I think Jeanine found me entertaining as the other half of the comedy act, the one that no one else finds funny."

"The Liz-and-Erika show was always entertaining. Funny? Not so much. But tell me about Jeanine. Erika didn't really say much except that they both had multiple partners."

"Erika was very discreet."

"But I bet she told you."

"Of course, she did," said Liz with a sly look. "She was my wingman, and I was hers. Erika adored Jeanine, who was a real character, but she was considered quite talented…that is, if her Cubism-redux style appeals to you."

"It doesn't. Erika kept a few of her paintings for sentimental reasons, but honestly, I don't really care for them."

"What's not to like about colorful images of morbidly obese women with abundant pubic hair? Or as your father-in-law used to say, 'fat women with hairy vaginas.' Sometimes, he used the other word."

"I don't believe it."

Liz laughed. "You didn't know Stefan in the old days. If you don't like the paintings, you should donate them to a museum or sell them and give the money to Erika's foundation for female artists."

"Good idea."

Liz put her hand on Lucy's thigh. The unexpected touch made her twitch. She tried to ignore the hand's warm presence, but she couldn't.

"Will you miss me while you're in New York?" Liz suddenly asked.

"Of course, I will. You could come visit me."

Liz nodded, considering the idea. "I'm on call this weekend, or I would."

"You could pick me up. I know it's a long drive, but the Amtrak ride is even longer."

"I can probably scare up some theater tickets. A few of the theaters have reopened. We could make it a date."

"You're taking this dating thing very seriously, but you should keep your hands on the wheel. There's a lot of traffic tonight," said Lucy, giving Liz's hand a squeeze before lifting it off her thigh.

"Glad I made reservations," Liz said, pulling into La Scala's packed parking lot. She drove around three times before finding a spot. "I hope it's not too tight, and you can get out."

"I may not be able to get out of a truck without showing my underwear, but being small has other advantages."

It was noisier inside than Lucy would have preferred after such a busy and contentious day, but like every Hobbs restaurant in the summer, La Scala was jammed with tourists. Liz glanced at the specials sheet and announced, "I know what I'm having."

Lucy didn't have to guess, or even say it aloud, but she did. "Lobster."

While Lucy figured out what she wanted to order, Liz intently studied the wine list. She ordered a super Tuscan. Out of curiosity, Lucy picked up the wine list to learn more about the wine. Her eyes flew open when she saw the price.

"Liz, that wine is crazy expensive. You don't need to impress me."

"I'm not. It's a good wine, and it's a special occasion. Besides, what am I saving my money for? Life is short." Liz said it innocently, but the idle sentiment instantly brought thoughts of Erika to Lucy's mind. Yes, life was short.

Because it was so busy, there was a long wait for their entrees. Liz had ordered the lobster scampi-style, and Lucy was glad there was no shell involved. "Remember the time you cracked your lobster claw and shot juice all over Tom's glasses?"

Liz laughed. "I'm surprised he ever forgave me for that. It was kind of obscene." She lewdly raised a brow.

"You really enjoy being naughty, don't you?" asked Lucy, expertly winding her pasta in her spoon. "What's that about?"

"Lucy, I'm eating," warned Liz. "*Don't* shrink me." Her impatient tone bordered on hostility. Lucy looked up to see where it came from, but Liz quickly changed the subject to the long-term mental effects of COVID. "Sorry to bore you with the medical talk," she said, breaking off a piece of ciabatta and dipping it in the scampi sauce. "Jenny and I used to talk about medicine at dinner. Sometimes I miss it."

"Did you talk to Maggie about medicine?"

"Not unless it directly pertained to her case, and then she had a limited tolerance for it. She said it bored her." Liz glanced around. "Did you know this is her favorite restaurant?"

Lucy did know because, when she and Maggie used to shop together, they liked to have lunch there. "How's she doing?" Lucy asked casually.

Liz shrugged. "Okay, I guess. I'm watching the kids this weekend while she and Alina go to New York to finish cleaning out storage space at her co-op." Liz peered at her. "You're her friend. Don't *you* talk to her?"

"I've called a few times to see how things are going. Otherwise, we haven't talked."

"She's not exactly what I'd call an attentive friend. After she moved in with me, she invited her so-called best friend at NYU. She came up once. Then I never saw her again. With Maggie, relationships are mostly transactional."

The coldness with which Liz dissected her ex-wife made Lucy look up from her dinner. Although Liz never missed an opportunity to disparage psychotherapy, her psychological assessments were insightful.

"What time is your train tomorrow?" Liz asked, unaware that across the table, Lucy was analyzing her. "I'll drive you to the station."

"Abbie said she'd drive me."

"She has her old mother to worry about. I'll drive you." Liz's tone was absolute. She clearly didn't expect an argument.

"You'll miss your morning walk."

"I'll walk at lunchtime."

Lucy could think of other reasons to turn down the offer. She was tempted to persist before she perceived why Liz was being so adamant. The status of their relationship had changed. They were dating, so Liz considered driving Lucy to the train her duty. It was an ethnic trait, something Erika would have done, but Erika was less stubborn about such things than Liz. *You have to stop comparing them*, Lucy thought.

For dessert, they split a molten chocolate cake with raspberries. Liz caught the last raspberry on her spoon and offered it to Lucy. It seemed a very intimate thing to do in a crowded restaurant in a town where so many people knew them, but Lucy opened her mouth to accept the fruit. Liz watched intently as her lips slid off the spoon.

"You took the last one! Now, you're the old maid!" Liz crowed.

"You tricked me! I can't believe anyone remembers that old game! And here, I thought you were being romantic."

"I was being romantic," Liz said. Her smoldering gaze over the teasing smile was confusing. As Lucy gazed into her blue eyes, warm arousal gathered between her legs. Physically, she was so ready to make love, yet she couldn't shake the idea that she should wait. In her bereavement groups, she always advised people to avoid jumping into bed after the death of a partner. Love chemicals could temporarily block the pain of loss, but left it unresolved, which could leave the new relationship on shaky ground.

"What are you thinking about?" Liz asked softly. "Don't tell me you hate raspberries."

"No, I love them, especially when a beautiful woman feeds them to me with her own spoon, but we should go. I haven't finished packing, and that train is leaving tomorrow morning with or without me."

Liz looked disappointed, but she signalled to the waiter to bring the check. On the way home, she suggested they drive along the ocean road. Lucy knew exactly what she had in mind when she pulled over to park by the seawall. She opened the windows to let in the ocean breeze. "I don't want this evening to end. You don't mind if we sit here for a few minutes?"

"As long as we're not parking to make out like two kids where everyone can see us."

"That's exactly what we're going to do." Liz turned off the engine. She unbuckled her seat belt and leaned over the console. The lobster had imparted a faint whiff of fish on her lips. Lucy thought of the raspberry Liz had fed her from her spoon, which made her open her mouth to invite her in. The interior of her mouth tasted tangy from the wine and the lemon in the scampi sauce. Lucy knew she should swat away the gentle hand caressing her breast, especially when it pinched her nipple and made it pucker. She felt her body opening, ready to welcome Liz inside, but she knew that if she gave in to her desire tonight, they'd both be miserable while she was away. She ended the kiss as gently as she could.

"Take me home, Liz. I have an early morning tomorrow."

Liz turned her face away, but Lucy turned it back. "Don't turn away from me. I know how hard it is to wait. It's hard for me too. I love you, but we're not making love tonight." Lucy gave her a gentle kiss on the nose. "Please be patient. I promise I'm worth the wait, and so are you."

Liz compressed her lips, but she put on her seat belt and started the engine.

When she got upstairs, Lucy undressed and removed her makeup. The image in the mirror confirmed that she was no longer young. So much of her time on this earth had already been used up. It was finite. Erika's premature death had proven there were no guarantees. Maybe she was wrong to make Liz wait. She reflected on how tenderly Liz was courting her as she got into bed.

The queen-sized bed still seemed so enormous without Erika, but after almost six months of her absence, Lucy was getting used to it. Lucy patted the space where her wife had once lain and wished her goodnight… wherever she was. She closed her eyes, but scenes from her evening with Liz kept replaying in her mind. She remembered Liz's blue eyes intensely holding her gaze as she offered the last raspberry off her spoon.

"Oh, Liz," Lucy whispered into the dark. She sat up and tapped open Liz's contact on her phone and requested a video chat. When it opened, she saw a sleepy, gray-haired woman, wearing a faded T-shirt.

"Lucy, is everything all right?" Liz asked anxiously.

"Yes, everything's fine. I wanted to thank you for a beautiful evening, and I have a confession to make."

Liz looked even more anxious.

"I'm not being honest with you. My therapist's head keeps urging caution, but if I listen to my body, it tells me how much I want you."

Liz's mouth twitched into an endearing off-centered grin. "I can be there in five minutes."

Lucy laughed. "Not tonight. We both have to get up too early. When we make love, I want to take my time. In fact, I might never let you out of bed again."

The smiling blue eyes grew serious. "I love you, Lucy."

Lucy brought her lips close to the screen and made a kissing sound. "I love you too. Now, go to sleep. I'll see you in the morning."

"You think I can go to sleep now?"

"Sure you can. Think of me holding you in my arms."

"That's not all I'll be thinking about."

Lucy air kissed the phone. "Sleep tight." She closed her eyes and tried to sleep, but she found herself imagining what Liz must be doing. *Oh, why not?* thought Lucy, reaching under her nightgown.

12

Melissa put on her mask as she watched her mother's car drive out of the train station. She'd given up her car when she'd moved to Boston because parking was outrageously expensive. Public transportation or taxis got her around the city, and if she needed to get out of town, she rented a car. So far, the arrangement had saved her a small fortune, but if she intended to move up to Hobbs, she couldn't expect her mother to get up early to drive her to the train.

She glanced at her phone. She was ten minutes early, but if she missed this train, the next one didn't get into Boston until almost eleven o'clock. The partners' meeting, their first in-house since the pandemic had begun, had been scheduled to start at nine-thirty. Mike Danvers, the senior partner, had made it clear that everyone was expected to be there. *Everyone.*

Melissa was surprised to see so many people waiting. She wondered if there were more commuters in the summer. This would be an interesting experiment. As a visitor, she'd only taken the train during off-peak hours. The commuter run made limited stops, but the trip to Boston took about two hours. It wasn't an unreasonable commute, but it meant getting up at four-thirty. Melissa groaned at the thought.

She walked to where a knot of people stood, assuming they knew the best position to wait. When she glanced up from reading her emails, she noticed an Audi SUV pull into the passenger drop-off area. Melissa squinted and recognized the driver as Liz Stolz. Sitting in the passenger seat was another familiar figure, the Episcopal rector, Lucy Bartlett. As she watched, the doctor leaned over and gave her passenger a prolonged kiss. Melissa found herself thinking how cute they were, then scolded herself for ageist thinking. *If they're lucky enough to find love, good for them.*

The doctor got out and took a rolling suitcase from the back of the SUV. She handed it off with another kiss, this one on the cheek. The priest was wearing her collar. Wherever she was going, it was on official business.

"Good morning, Rev. Bartlett. I see it's an early morning for you too."

"Melissa! How good to see you."

"You too. I like your mask. Treble maker? Hah! I get it. Because you're a soprano. Right?"

"My daughter gave it to me."

"From what I hear from my sister, the pun applies too."

"Like John Lewis, I only make good trouble." Lucy reached out and patted Melissa's arm. "Where are you heading this morning?"

"Boston. My firm called an in-house meeting of all the partners. How about you?"

"New York."

"Wow! That's a long trip."

"Oh, it is, but it's better than driving and trying to park my car in Manhattan."

"You're lucky to have your chauffeur drive you to the station. I hear it's hard to get a parking spot in the summer."

To Melissa's surprise, the priest blushed all the way to crimson. Maybe she had just come from spending the night with the doctor.

"It's a longer trip," said Lucy, skillfully deflecting, "but if I ride the train, instead of drive, I can study. I'm working on my doctorate at Union Theological."

"I heard that. Good for you, Rev. Bartlett."

"Please, call me Lucy. Your sister and I have become such good friends, and I hope we will be too."

"Thank you, Lucy. I hope so too." She sighed. "Too bad you have to study. When I saw you, I was hoping for an excuse to avoid reading case files."

"I have a very long trip to New York. I'm sure I can spare the time it takes to get to Boston. Fortunately, the pandemic gave me a reprieve from the residency requirements. Otherwise, I couldn't even consider going back for my degree."

"I've been lucky too. The firm has let us work from home since the pandemic began, but there's talk everyone will have to come back to the office."

"You don't like that idea," Lucy guessed after studying Melissa's face.

"It does wreck my plans to help my mother get adjusted to life in Maine. I was hoping to give her some company for the summer."

"Hold that thought," said Lucy as the train rumbled into the station.

Through the passing windows, Melissa could see the train was already crowded. She deliberately blocked the path of an aggressive, young man so that the priest could board with her suitcase. "Thank you for running interference," Lucy said over her shoulder, rolling her bag down the aisle. She stopped at two facing seats. "Here good?"

"Perfect." Melissa tossed her bag on the seat to lift Lucy's into the luggage rack above.

"You don't need to do that," Lucy protested.

"I know, but my mother taught me to be respectful to my elders."

There was suddenly fire in Lucy's green eyes. "I'm often lucky to get an assist from tall people because I'm short, but not because I'm old." Although her voice remained friendly, it had a slight edge.

"I'm sorry," said Melissa. "I didn't mean anything except to be helpful. I've gotten into the habit of doing things like that because of my mother."

"Be careful, Melissa, or you'll make her old before her time," warned Lucy.

"I hadn't thought of that." Melissa took the seat facing forward because the train moving in the wrong direction always disoriented her. "Now that Dad's gone, I'm just trying to help her."

Lucy settled in the opposite seat. "Does your mother act like she expects you to care of her?"

"Yes, I guess she does," Melissa said. "My father was very attentive to her. She's what you call 'a high maintenance woman.' There are other names for what she is, but they're pretty mean, and there's enough name calling right now."

"I think I know which name you're referring to." Lucy raised her auburn brows. "It's pretty nasty."

"I don't know why some Jewish women were raised to expect so much attention," Melissa said with a frown.

"You weren't?"

"No, actually. I showed interest in law early, so Dad brought me to the office and talked to me about his cases…in a general way, of course, not breaking any confidentiality."

"So, your father was your role model?"

"He was. He's the reason I became an attorney." Melissa reminded herself that the priest was a trained psychotherapist, which explained the leading questions. Melissa was used to being the one doing the interviewing, but she sensed Lucy's gentle probing came from kindness, so she didn't mind being open with her. "My mother wasn't always so demanding. It's been hard for her, moving into a new community while she's still grieving, especially during a pandemic. I'm only trying to help her get through this rough patch."

"It seems like that now, but it could become an established pattern. Unless your mother starts taking responsibility for finding her way, you may get stuck enabling her." Lucy frowned. "Apologies for the unsolicited advice."

"No worries. I appreciate it." Melissa looked into the green eyes that were so full of warmth. "I heard you were recently widowed. How did you cope with the loss?"

Lucy swallowed audibly and looked out the window. When Melissa realized there might be tears involved, she regretted saying anything. Finally, Lucy turned and said, "My situation is different. My wife and I both led independent lives before we met. It's different between two women."

"I'm gay," Melissa blurted out.

"I think I knew that," Lucy replied matter-of-factly.

"My sister has a big mouth."

Lucy's eyes smiled. "I didn't need her to tell me."

"I read that much?"

"Not especially. In fact, most people would never guess, but I saw you with your friend, the new assistant principal. That clued me into your preferences. And Liz invited you to her boat. Her gaydar is pretty reliable."

Now, it was Melissa's turn to blush. "You're very observant."

"It's my job," said Lucy with a shrug. "You asked how I coped with my loss. It took a village. I mean, literally. I was lucky to be part of a tight-knit group of women, who were there for me. I was a wreck. After the Christmas service, I literally had to be picked up off the ground. I kept trying to prove I didn't need help, but they gently insisted I accept it. The best thing about a community is everyone helps a little, so no one has to bear the entire burden."

"You're lucky to have such good friends."

"I know. They kept me going when I couldn't. When I started to feel like myself again, I asserted my independence, and they respectfully stepped back. That's how it's supposed to be. People support you in your grief, but eventually, you need to find your way."

"I heard you're an expert on grief."

"I run a bereavement group. That's not the same. There's no such thing as an expert in grief. Everyone grieves differently. Everyone's timeline for grieving is different. People probably wonder how I recovered so quickly. Maybe they think it means I didn't really love my wife, but I did, and I do. We had so much love in our short time together. I miss her terribly, but every day, the pain is a little less, and the happy memories make me cry more often than the sad ones."

"That's beautiful," Melissa said. "It makes me want to cry."

Lucy reached over and patted her hand. "I'm sorry. That wasn't my intention."

"My mother is still so angry at my father for dying young. They were supposed to grow old together. Now, she's a widow at sixty-six."

"What's that old saying? 'Man proposes and God disposes.' Anger is part of the grief process. At first, I was angry that Erika died so suddenly. I never even had a chance to say goodbye. Fortunately, the anger didn't last long. I couldn't indulge it. I had to help other people dealing with the loss. Erika's father is still alive. He's in his nineties and fragile. Erika and Liz were friends for over forty years. She was grieving too. We could comfort one another by sharing our love for her as well as our grief."

Sometimes, the things religious people said, including her own sister, annoyed Melissa because they sounded so trite, but Lucy's words rang true because they came from experience.

"I thought that's what we were doing with my mother, sharing our love for Dad, but now she's just turning us into a substitute for what she's missing in her life. She's desperate to meet a replacement for my father, as if that will make it all better."

"The shock of being alone is the hardest thing after losing a spouse," Lucy said, "especially if they've been married for a long time."

Melissa smiled, wondering how much she should say about her observations. Lucy seemed to be sharing more with Liz Stolz than love for her deceased wife. "You seem to have that problem solved. Are you with Dr. Stolz now?"

Lucy gave her a sharp look, but she answered the question in an even tone. "We're exploring the potential for a relationship. Obviously, that's not for public consumption."

I've stepped on her toes, thought Melissa, *I need to reassure her.* "As you probably know, attorneys are bound by confidentiality like clergy. Your secret is safe with me."

"It's a poorly kept secret, but given my public role in the community, discretion is in order."

"Not that my opinion matters, but you make a sweet couple."

"Thank you." Melissa felt Lucy studying her carefully. "And how is it going with the school principal?"

Melissa glanced away to avoid Lucy's inquiring gaze, but when she turned back, she saw that Lucy was still waiting for an answer. "It may have potential for a relationship. I don't really know yet. We've just started seeing one another. Today's meeting may decide whether I can pursue it."

"Why is that?"

"If they force us back into the office, it could be a problem of geography. I'm not a big believer in long-distance relationships. I tried it once, and it was a disaster. Distance may make some hearts grow fonder. Sometimes, it makes them cheat."

"But not always."

"No, of course not. There are other logistical problems. I'd have to get a car again. I'd be living in two places, it's a long commute, especially in the summertime when there's so much traffic."

Lucy watched Melissa's face while she ticked off her issues, but she didn't look impressed. "You've certainly come up with lots of reasons why the relationship can't work. Are there any reasons why it can?"

"Why did I think it was a good idea to spend the ride to Boston with a therapist?"

Lucy's merry laughter was musical. "I don't know. Why did you?"

"Because I always feel good after I spend time with you. I can't see it now, because of the mask, but you have the most amazing smile. I bet people tell you that all the time."

"They do, but it's just my smile. When I was on the stage, people tried to tell me how to smile, which was weird."

"I hate plastic smiles," Melissa agreed.

"My mother was a model, but her smile was always genuine. That's the smile I remember and try to emulate."

"You do it well."

"Thank you," Lucy said. "So, are you going to tell me the reasons why the relationship *can* work?"

Melissa had been warned by her sister that St. Margaret's rector was a force to be reckoned with, so she wasn't surprised that Lucy was persistent. "I need to think about it for a moment."

"Take your time, and you don't have to tell me unless you want to," said Lucy casually.

Another therapist's trick. Act indifferent.

"We're very attracted to one another," Melissa said.

Lucy shrugged. "That's good, but everyone is very attracted in the beginning."

"She has a child. I like kids, but I don't know if I consider myself parent material."

"Erika was worried about being a parent, but she was surprisingly good at it. Because she'd taught college students for years, she was wise to the ways of adolescents. I was grateful for her support, especially considering the difficult circumstances."

Melissa waited for her to say more, but Lucy merely smiled, forcing her to ask, "What circumstances?"

"My daughter is on the autism spectrum, but she's super bright, a math genius. She's already been accepted for a PhD program at Yale. Fortunately, my wife and father-in-law were mathematicians. Erika changed to philosophy, of course, but she could communicate with my daughter on her level."

"Is it harder to communicate, now that she's gone?"

"Emily and I speak our own language. She has musical talent. We share that."

"You've led a charmed life, Lucille Bartlett, former opera star, now priest."

"I have, but nothing has turned out the way I expected. Life always has surprises for me. I try to accept them gracefully."

13

Kaylee collected some corn chips into a plastic bowl and spooned some salsa into a small dish before making a beeline to her room.

"Is she trying to tell us something?" asked Melissa, reaching for a handful of chips.

"I think she wants to give us privacy."

"That's nice of her. Have you told her about us?" Melissa bit into a chip.

"No, but she's a smart kid and has probably figured it out." Courtney peered at Melissa. "Is there an 'us' to tell her about? I didn't know we were that far along. That's part of the reason I haven't said anything."

Melissa scooped up some salsa with a chip. "I don't know. What do you think?"

"That's not fair. I asked first." Courtney turned and leaned back against the sink, waiting to hear what Melissa would say.

"Yes, you did. And I suppose we should try to figure it out because when there's a kid involved, things are more complicated."

"I'm glad you finally noticed the kid," replied Courtney, instantly sorry it sounded so sarcastic.

"Of course, I noticed the kid. I've even had conversations with *the kid,* who's smart and very together for a twelve-year old. That's your doing I suspect."

Courtney shrugged, but she was pleased to hear her daughter complimented. Kaylee was a good kid, compared to others she'd seen. "I'm not sure I need to make an announcement that we're seeing one another. Kaylee knows I've been involved with women before. She saw some photos of the woman I was with before I married Doug and asked a lot of questions."

"What did you tell her?"

"The truth. It didn't faze her in the least. Young people grow up seeing LGBTQ people on TV, in the news, in politics, everywhere! It's normal to them."

"That's what we've been trying to achieve, isn't it? Visibility? Parity?"

"I suppose so." Courtney glanced down the hall toward Kaylee's closed door. "She's probably better adapted to the idea of us getting together than we are."

"Maybe we're overthinking this." Melissa made a racket digging into the chips. "We've barely kissed, and we're worrying about what comes next."

"When you get to be our age and have responsibilities, you don't just jump into bed and hope for the best. It's important to think things through."

"Really? I've spent my whole life thinking and planning and strategizing. I made sure I joined the right clubs in high school and did the right community service, so I could get into an Ivy League college. I studied like a maniac to get good grades and ace the LSATs. I worked my ass off to make law review, then used my father's contacts to get into the right firm. Finally, I worked my way up to partner. And where am I now?"

"You're a partner in the right firm, and I bet you make buckets of money."

"I do. But so what? I work absurd hours and pay ridiculous money for a tiny apartment in one of the most expensive cities in the country. I don't really have time for my friends…never mind a girlfriend. And now, they want us to come back into the office…just when I was beginning to enjoy life a little."

Courtney tried not to let her anxiety show on her face. "You have to go back to the office?"

"They're still talking, but it sounds like I will."

"That sucks."

"It does. The commute will be brutal. There's got to be more to life than work. Otherwise, why bother?"

"I know. I work my ass off and make shit money. I don't have any time to myself between my job and my kid, who's in every sport they offer, and girl scouts, and now wants to learn how to sail."

"It could be worse. She could want dance lessons."

"Who says she doesn't want dance lessons?" Courtney opened the oven door to check on the sheet-pan dinner she'd prepared. "Whoever invented the idea of cutting up all the ingredients for a meal and throwing them on one pan was a genius."

"It smells so good," said Melissa. "I'm salivating."

"It does smell good," Courtney agreed, stirring the contents of the pan.

"I'm salivating even more for that cute ass I see every time you bend over to look in the stove." As if she'd been goosed, Courtney instantly stood up straight. Melissa laughed. "That got your attention!"

Courtney brought her finger to her lips. "Keep it down. She only pretends to be deaf."

"Does that mean I can't talk dirty to you?"

"You're bad. Let's see what happens later. Can you hang until Kaylee goes to bed?"

"When will that be?"

"Around nine-thirty, ten…"

"I don't know. I got up really early this morning. I never realized how complicated it would be to date a woman with a child."

"Be glad Kaylee's not younger. I'd be keeping one ear alert to make sure she's not into mischief. Try having sex with a toddler in the house."

"No, thanks. I'm glad Kaylee is past that stage."

Courtney was aware of Melissa admiring her backside while she took dishes down from the cabinet to set the table.

"I suppose I could get up and help you," Melissa said in a half-hearted voice.

"You could, but you've been down in Boston all day, so you get off easy tonight." Courtney planted a kiss on the top of Melissa's head before laying out the plates on the table. "Next time."

"Thank you for letting me come over tonight. I needed someone to talk to who's not my mother, but I had a nice chat with the Episcopal rector on the way down."

"Mother Lucy?"

"Is that what they call her? That's perfect. She's very motherly without being overbearing. If I were Christian, I might even consider going to her church."

"What did you talk about?"

"Enabling people. Being widowed. Grief," Melissa listed the weighty topics so casually. Courtney stopped setting the table to stare at her.

"That counts as a pleasant chat?"

"I don't waste time on small talk. Apparently, neither does she. She gave me some good advice about my mother though. I shouldn't cater to her. That's enablement. The problem is, Mom does guilt very well…like most Jewish mothers."

"Can't you offload some of the responsibility on your sister?"

"She's busy too, and she has a family. If Mom could only meet a nice, Jewish guy. Unfortunately, the nearest Reform synagogue is in Portland. Damn. I meant to ask Lucy if she knows someone from her bereavement group."

"Why does he have to be Jewish?"

"You don't understand."

Maybe Courtney didn't understand, but she was beginning to get the picture. "Does it matter that I'm not Jewish?"

"Not to me, but it probably matters to my mother. I haven't talked to her about it, so I don't know."

"I'm glad it doesn't matter to you. I'd be really worried if it did."

"To some people, religion is a big deal."

"I know," said Courtney, thinking of her mother as she filled glasses with water from the refrigerator. She shouted down the hallway, "Kaylee! Dinner's almost ready!" She turned to Melissa, who shook her head as if her ears were ringing. "Sorry to shout. If I'm not loud, she doesn't hear me, and I usually have to call her at least twice before she shows up."

"Is she deaf?"

"If ear pods count as deafness, I guess so." Courtney took the dinner out of the oven and set it on the stove top. Out of the corner of her eye, she could see Melissa sniffing the air appreciatively. "Kaylee! Dinner's ready!"

"I'll go down and knock on her door," Melissa offered.

"Thank you."

By the time Courtney distributed the food onto the plates, Melissa and Kaylee had arrived at the table.

"Looks good, Mom. This is my favorite."

"It smells delicious," said Melissa, sitting down. "Thank you for having me. You're always cooking for me. Maybe, sometime, you can come to my house, and I'll cook for you."

"Your mother won't mind?"

Melissa shrugged. "How about Saturday?"

"I'll have to look at the schedule. I think Kaylee might have a game."

"I do," said Kaylee, nodding. "Two."

"See what I mean?" Courtney said. "Are you sure this is what you signed up for?"

"No, but let's see how it goes."

"What will you do if they decide you can't work from home?" asked Courtney casually to disguise her concern. This friendship had looked like it had so much potential.

"Try to work it out, I guess. I can't commute on the train every day. I'm sure I would get a lot of work done in the five hours I would waste on trains every day, but that schedule would kill me. Driving is faster, but it's a waste of time and gas. Either way, I'd have to get a car and probably keep my condo going, because there would be times I'd have to stay in Boston for late nights with clients or meetings."

As Melissa laid out her options, Courtney realized she'd already given them careful thought. She'd analyzed the situation and formulated a plan. That gave Courtney reason to hope.

"The one thing I can't do is quit," Melissa continued as she put a piece of roast sweet potato into her mouth. "I've put too much effort into becoming a partner and building my clientele. Besides, I could never make that kind of money up here. Salaries are only seventy-five percent of what they are in Boston."

"I didn't know that."

Melissa, who was chewing, only nodded.

"But if you don't have to pay to commute and keep an apartment in Boston, it might be a wash."

"True." Melissa gave her a hard look. "You figured that out fast."

"I used to be a math teacher."

"Of course. I forgot." Melissa reached over and touched her hand. Courtney glanced at Kaylee and realized she had noticed but was pretending she hadn't, which counted as impressive sensitivity for a twelve-year-old. She smiled at her daughter.

"Won't you miss Boston?" Courtney asked.

"It's only two hours away. An hour and a half by car."

Courtney laid down her silverware and leaned on her hand. "Why do you want to move up here? Is it because of your mom?"

"Honestly, it's because I love it up here and always have. We came up here every summer when I was a kid. I'd never been in a more beautiful place, especially living in Manhattan. It was always a dream of mine to move up here, but Boston was as close as I ever got until now."

"But you could always stay with your mother."

"I could. That's why she built that big house, so we'd all come visit. But if I lived here, I could spend more time hiking and kayaking and doing the things *I* want to do. Maybe I'll get a boat like Liz Stolz."

Courtney was waiting to hear that she was one of Melissa's reasons for wanting to move. She couldn't decide if she was disappointed or relieved when she didn't.

"I hope you get a boat," said Kaylee. "That would be so fun!" Courtney studied her daughter, who'd been quietly eating while the adults talked. As Courtney suspected, she'd been paying close attention to the conversation.

Melissa looked at Kaylee. "I know someone who has a boat. Want me to ask if she'll give us a ride?"

"Yes!" the girl declared.

"Who do you know with a boat?" asked Courtney, not that she doubted her, but she was curious.

"Liz Stolz, and she owes me a favor for some legal work I did for her."

"You wouldn't really ask her?"

Melissa shrugged. "Why not? What do I have to lose?"

"You're too much sometimes."

While Melissa washed the dishes, Courtney helped Kaylee with her homework. The faint clatter of dishes was comforting because it meant Courtney wouldn't have to worry about them later. Remembering she was down to her last pair of panties, she considered throwing in a wash while she worked with Kaylee. Then she remembered the pump couldn't handle running water for the dishes and the washing machine at the same time.

The noise from the kitchen stopped, replaced by the pleasant sound of Melissa's voice speaking softly. The conversation went on for some time. Although it wasn't really Courtney's business, she wondered who Melissa was talking to. A moment later, Melissa poked her head into the room. "Sorry to interrupt, but Liz Stolz says we can go out on the boat with her on Sunday afternoon. She's watching her granddaughters this weekend, and the idea of having more adult eyes on them was appealing. She says they're pretty lively." Courtney wasn't looking forward to watching someone else's kids on her day off, but if it meant a boat ride for Kaylee, she'd go along with it.

Kaylee asked if she could stay up later to finish the book she'd been reading. Courtney would have preferred to have lights-out at the regular time so she could spend some private time with her guest. "No later than ten, okay?"

"Okay, Mom."

Courtney remembered that she'd meant to throw a load in the washer, so that it could go in the dryer before she went to bed. She reached into the container of laundry pods and found only one left. *How did things get so out of hand?* She pitched the lone detergent pod into the washing machine and turned it on.

Melissa had made herself comfortable in the living room. She'd taken off her shoes and had her feet up on the hassock. She was dozing. Instead of waking her, Courtney sat down in the opposite chair and took the opportunity to admire her.

Although Melissa was attractive, she was not a classic beauty. Obviously, she wasn't trying to be. She'd let her eyebrows go wild, and her dark hair wasn't styled, just pulled back behind her ears. She had a charming mole on her left cheek. Her figure, however, was absolutely perfect. Courtney allowed her eyes to wander the landscape of Melissa's body from the toenails painted pale rose, up her long legs, into the inviting darkness under her skirt. They lingered on her breasts, rising and falling gently with her breaths. When her eyes reached the sensual lips, smiling slightly in sleep, Courtney couldn't resist any longer. She got up and kissed them.

Melissa's eyes flew open. She flicked her tongue over Courtney's lips until they parted. The kiss was deliciously deep. When Courtney leaned closer to get more, she lost her balance. Laughing, she fell into Melissa's lap.

"Can you stay the night?" Courtney asked, reaching under Melissa's top. She ached to feel the softness hidden there. It had been so long since she'd touched another woman's breast.

Melissa pulled her phone out of her pocket. "Let me call my mother to say I won't be home."

14

Liz stretched out on the sofa. "Oh, Lucy, this is torture. Two weeks! I don't know if I can last that long."

A deep sigh was audible through the phone speaker. "It's hard for me too, but I have studying for my exams to distract me. What can we do to help you?"

"Phone sex?" Liz wanted to bite her tongue. She'd been trying so hard not to make suggestive remarks. Now that she didn't have Lucy's smiling face to remind her of why she was on good behavior, she'd instantly reverted to type.

"Hmm. Not a bad idea," said Lucy.

"What?" asked Liz, sitting up in surprise.

"Do you think of me when you masturbate?" Lucy asked matter-of-factly.

"What?"

"You heard me. If we're going to have a sexual relationship, we should be able to speak openly about sex. Talking dirty in bed is fun, but discussing your sexual needs with your partner is essential to a good relationship." Lucy was lecturing her about sexual communication. Liz was suddenly speechless. "Do you think of me when you masturbate?" Lucy repeated.

"I hate the word masturbate. It sounds like making yourself come is dirty."

Lucy's chuckle was low and sexy. "I bet you're blushing."

"I am not!"

"You are a study in contradictions, Elizabeth Stolz. Maybe that's why you fascinate me. However, I expect you, a doctor, to talk about sex using proper terminology."

"Of course, I do…with patients. But what works in the exam room, sounds cold in the bedroom." Except Lucy talking about sex sounded anything but cold. Liz slid her hand into her pants and confirmed that it was having exactly the intended effect. "Do you think of me when you make yourself come?" Liz asked.

"I do. I find it very stimulating to imagine you touching me. When I think of the ways I'd like you to make love to me, I come really fast." Liz imagined Lucy touching herself, an intense look of concentration on her face instead of a smile. A preview of Lucy in a moment of passion. "I hope you won't be hurt to know that sometimes I think of Erika," Lucy added.

Liz withdrew her hand. Touching herself while talking about Erika didn't seem right. "I do understand. You miss her. Does it make you feel closer to her to think of her when you…masturbate?"

"Sometimes. Sometimes, I can't because…"

"I know," Liz said gently, wishing she could reach through the phone and put her arms around her.

"I had a dream last night that I was singing *Otello* at the Met. You and Erika were in the audience."

"Well, we were. At least, on one of those nights. Those last-minute tickets cost a mint, but they were so worth it. Nothing could cheer up Erika faster than music, and she really needed cheering up. Her ex would call at all hours of the day and night. Usually, Erika would listen, but she was working on an important paper, so she cut her off. A couple of days later, we heard the woman had slashed her wrists."

"She told me about that, but Liz, what were you thinking? Erika was upset, so you took her to a tragic opera?"

"It makes perfect sense if you think about it. We're cerebral, so we sublimate strong emotions through music. And if I hadn't taken her to the Met that night, we might never have heard you sing. Of course, we both fell in love with you. We talked about you the whole way back to New Haven."

"In my dream, I was naked," said Lucy. "So were both of you."

Liz chuckled. "I wonder what Freud would think about that."

"Who cares? Freud was an idiot," Lucy said dismissively.

"Mother Lucy! Let's be charitable," Liz mocked.

"You be charitable. I try not to hate anyone, but Freud's theories did so much damage…to women, especially. He deserves whatever he gets." Lucy's sudden candor made Liz feel privileged. Apparently, Lucy now felt comfortable sharing her real opinions instead of the Christian party line.

"Was your dream a fantasy about a ménage à trois?" Liz wondered aloud. "It would complete the circle. Erika and I once slept together. Erika gave you permission to sleep with me. Maybe you subconsciously wish the three of us could have slept together."

"Have you ever been in a ménage à trois?"

"I'm taking the fifth."

"Well, that's like admitting it. Come on. Tell me."

"Nope."

"Never mind. I'll get it out of you," said Lucy with a low chuckle. "I never got as far as imagining the three of us together, but now that you mention it…."

"Lucy, remember you're in the dormitory of an Episcopal seminary."

"So? Who says we can't have phone sex in an Episcopal seminary? Tell me. If we were together right now, what would happen?"

Liz answered without a second thought. "I'd be kissing your breasts. You have perfect breasts."

"What makes them perfect?"

"They're yours."

"I mean, objectively."

Liz thought for a moment. "They're slightly too large for your body, which makes them seem big. In fact, they're exactly the right size to fill my hands. At our age, most of us sag, but your breasts are still perky. I like the way they jiggle when you walk. How the nipples get so hard and show through your top when you're cold."

"You've spent a lot of time studying my breasts," Lucy observed after a thoughtful silence.

"I adore them. Your lips are perfect too."

"I love the way you kiss."

"I meant the other lips."

"Oh!"

"Can you feel my tongue on you? Inside you?"

"Okay, Liz. That's enough. Now, you're torturing me."

"No, you're torturing *me*! Hey, you started it. Why wouldn't you let me make love to you before you left?"

"Because then I wouldn't want to leave. When I get you into bed, I won't let you out again. You'll be my prisoner!"

"Can we make love when I pick you up in New York?" asked Liz in a hopeful voice.

"We'll see."

"Lucy!"

The extravagant laughter let Liz know that Lucy was done with serious topics and probably the sex talk. When she changed the subject, Liz knew that her assumptions had been correct. "I had a pleasant traveling companion on the train this morning…" Lucy said.

The extended pause meant Liz was supposed to ask, "Who?"

"Melissa Morgenstern. Her partners called a meeting to discuss returning to the office."

"Oh, I bet she doesn't like that idea. She wants to stay in Hobbs." Lately, the news was full of reports about people's reluctance to give up working at home, especially women. Going back to a workplace meant sending their children back into childcare, which was expensive and risky with the virus still spreading. The possibility that working remotely would continue had driven a real estate boom in Hobbs, where the price of houses had skyrocketed.

"If you've considered selling the beach house, now would be a good time," Liz said, speaking aloud what she was thinking.

"What?" asked Lucy. "Where did you get that idea?"

"Real estate has shot up in value. It could be a bubble. Now would be a good time to unload the house, if that's your plan."

"I don't have a plan, Liz," said Lucy in a testy voice. "I never even considered selling the house! Erika remodeled it so that there would be a place for Emily and me to live after we married. You and Sam built that beautiful practice room over the garage. It was Erika's last Christmas gift to me."

"I didn't know you were so sentimental."

"Liz! It's not sentimental to want to live in the home I shared with my wife. You were the one who encouraged Erika to buy that house!"

"Yes, I did, but you could make a lot of money if you sold now."

"It's not about the money. I'm not ready for a big change like that. I advise the people in my bereavement group to hold off on big decisions until things settle down. Losing a life partner changes everything…how you live, how you sleep, even how you eat. It's hard to deal with so much change."

"And you were still getting used to living with Erika."

"Oddly, that makes it easier. I wasn't used to seeing her every day and sleeping beside her every night. It was still new and a little strange. Imagine what it's like to lose your partner after ten, thirty, fifty years? That's devastating."

"Losing your partner, no matter how long you lived together, is devastating."

There was a long silence. "You miss Maggie, don't you?" asked Lucy in a gentle tone.

"Yes, of course, I do. Our lives were intertwined."

"Losing a spouse is hard for anyone. It's not just the person you miss, but your life together." While Liz was thinking about what she missed about her life with Maggie, Lucy suddenly asked, "Do you know any single, Jewish men your age? Bonus points if he's a successful professional."

"My age? Do you need to remind me I'm older than you?"

"Eight years isn't much. Besides, you're young, Liz. I don't want to hear any of that old lady talk."

Liz scanned her mind for eligible men who fit Lucy's criteria. "There's a plastic surgeon I worked with at Southern Med when I was still doing a lot of breast surgery."

"That sounds promising. Tell me more."

"This guy has quite a backstory. He's an Ashkenazi Jew by way of Portugal. His father was a diplomat. His mother was a famous physician in her home country. His grandmother was half-Chinese."

"Not exactly your Jewish boy next-door."

"Is this guy supposed to be for Melissa's mother? I thought you just married them, Lucy. I didn't know you provided matchmaking services too."

Lucy began to sing the "Matchmaker Song" from *Fiddler on the Roof.*

"All right, Yente. I'll call Jack. He always wanted a boat. When we worked together, he was always angling for invitations to mine. Melissa called to invite herself earlier. I'll tell her to bring her mother along."

"That's perfect! Oh, Liz, I hate to cut you off, but I have to study."

"I'll miss studying with you after you pass."

"Oh, this is just the beginning. I have a long way to go. And think of all the theology you'll have to read to catch up with me."

"I think I've had my fill," Liz replied dryly.

"I doubt it. You're a very curious person. You like to learn new things. Besides, you'll enjoy the conversations we'll have."

"I'd rather talk about sex."

"I'm sure you would." A video chat request appeared on Liz's phone. She tapped it open and saw Lucy's face. Lucy had already taken off her makeup, revealing her abundant freckles. Her green eyes were full of mischief. "I don't know why we didn't think of this earlier," Lucy said. Her eyes grew serious. "Oh, Liz. I miss you so much."

"You have no idea how much I miss you."

"I do, but I'm going to give you a kiss and say good night." She brought her lips close to the screen and mimed a kiss. "Don't masturbate too much while I'm gone. Save some for me!"

Liz heard peals of laughter as Lucy closed the call.

15

Liz studied the young woman sitting in the visitors' chair. She guessed there had been work done on her face, probably bone shaving to narrow the jaw and create a more feminine chin. Liz searched the file and found the reference to some cosmetic surgery done two years earlier. She scanned the notes quickly. "I'm sorry I haven't had time to review all your history, but my partner's out today, so I'm covering her cases."

"Take your time," said the patient. "I want you to be fully informed. You need to know what you're getting into."

The file went on for pages. Reading all the history in one sitting would be impossible, even for a fast reader like Liz. She'd have to go back to it when she had more time, which was not going to be this morning. If she didn't move on to the examination, she'd be so behind schedule she'd never catch up. She quickly scanned the remaining notes for any red flags. Finally, she closed the laptop.

"What made you choose me as your primary?" Liz asked, folding her arms on her chest. She could almost feel Lucy nudging her to assume a more welcoming pose, so she unfolded her arms and sat up straight.

"Mother Lucy recommended you. She says you're the best doctor in Hobbs, but before I commit to this practice and you, I want to make sure you don't object to providing healthcare for a trans woman." Below the assertive tone, Liz detected an undercurrent of bravado. As a musician, the young woman would need an overdeveloped sense of confidence, but dealing with a healthcare system that wasn't always sympathetic, never mind supportive, made it mandatory. "I need you to be honest with me, Dr. Stolz. I've had some bad experiences with doctors."

"I'm sorry to hear that. What happened?"

The patient shifted in her seat. The old-fashioned molded plastic chairs were unyielding, and people often squirmed in them. "I had serious in-flammation after my implant surgery. I ended up having to see another doctor, not the surgeon who'd operated. The doctor on call was dismissive and told me there was nothing she could do except recommend cortisone and painkillers. You're a breast doctor. Is that true?"

"It depends on the cause of the inflammation. I only performed mastectomies for breast cancer. A plastic surgeon handled the implants."

"But you're an expert on breasts. There's a whole chapter on implants in your book. What aren't you telling me, Doctor?"

"I don't pretend to understand why people would alter their gender. As someone who had to perform mastectomies to save a life, I don't know why anyone would voluntarily remove a healthy body part. But that doesn't mean I can't provide good healthcare to you or any other trans person."

The patient studied her carefully. "That's an honest answer, Dr. Stolz. I can't tell you how much plastered-over, fake professionalism I've had to deal with."

"I'm sorry to hear it. No matter what the doctor personally believes, everyone should be treated with respect. If you're concerned, there are other doctors in this practice. They might be less opinionated than I am."

"No. I know where you stand, and I can live with that. Plus, you're a surgeon, so you'd be more attuned to my post-operative concerns." The patient finally smiled. "If Mother Lucy trusts you, I trust you." Liz didn't know whether she should thank Lucy for the recommendation. Sometimes, it seemed she deliberately put her in these difficult situations.

"I can promise that my personal feelings will never interfere with my professional judgment."

"I believe you, Dr. Stolz. You have an honest face."

Probably too honest, Liz thought as she focused on the intense blue eyes skillfully enhanced with makeup. The woman made a great deal of effort to pass, from wearing her nails painted red to the pretty dress and open-toed sandals she wore. Most women in Maine dressed more practically, but the feminine adornments drew the eye away from Denise's broad shoulders and the large bones in the wrists and knees. If Liz hadn't been told Denise was trans, she would have guessed right away, but most people never looked that closely.

While the assistant drew blood and got the patient ready for her exam, Liz went next door to see Cathy Pelletier's pediatric patient who had an earache. Fortunately, it was simple swimmer's ear, easily treated with alcohol drops. The assistant still hadn't called her, so Liz looked in on the next patient, an elderly woman with a tick in her shoulder. While Liz stood in the hall, sending a script for prophylactic antibiotics from her phone, the assistant approached. "*She's* ready for you," she said, raising her brows and rolling her eyes in the direction of the exam room.

Liz beckoned the assistant further down the hall to get away from the door. "Janna, I don't want to see any more of that from you. No faces. No gestures. No comments. We treat all our patients with respect."

"I'm sorry, Doctor," said the young woman, clutching her hands. "I just never saw one of those people before." With great effort, Liz restrained herself as the assistant babbled on. "I mean, it's not something we see here every day. I didn't mean anything by it."

"I hope not, and remember, our job is to provide healthcare, not opinions. Understand?"

The young woman nodded. Liz watched her hurry down the hall, probably heading to complain to the other assistants. Gone were the days when Liz had to savage junior staff to make a point, but Ginny often told her that she was too fierce. Maybe by the time she retired, she'd find the right balance.

Liz knocked on the door to announce her arrival. The preoperative physical for sex reassignment called for a classical examination, so Liz began with listening to the patient's chest sounds. "Do you have any specific complaints today?"

"No. None." Liz pulled up the leg support, so the patient could lie down. She closed her eyes to focus as she palpated the abdomen. The muscles were taut and toned, but there was a soft layer of fat below the skin, the hormones doing their work. Liz looped her finger into the waistband of the panties. "Do you mind?"

"No, go ahead. I expected that."

Liz's examination revealed nothing but exceptionally healthy male genitals. "No regrets?" she asked, pulling up the lace panties.

"No regrets," said the patient without hesitation.

"Have you had a recent PSA test?"

"Yes, all in the normal range."

"Okay, then no rectal exam today."

"But I want to get my money's worth." The patient grinned.

Liz laughed. "So, you want me to do a rectal exam?"

"No, thanks. I'll pass."

"You don't mind if I take a look at the implant site that was inflamed?"

Denise modestly pulled down the paper gown. Liz inspected the incision carefully hidden under the curve of the implant. The overall cosmetic result was perfect. "It's healing well."

"The inflammation wasn't the worst part. It was the attitude of that snotty doctor."

"I'm sorry you had that experience. There's never any excuse to be unprofessional." Liz pulled the paper gown back into place. "You look fine. Once I get your blood work back, I'll sign off on the procedure. You can get dressed now."

"Thank you, Dr. Stolz."

"Call me Liz. Everyone does." Liz reached out her hand. "Good luck with the surgery. I'll see you afterwards."

Liz went back to her office to write up her notes. The intercom line lit. She pushed it down forcefully. "Yes, Ginny?" she asked as she typed.

"Ms. Enright is on the line."

"Is it important, Ginny? I'm drowning here."

"I'll ask."

Liz let her head fall back and gazed at the ceiling while she continued to type. The intercom squawked. "She wanted to invite you for lunch, but I told her you're swamped, so she invited you to dinner instead. She said to come over when you're done here."

"Whenever that is."

"What should I tell her?" Ginny asked.

"Tell her I'll be there around five."

The rest of the day was so busy that Liz skipped lunch, but she had gotten to the end of her appointments, seen her patients relatively on time, and hadn't killed anyone. In all, a good day. She took a long, hot shower in the doctor's bathroom at the back of the building and changed into the spare outfit she kept at work in case patients splashed their bodily fluids on her clothes. Olivia, as usual, would be dressed to the nines, but she'd have to put up with her guest wearing a polo shirt and cropped pants.

Liz decided to stop at the supermarket to buy a bottle of wine to bring along. She tapped Olivia's number as she walked through the Hannaford parking lot.

"Don't tell me you're not coming," Olivia said in a droll voice.

"I'm coming. I'm getting wine. Red or white?"

"White. Seared scallops with wilted greens."

"Oh, Liv, I love you," Liz replied with faux ardor.

"I won't tell Samantha."

"Good. She doesn't need to know everything."

Liz smiled at the banter, still amazed that she and Olivia had become such good friends. They had Sam in common, of course, but that only went so far. Lucy had a succinct explanation for the improbable friendship. Psychologically, Olivia and Liz were mirrors of one another, both powerful women driven to succeed. Each had made her way in life through her own efforts.

Olivia air-kissed Liz on both cheeks like the society lady she had learned to be, but she responded with a sigh of pleasure when Liz enfolded her in a full body hug.

"Liz, you look absolutely exhausted," said Olivia, standing back.

"My partner has been out with gastric issues," Liz explained, handing the wine to Olivia. "I'm honored to be your date tonight." She followed Olivia into the kitchen and watched her open the wine. "Where's Sam?"

"Oh, she's working on that new monstrosity on the other side of the harbor," said Olivia, offering a glass of wine. "She works late every night. Sometimes, she calls after midnight to apologize for never seeing me. The owners want it done by Fourth of July. Those rich people are so demanding!"

"Yes, they are," said Liz, raising her glass to the fabulously rich founder of the Enright Fund. "Takes one to know one."

Olivia made a face. "And the kettle calls the pot black. Let's go outside. Bring the tray, will you?"

They settled on the deck. It had been a warm day, and the breeze off the ocean felt good. Olivia moved the charcuterie tray closer. "Try the garlic olives. I got them in the deli in Webhanet."

Liz ate one, and it was delicious. She briefly worried about garlic breath before remembering that there was no one at home to kiss, so she helped herself to another.

"Thank you for inviting me. It's nice to eat with other people for a change."

"I feel the same. I wish Samantha agreed."

"Have you worked anything out yet?" asked Liz, snatching another olive from the dish. They were addictive.

"Not yet. And we may never," said Olivia with a shrug. "We don't need two separate houses. Look at all this space. You'd think it would make sense to move in together."

"I told Lucy she should sell while the market is high."

"Shame on you, Liz. She's only been widowed since Christmas. She shouldn't rush into things. That house is a showpiece, and the location couldn't be better. It will retain its value. And where is she going to live… with you?"

"We're not that far along yet," Liz conceded, admiring the moonrise over the ocean. "It's so nice and cool here at the beach."

"I'm surprised you never bought waterfront property."

"I built on high ground. I figured if global warming continues at this rate, I'll have waterfront property by the time I die."

"Now, *that's* what I call long-term planning."

Liz sipped the wine. It was a new label and better than she'd expected. She never trusted the ratings posted on the shelf talkers. Who really cared if a wine had won five gold medals at some obscure vintner's fair? "I doubt Sam will ever give up her house. If you don't mind advice, don't push her for a commitment. She doesn't like being pressured. You don't have to live together to be happy in a relationship."

"I'll remind you of that when you keep encouraging Lucy to sell her house."

"I don't want her to miss the boom."

"Right," said Olivia curtly.

"I hope you're giving her good financial advice," said Liz, reaching for another olive.

"Don't worry. She's making big money in this recovery, and Maggie too."

"Is her little boy-toy still hanging around?"

"You know I wouldn't tell you if he is. You're divorced. It's none of your business."

"You're right, of course, but it still pisses the hell out of me."

Olivia peered at Liz with her penetrating blue eyes. "Liz, let it go. Just move on. You'll be much happier."

"Easier said than done."

Olivia scrutinized her with a raised brow. "Let's change the subject if you don't mind. I want your opinion about something. That's one of the reasons I invited you tonight." Liz suppressed the urge to smile. Olivia always had an ulterior motive. "There's a trend in small towns to create a department of safety services and put one person in charge. I'm thinking about promoting Brenda to senior safety officer and giving her authority over the fire department and the ambulance service."

"Brenda will be delighted with the promotion and perfect for the job. Duvaney will hate it. The fire department has been his territory for years."

"But it won't affect his job. It only means he'll be reporting to Brenda instead of to me. What difference does it make?"

"He and Brenda were equals before. Those lateral promotions inevitably create bad blood. That's why I always hired managers from outside."

Olivia munched on a piece of cheese while she thought. "Maybe you're right."

"I know I'm right. It's great to promote from within, except in situations like this. You have well-functioning, independent departments. They're small, but there is no economy of scale to be gained in merging the leadership, unless you merge their budgets too."

"I could."

"It will only make it harder to keep track of the spending. Sorry, Olivia. Doesn't sound like a good idea to me."

"I knew you would have the answer, Liz. Despite what you think, you're a good administrator. It's a shame Yale lost you."

Liz shrugged. "It was time to go, and I'm enjoying my second act. That's why I haven't retired." Liz took a sip of wine. "While I have the attention of the town manager, I want to tell you my concerns about this new delta variant. It's here in Maine and virulent. We have a high vaccination rate, and so far that seems protective. But with the tourist season revving up, there are a lot of people coming into the state."

"You don't think we'll need to shut down again?"

"Hopefully, not. I'm telling you now, because I think we need to pay attention. We don't want to get caught with our pants down like last time. We might need to go back to wearing masks indoors."

"Oh, God, I hope not."

"Me too," said Liz with a sigh. "I had enough of masks when I was a surgeon."

Olivia reached out and patted Liz's arm. "I'm glad you came, Liz. Not just for the advice, but I enjoy your company. I thought you might be lonely with Lucy away."

Liz shot her an impatient look. "Thanks. Are we that obvious?"

"To your friends, you are. Don't worry. I'm not judging you. By the way," said Olivia, helping herself to a rice cracker, "when I was up at the rectory talking to Tom about the endowment, there was a woman asking for Lucy. She said she knows her from school. She was wearing a collar."

"I hope Jodi didn't give her Lucy's mobile number. Her exams are tomorrow. She won't even talk to me."

"I think Jodi took a message and referred her to Tom."

Liz shrugged. "I'm sure they'll find each other."

16

Courtney watched Kaylee turn into a mother hen clucking over the younger girls. She'd always encouraged her daughter to include other children in her games, especially because she was an only child. While Dr. Stolz raced around the boat, getting it ready to go out to sea, Kaylee read aloud from the book Dr. Stolz's youngest granddaughter, Nicki, had brought in her colorful knapsack.

Meanwhile, Courtney sat alone. Melissa was preoccupied with her mother, who talked incessantly. Courtney found it irritating because it isolated Melissa from everyone else. Now that they were lovers, Courtney expected at least some attention.

The last-minute invitation was clearly a ploy to introduce Mrs. Morgenstern to one of Dr. Stolz's friends. Once Courtney learned he was Jewish, the scheme could not be more obvious. For everyone's sake, Courtney hoped it worked out. Maybe if Ruth had another interest, Melissa would have more time for her. As it was now, between Melissa's demanding job, her long commute, and her mother, she hardly had any time for herself, never mind Courtney. With Courtney's obligations to school and Kaylee's activities, dates had been hard to arrange. They hadn't even been able to find time to make love again.

Their first joining had been awkward, as first times usually are. Faced with enormous expectations but lacking knowledge about the strange, naked person in bed, how could it be otherwise? Courtney fumbled at first. It had been ages since she'd been with a woman, but there was no forgetting something so elemental. Fortunately, Melissa was a confident lover and patient when Courtney found it hard to relax enough to come. "We'll get there," she'd said and reassured her with a kiss.

Part of the problem was that Courtney was distracted. She kept listening for signs that Kaylee was awake and roaming the house. Once she'd heard the water run in the sink and the toilet flush in the bathroom next door, she knew her daughter was in bed for the night. Just as she began to relax, she heard the sound of the washer spinning and worried about wrinkled laundry. Melissa's lips on her nipple banished those thoughts.

Melissa took her time, which Courtney appreciated after years of hurried marital sex. A minute of foreplay, which always included a rough kiss, led to Doug nudging her legs apart with his knees. Sex had become a routine that occurred every weekend, whether she wanted it or not. Part of her still cared for Doug. If he hadn't wanted so badly to move to the "left coast," as he called it, they might still be married. After a dozen years, they were something of a habit. It hadn't started out that way. In the beginning, she'd found sex with him exciting, a raw carnal experience, so different from the deep feelings she'd had for women. When she'd discovered she was pregnant, they'd decided to marry because it was the right thing to do. Sometimes, what everyone tells you is right, isn't.

"Courtney, are you okay?"

She looked up into Melissa's curious eyes and smiled. "Yes, fine. Why?"

"You looked strange. I was worried you might be getting seasick."

Courtney became aware of the boat bobbing from the wake of another boat. She reached out and patted Melissa's arm. "Don't worry. I don't get seasick. I love boats. My father always wanted one."

"Everyone wants a boat until they discover how much work they are," said a nearby voice. Dr. Stolz was standing a few feet away, unwinding and rewinding a thick rope around a cleat. "Sorry it's taking Jack so long to get here. Northbound traffic must be bad today. Those damned summer people!" She shook her head in disgust.

"Weren't you one of those summer people before you moved up here?" Melissa asked.

"I was, but then, I had no idea how much the locals hated us."

"You don't really hate us," said Melissa. "Everyone in Hobbs is so helpful and friendly."

"That's our motto: 'Hobbs, the friendliest town in Maine.' Looks good on signs. Harder to put into practice."

"Dr. Stolz, you're in charge of the chamber of commerce, aren't you?" Courtney asked.

"Yes, but my term is up this year. And, Courtney, if you're on my boat, you need to call me Liz. Okay?"

"Yes, Dr. Sto... I mean, yes, Liz."

But Liz wasn't paying attention. "There's Jack!" Courtney followed her line of sight and saw a tall, slim man with salt and pepper hair standing at the parking lot fence. Liz cupped her hands around her mouth and shouted, "Hey, Jack! Down here!" She waved vigorously.

The man waved back. He picked up a knapsack and a canvas bag and nimbly ran down the stairs. Courtney glanced at Melissa and saw she was giving the newcomer a critical inspection. Jack Dreyfus might catch Courtney's eye because he was a handsome guy in great shape for his age, but to Melissa, he was a potential suitor for her mother.

Liz reached over the side and took the man's bags as he climbed aboard.

"Hello, everyone!" he said brightly. "Sorry to be so late. The traffic is a nightmare."

"You're forgiven," Liz said. "Now, get your bags stowed, so you can help me cast off."

"Hold on, Liz," said the man. "Aren't you going to introduce me to these lovely ladies?"

"I'm sorry. Forgot my manners." Liz led him to Mrs. Morgenstern, who was glowering suspiciously in his direction. "This is Ruth Morgenstern, her daughter, Melissa, who's been helping me out with some legal work. And Courtney Barnes, our new assistant principal at the elementary school." Jack shook each woman's hand in turn.

"And who is this gentleman?" Mrs. Morgenstern asked, although Liz had explained their connection before Jack arrived.

"Jack Dreyfus is the senior partner of Atlantic Plastic Surgery Associates."

"Soon to be retired senior partner," Jack corrected.

"You finally decided?" said Liz, looking surprised. "Good for you!" Liz patted him on the shoulder. "Stow your gear below, so we can get underway."

Jack raised his hand to his brow in salute. "Aye, aye, skipper." When he turned and winked at the women, Courtney saw the faint suggestion of Asian heritage around his eyes.

Liz had told his backstory like a thriller, including the part about his family escaping from Portugal to Belgium right before the Nazis arrived. They'd then headed to South America for safety. When Liz had mentioned Jack's half-Chinese grandmother, Mrs. Morgenstern's eyes narrowed markedly.

Liz went into the pilot house to start the engine. As the deck started to rumble, the girls squealed in delight. They'd been so patient during the long wait. Courtney sent a silent word of thanks to her daughter for keeping the younger girls entertained.

Courtney knew Katrina and Nicki weren't Liz's biological grandchildren. She'd heard about the divorce from one of the teachers, who knew Maggie Fitzgerald from amateur theater. Despite the rift, the girls seemed to have a close relationship with their step-grandmother. Too often, grandparents were cut out of the equation after a divorce. Courtney sighed at the thought of her own mother-in-law, who hadn't seen Kaylee since they'd moved.

After Jack helped Liz cast off the lines, he spent a few minutes talking to her in the pilot house. When he came down to the deck, he glanced around for a place to sit. Courtney considered it a favorable sign when Melissa's mother moved over to make room for him.

"What a great day for a boat ride," he said, beaming at the women with his movie-star smile. He had perfectly white, straight teeth. Courtney guessed that as a plastic surgeon, he probably needed to impress potential patients by looking his best.

"Where do you live in Hobbs, Mrs. Morgenstern?" he asked, turning to Melissa's mother, who now looked completely charmed by his attention.

"I built a house on Gull Island two years ago," said Mrs. Morgenstern. "It overlooks the salt marsh."

"I live in New Hampshire because of taxes, but I'm often tempted to move up to Maine. It's beautiful here."

Melissa was hanging on every word the poor man said. Courtney elbowed her as subtly as she could. "Come on, let's see what Liz is up to," she whispered.

Melissa looked reluctant to leave her mother's side, so Courtney gave her *the look*, which after years of teaching, she could do very effectively. Once they were out of earshot, she said, "Your mother looks interested. Give them some time to get to know one another. This is why you wanted Dr. Stolz to invite him. Right?" Melissa glanced back to where they sat. "And don't be so obvious that you're watching them!"

"But I don't know this guy."

"Liz likes him. He's a successful surgeon. How bad could he be? Melissa, you need to let your mother have a life." Courtney thought, but didn't say, *and she needs to let you have one too.*

"Hello, ladies. Thanks for keeping me company," Liz said, her eyes fixed on the path ahead as she navigated between the jetties to open water. All the pilot house windows were open, and the sea air was refreshing. "How's it going down there?"

"The kids are having a blast," Courtney said.

"I meant with Jack and Ruth."

"So far, so good," Melissa said. "Thanks for inviting him."

"I don't know why I didn't think of him right away. He's a great guy."

Someone was on the jetty, using a hoop to blow enormous bubbles that floated black over the beach.

"Look, Mom!" Kaylee called from the deck.

"I see, honey."

The little girls were squealing again. Even for a seasoned teacher, the ear-piercing screams could be hard to take, but Courtney had learned to tune them out.

"Thanks for inviting us today. Kaylee is so excited," Courtney said, settling into one of the seats behind the skipper's chair. Melissa took the other. "This is such a treat. Usually, on weekends I'm doing nothing but chores. It's so nice to have an excuse to relax."

"Thank your friend there," said Liz, nodding toward Melissa. "It was her idea, and I'm glad. Watching those little girls when I'm alone on the boat makes me really nervous. Katrina is a devil. She has never met mischief she didn't like."

"She seems well-behaved today," Courtney observed.

"I told her you're the school principal at Hobbs elementary. Apparently, that made a big impression."

Courtney laughed. "I wish it worked that way with other kids."

Melissa leaned forward. "Liz, I know I said you would return the favor, but I never expected this. It's perfect. What made you think of inviting Dr. Dreyfus?"

"Your new best friend, Mother Lucy. When she wants something done, it gets done."

"I noticed that."

"Jack's a great guy, and he does beautiful work. I'm glad for his sake that he's retiring, but sad for the profession. We'll miss him."

"It seems like a lot of doctors are retiring at the same time," Melissa said.

"Especially surgeons. They shut down all the elective surgeries in the spring. People put off procedures or were afraid to come into the office. Some medical practices were really hurting. Combine that with so many Boomers reaching retirement age, and you have a mass exodus."

"Are you going to retire?" Courtney asked anxiously.

"Eventually," said Liz, "but not soon."

"I hear it's good to work until you're seventy to maximize your social security," Melissa said.

Liz smiled. "That's not my reason." She stepped down from the skipper's chair. "We're in open water now. Who'd like to take a turn at the helm?"

"I'll try it," volunteered Melissa. Courtney was surprised. Melissa didn't seem like the adventurous type. *Is she trying to impress me?* Courtney wondered.

Liz held on while Melissa positioned her hands and got the feel of it.

"Steer straight ahead and try not to hit other boats. Think you can manage that?"

Melissa laughed and shot Courtney a quick look of excitement. "Look! I'm steering the boat!"

Courtney smiled, endeared by Melissa's childlike pleasure.

17

Melissa scanned the Dox.com rating site again. So far, she hadn't found a single negative comment. She'd already checked Jack Dreyfus through the background service her office used and searched the public and court records. The few details she'd been able to unearth were innocuous. Jack was divorced, but his wife had remarried, so he was off the hook for alimony. His two children were grown. One was an attorney; the other had followed in his father's footsteps and was a surgeon on the West Coast.

She glanced over the notes she'd scribbled on the legal pad. Only she could read her handwriting, which was why she typed everything for her legal assistants. Even so, she tore off the page and fed it to the shredder. She didn't want her mother to know she'd been researching Jack's background.

Ruth came into the spare bedroom where Melissa had set up a make-shift office. She was wearing a white skirt and a leopard-skin-print jacket. Melissa didn't have the heart to tell her that the fashion of wearing faux animal patterns had come and gone. In Florida, where Ruth had been living, the old ladies seemed to get stuck in the era when they'd moved south.

"Going out?" Melissa asked. She almost said, 'again,' but she'd caught herself just in time. Two dates in a week seemed excessive to her even though she, herself, had scheduled more when she'd first met Courtney.

"Jack invited me to dinner in Portsmouth. Supposedly, there are some great restaurants there."

"I heard that. Liz Stolz recommended a sushi place."

Ruth mocked a shudder. "I don't know how you can eat raw fish."

"You eat lox. It's raw."

"No, it's not. It's smoked."

"It's cold smoked. That means it's basically raw."

"I don't care. It tastes good. And we've always eaten lox."

Melissa decided it was a waste of time to argue with her mother about lox, or anything, really. There was no winning. "Are you coming back tonight?" she asked, trying to sound casual.

"What kind of woman do you think I am?" asked her mother. "It's only our second date!" Her exaggerated tone of insult was almost comical, but Melissa didn't dare smile. "No, I'll be home later. What about you? You've been spending a lot of time with that *Courtney*." The way her mother pronounced her name made her dislike obvious.

"What do you have against Courtney? She's a smart woman. She has a good job. She works hard for the community…"

"She's not Jewish."

"That doesn't matter to me."

"Well, it should." Her mother frowned. "How serious is this? When are you going to tell her that you have to go back to Boston?"

"She knows. We've talked about it."

"So, it is serious," said her mother, raising her brows.

"I don't know yet, Mom. And it's not settled that I have to go back to the office. Many big companies were saying they wanted their employees to come back inside but had to walk it back because of resistance. Google is a case in point, and we're talking about thousands of people."

"I'll miss you when you go."

"Oh, Mom, you're so busy with Dr. Jack, you won't even notice."

"Yes, I will," Ruth protested, "I like having you here. I wouldn't mind if you stayed." She wagged her finger. "You should be honest with Courtney. Don't string her along. It's not right." Now, she was acting like she liked Courtney. Melissa fought the temptation to roll her eyes. She'd long known that her mother's likes or dislikes were based on how they advantaged her. Ruth had probably just figured out that Courtney might help keep Melissa in Hobbs and could be useful.

"I've got to work, Mom," Melissa said, telling a white lie to end the conversation. "I'll see you later. Okay?"

Ruth stiffened and headed toward the door. Melissa felt angry with herself for being impatient with her mother, especially because she had been trying so hard to raise her spirits.

Of course, now that a man was in the picture, Ruth's attitude had noticeably improved. The situation had been entirely predictable, but it still disappointed Melissa. Ruth, who'd graduated summa cum laude from Hunter College and had wanted to become a history professor, still believed that she was incomplete without a man. Becca, the expert on feminism, had tried to explain it to her sister: patriarchal religions like Judaism taught that women exist to support men. Some women's identities were completely wrapped up in the males in their lives: fathers, husbands, sons. If their men succeeded, they succeeded.

But when Jewish women rebelled, they were a force to be reckoned with. It was no surprise that the founders of modern feminism had been raised in Jewish families. As a college student in New York, her mother had marched for the ERA amendment with Steinem and Friedan and Abzug. How could Ruth have forgotten her zeal for equality? Why did she think she needed a man to make her whole?

A text message flashed across her phone: *Hey. What are you up to?*

Melissa smiled. She decided to call instead of text her answer. "Hello, there! I'm playing sleuth and researching Dr. Jack's background."

"What did you find?"

"A couple of speeding tickets. Otherwise, he's a good, Jewish boy."

"It would be nice for your mother if it worked out."

"Yes, for me too." Melissa suddenly realized that her mother would be out late, so it was a perfect time to invite Courtney. "How would you like to come over for a cookout?"

"Really? You're inviting me to your house?" asked Courtney in a droll tone.

"Well, it's my mother's house." *Which she makes clear at every opportunity,* Melissa thought. She felt devious and slightly guilty for waiting until her mother was out to invite her girlfriend.

"What can I bring? I made brownies for the team dinner tomorrow night. There are way more than we need. How about I bring a few for dessert?"

"That would be perfect," said Melissa, smiling at the thought of Courtney baking for the twelve-year-old female athletes and their parents. Such commonplace suburban rituals were something she'd missed growing up as a Jewish girl in the big city, but she knew all about them from watching TV.

"I need to run to the store first," Melissa said. "Would you mind hot dogs and supermarket salads?"

"No, it sounds like fun. What time should we be there?"

"Give me a half hour to get my act together."

At the supermarket, Melissa grabbed a small cart and headed to the deli counter. The dispenser was out of tickets, which meant she'd need to elbow her way to the counter to stake out her claim. Then she noticed the salads to go in the refrigerated case. She'd rather get them fresh from the deli, but there wasn't much time. She headed to the meat counter for kosher hotdogs, but the neon color of the Maine "snappers" attracted her attention. The bright pink hotdogs had always intrigued her. According to Maine tourist websites, they had a unique flavor and snapped when you bit into them. *Oh, be daring,* she thought and put a package into her basket.

She berated herself for using the self-serve check out and pushing someone out of a job. She berated herself for offering her guests nothing but a deli meal after Courtney had cooked so many dinners for her. *Guilt is a Jewish girl's middle name*, she thought. As if she needed more, she felt bad about waiting until her mother was out to sneak Courtney into the house. How could she be forty-one years old and still need her mother's permission to invite her girlfriend for dinner?

Courtney's old Subaru turned into the driveway as Melissa was getting out of her mother's car.

"Melissa!" Kaylee squealed and ran to her, clutching her around the waist while her mother got the plastic container of brownies out of the backseat.

"This cookout came together out of the blue," said Melissa, affectionately rubbing Kaylee's back, "but I promise I'll cook you a real meal soon."

"Well, you can cook at my house any time you want," said Courtney, sounding casual, but there was a tone in her voice.

Melissa was about to kiss Courtney but changed her mind when she noticed Kaylee watching. She landed the kiss on her cheek instead.

"Does your mother really live in this big house all by herself?" asked Courtney, taking it all in. Melissa tried to see it from her eyes. Yes, it was obscenely huge, but it was a tastefully designed New England shore house, not a monstrosity like some of the new houses they were building.

"When I'm not here, yes, she lives here by herself."

"Why does she need so much room?"

"So that I and my sister will come to visit."

Courtney raised a skeptical brow.

"It's the potential that matters," Melissa explained, but Courtney's question was a good one. Why was one person entitled to so much space, while another lived with her child in a beat-up, cramped trailer?

"Must be nice to have all that space," Courtney said in a sarcastic, but slightly envious tone.

Melissa handed Courtney one of the shopping bags from the trunk. "Thank you for arriving right on time to help bring in the groceries. Look, I got these pink hot dogs." Melissa pulled the package out of the bag. "'Red snappers' they call them."

"Don't they use red dyes banned in the EU?" Courtney asked, eyeing them suspiciously. "Are you sure they're safe to eat?"

"No, but I'll try anything once. Hasn't killed me yet," said Melissa, but Courtney still looked doubtful. "Be brave. Everything I've read about them says they're amazing. It's supposed to be part of the Maine experience."

"Come on, Mom," Kaylee urged. "Try them. They're good."

"You've had them before?" asked Courtney, looking at her daughter with surprise.

"Yes, at the Girl Scout cookout."

"I guess I'm outnumbered," Courtney conceded. "Is your mother going to eat the pink hot dogs too?"

"She's not here. She's on a date with Jack. We have the house all to ourselves," she said, raising a brow suggestively.

Melissa saw Courtney's eyes glance in Kaylee's direction. "Yes, I know," she said in a low voice. "We can't do anything because we have company."

"I'm sorry. I know it's not easy," said Courtney, looking equally disappointed.

"Don't worry. It's all good," Melissa said, putting her arm around her.

18

Wrangling with the desk clerk at the Plaza Hotel had left Liz surly. To calm down, she stared out the window at the wooded lot behind the office.

For the outrageous prices the Plaza charged, anyone would think it would be easy to make a reservation, but Liz had specific requirements, namely a two-bedroom suite with a view of Central Park. The second bedroom was insurance, in case things didn't go as planned, and Lucy decided to sleep separately. With Lucy's history of sexual assault, she didn't want her to feel trapped.

All the park-facing suites had been booked for months, except one, a suite by the elevator that was outfitted for the handicapped. When Liz had first called, she'd left a deposit. Today, the clerk had impatiently explained that the hotel had to leave it open in case a handicapped guest showed up. "You have first shot at the suite, but we reserved a king-sized room on the other side of the building if it doesn't work out."

"But I have to cancel the other room by six."

"I'm sorry. That's the best I can do."

Not only was the policy stupid, it was completely irrational. Liz stifled her impulse to use the F-bomb, which she'd mostly edited out of her speech since she and Lucy had started dating, but there were exceptions. She really wanted that suite overlooking the park.

Although she hadn't stayed at the Plaza in decades, she could still visualize the view from the hotel window. The night she'd spent with Joyce Meckler in 1974 counted as a singular moment of joy in a year of abject misery. After Maggie left college, Liz was forced to room with students who liked to party. Desperate to connect with them, Liz made the mistake of coming out. Afterwards, they shunned her, and she felt even more miserable and alone.

Up to that point, Liz had been a straight A student. When she got a

C-minus on an organic chemistry exam, she flew into a panic, convinced she would never get into medical school. After checking the grades in the chemistry building, she returned to the dorm suite she shared with her new roommates. Heavy-metal music blared in the common room. A cloud of pot smoke floated overhead. Every surface was covered with open beer and wine bottles. Liz knew she had to get out of there or lose her mind.

Majority Report had recently run a story about the new lesbian bar that had opened on the Upper East Side. The Sahara was supposed to draw a classier clientele than the bars in the Village. Instead of the political lesbians trying to prove their socialist leanings by wearing work shirts and laced boots, Liz hoped to find a woman more like herself, someone bound for a professional career.

Liz gazed at herself in the mirror of her memory. At eighteen, she was a baby butch, hoping to look cool in a black-leather motorcycle jacket that closed on the bias. The snaps were designed to look like rivets. She was striking, taller than anyone in the room, flat-chested, and abnormally thin from lack of appetite since Maggie had left.

The Sahara lived up to its reputation. It was clean, elegantly furnished with potted palm trees and upholstered chairs and sofas. The atmosphere vaguely suggested the bar in *Casablanca*. It was hot inside, but the leather jacket was part of her costume, so she didn't take it off. She spotted an attractive woman with long, dark hair, sitting alone at one of the cocktail tables. Summoning her best butch bravado, Liz swaggered in her direction.

To her relief, the woman looked up and smiled warmly. She gestured to the other chair. "Would you like a drink?" she asked. Liz sat down and ordered a dry martini. She wasn't much of a drinker, but she was hoping to make a sophisticated impression. The gin went straight to her head. The woman leaned on her hand and listened politely while Liz babbled about the miseries of life as a pre-med.

"Only one in three ever makes it to medical school, and it's even harder for women. If I don't get straight A's, I'll never get in." Liz went on telling her story of misery to someone whose name she didn't even know. Finally, she got around to asking what the woman did for a living.

"I'm a doctor," she said and extended her hand, "Hi. Joyce Meckler."

Liz's face flamed as she stared at the woman's hand. She wished the ground would open up and swallow her. "You must think I'm a complete idiot," she mumbled.

The woman laughed. "No, I think you're cute." After another drink and more pleasant conversation, Joyce said she needed to get back to her hotel. She gave Liz a sly look. "You can come along if you'd like."

Foggy after two martinis, Liz accepted the invitation. They made love for most of the night. Finally sated, they watched the lights of the buildings around Central Park fade as the sun painted all the east-facing windows gold.

Liz closed her eyes and conjured the scene of holding Lucy in her arms as the sun rose over Central Park. She used what memories she had of Lucy's body to supply the details—Lucy's pale limbs sluicing through the dark water at Jimson Pond when they swam naked at Sam's place. Lucy, aware that Liz was admiring her, always dashed out of the water and wrapped a towel around her torso to hide her breasts and the thatch of red hair between her legs. Liz imagined lifting the towel and kissing the warm, hidden places. The expression: "wanting something so bad you can taste it," came to mind.

As a physician, Liz had seen Lucy's naked flesh. She'd palpated Lucy's exquisite breasts for lumps. She'd peered into her vagina with a speculum. In the examination room, her body was a collection of parts. Professional modesty required detachment. If they became lovers, Liz would insist that Lucy switch to another doctor—not only because ethics required it, but because Liz wanted to stop seeing Lucy's body objectively. She wanted to treasure it as a lover.

"Liz?" squawked the intercom on her desk. Liz identified the voice as her PA's. "Liz, are you there?"

"Yes, I'm here," said Liz, shaking off her daydream.

"I sent Cathy to the ED at Southern Med to get her belly pain checked out," said Cherie.

"You think it's a hot appendix?" Liz asked, trying to keep the irritation out of her voice.

"Yes, she finally let me examine her." Cherie explained. "I'm pretty sure it is."

"Shit. I told her it might be a bad appendix, but she wouldn't let me near it." Liz knew why. As a surgeon who'd performed hundreds of appendectomies, she would have insisted that Cathy go to the ED. As her doctor, she would have ordered it.

"She said she'd call us when she finds out more."

"Well, that sucks. Great timing with Bill on his fishing trip. Come down as soon as you're free, and we'll figure out how to divide her cases. We might have to cancel some."

Liz's gold Cartier began to beep. Her consolation prize from when she'd retired early from Yale had more bells and whistles than a space probe. She'd set an alarm to warn her an hour ahead of when she needed to leave to pick Lucy up in New York.

Cherie came in with her tablet to review Cathy's appointments. No matter how gloomy the situation was, her pretty face and unusual blue-green eyes made Liz smile. She had a weakness for female beauty, and Cherie's bi racial coloring and honey-blond hair made her especially attractive.

"We're probably going to have to reschedule some of Cathy's appointments. There's no problem with the routine follow-ups, but what do we do if she needs surgery?"

Liz sighed. "If she needs surgery, we'll do the best we can. What else can we do?"

"But you made all those plans," said Cherie with a sympathetic look.

"Well, that's the life of a family doc…interrupted."

"I'm so sorry, Liz," said Cherie, laying a gentle hand on her arm. "I know how much you were looking forward to seeing Lucy."

"I wanted this weekend to be special because she passed her exams." Why did she feel the need to explain? Of course, Liz had other reasons for making it special, which Cherie probably suspected.

"Hopefully, Cathy's problem is simple gastric distress, and she's okay to come in tomorrow."

Liz doubted it. Cathy had been complaining about pain in her lower abdomen for over a week. Like many busy professional women, she tried to ignore symptoms until she just couldn't anymore. Being a single mother of two teenagers was additional incentive to avoid a trip to the hospital. Who would keep an eye on them while she was away?

Liz and Cherie divided up the cases as equitably as possible. Cherie took the routine cases and Liz took the more problematic ones. They made a list of appointments to be rescheduled, including those for the next morning. Fortunately, they were only open until noon, so there weren't many.

"If you're rescheduling tomorrow's appointments, you're assuming Cathy's not going to be back tomorrow."

"Even if she doesn't need surgery, if she's hurting enough to go to the ED, she's probably not going to feel up to working tomorrow."

"I could take her appointments," said Cherie.

For a moment, Liz was hopeful, then she remembered her own rule. "There's always supposed to be a doctor here."

"There's supposed to be a doctor available for consultation," Cherie reminded her, "not necessarily on-site. We could do telehealth, if necessary."

"Let me think about it," said Liz, but she didn't like the idea. She disapproved of physicians who dumped their responsibilities on their support staff.

As Liz raced through her appointments, she tried to think of ways to save her weekend plans. Between digging a fishing hook out of a boy's thumb and evaluating a vaginal infection, Liz phoned Libby Kent, the internist at the urgent care and explained the situation.

"I'm sorry, Dr. Stolz, but my parents are coming up this weekend. It's the first time I'll see them since the pandemic began. I'd really like to help you out, but…"

"I understand, Libby. Enjoy your visit with your parents."

The practice manager came down the hall while Liz was on the phone.

She waited for the call to end before telling Liz, "Cathy called. They're taking her into the OR in a few minutes."

"So, it was her appendix. She shouldn't have waited so long."

"You should talk, Liz. You never slow down to take care of yourself."

"Thanks, Ginny, I didn't need to hear that today."

"Yes, you do, but you never listen!"

"Did Cherie give you the list of reschedules?"

"Yes, I'm working on it. I think we could cancel a few of tomorrow's appointments or send them to urgent care."

"I hate to do that. We worked so hard to get everyone back after we reopened the office."

"I'll do whatever you tell me, Liz." Ginny stood in the doorway, waiting for instructions.

"Do today's reschedules. I'll figure out tomorrow in a little while. I'm trying to see if I can find someone to help Cherie. She volunteered to come in on her day off. I'll let you know."

The assistant was waving her into the examination room. Fortunately, it was one of Liz's own patients. Getting up to speed on Cathy's took twice as much time.

Between patients, Liz tried to think of other doctors who could fill in for her. Alyson Gagnon, her ex, came to mind, but a radiologist couldn't really fill in for a family doctor. She thought of Jack Dreyfus, but a plastic surgeon was only a marginally better choice. Certainly, he could remove fishhooks, but he wouldn't have a clue about Cathy's heart patients.

Finally, Liz conceded defeat. After her next patient, she looked up the phone number of the car service in Hobbs. "Can you pick someone up from New York?" she asked when a brusque male voice answered.

"Where in New York?"

"The city," said Liz impatiently. There was a long, puzzled silence. "New York City," she explained.

"Who's calling?"

"Dr. Stolz, Hobbs Family Practice."

"We usually only go to Boston. New York is a long trip. What date are you looking at?"

"Today."

This time, the silence was even longer. "Okay, but it will cost you." That didn't faze Liz. She knew it would be expensive.

"I understand, but I promised to pick up someone. The driver probably needs to leave now, so he can get there in time." Liz gave him the address of the dormitory at Union Theological and tried to give him her credit card number.

"I know where you are, Dr. Stolz. I'll give you a discount for cash. I can pick it up tomorrow." In any other place, she'd be expected to pay up front, but the people in Hobbs still trusted one another. *Amazing*, Liz thought.

The mention of credit cards reminded her that she needed to cancel the reservation at the Plaza. She imagined the view of Central Park once more before allowing the scene to dissolve.

19

Lucy studied Professor Spangler's face, thinking how much he'd aged since she was a divinity student. Her thoughts weren't uncharitable. She was fond of the man, whose words had inspired her long after she'd gotten her degree. His theology focused on the real, physical world instead of getting lost in the clouds. As he liked to say, "Even clouds are physical, water vapor collecting in the atmosphere." He'd been an evolutionary biologist before turning to God and studying theology. His hero was the Jesuit paleontologist, Teilhard de Chardin, and he encouraged all his students to read Teilhard's work.

The deep lines at the sides of Spangler's mouth proved how much he liked to laugh. He always wore a slight smile, even when he was intently focused on some theological conundrum. His was a happy theology, a story of unfinished business that God had put in motion and was constantly perfecting. The idea that God sometimes made mistakes and headed in another direction was controversial.

He looked up from Lucy's manuscript with merry eyes. "Lucy, I'm always amazed at how you can say the most outrageous things but leave everyone feeling better." Even though Lucy heard the compliment, she waited for the proverbial other shoe. It dropped gently. "You summarized my thinking about how God uses evolution to work out design problems very well, but I'd like to see a little more original thinking."

"Yes, Jerry." Lucy still wasn't completely comfortable with the idea of calling her professor by his first name, as he'd asked. She sometimes had to force her mouth to form the word.

"Overall, I think it's fine work. I took the liberty of sending the early chapters to someone I know at Highroads Press. They're interested but want to see more. I'll email you the editor's response so you can have his contact information. If they take it, your book could be very popular."

Lucy tried to control her excitement. She'd hoped that her book would reach a wide audience, not sit unnoticed in the dusty collection of doctoral dissertations in the school library.

Spangler offered another smile. "I won't keep you longer, Lucy. I know you've had a busy week, and I'm sure you're anxious to get home. It's a long way to Maine." He pushed the stack of paper across the desk. The top page was covered in red scribbles. Lucy knew from experience not to worry too much. Spangler liked to comment extensively on student papers, but the comments were more likely to be, "Yes!!!" or "Exactly!" than something negative.

After Spangler told Lucy about the publisher's interest in her book, she was walking on air, but by the time she got back to her dorm room, her balloon of joy had completely deflated. Not only was she exhausted from preparing for her exams, she'd stayed up past one to finish her last paper.

She considered taking a nap, but she'd already stripped the bed and stuffed the linens into the pillowcase. All her clothes were packed except the green dress she'd left out for her big date with Liz. The details were supposed to be a surprise, but Liz had let it slip that she'd gotten tickets for an outdoor performance of *Wicked*, which featured "For Good," one of Lucy's favorite Broadway duets. She used to love singing it with Maggie Fitzgerald. Hearing it tonight would be ironic and bittersweet.

They probably wouldn't eat until after the performance, and if the evening ended as Lucy expected, it would be a very late night. She pulled out the tab collar and decided to take a nap. Before she added her clerical blouse to her laundry bag, she yanked the sheets out of the pillowcase and indifferently made the bed.

Drowsing, she thought of Liz. Neither of them had acknowledged the plan to consummate their love, but they both silently knew it would happen. Liz couldn't wait any longer, and frankly, neither could she. Her body was so ready, practically screaming to feel Liz's touch.

Lucy wished she could be sure it was more than raw physical need. Their tentative conversations about a commitment had been promising, but Lucy still worried they might be getting ahead of themselves. She really wanted this to work for both their sakes. She was still in pain from Erika's death. Liz remained angry and spiteful from her divorce. Emotionally, neither of them could afford a mistake. They had to get this right the first time.

The subject was too troubling before sleep, so Lucy turned to something more pleasant. She imagined Liz's body. She'd seen it when they swam naked with the others at Jimson Pond. Her shoulders and arms were muscular, but her breasts were full and soft, and her little belly from too much beer was endearing.

Lucy wondered what kind of lover Liz would be. She'd probably want to have the upper hand, whereas Erika had always found it amusing when Lucy flipped her over in bed. Often, Lucy did it simply to hear Erika's laughter. She could be so straitlaced at times, and sex should be joyful.

Liz had learned to be bold from her profession, but being too aggressive could be a problem for a partner who's been raped. Lucy had nearly dislocated Liz's shoulder when she'd tried to kiss her before she was ready. The fact that Lucy's martial arts training had made her so dangerous sometimes frightened her. She shuddered at the thought of hurting anyone, never mind someone she loved so much.

Lucy touched her nipple and imagined the sensation of Liz's lips tugging gently, her sensitive fingers kneading her flesh. *Keep thinking about this and you'll have to make yourself come,* Lucy told herself. *Save your excitement for the real thing.* Eventually, she drifted off to sleep.

When her phone rang, she was in such a stupor she had no idea where she was. The loose sheet had come away, revealing the blue stripes of the mattress. She was still in her dormitory room. Although the building was mostly empty, she hurried to answer the phone before the loud ring disturbed anyone.

"Lucy, I'm so sorry, but I can't pick you up tonight." The solemn tone of Liz's voice alarmed her.

"Oh, no!" she exclaimed. "What happened?"

"One of my partners was taken in for emergency surgery, so I can't leave. I hired the Hobbs car service to pick you up instead."

"I could have taken the train."

"No, I promised to pick you up."

"But it will be so expensive!"

"When I told him that you'd be his passenger, he gave me a discount. You have all your parishioners wrapped around your finger." Despite the gentle teasing, Lucy could hear Liz's regret. "I'm so sorry."

"Stop apologizing. When I started dating a doctor, I knew these things might happen." Now that she'd absorbed the news, Lucy sank back on the bed. "When will the driver be here?"

"Around the time we arranged. Six o'clock. I'm so bummed. I had such a wonderful night planned for us."

"Tell me about it," Lucy encouraged because Liz sounded so utterly disappointed.

"If I tell you, it will spoil the surprise for next time."

"I'll pretend I'm surprised. Tell me."

"You knew about the play. I made reservations for the tasting menu at Le Berniden, and I got a suite at the Plaza, but don't worry. It had two bedrooms."

Lucy smiled at the cleverness of Liz's plan. "Why would we need two bedrooms?"

"Well, you know. I didn't want to presume." Lucy could imagine Liz blushing. When she blushed, her eyes became so blue. Lucy longed to see them, so she requested video chat.

"One bed would have been fine," she said when the chat window opened. She could see Liz's diplomas over her shoulder, which meant she was still in the office.

Liz's smile claimed her entire face. "Does that mean you'll come to my house tonight?" she asked with growing excitement.

"Oh, sweetie. I'm going to be exhausted after the long car ride."

"But Lucy, I miss you so much!"

"Liz, we've waited this long. We can wait another night. I want to be fully rested and alert, not falling asleep in your arms. Actually, falling asleep in your arms sounds pretty good, but not tonight."

"Tomorrow night? Please?"

Usually, when Liz pleaded, it tugged at Lucy's heartstrings, but now that they'd acknowledged what lay ahead, she found her childlike begging endearing rather than painful. She smiled indulgently.

"Maybe. I'm sure I'll have all sorts of things waiting for me when I get home. I promised Tom I'd take the worship services on Sunday. He's going to Connecticut to see his mother. He hasn't seen her since the pandemic began. My sermon is only half done. I didn't want to stop to write it in the middle of studying for my exams. Will you come?"

"Oh, I'd love to come," said Liz, grinning.

"Liz! I meant to my worship service on Sunday!"

"I knew what you meant. Yes, I'll be there." A deep sigh was audible. "Oh, Lucy, I had such plans for us tonight!"

"I'm sorry too, but we can do it next time."

"Next time won't be the same."

"Oh, sweetie, I know," said Lucy with a sympathetic look, "but maybe it will be even better." A mischievous thought played in Lucy's mind. "We could wait, you know…until we can come back to New York."

"No!" protested Liz as if she'd been stabbed. "I've been waiting and waiting. I can't wait *any* longer."

"Let's see what happens. We're both adults. What's that old expression, 'good things come to those who wait'?"

"Invented by someone who has never been horny." Liz pouted, her bottom lip pulled up over the top one like a petulant child.

"I won't call you tonight because it will be late when I get in. I'll send a text to let you know I arrived safely."

"Call me anyway," Liz ordered. "I want to hear your voice."

Although Lucy liked the idea of someone caring enough to want to know when she got home, a part of her rebelled. She didn't promise. She threw a kiss to the screen before tapping off the call.

Her hand searched on the bed stand for her hair clasp. There was no need to rush now that the date was off. She could even skip washing her hair. A sigh escaped as she looked at the green dress hanging on the back of the closet door. She'd probably sleep on the long ride home, so she'd wear yoga pants and a knit top to be comfortable.

Before she locked her phone, she noticed the banner indicating a text message. It was from Tom: *I made an executive decision and offered one of the curates' studios to a priest who says she's an old friend of yours. Her name is Susan Gedney. I'll explain when you get home.*

Lucy's eyes widened. *Susan? Susan, her first lover, the woman who'd inspired Lucy to become a priest…who'd taken a curate's post in the Midwest and never let anyone know where she'd gone? Susan was there…in Hobbs?*

Lucy's mind raced as she tried to make sense of this development.

20

Don't be ridiculous, Susan Gedney told herself as she put back the milk and chose a small container of half-and-half instead. The difference in price was barely fifty cents. Yes, she had to watch every penny until she found a job, but for her, coffee with real cream was a necessity, not a luxury. Besides, she was having a guest for breakfast.

Fortunately, Susan now had a place to lay her head at night and not a moment too soon. The people at the campground were beginning to look suspicious whenever she drove in to use the showers. The place had a limited staff, so it wasn't easy to hide the fact that she wasn't a paying customer, but it was worth the risk. The hot water in the communal shower felt so good, even if it did remind her of being in the convent.

Thanks to Lucy's associate rector, Susan now had a comfortable little studio with plenty of hot water and her own efficiency kitchen. It even had internet! Tom Simmons seemed like a kind man. He'd bought her story about the lack of vacancies in town because it was entirely plausible. "The motels and B&Bs are always overbooked for Fourth of July week," he'd said, instantly commiserating. "The summer people all descend on us at the same time."

She'd told Father Simmons that she'd decided to come back East to spend the summer. Of course, she couldn't be so near and not look up Lucy Bartlett, her old friend from divinity school.

"I'm between assignments," Susan had said when he'd asked the name of her church.

"You should sign up for our diocesan newsletter, the Maine Dio-log. They post all the clergy vacancies there. Let me give you the internet password, so you can get online and take a look." He wrote down the password and handed her a numbered security key like those used in college dormitories in another era. The charm on the key chain was a stylized cross. When he'd put it in her hand, Susan had clutched it like a lifeline.

She'd worn her clerical collar when she'd first come to St. Margaret's looking for Lucy. People made assumptions when she wore it. She was still listed on the staff page of her last church. The woman in charge of the website had limited skills and would do anything to avoid updating it. If Father Simmons needed additional verification, he could look her up on the Union Theological alumni page.

Although some parts of Susan's story didn't match her current circumstances, she was an ordained Episcopal priest. Ironically, she, who'd encouraged Lucy to become a priest, had remained a deacon longer. Susan had once been such a devout Catholic she'd entered a strict order of nuns. Even while she was studying for her divinity degree, she'd remained stuck in the idea that only males could be ordained. Her teachers at Union Theological had tried to explain that Anglican bishops had apostolic succession and could legitimately ordain women. Even Lucy, who was never good at making theological arguments, had tried to persuade her. Susan had finally applied for ordination, but it had required a leap of faith.

Susan realized that the friendly woman at the checkout was still waiting for payment. Two lone dollar bills remained in her wallet. She handed them over and counted out coins for exact change. Since leaving South Dakota, she'd tried to limit herself to a set amount of cash each week. The money she'd withdrawn from her retirement account had to last until she figured out what to do.

As she drove back to the rectory, she remembered her joy at seeing Lucy. She had appeared at her door close to midnight, wearing that fuzzy look which meant she was long past tired. She stood in the hall, waiting for an invitation to enter. Naturally, after so many years of silence, they were both awkward and unsure.

"Don't worry. I've had my shots," Susan said, but she didn't dare approach. Instead, she waited for Lucy to make the first move.

"I thought I'd never see you again!" When Lucy touched her face as if not believing she was real, Susan pressed her hand against her cheek to get more of her touch. How she'd missed it!

"Can you stay for a cup of tea?" she asked. "Or a glass of wine?"

"Not tonight. I'm really tired. My residencies at Union are exhausting. Tom told you I've gone back to school?" The dark circles under Lucy's eyes meant that she still over-studied because she lacked confidence. "We can catch up tomorrow after I get some sleep."

"Come for breakfast?" Susan asked in a hopeful voice.

"What time? I usually get up to watch the sun rise."

"That's early for me. How about seven?"

Lucy nodded her agreement and looked around the small room. Susan was glad she'd tidied that morning. "Are you comfortable here?" Lucy asked.

"Yes. It's a cozy, little place. I have everything I need and more. Even web access."

"My daughter lived here when we first brought her to Hobbs."

"Your daughter? What daughter?" Susan's shock had shown on her face, despite her best effort to control it.

"Emily. My daughter. That's right. You don't know about her. I'll tell you about it, but not tonight."

Before Lucy left, she caught Susan by the arms and trailed down to her wrists, holding them lightly. "It's so good to see you again."

Their reunion could have been a disaster, so the warm welcome had come as a relief. After being abandoned, Lucy had every right to be angry. Fortunately, Susan's faith in Lucy's generosity and kindness had been proven right.

When Susan got back to the rectory, she carried the spoils of her frugal shopping expedition into the studio apartment. She put the perishables into the refrigerator. Fortunately, it was a full-size refrigerator, not one of those compact "dorm-room" fridges like the one they'd lived with for two years until Lucy had insisted that they move into a real apartment on the upper West Side.

Susan washed the blueberries in a plastic colander she'd found in one of the cabinets. She'd found a local granola on sale. Everyone seemed to be into healthy living in Maine. The "Buy Local" signs on the shelves in the supermarket celebrated Maine farms. South Dakota had been farm country too, but no one made a fuss about the local farmers, maybe because they sold all their livestock and produce to big distributors.

The thought of South Dakota chilled her to the bone. The long winters were so depressing, especially in the remote, rural community where she'd served. The vast expanses of snow-blanketed fields were so desolate. Maine had long winters too, but at least, it had the ocean and its restless beauty to make it tolerable. Now that she was no longer living out of her car, Susan looked forward to long walks on the beach.

There was a soft knock on the door. When she opened it, she saw the Lucy she remembered, not the sleepy, overtired woman who had appeared the night before. After rest, the dark circles under Lucy's eyes always disappeared. Her makeup was perfect, including her signature red lipstick. Long after Lucy left the stage, she could still create operatic glamor.

"Come in," said Susan, reaching for her hand. She gestured to the little table for two. "It's a simple breakfast, but I can fry some eggs." It would be a sacrifice because she'd been eating omelets for dinner to save money.

"I don't really care what I eat," Lucy said. "I just want to look at you and catch up."

"Me too," Susan replied. "Sit down. Will you have some coffee?"

"Oh, please!" Lucy glanced around. "I hope you're comfortable here. No one's been here since the pandemic began. I hope it wasn't dusty. We try to keep it clean."

"Oh, my word! I'm so grateful to have this wonderful place to live. There were no vacancies in your town."

"How did you know I love beach roses?" asked Lucy, smiling as she turned the water glass to admire the pink and white blossoms.

"They were there, so I picked them. I hope that's allowed."

"They grow wild here. They're everywhere."

"How did you land in Maine?" Susan asked, pouring the coffee.

"My rector in Boston encouraged me. He said I was ready to step up into leadership. He showed me the opening in Hobbs. When I applied, I never expected to be accepted."

"Of course, they accepted you, Lucy. You are a natural leader, and you radiate. No one can resist your light."

"I don't know about that," said Lucy, making herself small by slouching in her chair.

"Oh, don't try that with me, Lucy. You know that people would follow you anywhere! When you speak, you have everyone's attention. Don't you realize how much power you have?"

There was a slight pucker between Lucy's auburn brows. "I don't think of it that way."

"God called you, Lucy. There's a reason you were given all those gifts."

"I try to be grateful," Lucy said in a soft voice, "and use them well."

Susan studied Lucy, wondering why she was still so insecure about her abilities as a priest. When she'd first seen Lucy on the stage of the Met, she'd seemed so confident.

Susan had been her fan since she'd first heard her sing on a recording. When she'd read that Lucy was singing in *Madama Butterfly* at the Met, she'd stood at the velvet railing in the back for the entire three-hour performance. Even if she could have afforded a seat, there was none. The performance had been sold out for months, but Susan would have stood until she fainted to hear Lucille Bartlett sing Cio-Cio-san. Years later, when Susan had heard from another divinity student that Lucille Bartlett was singing for an ordination, she'd lobbied the liturgy committee for tickets until she made a pest of herself.

Susan spooned Greek yogurt into Lucy's bowl, added some blueberries, and topped it with some granola. "It's simple, but I remembered that it's one of your favorite breakfasts."

"Thank you for remembering."

"Let's eat, and then, maybe, you can show me your beach."

"Oh, I would love that!"

"But first, tell me about this daughter. Who? What? How?"

Lucy's hand tapped her chest in apology. "I'm so sorry I never told you. It needed to be a secret…to protect the adoption and keep her away from him."

"Who? The man who raped you?"

Lucy stared into her bowl. "I didn't want him to know I was pregnant. I didn't want him to interfere or sue for parental rights. He was so controlling."

"I can understand not wanting your rapist involved in your daughter's upbringing, but why didn't you tell me? You told me everything else. I thought you trusted me."

Lucy looked into her eyes. "There's more. I considered an abortion, but when the time came, I just couldn't." That came as no surprise. Lucy was so kind. Susan couldn't imagine her killing anything. "When I gave her up for adoption, the lawyer swore it was sealed, but New York allows adopted children to search for their birth parents."

Susan took a deep breath, trying to absorb all the news. "So she found you. Were you happy about that?"

"Of course, but I thought I'd put that part of my life behind me forever, so it was a shock. It almost ended my relationship with Erika before it got started, but I had no choice. She was only sixteen and living in a homeless shelter. The people who adopted her were Jehovah's Witnesses. They don't believe in higher education and wanted her to quit high school to work in her mother's cleaning business. That's why she became an emancipated minor and looked for me."

"What a horror. The parents sound like the Taliban."

"Not quite, but their beliefs were especially difficult for Emily. Her IQ is off the charts. She's a math and music genius."

"That's wonderful!"

"Yes, it is wonderful, but she's on the spectrum. She has high-functioning autism."

"I'm so sorry," said Susan. She'd briefly worked with autistic children as a teacher and knew how challenging they could be.

"Don't be sorry. My beautiful, brilliant daughter is a gift. I only wish I could talk to her on that level. My wife could and her father. Stefan Bultmann was Clemson Professor of Mathematics at Yale and shortlisted for the Fields medal."

"Do you have a photo of Emily?" asked Susan.

Lucy's face lit up like any mother's when someone shows interest in her child. She flipped through the photos on her phone. "This is Erika," said Lucy, gazing lovingly at the picture before turning the screen toward Susan. The smiling woman in the photo had white-blond hair and pale blue eyes.

"She was an attractive woman."

Lucy smiled when she found a photo of her daughter. Susan gazed at the image of a sweet-faced young redhead, shocked to see how much the girl resembled her mother. "She's beautiful," Susan said. "What gorgeous blue eyes."

"Her father had blue eyes." Lucy locked the phone and put it into her pocket.

Susan nudged Lucy under the elbow. "Eat. You're too thin."

"Everyone keeps trying to feed me. I suppose I should feel loved, and I do." Lucy picked up her spoon and put it into her yogurt. "How did you find me?"

"After I left, I'd heard that you'd gone to a church in Boston. I subscribed to the church bulletin. I saw the announcement when you accepted the post of rector here in Maine, so I signed up for your diocesan newsletter and followed you. When I saw the post about your wife's death, I wanted to come right away, but I wasn't sure you'd want me here." Susan watched Lucy slowly eat the bowl of blueberries and yogurt. "I'm sorry. Did I say the wrong thing?"

Lucy shook her head. "No. I just wish you'd let me know you were okay. You seemed so upset when you left."

"I thought a clean break was better."

"For you, maybe."

"Will you ever forgive me?" Susan asked hopefully.

"Oh, Susan," said Lucy with sigh. "I forgave you a long time ago."

"So, you don't mind that I'm here?"

Lucy looked at her with a strange, puzzled expression. "I'm not sure. I'm glad to see you, but so much has changed." Lucy's ambivalent answer made her uneasy. Evidently Lucy sensed it because she reached out for her hand. "Yes, of course, I'm glad you're here. Concelebrate with me tomorrow."

Susan tried to keep smiling, but Lucy's earnest eyes forced her to look away. "Another time. I want to introduce myself to the bishop first."

"There are provisions for visiting clergy."

"I'm sure. I'll serve as your acolyte. As a deacon."

"All right," said Lucy, "if that makes you more comfortable."

21

For the sake of her patients, Liz forced herself to calm down. She reflected on the unfairness of it. If not for Cathy's appendicitis, she and Lucy would be having breakfast at the Plaza. After a night of passionate sex, room service would have been ideal, but they also could have enjoyed a leisurely meal in the hotel restaurant. The breakfast buffet featured exotic specialties like blini with crème fraîche and caviar. Liz salivated at the thought. Stuck in her office in Hobbs, she had wolfed down a yogurt at her desk.

Dealing with her disappointment over the ruined plans for the weekend was hard enough, but now Lucy had a surprise guest staying at the rectory, some old friend from divinity school. After they'd been separated for two weeks, how could Lucy even think of spending the day with this friend? Liz seldom showed Lucy her anger, but she was too frustrated to hold back. Lucy responded with characteristic understanding and generosity while Liz snarled.

"Liz, I love you, and I miss you so much. We'll be together soon. I promise."

"*Together* together?"

"When the time is right, yes."

"Come over after your dinner with your friend."

Liz sensed Lucy's indecision before she finally said, "I'll see you on Sunday morning. Afterwards, we'll talk."

Liz stifled a grunt of anger. "Who is this friend that she's so important?"

A deep sigh was audible through the phone speaker. "Susan helped me through a very difficult time in my life. She pretty much scraped me off the ground and helped me find my way. I owe her so much."

Liz was almost afraid to ask the question that had been nagging her, but she did. "Were you lovers?"

The long period of silence made Liz even more anxious. Finally, Lucy answered, "Yes."

The jolt of anxiety that went through Liz felt like touching a live wire. "Should I be worried?"

"No."

"Are you sure you're not still interested in her?"

"Liz, I haven't seen or heard from her in seven years. No, that ship has sailed."

"Does she know that?" Liz asked curtly.

"I don't know. She's the one who broke it off. She left because she felt she needed to be celibate. That's what the Church taught at the time. She thought being near me was too much temptation."

"Maybe she's changed her mind."

"Maybe she has, but that has nothing to do with me…or with us."

Liz liked the "us" part of that statement, but she cautioned, "Be careful, Lucy. That blast from the past can be very seductive. Look what happened to me and Maggie."

"But you were meant to explore that relationship, Liz. She really needed you, and you were there for her. It was meant to be."

"Just watch out, Lucy. You have such a kind heart."

"Don't worry, Liz. I can look after myself."

Liz wanted to say, I hope so, but she didn't. She needed to dial back on the advice, especially because she knew Lucy didn't respond well to pressure.

Kristy, the new assistant, knocked on her open door. "Dr. Stolz, you have a patient in two and another in five."

"Thank you. And dammit, call me Liz, will you?"

The young woman backed up a step. Liz knew she had to stop being so irritable, but who the hell decided to schedule the newbie while Cathy was out? "Hold on, Lucy." Liz muted the call and said she'd take the patient in exam room two first. "Gotta go, Luce. Call me later when you have time to talk to the woman who loves you." Liz despised passive-aggressive be-havior, so she regretted rubbing in her disappointment.

"Liz, I know you love me. I love you too, but I need to deal with this. I hope your day isn't too busy without Cathy there." Liz sensed Lucy's an-noyance in her tone, but there wasn't time to sort out the misfire. A patient was waiting.

Liz hurried down the hall to the exam room. She gave her usual warning knock and found Denise Chantal sitting on the table. "I didn't expect to see you back so soon," said Liz, offering her hand and taking a seat on the stool. "Your post-op follow-up isn't for a couple of weeks."

"I know, but I was uncomfortable, and when I found out you were on call, I made an appointment right away. I didn't want to take my chances with urgent care."

"What seems to be the trouble?"

"I can't stop peeing. After surgery, I was so happy that I could pee, but that didn't last long."

"Well, urinating is better than not urinating. They rerouted a lot of your plumbing. Have you been keeping everything clean as they instructed?"

"Absolutely."

"Hygiene is different for women. Now, you know what it's like to live with our geography."

"Believe me when I say I've looked forward to it for years."

Liz patted Denise's arm to reassure her. "We'll figure it out." Denise's symptoms sounded like a simple UTI, but this was a unique situation. Liz pulled up the leg support. "Lie down, please. Besides the urinary symptoms, how are you feeling today?"

"Pretty good. I'm so glad it's over. I've waited so long for this."

Liz inspected the surgical site, still amazed that surgeons could achieve such good results in a surgery that basically turned the penis inside out and constructed a working vagina and labia. The urethral opening seemed clear and healing nicely. She was relieved to see there was no sign of overt infection.

"Any urinary incontinence?"

"No, only urgency."

"Sounds like a simple infection, but I'd like you to give a sample for culture. Sometimes, people pick up exotic bacteria in the hospital. While we're waiting for the results, I'll prescribe a broad-spectrum antibiotic. It should help you feel better by tonight. If not, call me. You should follow up with your surgeon too. He'll want to know about this."

"She," said Denise. "I chose her because she's trans too."

Skill and experience were probably better criteria for choosing a surgeon, but plenty of patients had admitted they'd chosen Liz as their breast surgeon because she was female. People often had strange reasons for choosing doctors.

"You can get dressed now," said Liz. "Kristy will be back in a few minutes and give you a specimen cup. There are wipes in the dispenser on the wall. Be gentle. I'm sure it's still raw. Thanks for coming in today."

As Liz headed down the hall to her next patient, she realized that thanking someone for taking care of their own health would have sounded strange before the pandemic, yet she was still saying it a year after they'd reopened the office. By now, it had become a part of her regular script.

Fortunately, none of the patients Cathy had scheduled for Saturday morning were particularly interesting or demanding. They always had a few walk-ins during the summer season. People who were on vacation sometimes forgot their medications or developed sudden symptoms. Sprained ankles from walking on the rocks at the beach or pulled tendons from bicycling for the first time in years were common. They saw the Hobbs Family Practice sign on the way to the beach and stopped in looking for a doctor.

As Liz locked up the office, she wondered what to do with herself for the rest of the day. She wouldn't have minded some company, but Sam was still working on her big renovation every day of the week. That meant Olivia was available, but she always wanted to talk about town business, and Liz wasn't up for that. Brenda was busy training rookie cops today.

Liz was twitchy knowing Lucy was with *that woman*. She needed to *do* something to keep her mind occupied. She remembered that the bulkhead door still needed scraping. After she changed, she grabbed her favorite sander out of her shop and headed to the harbor. On the way, she stopped at the food truck on Route 1 for a lobster roll. As she ate it, she found herself wondering what Lucy was doing with her old "friend." Liz, who'd mostly had open relationships, wasn't the jealous type. The only one exception was the idea of Maggie being with a man. That drove her crazy.

She popped the last tasty bit of lobster roll into her mouth and noticed a familiar girl and a man coming down the dock. As they came closer, she recognized Courtney Barnes' daughter, Kaylee.

"Hey, Dr. Stolz," the girl called, waving.

"Kaylee. What brings you down here?" Liz kept smiling, but she eyed the man with Kaylee. He was a good-looking man in his forties. He had a muscular physique and moved with an athlete's confidence. She'd never seen him before, but that meant little. During the summer, the town was full of strangers.

"I told my dad about your boat, so we came to look at it. Is that okay?" Kayle called back.

The man smiled and waved. He had a pleasant face with friendly, blue eyes, and thinning, sandy hair. Liz could see the resemblance between father and daughter. "Hello, Dr. Stolz. Nice boat."

"Want to come aboard?"

Kaylee grinned. "Yes!"

"Kaylee, show your father where the ladder is." The man let Kaylee board first. Liz reached down to help her up.

"Kaylee really wanted me to see your boat," said the man, offering his hand. "I'm Doug Barnes. Thanks for having us, Dr. Stolz."

"Call me Liz," she said, giving his hand a firm squeeze and looking directly into his eyes, but she didn't perceive any threat. Kaylee seemed relaxed and looked at the man affectionately. Liz finally lowered her guard. "Can I offer you something to drink? How about an iced tea for you, Kaylee?" The girl nodded enthusiastically. "A beer, Doug? I have lagers, Pilsners, IPAs, wheats…"

The man laughed. "I'm no expert on beer," he said cheerfully. "Pick for me. Nothing too bitter, please."

In the galley, Liz found some bags of pretzels and chips. She chose a citrusy wheat beer for Kaylee's father and peach-flavored iced tea for the girl.

"Thanks," said Doug. "It's really nice of you to allow us to invade your space while you're working," he said, peering at the dusty sander bag on the deck.

"Sanding isn't my favorite thing."

"I'm with you on that," he said, raising his glass. "This boat looks brand new."

"It's not, but it was hardly used. A lot of people buy boats but don't have time to use them. There's still some work it needs, mostly minor stuff. The engines were in great shape."

Doug glanced toward the fore deck. "I bet a boat of this size burns a lot of gas."

"It does. And gas prices are going up again."

The man huffed out a sigh. "Tell me about it. I just drove back from Oregon."

"Oh? That's a long drive."

"The coaching job I thought I had there fell through. College sports programs are cutting back because they lost all of last year's season."

"Sorry to hear that."

The man shrugged. "It happens. I had nothing better to do, so I came back East. I haven't been to Maine since I was a kid, so I figured I'd come up and look around. I'm a phys ed teacher. Maybe I can find a high school job."

"I hear they're hurting for teachers up north. Unfortunately, they don't pay well, which probably explains why."

"College coaching jobs certainly pay better."

Kaylee plopped down in the sling chair near her father. "I wish we could take a ride," she said with a sad pout.

Doug frowned disapprovingly at his daughter. "Kaylee, let's not complain. It was nice of Dr. Stolz to let us come aboard and give us snacks."

Liz hadn't planned to take *The Wet Lady* out today, but the sea was calm and the sun glittered brilliantly on the surface of the water. She suddenly decided she wouldn't mind a brief run. Anything to avoid breaking out the sander.

"We could take a quick ride up to Kennebunkport and back. You okay with that, Doug?"

"Sure, why not?" he replied with a big grin. "Let me run up and close my car windows in case it rains."

After he climbed down the ladder, Liz smiled at Kaylee, who had finished one bag of chips and was working on another. "I have some salsa to go with those chips. I should have brought it up."

"I'm fine."

"You seem happy to see your dad."

Kaylee nodded enthusiastically. "I haven't seen him since we moved."

Liz uncovered the instrument panel and started the engine. She was pleased when Kaylee came into the pilot house to sit in one of the passenger's chairs.

"When did your dad come?" asked Liz.

"This afternoon. I was supposed to spend two weeks with him in Oregon at the end of the summer. Now, I don't have to wait that long. I really missed him."

Liz found herself enjoying the ride and wondered why she hadn't decided to do this from the beginning. Why did she work so hard? She knew it was the work ethic ingrained in her by her grandmother. When the woman wasn't cleaning or digging in her garden, she was crocheting afghans like a human loom. The only time Liz had ever seen her relax was when she watched her daytime soap operas.

After they got underway, Kaylee and her father sat with Liz in the pilot house. Listening to the girl describe the purpose of the instruments to her father, Liz was amazed at how much the girl had learned from her last boat trip. "Wow, Kaylee, you know so much about boats!" Doug said, beaming with pride after she showed him how the fish sonar worked.

Liz was reluctant to return, but there wasn't much gas in the tank, so she headed back to Hobbs. As she backed into her mooring, she noticed people running down the dock. One of them was Brenda Harrison. The other was Kaylee's mother.

"Hi, Mom," Kaylee called brightly as Liz looped the lines over the piers. "Dr. Stolz took us out for a boat ride!"

"Kaylee! You had me worried to death!"

The girl's enthusiasm instantly deflated. Her face went white.

Doug leaned over the railing. "I'm sorry, Courtney. It's my fault."

"You!" she said with venom in her eyes. "What the hell did you think you were doing?"

"Nothing. Kaylee wanted to show me her school and around town. I didn't mean anything by it."

Courtney glared at him. "You could have called to tell me you were coming." Then she turned her furious eyes on her daughter. "I came home, and you were gone. I called and called you. You never answered."

Kaylee took out her phone and looked at it. "Sorry, Mom. I turned off the ringer by accident."

"Why didn't you call me?"

"I forgot. I was so happy to see Dad."

Kaylee took a step closer to Liz and looked up to plead for her support. Liz put her hand on the girl's shoulder.

"I'm sorry, Courtney," Liz called down to the angry woman. "I should have asked if you knew she was here before I took them out."

"That's not your job, Dr. Stolz. She's old enough to know better. She should have called me before she went off with *him*." Courtney glared at Doug, then at her daughter. "Come down here this minute!"

"Thanks for the ride, Dr. Stolz," murmured Kaylee.

Liz patted the girl's shoulder. "Sorry I got you in trouble."

"You didn't." Kaylee headed to the ladder.

Frowning, Doug watched the scene below. He eyed Brenda, who was busy talking on her radio. Liz guessed she was calling off a search for the girl. She hoped it hadn't gotten as far as an Amber Alert.

Once Kaylee was in reach, Courtney grasped her daughter's arm and yanked it before leading her up the stairs to the parking area.

Doug turned to Liz with a lame smile. "I asked Kaylee to text her mother and tell her where we were going. She probably just forgot."

Liz gave him a hard look. "Really? She seems like a good kid. Very responsible."

"Maybe she didn't want her mother to know she'd gone off with me."

"Is there a reason for that?" asked Liz, unwilling to let his actions go without comment. Maybe she shouldn't have made assumptions. She frowned so that Doug understood that she was suspicious. Cases of parents kidnapping their children after a divorce were, unfortunately, much too common.

"No. I mean. I don't know. Kids have their own reasons for doing or not doing things."

"Is there a reason Courtney wouldn't have wanted Kaylee to come down here with you?"

Doug shrugged. "If there is, I don't know about it. Our divorce wasn't especially nasty." He gave her a quick anxious look. "I should go. Thanks for the boat ride."

Liz tried to decide what she thought about the man as she watched him walk down the dock to the stairway.

22

Melissa wanted to sink into the car seat while Courtney berated her daughter. In her shoes, she would have been furious too. For the brief time before the police chief arrived at the house, Melissa had to stifle her own anxiety to calm down the girl's mother, who was trembling and buckled over with worry. Melissa's soothing words and hugs had done little to comfort her. Fortunately, the police arrived quickly.

Chief Harrison's slight Brooklyn accent made Melissa a little homesick. When the chief took off her gray campaign hat, Melissa noticed that her blond hair needed a dye job. She wasn't young, probably mid-fifties. Melissa instantly liked the tall woman, who was as buttoned up as any New York City cop, but the relaxed pace of Maine seemed to have rubbed off on her. She exuded laid-back but professional calm.

The chief had two rookie cops in tow. She explained that she'd been training them and asked Courtney if she minded if they stayed. Courtney probably would have agreed to anything if they would only find her daughter. After the brief interview, the police chief sent the junior patrol officers to search Kaylee's school and the ball fields where her team played.

"We'll find her," said Chief Harrison confidently. "She can't have gotten far."

"I shouldn't have left her home alone," said Courtney. "She's too young."

"Heck, at that age, I was already babysitting," Chief Harrison said with a smile. "Don't worry, Ms. Barnes. I have the State Police tracking her GPS. We should hear from them soon."

The chief's scanner began to chatter. She took it out of its holster and stepped out of the room to speak privately. When she returned, she said, "The state police have located her signal. They're sending your daughter's coordinates to my phone." She took out her phone and pinched it open to look at the map. "She's in the harbor." She pinched again to enlarge the detail. "Looks like she's on the boat dock. The signal is coming from one of the berths. Now, it's moving."

"Someone's taking her away!" Courtney wailed, her eyes wide with alarm.

Chief Harrison's blue eyes steadily held Courtney's gaze. "That's Liz Stolz's berth. Let's check the harbor webcam." She made some taps on her phone. "Yep, that's *The Wet Lady* heading out to sea. Your daughter is probably with Dr. Stolz."

"Oh, thank God!" exclaimed Courtney. "But how did she get there?"

"Good question. Let's head down to the harbor and find out. Will you run me by the police station, so I can pick up my squad car?" She smiled. "No rush. If they're heading where I think they're heading we have plenty of time."

Now that Kaylee had been found, Courtney was much calmer, but Melissa could tell that her stress level was still high. As she drove them back to the trailer, she kept babbling about a tracking app some mothers used to keep tabs on their kids. She hadn't activated it because she didn't want Kaylee to feel like she was spying on her. "If the state police hadn't been able to track her GPS, we still might not know where she is."

"Hobbs is really lucky to have a seasoned police chief like Brenda Harrison," said Melissa but there was no response. Melissa realized Courtney was probably still wrapped up in her worry. Equally likely, she was trying to figure out how to punish Kaylee. Melissa glanced over her shoulder to the backseat where Kaylee sat with her arms folded, looking out the window. She obviously knew she was in big trouble and was trying to avoid attention by being unusually quiet.

Melissa reached over and patted Courtney's thigh. "All's well that ends well."

"He could have warned me he was coming to Maine," Courtney muttered under her breath.

"I thought you parted on good terms."

"We did, but our communication was never great. He and I need to have a little chat after our young friend back there has gone to bed. I want to know what he's up to."

"Can't it wait until tomorrow?" Melissa asked. "I was kinda, sorta…you know…hoping I might get an invitation to stay the night. It's not a school night or anything, and I don't have to work tomorrow."

"Maybe that could be arranged," said Courtney. "But I do have some work to do this weekend. Principals don't get the summers off like teachers do."

"Too bad. I was hoping we could spend more time together."

"I get two weeks off at the beginning of August. Maybe we could plan a trip to Acadia or Moosehead Lake. I've never seen a real moose in the wild, but I've always wanted to."

"Sounds like fun," Melissa agreed. "I've been thinking of getting some kayaks. The guy who rents them in the harbor has good deals on the used ones. Maybe at the end of the season, we could get a couple and leave them at my mother's house."

Courtney looked in the rear-view mirror to check on Kaylee. "Has your mother decided yet if she likes me?"

Melissa turned sharply. "What brought that on?"

"You didn't even invite me to her house until you knew she was gone." The chilly tone made Melissa sit up straight. "Never mind. I'm just stressed. Let's talk about it when we don't have an audience."

"She's asleep," Melissa said.

"Don't be fooled. Kids' ears never sleep."

"Okay. But I don't want to have a big fight after you were scared out of your mind."

"Thank you. I don't either."

They turned on the road that led to the trailer. Melissa studied the other houses on the street. Few were as rundown on the outside as the one Melissa was renting, but they all looked pretty sad. "Have you found any places to rent yet?"

"Now's not the time to look. Summer is the worst time to find a place in Maine."

Courtney pulled into the driveway. "Kaylee, we're home," she said in a tone that Melissa recognized as her stern-parent voice.

The sleepy girl in the back seat opened her eyes and looked out.

"Here's the key," said her mother handing it over. "Open the door, please."

Kaylee took the keys and headed up the gravel path to the door.

"I need a few minutes to speak to her about her behavior," said Courtney in a low voice. "Do you mind waiting out here?"

In fact, Melissa was glad to be spared watching Courtney discipline her daughter. She sat in one of the sling chairs Courtney had set up around a fire pit she'd found on sale at Marden's. It gave the yard a woodsy, campground feel but only reinforced the transient nature of Courtney's occupancy. Melissa heard the raised voices from inside the trailer, followed by crying. Melissa wondered what Kaylee's punishment might be. Grounding or taking away phone privileges were popular in her day, but in the age of mobile phones, how did that work?

A few minutes later, Courtney came out of the house with a bottle of wine and two glasses. "I need some alcohol. How about you?"

"You'd better believe it."

Courtney dropped into a neighboring chair and sighed. "I'm angrier with Doug than with Kaylee. She's just a kid. How dare he show up where I live without warning me he was coming!"

"I thought you had an amicable divorce."

"We did mostly, but he put up quite a stink about custody because he thought I was having an affair with a woman. I wasn't. We were just good friends. But Doug knew I'd been involved with a woman before we got together."

"Does he have an issue with you being with a woman?"

"He's kind of intrigued by it. You know how guys are about women having sex together."

"He's not going to make trouble for you, is he?"

Courtney frowned and looked thoughtful. "I doubt it, but I felt more comfortable with him being thousands of miles away in Oregon. Then he couldn't see what I do."

"Well, you don't know what he's planning. Maybe he won't stay. You told me he really wanted to be on the West Coast."

"That's what he said, but Doug's never been too sure of what he wants. He can change his mind in a heartbeat." Courtney eyed her cautiously. "The bi thing really bothers you, doesn't it? Are you worried?"

"Not about your ex-husband. Sounds like you're done with him."

"I am. I married Doug because I got pregnant with Kaylee."

"But you stayed with him for over twelve years. Obviously, you were attracted enough to sleep with him."

"Yes, I found him attractive…in a jock kind of way. I slept with both men and women in those days."

"What about now?"

"Now, I'm sleeping with you, and only you. I'm attracted to you, and only you. Any more questions?"

"Just one. You've already had a really hard day. How about we go out to dinner tonight. My treat. I think we can all use a break."

Courtney reached across the seat and took Melissa's hand. "Thank you. That's the best news I've heard all day."

"I think the best news was when Chief Harrison said, 'we found your daughter.'"

"You better believe it!"

23

Lucy, sitting beside Susan during the readings, watched her rearrange her stole for the umpteenth time. She picked at the embroidered brocade as if she were allergic to the fabric. Scanning the congregation, Lucy noticed Liz in the back, glowering at Susan with undisguised menace. Lucy gazed over the seawall and prayed for patience. Having one anxious woman at her service was uncomfortable but having two was distracting.

At communion time, Liz didn't budge. Lucy waited until it seemed unnatural before returning to the altar. *Liz, you're not hurting* me *by staying away. You're not going to win this tug of war. Stop being so gosh darn stubborn!*

After the service, Lucy greeted the people in her congregation, introducing Susan as a visiting priest. She noticed Liz watching from a distance with her arms folded on her chest.

"Who is that?" Susan murmured, nodding in Liz's direction.

"That's Liz Stolz," said Lucy, leaning forward to fist bump a boy from the youth group. "The town doctor."

"She keeps watching us. Why doesn't she just come over?"

"She's territorial. She's probably waiting for us to go over there." The line finally wound down to the end. "Come on," said Lucy to Susan. "Let's get changed."

By the time all the vestments were hung up in the closet, there was a knock on the open door. Liz regarded Susan with a cold stare as she stepped into the room. Lucy recognized it as Liz's 'I'll show you who's boss' look, left over from her days as a surgeon. Before Lucy got to know Liz, even she could be intimidated by it.

"I was wondering when we'd see you," Lucy said sarcastically as Liz bent to kiss her on the cheek.

"I didn't want to interfere." Liz's eyes narrowed as they engaged Susan's. She offered her hand. "I'm Liz Stolz." Her tone was civil but not friendly. As if Susan weren't standing there, Liz directed her comments to Lucy. "I came to invite you to brunch at Cliff Manor."

"Susan too?"

"Yes, of course," said Liz, glancing at her.

"Are you sure we can get in there?" asked Lucy. "It's always so crowded in the summer." The restaurant had the best brunch in the county and was known for its spectacular view from Webhanet's rocky cliffs.

"I made reservations," replied Liz. "The parking lot will be full. I'll pick you up at the rectory, and we can drive together. My MD plates always guarantee me a place to park."

Liz almost never flaunted her influence, but she was not above using it when it suited her purposes, like getting Lucy into the hospital when Erika was dying. Lucy had never seen her use it to impress people. Susan must be making Liz feel really insecure.

Lucy glanced at the slight woman with fading blond hair. Her gentle eyes gave her face a saintly quality. Her attitude was unassuming. She looked like a beloved elementary-school teacher, a role she'd taken to support herself since she'd left the convent. Lucy wondered what Liz saw.

They agreed to meet Liz at the rectory. When Lucy drove into the parking lot, she wasn't surprised to see Liz already waiting. She knew every back road in town and always drove too fast.

Lucy noticed Susan eyeing the expensive Audi SUV. "I guess family doctors do well in Maine."

"Actually, they don't. Liz used to be chief of surgery at Yale before she moved up here. She calls Hobbs Family Practice her retirement business."

"She's a little old for you, isn't she?"

Although Lucy hadn't said a word about her relationship with Liz, she wasn't surprised that Susan, who was perceptive, had already figured it out. Lucy merely shrugged in response to her comment.

On the way to the restaurant, Liz pointed out sights along the way like a tour guide. Lucy silently commended her for making an effort to appear friendly, despite the undercurrent of hostility.

While they ate the ridiculously expensive breakfast, Liz interviewed Susan as thoroughly as if she were taking a medical history. Lucy's role in this conversation was to listen, and she was attentive because Liz's relentless inquiry unearthed facts she hadn't heard before. Susan's sister had recently died after a heart attack, which meant she had no living family. Sympathetically, Lucy reached under the table for her hand. Liz didn't notice because she was lecturing Susan about the importance of cardiac screening.

Susan drank three mimosas in quick succession and soon became obviously giddy. Liz, watching her, called for the check so they could leave.

When they arrived back at the rectory, Susan went in right away. Lucy decided that she and Liz needed to talk, so she remained.

"I know you're being on your best behavior, Liz."

"But what? It's not good enough?"

"No, it's very good. That's what worries me."

Liz laughed. She gazed at the rectory door through which Susan had disappeared. "I just can't figure her out. What does she want?"

"I'm not sure I know either. But I can see she's having a hard time. She's looking for a new job, which can be a long process. I want to be supportive."

Liz turned to her and gave her a penetrating look. "Are you sure you're not interested in getting back together with her?"

"Once upon a time, maybe, but not anymore."

"But *she's* interested. That's obvious from the way she looks at you."

While Liz's gaze was focused on the rectory door, Lucy admired her handsome profile. "It doesn't matter what she wants. I've moved on. I always thought there was so much unfinished business. Sometimes, the need for closure is just an excuse for irrational hope."

"That's good," said Liz, finally turning in her direction. "Are you going to spend the day with her? Your *guest*?"

"No, I was going to spend the day with you. That is, if I'm invited. I haven't seen you in weeks."

Liz smiled. "We can go out on the boat."

"I'd rather stay home with you and talk. I think we need to talk."

Liz mimed a look of horror. "Oh no, *the talk*! Erika dreaded it. She was terrified you'd try to convert her."

"I don't try to convert people. I model the greatest love of all time and make it so attractive that people find it irresistible."

"Resistance is futile. Erika always compared you to the Borg queen."

"Did you two talk about me a lot?"

Liz grinned. "Let's just say, you were a frequent topic of conversation."

"Like two little boys talking behind a pretty girl's back?"

"Something like that."

Lucy opened the car door. "Let me take off my work clothes. I'll be over in a little while." She got out and blew Liz a kiss. "See you later."

As soon as she got home, Lucy took off her collar and black blouse, which was so hot in the summer weather. Naked except for her black lace bra and panties, Lucy stared into her closet. She took out one of the pastel-colored clerical shirts that Erika had encouraged her to buy for summer wear and a black skirt. She realized that by packing clothes for the morning, she was acknowledging that she would spend the night with Liz. Even though they both knew that sex was likely during their big date in New York, the act would have been more spontaneous, a celebration as well as a consummation. Now, it would be more purposeful because they both needed this affirmation. Susan's confusing reappearance had made it even more necessary.

Lucy had said they needed to talk, but she doubted there would be much talking this afternoon. Besides, it was too soon to talk to Liz about marriage. After her divorce, she was understandably "gun shy." Lucy would happily enter another marriage, not to replace her wife, but because she loved her so much. She knew Erika loved her too and would have wanted her to be happy.

When Lucy arrived at Liz's house, she wanted to avoid being obvious about her intentions, so she left her overnight bag in the car. She had the key to Liz's house, but she respectfully rang the bell.

Liz was barefoot when she came to the door. The plaque inside proclaimed, "This is a barefoot home." Lucy took off her sandals and put them on the rack. She felt Liz's eyes looking her over appreciatively. "Pretty dress," she murmured, as she offered a quick kiss of greeting that left Lucy wanting more, but Liz seemed almost shy.

Lucy was a little surprised that Liz had made no special effort to dress up for the occasion. Her shorts were a little threadbare in places. Her faded T-shirt had gone through the washer too many times. She looked like she would on any other lazy Sunday afternoon.

"I'm out on the deck," Liz explained, gesturing in the direction. "I opened some wine."

"I'm sorry, but I've come empty-handed."

"Lucy, you're a member of the family. I don't expect anything. And after all, you invited yourself."

"You'll still feed me?"

"As long as you don't mind leftovers."

"I enjoy everything you cook."

Liz's blue eyes smiled into hers. Since they'd parted, all the thorniness of the morning had vanished, which made Lucy suddenly think of Erika cutting roses from her garden for the kitchen table. Lucy always felt sad that the flowers would be deprived of sunlight and the quenching morning dew, but Erika reminded her that, either way, their beauty was brief.

"I snuck in a cup of coffee before you came," Liz explained. "I'm not used to drinking alcohol so early in the day. I bet your friend takes a nap this afternoon. If you weren't coming over, I probably would have taken one myself." Liz handed Lucy a glass of wine and sat across from her. She stared at Lucy's red toenails. "I like your nail polish."

"I thought you might. I put it on for our date. I was going to color my fingernails too, but I knew I had this morning's service. I don't want my fingernails to be a distraction."

"They certainly would have distracted me." She gave Lucy a canny look. "You were planning to make love that night."

Lucy smiled. "I'd hoped we would."

"Then what are we waiting for?"

"I'm enjoying sitting here in the sun with you, talking about nothing. I want to look at you and get to know you again. I haven't seen you for weeks." Lucy reached out her hand. "Talk to me. Tell me how you've been."

"It was hard to be without you. I was so disappointed I couldn't come to New York."

"But now, we have all day…and all night."

Liz flashed a smile. "You're staying?"

"Of course, I'm staying. You think I'm going to leave after we make love?"

Liz put down her glass and moved to the chaise lounge where Lucy sat. "I'm sorry, Lucy, but I can't wait any longer."

"Sure, you can."

"Nope. Not one second longer."

Liz's kiss made her head swim, but when an eager hand tried to find its way into the neckline of her sundress, Lucy gently pulled it out. "Liz, I can't wait either, but I'm not making love on the deck. Let's go to bed."

24

Liz was too impatient to take the three flights of stairs, but once inside the small elevator, she wondered why she thought it would be faster. Like most residential elevators, it rose at a glacial pace. She stared at the panel, trying to will the numerals on the display to move.

"Why are you so far away?" Lucy asked. "Think I'll bite?"

Liz shrugged. "I don't mind hickeys…in discreet locations."

Lucy gave her a hard look. "I think you're afraid of me."

"I am not!"

Lucy dropped her chin and gazed at her from under her eyebrows. "Liar."

"All right. If you have to know. I'm still a little afraid of what might happen when you get your priest's hands on me."

"My priest's hands?" Lucy laughed. "What do you think they'll do to you?"

"Turn me into a vampire? Maybe I'll be struck by lightning or vanish in a puff of smoke."

"I'm a priest, not a magician. My hands, my fingers, and my lips only want to love you." Lucy's fingers walked along the railing and interlaced themselves with Liz's.

"Sure you won't put a spell on me?"

"Okay, Liz. Enough of this!" Lucy leaned on the button to stop the elevator. She placed her hand over Liz's chest and pushed her back against the wall. She closed her eyes.

"What are you doing?" asked Liz.

Lucy raised a finger to her lips. "Sh! I'm blessing you." Liz saw Lucy's lips moving. Her hand over Liz's heart made the skin beneath tingle a little, but it had nothing to do with divine forces. Finally, Lucy opened her eyes. "See? No lightning. No smoke. Just you and me." She smiled and took away her hand. Liz reached over her to start the elevator again. Finally, the door opened on the third floor.

Liz had neatly turned down the bed that morning to let it air. The sheets were smooth, and the pillows propped up, but she felt a little embarrassed that the bed wasn't made. Lucy wasn't the tidiest housekeeper, so she probably wouldn't even notice. Instead, her eyes were drawn to the view of the ocean through the window. "How beautiful! I know you planned to share the Manhattan skyline, but I just love this view."

"Have you been up here before?" Liz asked with a frown. She considered her bedroom, along with her office, her private space, never shown on house tours or allowed access by guests.

Lucy turned around. "Yes, remember? Maggie brought me up here to do yoga with her." That was the day when Maggie had confronted Lucy about her feelings for Liz, beginning a series of events that had led to this moment. "Where have you gone?" Lucy asked, looking at Liz curiously.

"Thinking of how weird it is that you're here in my bedroom. Did you know *wyrd* means fate in Old English?"

"You and Erika and your scholarly lectures at the strangest moments."

"Encyclopedias of useless information."

"Interesting and sometimes useful," Lucy corrected.

Although her backyard was perfectly private, Liz stepped away from the window to undress. She peeled off her T-shirt and tossed it on a nearby chair. She shrugged off her shorts. A kick skillfully landed them on the chair seat. She turned around to see Lucy staring at her with a frown.

"Something wrong?"

"You could have waited and let me undress you. You act like you're getting ready for a swim."

"I'll undress you," said Liz, approaching. "How's that?"

Liz unbuttoned the front of Lucy's dress and pushed it off her shoulders, so she could step out of it. Instead of flinging it aside, she carefully draped it on the back of the chair. She paused at the black lace bra to admire it before unhooking it. She planted a sweet kiss on the top of each breast.

She'd waited so long for this moment, she almost didn't know what to do. "You're so beautiful," she breathed in a whisper.

Lucy nudged her with a light touch at the back of her head. "You can touch them. They're for you."

Liz wanted to devour them. She sucked on one breast while she pinched the nipple of the other, hungrily going from one to the other.

"Liz! Liz!" said Lucy, raking her fingers through Liz's hair and giving it a little tug. "Slow down!"

Liz looked up. "I'm sorry."

Lucy laid a warm hand on her cheek. "You're moving too fast. I'm excited too, but there's no need to rush. Let's savor the moment." Lucy got into bed. Settling beside her, Liz gazed into her eyes. They were like miniature lakes, green pools with little islands of brown and gold flecks. Liz was mesmerized. "I want you to love me slowly. I want to make love all day… and all night," Lucy said.

"We might get hungry."

"Then we'll eat." Lucy's eyes were suddenly full of mischief. The amusement faded, replaced by frank desire. The intensity was too much for Liz. She nuzzled against Lucy's cheek to hide from it.

Lucy held her closer. "You're still afraid of me, aren't you?"

"No," said Liz, deliberately lying. "I'm just so excited."

"Let me make you come. It might calm you down." Lucy's warm breath in her ear left Liz even more aroused. "After you're more relaxed, we can take our time."

Liz suddenly found herself on her back. Lucy had deftly flipped her with one of her martial arts moves. Smiling triumphantly, she sat on Liz's hips, pinning her on the bed. "I like surprises in bed. Don't you?" Lucy tilted her head to one side, then the other, studying her. "What do you like? Do you like to be barely touched? Or do you like it hard and fast? Penetration or not? Hmmm. Only if you're really excited." Lucy stroked her chin in an exaggerated display of thought. "I know! You like to be kissed all over…Am I right?"

Liz, unable to speak, nodded. Lucy lay alongside her and blew a warm breath into her ear. "You like your ears kissed, don't you?" She nibbled Liz's earlobe gently. Her tongue delicately defined the outside edges, then investigated the ridges and folds. Finally, it languorously found its way inside until Liz writhed with pleasure. "Yes, you like your ears kissed," Lucy pronounced with satisfaction. "Where else?" Lucy leaned on her elbow and surveyed Liz's body, gently stroking wherever her eyes landed. "Your boobs, of course," she said, lightly teasing a nipple with her fingertip. "They're beautiful. I admire them when you're not paying attention. When you're thinking, you disappear into your head and have no idea what's going on around you." She gave each breast a kiss as if they were two children ready for bed. "I really like boobs, but I'm not obsessed with them like you are."

"I'm not obsessed with breasts," Liz protested indignantly.

"No? You built your career around them."

Liz opened her mouth to explain, but Lucy giggled and kissed her. "You don't need to tell me. I already know why, but you stare at mine… all the time!" Lucy sucked gently on one breast, then the other. "Why do you always hide these under baggy tops? You should show them proudly!" Lucy brought her face closer. "I like inspiration too." Lucy's fingers wandered into Liz's panties. "I can feel you're already inspired…and so wet!" She gazed directly into Liz's eyes as she stroked her. "I bet this is where you really like to be kissed, isn't it?"

Liz tensed because Lucy's gentle caresses were almost painful. "Don't worry. I won't torture you," Lucy said.

"Please torture me," Liz begged.

Lucy's chuckle was full of mischief. "Later." She pulled off Liz's panties and flung them onto the pile on the chair with impressively accurate aim. Climbing down Liz's body, she nudged her legs apart with her elbows and enlarged the space with her shoulders. The warmth of her breath was exciting as she gently blew on Liz's clitoris. After that, all it took was a few delicate strokes of her tongue to ignite an orgasm that made Liz see stars.

"Wow," said Lucy, leaning up on her elbows. "You took off like a rocket!"

She found her way back up Liz's body and pressed her freckled nose against Liz's. Her eyes merged, and she became a green-eyed cyclops. The single eye blinked. Liz could feel rather than see Lucy smile. "Feel better now?"

"Much better." Liz rolled her hips to move her off her body. "Now, you."

"Now, both of us," said Lucy and boldly parted Liz's lips with her tongue. The assertive kiss threw Liz off balance because she'd never seen this side of Lucy. She took it as a challenge and returned the kiss with equal fervor. She opened Lucy's legs with her knees and lay down between them, pressing against her with her pubic bone.

"Yes!" said Lucy with a little gasp, but the single point of contact wasn't enough. Liz needed to be closer, so close there was no separation between them, like they were two halves of the same body. She had to be inside her. Lucy's legs, wrapped around her waist, squeezed her. As Liz drove her fingers into Lucy's warm interior, she felt herself being caressed. She was instantly skeptical that this activity would lead anywhere. Coming together was an art learned from long experience of a partner's needs. It took incredible sensitivity and focus to pace the excitement and to release it at the same time.

Lucy's fingers continued to work, inside, then outside. *She's teaching me how to make love to her,* Liz thought with stunning clarity. She mirrored everything Lucy did, precisely following her lead, as if letting her direct the movements and rhythm of a dance. Their excitement grew and spilled over, but they stayed with one another until Lucy begged her to stop. Liz gingerly lowered her weight on her body.

"Tell me if I'm too heavy."

"You're not," said Lucy, still panting. "Hold me tight." When she wrapped her arms around Liz's neck, Liz could smell her exertion, her own special Lucy scent.

Liz sat up and allowed her eyes to savor the beauty of Lucy's body. She wanted to know all its nooks and crannies, every mole, every freckle, every vibrant red hair. Liz's fingers tenderly traced the faint, silvery streaks on her belly. As a new patient at Hobbs Family Practice, Lucy had skipped the pregnancy question in her medical history, but Liz's eyes and hands had told her all she needed to know. She'd pushed for candor, asking persistent questions, because it was important to have trust between a patient and her doctor. Liz had to deadpan when Lucy first told Maggie about Emily.

"Thank you for keeping my secrets," Lucy said, watching Liz's face. "I was so afraid you would tell Erika while we were dating."

Liz kissed the soft, white belly and teased her navel with her tongue. "Who can you trust with your secrets, if not your doctor?"

"Your priest?"

"You kept Maggie's secret. You didn't even tell me."

The expression on Lucy's face noticeably changed, and she shivered.

"Are you cold?" Liz asked, concerned.

"I'm still recovering from that orgasm, but I wouldn't mind a blanket."

"You're so small. Your body can't hold the heat." Liz reached down for the covers and drew them over their naked bodies. She pulled Lucy into her arms and held her close to warm her. She kissed her forehead and her eyelids. "Was it like you imagined?"

"Exactly. Like when two atoms collide and release energy as brilliant light." Liz visualized the image in her mind. "I knew it would be perfect because I love you so much," Lucy said, reaching between Liz's legs.

"Again?" Liz asked, surprised.

"Yes," said Lucy, smiling. "Again and again."

This time their lovemaking was more leisurely. Lucy's fingers played in Liz's hair while she teased her with her tongue, inhaling her scent and savoring her taste. When Lucy came, she smiled with sublime pleasure and laughed softly. Liz added this smile to the mental album she kept of the many faces of Lucille Bartlett going all the way back to the photo in the opera program.

When she returned to Lucy's arms, she was rewarded for her efforts with a deep kiss.

"If you want to do this all night, maybe we should take a little nap," Liz suggested.

"Before we nap, let me take off my makeup. My eyes get gummy if I sleep with my mascara."

"Be my guest. There should be some makeup remover in the top drawer on the right, and use the toilet while you're in there."

"What?" exclaimed Lucy, her lips parting a little in surprise.

"You heard me. Urinating after sex prevents UTIs. I'll use the downstairs bathroom."

Lucy raised her eyes heavenward. "Thank you for sending me a doctor to love, but could you make her a little less direct?"

"Direct is good. It avoids misunderstandings."

Shaking her head, Lucy headed to the bathroom. When she returned, she insinuated herself into the curve of Liz's body.

"Another one who likes to cuddle," Liz grumbled, blowing red hair out of her mouth.

"I love to cuddle. Don't you?" Lucy tucked her rear deeper into Liz's lap.

"Cuddling is okay, but I don't like people touching me when I sleep. However, I've learned to adjust."

"That's good. Glad to know you're flexible," said Lucy with a yawn. Barely a moment later, Liz realized the woman in her arms was sound asleep.

When Liz awoke, she saw that Lucy was wearing the oversize T-shirt that had been hanging on the back of the bathroom door.

"I see you've made yourself at home," Liz said. "I've been sleeping in that shirt. It's not clean."

"Doesn't matter," Lucy said, pulling the fabric to her nose. "Smells like you. That's okay."

The sound of rapid typing made Liz curious. "What are you writing?" Liz asked, raising herself on her elbows to see.

"Some notes for my book."

"Not really?"

"It's a book about sex. Making love with you inspired me." Lucy combed through Liz's gray curls. "When I woke up I was watching you sleep, and I had an idea about teaching someone your rhythm. Of course, the other person has to be willing to learn. And you have to be willing to adjust to theirs. Sometimes, we have to adjust to God's rhythm too, and it's not always easy."

The last thing Liz wanted to talk about in bed was God, so she got up. "How about a glass of wine?"

"Sounds wonderful."

Liz opened a drawer and tossed a folded T-shirt on the bed.

"Uh-uh," said Lucy, shaking her head, "I'm not giving up your shirt. When I'm ready to get dressed, my clothes are in the car."

Liz smiled, realizing that Lucy really had planned to stay. "Is it locked? I'll bring them in."

"No, it's not locked."

Liz dressed and went downstairs. She turned on the oven and put in the chicken stew to heat up. She felt lazy offering Lucy leftovers on such a momentous occasion. Fortunately, chicken cacciatore was one of those dishes that improve after sitting in the refrigerator overnight. She went out to Lucy's car to bring in her bag. When she returned to the kitchen, she put two glasses and a bottle of pinot grigio on a tray. Before she went upstairs, she took the time to make a salad for dinner. The savory aroma emanating from the oven made her think of Erika. Liz had given her the recipe. Erika had probably cooked it more often than Liz did.

The tears took Liz completely by surprise. Timid at first, they began to stream down her face like rain in a summer cloudburst. Her chest suddenly heaved with sobs. Liz had to put down the corkscrew because she couldn't see what she was doing.

"Liz?" asked Lucy from the kitchen door. "Liz, are you okay?" Liz turned to hide the evidence and held her breath to get control of the sobs. A few escaped, sounding more like hiccups. Lucy touching her shoulder made it worse. "Oh, sweetie, what's wrong?" asked Lucy, hugging her from behind. "You were gone so long I came down to see why."

Liz furiously ripped a paper towel from the roll to mop up her face. "Your bag is in the hall."

Lucy pulled on Liz's shoulder until she turned around. "What's going on?" she asked, wiping Liz's cheeks with the back of her hand. "Why are you crying?"

"I remembered that Erika made my recipe for chicken cacciatore for your first dinner."

"Yes, she did, and it was delicious."

"We're having it tonight."

"Oh," said Lucy as understanding dawned.

"I didn't plan it that way, but I wasn't kidding when I said I was giving you leftovers. You don't mind?"

"It's one of my favorites!" Lucy wrapped her arms around Liz's waist. "Oh, sweetie. Things that remind me of Erika make me cry too, but that's okay. I thought any reminders would make me sad, but sometimes, they make me happy. Plus, I love chicken cacciatore. Will you teach me how to make it?"

"Of course." Liz finished drying her face on the shoulder of her T-shirt. "It's a nice evening. Would you like to sit outside?"

"Yes, lets."

They settled on the deck. After pouring the wine, Liz raised her glass. "To Erika," she said, "an amazing cook, brilliant philosopher, and my wingman."

"To Erika, my dear wife. I love you and miss you so much!"

They both drank. Out of the corner of her eye, Liz noticed Lucy looking at her with what she would belligerently call her 'shrink face.' "Oh, no. Now what?"

"You don't think you're betraying Erika by making love with me?"

"I don't do guilt," Liz replied sullenly.

"Everyone 'does' guilt," Lucy said. "Even you, Dr. Stolz, skeptic and atheist. But there's nothing to be guilty about. Erika loved you. She loved me. She probably wants us to be together."

"She asked me to take care of you if anything happened to her."

Lucy studied her with a long, thoughtful look. "She asked me to take care of you too."

"Do you believe in messages from the beyond?"

"Not usually, but when I see an obvious example, I don't argue with it." Lucy gazed up at the sky and raised her glass.

25

Lucy sang as she drove to Southern Med to make hospital visits. Susan always knew when Lucy was singing because she was happy. While she was recovering from the rape, Lucy only sang to maintain her voice. It had been pitiful to hear her sing with such effort and sorrow. All the songs she chose were sad. When she'd turned a corner in her therapy, she finally sang for pleasure. Today, it was obvious that she was singing with pure joy.

Lucy's effervescence confused Susan. She'd expected to find her friend a physical and emotional wreck from the death of her wife. After reading about it in the diocesan newsletter, she'd wanted to drive straight to Hobbs to comfort Lucy, but she couldn't abandon her students or her church and ever hope to return. Now, of course, it didn't matter. She was never going back to St. Anselm's or the Greenleaf public school system. Those doors were closed for good.

The aria ended. "I hope I wasn't too loud," Lucy said. Susan smiled because Lucy always asked that question when she had an audience in a small space. Her powerful voice was stunning even when she sang sotto voce.

"I love to hear you sing, Lucy. It can never be too loud."

A radiant smile was Susan's reward for saying exactly the right thing.

"You're so happy this morning," Susan observed.

"It's a beautiful summer day, the sun is shining brightly, and I can make music! Yes, I'm happy."

Lucy was the sunniest person Susan had ever known, but this morning, her joy was simply overflowing. Susan wondered what had happened since they'd parted yesterday.

Susan's afternoon had been miserable. When she'd awakened from her nap, the memory of getting so tipsy in front of Lucy's friend was mortifying. She'd considered calling Lucy to apologize, but her burner phone was almost out of minutes. She needed to save them for her job search.

But she couldn't sit still. She had to know that Lucy would forgive her for making such a fool of herself.

She decided that making her apologies in person was best and drove to Lucy's beach house. From the street, she could see that no one was home. When she returned a few hours later, she worked up the courage to ring the bell, but no one came to the door. She prayed that Lucy would come home soon. Only Lucy could reassure her that they were okay. Only Lucy could make her whole again, Lucy's smile, Lucy's beautiful voice…Lucy's sweet kiss. Oh, that kiss!

On the way back from Lucy's house, Susan passed the supermarket with the sign out front indicating it was a Maine Liquor Store. Temptation was everywhere in this state—in supermarkets, convenience stores, even pharmacies. Susan hadn't touched a drop of alcohol for almost two weeks, but those mimosas had gone down so easily.

She wrestled with herself in the supermarket parking lot for over ten minutes before she went into the store and found the wine aisle. She passed up the flasks of vodka on sale. That was for cheap drunks. Instead, she bought two bottles of Australian merlot for only $4.99. One was gone already.

She hoped Lucy hadn't noticed her bloodshot eyes. When she had a chance to get to the drug store, she'd buy some of those eye drops that hide the redness.

"Is there something special you'd like to hear?" Lucy asked brightly.

"'*Qui la Voce*' from *I Puritani*? I loved you in that opera."

"Let me see if I have the voice for it this morning." Lucy cleared her throat a few times. Finally, she began to sing.

Susan closed her eyes and savored the sound of Lucy's full, round soprano embracing the delicious notes. When Lucy finished the aria, she said, "Oh, that felt good!" She flashed a smile in Susan's direction.

"Your voice hasn't darkened a bit. It sounds as bright as ever."

Lucy gave her a skeptical look. "You're prejudiced. I know my prime has come and gone. I do all the exercises to keep my high notes, but some days, they're not there. If I were still on the stage, I'd be exploring a different repertoire." She looked reflective as she focused on the road ahead. "I'm glad I was able to have a career so early. I'm especially glad that my mother lived to see me on the stage of the Met."

"She was taken too soon," Susan said in a sad voice.

Lucy momentarily took her hand off the wheel to pat Susan's arm. "I'm sorry I wasn't there for you when your mother died."

Susan caught a glimpse of her mother's face. She'd suffered terrible pain, despite the morphine drip. There were tubes coming from everywhere. Then the memory of her mother dissolved, replaced by the many faces of Lucy—Lucy weeping, Lucy almost destroyed by the probing of discernment, Lucy coming in her arms. Lucy's face during a climax had become Susan's metaphor for the experience of the beatific vision.

That was heresy, of course, like so many heresies Susan had embraced. If she hadn't felt she'd been called to the priesthood, she would never have switched. The Episcopal liturgy was almost identical to the Roman Catholic Mass. Despite the similarities, Susan had gravitated toward a stricter church. She couldn't imagine serving in an ultra-liberal parish indistinguishable from the Unitarians. The 'anything goes' approach to religion had never sat right with Susan.

"Thank you for coming on my visits today," said Lucy with another brilliant smile. "Maybe you can help us out while you're here. There are so many people who still won't come out of their homes, despite the loosened COVID restrictions. Tom and I can't visit them all."

"I'll help as much as I can, but I really need to find a paying job."

"Would you go back to teaching? I know the assistant principal at the elementary school. I could ask if there are any openings."

A little shiver of fear rippled through Susan. A job in any public school system would require a background check. "Thanks, but I'm done with teaching," Susan said quickly.

"But if you don't teach, what will you do?"

"I saw the sign at McDonald's. They're paying fifteen dollars an hour and a signing bonus."

Fortunately, they were stopped at a light because Lucy turned and stared at her. "You would really work at McDonalds?"

"Of course. It's honest work. Lucy, I can't believe you're shocked."

"I'm shocked because you have so much education and training. You have two master's degrees! You can do better. Much better!"

"Lucy, that's an elitist view. I need money. They're paying a decent wage." She shrugged. "And I like to cook."

"I can't believe I'm hearing you say this. You're the one who kept pushing me to go back to the Met."

"Of course, I did. You should have never left. You would still be singing if it wasn't for that horrible man trying to destroy your career. I can't believe people listened to your rapist instead of you."

"That's the way it was then. Powerful men believed other powerful men, not the women they abused. They still do. Look at all the lawsuits against the former president. None of them stuck. Look at that poor woman who testified against Kavanaugh. She told her humiliating and painful story in front of millions of people. Our senator, a woman who claims to be for women's rights, stood up in the Senate and defended him. Nothing's really changed."

"You gave up too easily. You should have sued him."

"I'd already spent too much money on lawyers." Lucy shook her head. "Sometimes you have to cut your losses and move on."

"The City Opera wanted you to sing."

"The City Opera," repeated Lucy in a disparaging voice. "The City Opera was teetering on bankruptcy. They wanted me because they were desperate."

"You could have gone to Europe. I would have gone with you."

"I wouldn't have let you. You'd found your calling. How could I take you away from God?"

"Then He found you too."

"She," Lucy corrected.

Susan stared at her. "Lucy, you can't just change dogma to suit your personal beliefs."

"Paul says, in God, there is neither male, nor female. Our bishop calls the Spirit, 'she.'"

Susan knew she would never win this argument. She gazed out the window to calm down. The traffic in the northbound lane of the interstate was bumper to bumper. "It seems like everyone wants to come to Maine."

"Now, you've seen it and know why."

"It's beautiful here. The ocean is so healing, especially after the desolation of the plains. The heartland has its own natural beauty, but the winters are so long."

"Don't be fooled by this beautiful weather. Our winters are long too. Would you ever go back?"

"I don't understand those people. Their religious views are conservative like mine, but they're so right-wing, and that governor! I can't minister to people who refuse to believe basic facts."

"But Susan, you are so loving and so caring. You're one of the best communicators I know. You aced our preaching class."

"When I'm inspired, I can write a great sermon, but my rector insisted I preach from the lectionary. One year, I gave a sermon on the role of mothers on Mother Day's. Well, you should have heard him. I thought I'd need to pack my bags on the spot. After I fell into line, he backed off. All that obedience training in the convent helped me, I guess."

"Weren't there any people like you? How about where you taught?"

"The school was very small. They knew I was a priest and couldn't figure out what to make of that. To answer your question, no, I didn't have close friends at school. It's hard when there are no others like you for miles and miles, and you're the only one."

Lucy glanced at her with a sympathetic look. "Oh, Susan, you must have been so lonely out there."

"I was, but I kept trying to fight the good fight. As you know, it's not always easy."

Lucy turned into the front entrance of Southern Medical Center. She showed Susan the parking space set aside for clergy in the staff lot. "…for when you come here by yourself," said Lucy with one of those brilliant smiles that could make anyone do anything.

Lucy opened the lunch cooler she'd used to transport Communion and counted the small plastic containers inside. Susan's mouth gaped when she realized they held consecrated wine. She managed to keep her mouth shut until they were alone in the elevator. "Lucy, you put the communion wine in Chinese restaurant cups?"

"Yes, why? I felt sad that our Communion was restricted to one element. I got the idea when we had Chinese takeout one night," Lucy explained. "We use individual hosts, why not individual cups? You don't really think it's sacrilegious, do you?"

Susan didn't know what to say. Yes, the idea of the sacred blood being delivered like duck sauce horrified her, but she smiled and said, "You are so inventive."

The hospital visits were brief, but Lucy spent extra time with an elderly woman who had survived COVID only to lose her daughter to the virus. "I'm all alone now," she confided to Lucy as she held her veiny, large-knuckled hand.

"You're not alone," Lucy countered. "You have us, your St. Margaret's family." When most clergy said things like that, they sounded like platitudes. When Lucy said them, they rang completely true.

The home visits went pretty much the same way. Lucy spoke to the members of her congregation as if she really knew each one of them. Apart from the Communion wine in the Chinese condiment cups, everything Susan had witnessed so far was like her own pastoral visits, but the last one threw her completely off balance. This parishioner, who was also the church music director, was a transsexual recovering from "bottom" surgery. Lucy shocked Susan by treating him…her—it still stuck in Susan's throat to say it—like it was the most natural thing in the world.

"Thank you for sending me to Dr. Stolz," said the trans woman. "I'm so sick of doctors pandering to me to be politically correct. She put her concerns right out there."

A worried look briefly crossed Lucy's face. "Dr. Stolz can be pretty direct."

"I like that about her. She's direct, but she really listened to me when I said I had a problem. When I called the surgeon's office, they said my symptoms were normal. I know my body. My symptoms weren't normal, and it turned out I was right."

"Welcome to our world, Denise. Doctors don't always pay attention to women's medical complaints. Sometimes, you have to be a pest to get them to listen."

Denise frowned. "So I'm beginning to learn, but we're lucky to have Dr. Stolz in town. I hope she doesn't retire soon. I think she's close to retirement age. Is she?"

"Yes, but I don't think she has any plans to retire soon."

Susan's mind wandered while they discussed vocal exercises. She waited until they were in the car to say anything about the trans woman. "I can't believe the vestry let you hire that man…uh…woman."

"It was a struggle to win them over," admitted Lucy, starting the car.

"I bet the conservative people in your vestry were alarmed when you told them she's not a *real* woman."

"I didn't tell them. That's not my place. And she is a *real* woman." Lucy turned to her with a frown. "Susan, do you have a problem ministering to trans people?"

"No, of course not! They're God's children too."

"Yes, and it's important to always remember that." Lucy's auburn brows dipped toward the base of her nose. "You've changed, Susan."

"I'm sure we've both changed." In fact, the further Susan had gotten from the liberal theology they'd taught in divinity school, the more she'd reverted to the strict Catholic beliefs of her childhood. But that was a conversation for another time. "Why don't we have dinner tonight and talk about it?"

"I'm sorry, Susan, but I can't tonight. I invited a friend to dinner. I'm going to cook, which I still find nerve-wracking. Erika was a great cook, so

I never had to worry about it while she was alive." Lucy sighed and glanced out the window. Susan perceived she was revisiting her grief.

"If you ever want to talk about it," Susan said gently, "I'll be happy to listen."

"Thanks," replied Lucy briskly. She engaged the gearshift to back up. Susan waited for Lucy to say more, but she didn't.

26

Melissa looked for the green Subaru in the parking lot. It was easy to spot Courtney's car because there were so few painted that color. The company had long since retired it, which Melissa only knew because she'd been searching for a used car, a beater to get to and from the train station. She'd read that Subarus were the most popular brand in the state. The salt from the ocean and the saline spray to prevent icy roads were hard on cars. Even in a frugal place, where people repaired everything until it literally fell apart, that shade of Subaru green was rare.

Courtney was busy on her phone when Melissa approached her car. She could see Kaylee in the back seat. Courtney dragged her everywhere now. The incident with her ex had made her less trusting. Melissa was sympathetic to Kaylee's situation and understood why she would go off with her father without thinking. Melissa had idolized her father and would have followed him anywhere. She thought Courtney was being too rigid, but she was smart enough to stay out of it.

This was her first relationship with the mother of a child, and it presented dilemmas she had never even considered. Who, in this era of sexual freedom, when lesbians were openly portrayed on TV, hid physical affection in her own home? Obviously, the presence of a curious adolescent imposed some limits. Waiting until she went to bed to have sex was one of the many inconveniences. More intrusive was the fact that they were never completely alone.

Melissa had seen an ad for a summer camp in Rangely and showed it to Courtney. To Melissa, it is seemed an ideal way to give Kaylee a break from her mother and provide them with some much-needed privacy. Courtney had instantly dismissed the idea. "That's a luxury I can't afford right now, especially with Doug out of work and not paying child support on time. I need to save money for the deposit on a place to live."

"I could pay for the camp," Melissa offered. "It's not expensive."

Courtney snapped back, "Not to you, maybe, but four hundred dollars pays for more than a week's groceries."

Melissa was surprised by the sharpness of her response until she realized that she'd stepped in it by calling attention to making more money—much more money than her girlfriend—and questioning the fragile economic independence Courtney had struggled to establish. Interfering with her child rearing counted as an even bigger mistake.

It seemed that the stars weren't aligning for this relationship. At the partners' meeting in Boston, the managing partner had outlined the plan to reopen the office. Everyone was expected to come back full-time, no exceptions. Her face had probably revealed everything she was thinking. After the meeting, Mike had come to her office to take her temperature.

"You could have given me a heads-up," Melissa said in an irritated voice. "At least, if you allowed *some* exceptions…"

"Melissa, half the office doesn't want to come back. I had to put my foot down. And you know how it is. Clients feel better about a firm when they see their attorney in a luxurious office. If you only meet your lawyer on Zoom, he could be a fly-by-night operating out of a van in Miami."

The hyperbole forced a smile out of Melissa. "I know everyone is sick of Zoom meetings. We just want to see and touch flesh-and-blood people. That firm handshake is important. I don't dispute any of that."

"Then what's the problem?"

"I really want to move to Maine. My mother lives there, and I have other interests in the state."

"Ah ha," said Mike, raising his brows. "Personal interests, I take it. Is this interest important enough to give up a career as one of the best trust attorneys in the country?"

"I have no intention of giving up my career for anything or anyone. I've worked too damn hard to get here."

"Can't you commute? There's a train from Hobbs. I hear people commute from Maine on a regular basis."

"There's one commuter train a day. If you miss it, you're screwed."

"But there is a way to get here. And, in a pinch, you can drive. It's not that far. I know you're not an early riser, Melissa, but work with me here."

"If I agree to come back full time, can we talk about other arrangements down the line?"

Mike never blinked while he returned Melissa's stare. "Maybe," he finally said. "That's all I can promise."

"If I want to come in part-time now, what will happen?"

"Well, you're a partner, and we expect all partners to contribute more than the minimum revenue and billable hours..."

"I get it," Melissa said in a resigned voice.

Mike smacked his knees and rose from his chair. "Let me know what you decide."

"Oh, I think you know what I'll decide."

He smiled. "I do, and I'm counting on you to set a good example."

After shouldering that burden, Melissa had spent most of the time on the train home working out her plan B. Commuting every day, whether on the train or driving, would be a nightmare. That's why she'd been willing to pay top dollar for an apartment in town rather than finding a cheaper place in the Boston suburbs. The longest period she'd ever commuted was when she was fresh out of law school. She'd moved back to her parents' Floral Park home. It was a great arrangement that allowed her to recharge her finances after paying the steep tuition. The housekeeper kept Melissa's room clean and was a great cook. Melissa would have stayed forever, but the need for a place to bring her dates finally made her find her own apartment.

One option was commuting some days and living in her Boston apartment the rest of the week. She could come back to Hobbs for weekends. That scenario made the most sense, but she would still need a car. She would have car payments and train fare in addition to the mortgage and maintenance charges on her condo, which would take a big bite out of her paycheck. Melissa's back-of-the-envelope calculations revealed it would be tight, but she could take on more clients to make up the difference.

Now that her mother was so involved with her new boyfriend, she was increasingly becoming a minor reason to move to Hobbs. Ruth's new romance only underscored her daughter's failure to sustain a relationship. After college, Melissa was too busy in law school and building her legal career to find dates for the weekend. Things finally settled down when she'd moved to Boston, where she'd had a series of short-term relationships. The last one had lasted three years, a record. For the last two years, they had lived together, which had probably been their undoing. They were complete opposites where housekeeping and finances were concerned, proof positive that opposites may attract but don't always make good roommates, no matter how good the sex is.

Sex. The sex with Courtney was wonderful. She was a generous lover, capable of passion, but she also enjoyed long, leisurely sessions of lovemaking. The only thing that would make the sex better was privacy. Melissa was a moaner, and she hated to stifle herself when she came.

Melissa stood directly in front of the car, waiting for Courtney to look up from her phone. The warm smile that had first drawn her to this woman made the wait worth it. When Melissa heard the door locks click open, she headed to the passenger side. She wished she could kiss Courtney at the train station the way a straight partner would, but the new assistant principal insisted on keeping a low profile. Instead of a kiss, they held hands for a moment before Courtney started the car.

She headed to join the cars lined up to get out of the parking lot. As usual, there was a long wait. "Busy day? You look frazzled."

"Really? I tried to get my act together on the train. I even put on more mascara and lipstick, so I'd look good for you."

"You look delicious, but I can see there's something on your mind."

"The senior managing partner dropped the bomb. Everyone has to come back inside. No exceptions."

Courtney shot her a quick, anxious look. "Does that mean you're moving back to Boston?"

Before Melissa replied, she glanced over her shoulder. Kaylee had taken out one of her ear pods to listen. She smiled at the girl, who looked out the window instead of meeting her gaze. Kids were so clever.

"There are several options. I'll tell you later."

"Probably a good idea to hold it for later. I have some news too."

"Oh?"

"Doug got a job with Hobbs Parks and Recreation. He's decided he likes it here and wants to look for something more permanent."

"If he gets a job and pays on time, that's good news."

"That's true." Courtney glanced in the rear-view mirror. "Except I heard this from Kaylee instead of her father."

"Oh, I see," said Melissa. "That may be poor communication, but legally, he's not obligated to discuss his plans with you."

"I know, but *some* communication would be nice. He put up quite a stink about custody during our divorce. I wonder what he's up to."

"He probably just wants to be closer to his daughter." Courtney seemed outwardly calm, but Melissa could see how much this development disturbed her. "I wouldn't read too much into it."

"I just thought things were settled. I wish he'd talk to me about his plans. I'm dependent on the child support to keep us going."

"It's a shame Maine doesn't pay higher salaries to teachers."

"If I were still a teacher and not a principal, I couldn't even afford the rent."

"Maybe we should look for a place together." After she'd said the words, Melissa couldn't believe they'd come out of her mouth.

Courtney turned to her in surprise. "Are you sure we're ready for that?"

"No. I don't know where that came from, but I mean it."

Looking stunned, Courtney focused on the road ahead. "Let's talk about it tonight after our young friend goes to bed."

27

A hand moved Courtney's long hair away and placed a soft, warm kiss at the nape of her neck, which could instantly arouse her. Melissa had cleverly figured that out on her own. What a nice change to have a bed partner who paid attention to what she liked.

Courtney stopped chopping onions because the new knives she'd bought when she'd moved were extremely sharp. Melissa's hands moving toward her crotch were distracting her, and she didn't want to sacrifice a finger tip for a moment of passion. "Don't worry," said a whisper into her ear. "Kaylee's locked in her room. I checked." The curious fingers found their way up the leg of Courtney's shorts into her panties, stroking very lightly but strategically. Courtney put down the knife and leaned against Melissa.

"We can't have sex now. I have to make dinner."

"I can make you come really fast." Melissa's warm tongue probed her ear. Courtney felt faint as the gentle fingers continued their seductive work.

"You're naughty."

"I know, but you like it, don't you?"

"What if Kaylee comes out of her room?"

"Shh, feel what I'm doing to you. Doesn't it feel good?" The pressure increased slightly as well as the tempo. Courtney leaned into Melissa's body.

"Yes, good," said Courtney, moving her pelvis to the rhythm of Melissa's stroking.

"That's what I like to hear." The tongue teased her ear again. Melissa's unoccupied hand found something to do. The nipple pinch was right on the edge of pain, but exciting. The pressure became more intense along with the pace. Courtney felt faint, but Melissa supported her with an arm around her waist while she came.

"Well, that was a nice start to the evening," Courtney said, standing straight. She mocked a shiver. "Your magic touch can make me come anywhere."

"When you're with a lady who has a kid, you need to make the most of every opportunity." Melissa grinned and snatched a piece of bright red pepper from the pile of colorful sliced vegetables and nibbled on it. She leaned her backside against the cabinet.

Courtney resumed chopping onions. "Does it really bother you that I have a child?"

"I'm adapting. It's not easy keeping my hands off you. I want to touch you all the time." The statement sent an instant pulse to Courtney's clitoris. She reminded herself that the knife was sharp. "It's hard to pretend we're making ordinary conversation when I really want to rip your clothes off."

"Keep talking like that, and I'll have to get into your panties."

"Anytime you want." Melissa nabbed another piece of pepper from the cutting board.

"Hey," said Courtney, slapping her hand, "I just cut that for our dinner. How about you do something useful? Pour us some more wine."

Melissa got the wine bottle out of the refrigerator. "Thank God for Friday nights!"

"I couldn't agree more." Courtney opened the package of chicken sausages and began to slice them. "Were you serious about looking for a place together?"

"It just came out. I didn't really think about it." Melissa reached for another piece of pepper, but Courtney gave her a filthy look.

"Leave some for dinner." She resumed slicing the sausages. "What will you tell your mother?"

"I'll say I'm moving in with you. She won't care. It's not like I'm paying rent to live there."

"No, you're just visiting for the summer, right?"

"Right." When Courtney's back was turned, Melissa grabbed another piece of pepper. "Maybe we can find a nice little place down by the train station so I can walk. I'll still need to get a car, I guess."

"You can't really get far around here without a car, so yes, I guess you would."

"I've been looking at Subarus online. I want to buy used, so I don't get hit by that big excise tax they charge up here. Did you know your car is considered an antique? You can tell by the color."

Courtney shrugged. "Who cares? It still runs well. I haven't had to put much money into it. I think I'll keep it."

"I would."

"I'm still paying off my student loans from graduate school. I'll be paying them until I die." Courtney's mind went numb at the thought of paying off that loan. "The things that matter like housing and education have gotten so expensive. How can anyone ever get out of the hole?" She heated the oil in the skillet and tossed in the onions and peppers.

"That's why it would make sense to pool our resources. You could afford a better place to live, and I could help with your other expenses."

"What do you get out of it?"

"Sex." Melissa grinned and rakishly wiggled her brows.

"That's all? A pretty girl like you should be able to get that anywhere."

"Maybe, but it's really good with you," said Melissa grazing Courtney's crotch with her fingertips. "I think regular sex is important. If I go too long without it, I get grouchy. But I have to warn you my track record with relationships isn't good."

"Why is that?" asked Courtney, tossing the zucchini and sausage into the pan and giving it a shake.

Melissa shrugged. "I have high standards. I expect people to pull their weight."

"Then don't look at me. You probably make ten times what I make."

"Not even close."

"But I'm sure you make a lot more than I do."

"There are other ways to contribute besides money."

"You want me to be your cook?"

"You cook really well," said Melissa with a grin.

"You can cook. You don't need me for that. And I just came out of a marriage to a man, where I had to pick up his jock straps wherever they landed."

Melissa made a face. "Thanks, but I didn't need that mental image. I can't unsee it now."

"Sorry," said Courtney. "I can't unsee it either." She checked the rice. Almost done. "We can eat soon."

"I don't need you as a servant," said Melissa. "I'm not into that kind of role-play, although you in a sexy French maid's uniform might be fun."

"Really? The truth is, when I first met you, I didn't even think you were a lesbian."

"Why? Do I look femme?" Melissa pointed to her chin with her index finger and made a silly face.

"No, do I?"

"You look like a woman. A very pretty woman. In fact, a gorgeous woman," said Melissa, reaching for her face to kiss her.

Courtney backed up because they didn't have time for more play. "We can eat. Will you knock on Kaylee's door and let her know?"

Melissa sighed, but she headed down the hall to call Kaylee to dinner.

Courtney watched Melissa and Kaylee wordlessly inhale her meal. She wasn't a fancy cook, but she always liked to watch people enjoy the food she prepared.

After Kaylee cleaned her plate, she began to talk about one of her teachers. Courtney still tended to take complaints about teachers personally, but she always listened carefully to what her daughter said about school. It gave her a look into Kaylee's world and also provided helpful insights into how students saw their teachers.

"They were bullying this French-Canadian kid, but Mrs. Chase didn't do anything to stop them. She didn't do anything when they bullied the Indian kid either."

"Well, that doesn't sound right," Courtney said. "Did the teacher see the students being bullied?"

"No, but we told her about it."

"The children were the only witnesses. That puts the teacher in a difficult position," said Melissa, surprising Courtney with the fact that she'd been paying such close attention.

"Unfortunately, teachers are often put in difficult positions."

"Dad came to my game today," Kaylee suddenly announced.

Courtney felt herself tense when Melissa looked up from her meal.

"He wants to get a job at Bates if he can," Kaylee continued. "Where's that?"

"That's in Lewiston," Courtney said in an even voice. "Not far."

"I thought your father wanted to live on the West Coast," said Melissa, casually keeping the conversation going in an interested but not particularly curious voice.

"He said he missed me…and Mom."

When Melissa sat back and gazed at her intently, Courtney wondered if the bi issue had returned to make trouble. Courtney raised her open hands to protest her innocence. "This is the first I've heard about it."

"I think it's nice of your dad to come to your games," said Melissa directly to Kaylee.

"He gives me tips…because he's, you know…a baseball coach."

"Then I bet he gives you good advice," Melissa said. Hoping she'd let go of this topic, Courtney glared in her direction.

Kaylee tugged on the sleeve of her mother's shirt. "Can I be excused now? I told Hailey and Emma I'd text with them after dinner."

"Okay but lights out at ten."

"But Mom," whined Kaylee, "it's Friday night!"

"Ten o'clock," Courtney insisted.

Kaylee headed down the hall to her room, and Melissa got up to clear the table.

"You don't have to do that," said Courtney.

"I think I'm past being a guest, so yes, I do."

"Don't get me wrong. I love seeing you pull your weight," Courtney said with a smirk. "Who cleans up after you at home? Not your mother?"

"We have a house cleaner. She does many of the houses on Gull Island."

"You won't get that kind of service in my house."

Melissa ran water into the skillet. "There are some services I find more important."

"Oh, it's service now?" asked Courtney, reaching under Melissa's blouse. "Then I'll expect *service* in return."

28

"Luce, you have to let me go," Liz whispered in her ear. Lucy loosened her grip around Liz's neck. Her legs released Liz's waist. Then she realized Liz meant the muscles tightly clenching her fingers.

"I never want to let you go," Lucy whispered back.

"I know you don't, but I don't want to hurt you by withdrawing too fast."

Lucy focused on relaxing the muscles, but she felt sad when the warm fingers finally escaped.

Liz rolled over on her back and gave her a curious side-eye. "You look pensive. You're not going to whip out your laptop and start working on your book? Sometimes, I think you're only using me as a research subject."

"No, but I do get ideas when we make love…" Lucy gave Liz a quick kiss. "…because you're so sexy…and I keep learning from you… and not only new ways to make love." Lucy had punctuated her statements with kisses. "But I would like you to read something I wrote," she said, sitting up. "I'd really like your opinion."

"I'm not sure I'd have anything useful to say," said Liz, looking doubtful.

"Why not? You have something to say about everything else. Besides, I really need you now. I lost my other editor."

Liz smiled but her eyes were sad. "Erika probably ran out of tactful things to say about your crazy ideas. That's why she took the exit."

"That's not nice," Lucy replied with a pout.

"Sorry. I'm sure Erika would have preferred to hang around. I doubt she was ready to go. She was probably as surprised as we were."

As a priest, Lucy had often prayed with the dying and wondered what they experienced. What were Erika's thoughts and feelings in those last moments? Did she realize before the aneurysm burst that she was going to die?

Liz rolled out of bed and stretched, drawing Lucy's eye. She always admired her body covertly, knowing how self-conscious Liz was about being older. She'd been dieting to lose her beer belly, which made the flesh below the waist sag a little. Although Lucy had seen photographs of young Liz, a tall, extremely slender young woman with sleek, dark hair, she never tried to imagine her lover's younger body. She loved this body with all its imperfections, including the long scar on her arm, which Liz cut on a glass door as a child. The scars on her chin came from falling off her motorcycle. The scars were souvenirs of an adventurous life and told the story of the woman she loved, so Lucy cherished them.

"Mind if I use your shower?" asked Liz, interrupting Lucy's loving thoughts. "I don't want to smell like… uh…sex when your daughter gets here."

"You were going to use a different word." Lucy scrunched up her face in disapproval.

"Yes, but you're a priest, so we don't use those words with you."

"That's not what you say when you talk dirty to me."

"We make exceptions for moments of passion." Liz sniffed her arm and wrinkled up her nose.

"Stop! I don't smell bad!" Lucy threw a pillow at her.

Liz laughed. "No, you smell good, very good, but I'm covered in you. Are you still using that lubricant I gave you?"

"I don't need it anymore."

Liz beamed. Her pride in her sexual prowess was so easy to stoke. Sometimes, Lucy did it for fun, but this time, it was merely a statement of fact. Her new lover knew exactly how to get her ready for sex. Liz wasn't always patient, but sometimes her impatience was even more exciting.

The first time Liz had come on too strong, Lucy had caught her in a scissor grip and flipped her. Instantly, Liz had flipped her back. Resisting the need to re-establish the upper hand took a supreme act of will, but Lucy forced herself because she didn't want their sex life to turn into a wrestling match.

It had taken almost a year before she'd allowed Susan inside her body.

Erika always asked permission before any sexual moves and built the tension gradually. Liz was quirky and unpredictable. She could lie quietly and allow herself to be caressed or probe Lucy so fiercely she felt raw inside. Lucy never knew what to expect, but once she'd looked into those eyes and saw love instead of a need to dominate, she knew Liz would never hurt her or force her to do anything against her will. Instead of resisting Liz's passion, Lucy had discovered the pleasure of opening herself to it.

As soon as Lucy heard the shower go on, she pulled out her laptop and typed some notes. She felt a little guilty. She wasn't intentionally using Liz as a research subject, and she was telling the truth when she said their lovemaking inspired useful thoughts. She had already decided to write a chapter called "Surrendering to God's Desire." People always talked about accepting God's will, but what about God's powerful love?

While Lucy was typing, a text message from Emily popped up on her screen. *Just crossing the NH border. Be there soon.* Lucy's heart took a little leap. She hadn't seen her daughter in months. Although they video-chatted several times a week, it wasn't the same. She'd missed the first sixteen years of her daughter's life, and now, she couldn't get enough of her. The feel of her daughter's flesh against hers was like nothing else.

Liz came out of the shower with her wet hair combed back. The water still clinging to her body bled through her T-shirt leaving dark spots in the soft cotton. Lucy presented her with the laptop. "Read this while I take a shower." Liz saluted and climbed back into bed. She crossed her legs squaw-style and began to read. The little furrow between her brows meant she was focusing.

Whenever Erika read Lucy's work, she always wore her dispassionate, philosopher's face and gave herself time to digest what she'd read before offering a critique. Erika's words regarding her wife's sermons, outfits, cooking, or anything else potentially controversial were always measured.

Lucy wrapped her hair in a towel and put on her bathrobe. When she went into the bedroom to pick out clothes to wear, she found Liz scowling at the computer screen. "That doesn't look promising."

"I don't know anything about this stuff." Liz closed the laptop and set it on the night table.

"After speedreading all those theology books, I bet you know more than I do." As Lucy stepped into her panties, she noticed Liz giving her breasts an admiring look. Before she got any ideas, Lucy put on a bra. "I want you to tell me what you think."

"No, you don't." Liz crossed her arms on her chest.

Lucy tried to read the message. Maybe Liz hated it. That possibility had never crossed Lucy's mind. "All right. Now, you *have to* tell me."

Liz regarded her with a steady gaze. "If I'd written that, Erika would say, 'bollocks.'"

"What?" Lucy's eyes widened. "You're yanking my chain."

Liz shook her head. "I said you didn't want to hear my opinion." Lucy couldn't stop the hot tears that sprang to her eyes. They instantly got Liz's attention. She jumped out of bed. "I'm sorry," she said, trying to put her arms around her. "You asked."

Lucy shrugged off her arms and sank down on the bed. "Erika never would have said anything so hurtful about my work."

"Not to your face, maybe, but she said it to me all the time. When I sent my policy speeches to critique, she never minced words."

Knowing that Erika was more direct with Liz didn't help Lucy feel any better. The tears wouldn't stop. They were running down her cheeks faster than she could wipe them away with her fingertips. "I'm sorry to be such a baby. I know I'm not as smart as you and Erika."

"You're very smart, Lucy. Don't sell yourself short."

"You don't understand. That's why I want my doctorate, so people know I have a brain."

Liz snatched some tissues out of the box on the side table and handed them to Lucy. "Of course, you have a brain. You don't need more letters after your name to prove it. Everyone knows you're smart. Here, look." Liz opened the laptop. "There are lots of good ideas, but they're all jumbled up, so they don't make sense. You need to build your case logically, not just throw everything you think on the page."

"That's what you think I did?" Lucy asked in horror. "Do you have any idea how hard I worked on that?" The tears came again. Liz handed her more tissues. "You don't know how much effort it takes for me to write stuff like this!"

Liz regarded her with a sympathetic frown. "I'm sorry, Lucy, but you asked me to be honest."

"I asked you to be honest, not brutal!"

"Oh, Lucy, I'm sorry!" Liz said, pulling her closer. "I wanted to rip off the Band-aid and get it over with. I guess that was the wrong approach."

"You think?"

"Lucy, you're a lateral thinker. You think in poetry, not in prose, but when you write an academic paper, you have to put your ideas in some kind of logical order. Maybe, I can help."

"You can't write my book for me. That's cheating!"

"I'm not going to write the damned thing!" said Liz, visibly recoiling from the idea. "*I* know what you're trying to say because you've talked to me about your ideas. If you want other people to understand them, you need to organize them better."

Lucy sat up straight and grabbed more tissues to blow her nose. "This is my weak spot. I want to be as smart as you and Emily, to talk to you on your level, but I just can't!" She hugged herself and stared at the floor.

Liz leaned down to speak to Lucy's face. "Lucy, we can't talk to *you* on *your* level. You can sense people's feelings and pain and give them exactly what they need. You can interpret music and sing so beautifully my heart breaks. Your sermons move people. You have real gifts I don't have, or Emily or Stefan." Liz sighed, obviously frustrated. "Do you want my help or not?"

"I'm afraid," Lucy said. "Can you be gentle?"

"I'll try." Liz reached over Lucy to get her laptop. She copied and renamed Lucy's book files to a new folder. When Liz started moving things around, Lucy had to pay attention because everything was happening so fast. "This belongs here because it's a consequent, not a proposition. This sentence is your lead, don't bury it down here…Move it here…" She continued this process for the first couple of pages in the chapter. "See? I didn't cut a word. All your ideas are intact. Now, read it. Doesn't it make more sense?" She handed the laptop to Lucy. "Here. I'm going to dry my hair."

After Lucy had read what Liz had edited, she realized that she was right. Now that her thoughts had been organized, they made much more sense. She glanced toward the bathroom where the hairdryer droned. Despite the pain Liz's blunt words had caused, her intentions were good.

"So, did I wreck anything?" Liz asked, coming out of the bathroom with her hair dried and messed up again into its usual grunge style.

"No, you didn't."

"Next time, I'll try harder." Liz flopped down beside Lucy on the bed.

"I'd love your help, but you're so busy. When will you have time?"

"I'll make time. It only took a few minutes to edit that much, but I'd really like you to learn how to do it yourself."

"I don't know if I can."

"Sure you can." Liz's confident tone was encouraging, but Lucy was still unsure. "Anyone with a brain can be taught to think logically. By the way, I didn't understand everything I read, so you're going to have to sit with me to translate."

Lucy gave her a quick kiss. "Thank you. I'm sorry I was such a baby."

"Am I forgiven now?"

"Yes, I guess so. I was spoiled by Erika's gentler criticism."

"Erika had to develop a filter for dealing with her students. She couldn't be as blunt with them as she was with me."

Liz's words made Lucy realize how gentle and loving Erika had been to her, which made her miss her even more. "We were both lucky to have Erika in our lives," Lucy said. Liz looked about to choke up, but she compressed her lips into a tight line and held back the tears. Lucy rubbed her shoulder.

Liz loudly cleared her throat. "We should get our act together. Emily will be here soon."

"You're right." Lucy gave Liz a little hug around the waist.

"Are we good?"

Lucy smiled. "You bet."

In the bright light of the bathroom mirror, Lucy spread the foundation that covered her abundant freckles. From her years on the stage, she could put on her makeup in minutes. She looked through her lipsticks, choosing a shade paler than she usually wore, which she preferred in the summer.

She glanced out the window and saw a familiar Audi coming down the street. "Emily's here," she called to Liz.

"Well, at least, we're decent."

"We shouldn't stand around expectantly. That might be too much for her."

"I'll go into the kitchen and open some wine."

Lucy said a little prayer to center herself. She didn't want to overwhelm her autistic daughter with an emotional welcome, although she was practically bursting with anticipation.

The doorbell rang, and Lucy went downstairs to greet her daughter. She opened the door to a tall redhead, who resembled her mother even more than when she'd left for Yale in the spring.

"Mom!" Emily offered the smile she'd been trained to form on happy occasions. Lucy felt a pang of sadness because her daughter couldn't experience the spontaneous joy she was feeling. Emily continued to cling to the handle of her rolling suitcase while her mother kissed and hugged her.

"Oh, sweetie. I'm so glad you're home!" Lucy said, squeezing Emily with all her might.

Emily gingerly patted her mother's back. "I would have been here sooner, but there was so much traffic."

"It's the summer people," said Liz, bringing in a tray with wine and glasses. "I know you're not legal yet, but I thought you might like a glass to celebrate."

"Hi, Aunt Liz. I didn't know you'd be here." Emily looked to her mother for an explanation. While Lucy searched her mind for the words she'd prepared, Liz clamped her arm around her.

"Your mom and I are together now."

Emily looked from Liz to Lucy and back again. "Oh," she said. "That's nice." She glanced at her bag. "I've really got to pee. I'll bring my bag up to my room."

Lucy listened to her daughter's feet on the stairs. When she heard the door close, she said, "Liz! You could have waited."

"We said we would tell her right away."

"Not the minute she walked in the door! Sometimes, I think *you're* autistic."

Liz frowned and looked thoughtful. "I could be. Who knew about Asperger's in the 1950s? It's not like I was ever tested."

"You're not serious."

"I am serious. I often wondered about Erika too." Liz reached out her hand, but Lucy only eyed it with a raised brow. "I'm sorry, Lucy. I should have waited and let you take the lead. I can't seem to keep my foot out of my mouth today. "

Lucy sighed and shook her head. She accepted not only the outstretched hand, but also the kiss that followed.

29

Liz carefully tightened the bolts that held the toilet to the floor. "You can't overtighten these things or you crack the porcelain. It has to be just right." She gingerly gave the bolt one more half-turn.

"I'm so grateful that Hobbs has a doctor who moonlights as a plumber," Tom said. "When I saw that water coming down the wall in Lucy's office, I knew I was in trouble."

"Lucy's going to kill you when she finds out. When did you notice this leak?"

"Yesterday. It started as a little wetness around the base. The next thing I knew, the floor was flooded. Was it something I did?"

Liz laughed heartily. "Without getting too deeply into your bowel habits, Tom, I would say no. The flange rusted out and the bolts broke through. Good thing the hardware store is open on Sunday, and they had all the parts."

Tom made a face as Liz threw the old wax ring into a bucket. "Doesn't it bother you to handle that yucky stuff after needing to be so hygienic as a surgeon?"

"Tom, you have no idea how yucky the inside of a human body can be." Liz mopped around the base of the toilet with paper towels and wiped down her tools before putting them into her bag. She got up to scrub her hands in the lavatory sink. "I'll let you explain the emergency to Lucy. I left her on her deck with a bottle of excellent rosé. It's probably warm by now."

"I have a nice white in the fridge. Would you like to try it?"

"Why not?" said Liz. "Lucy's got Emily for company now."

Tom raised his brows. "I'm sure it's not the same. How's it going?"

"How's what going?"

"Oh, don't be coy, Liz. I can see you're involved."

"That's not good. We're trying to keep it on the Q.T. because…you know…your religion."

"Liz, you're divorced now. You're allowed to date."

"It's not me I'm worried about. I don't want to hurt Lucy's reputation."

"Lucy has to be discreet, just as I do, but you shouldn't hide. Everyone in Hobbs knows both of you. If you suddenly start acting strange, that will make people more suspicious."

Liz followed Tom into the kitchen. She put her tool bag and the bucket by the door.

"Sit down while I open the wine."

Liz took a seat at the kitchen table. "Why do I think you want to tell me something, Thomas?"

"I do want to tell you something." He poured the wine and handed her a glass. "I want to wish you and Lucy all the happiness you can have in this life," he said raising his glass.

"Thank you. To you and Jeff as well. How's that going?"

"It's coming along. I think it has potential."

"You're smart not to rush into a commitment."

"Oh, I'm afraid we're past that point."

"Is that good or bad?"

"Good."

"Tom, why are you making me play twenty questions? Will we be hearing wedding bells soon?"

"Maybe." The smile on Tom's round face reminded Liz of the Cheshire cat. He pulled out a chair from the table and sat down. "I'd offer you something to eat, but I need to get to the market today. The toilet disaster interrupted my plans."

"I know what you mean," said Liz. "So, will you move in with Jeff? That will leave the rectory empty."

"We do have our permanent guest in the curate's studio. The Rev. Susan Gedney." Tom's pursed lips indicated he had more to say but was trying to keep whatever it was to himself.

"You don't like her," Liz ventured.

"Let's just say, I'm not sure about her."

"Come on, Tom. This is me you're talking to."

"There have been a lot of empty wine bottles in the recycling bin," he said. "I'm the last one to throw stones. I like a glass of wine as much as anyone. I don't want to be a hypocrite."

"But you think the number of bottles in the recycling is excessive," said Liz, drawing conclusions. "Are you saying she has a drinking problem?"

"I don't like to assume, but I think so. And the stuff she drinks is the cheapest rotgut you can buy." Tom screwed up his face in exaggerated disgust. "She's in that little studio all the time. Unless she has appointments with Lucy, she doesn't emerge until noon, sometimes later. She says she's looking for a job, but I don't think her prospects are good keeping those hours." Tom's blue eyes, usually so merry, looked concerned. "What do you know about her?"

Liz took a sip of wine while she wondered what to say. She knew more, but she didn't want to betray Lucy's confidence. "What has Lucy told you about her?" she asked, deflecting.

"Not much. They were at seminary together. It was Susan who encouraged Lucy to pursue the priesthood. She's quite conservative in her beliefs," said Tom, twirling the stem of his wine glass.

"That's it?"

"No, there's more."

"All right, since we're gossiping, I'll say it," said Liz, putting down her wine glass. "They were sexually involved. She brought Lucy out."

"Did you also know she was in the convent before she left to become a priest?"

"The way I heard it, they asked her to leave because she was having an affair with another nun."

"Oh," said Tom. As if he needed fortification, he took a jar of peanuts from a cabinet and poured some into a bowl. "Sorry, Liz. It's the best I can do until I get to the market."

"I love peanuts. Don't apologize." Liz took a handful and ate them one by one. "So, we know this Susan's religious beliefs aren't as strict as she would like us all to believe."

"Maybe they are, but she might not come up to her own standards. That can cause a dangerous internal conflict," said Tom, reaching for the bowl of peanuts. "She could be one of those people who strikes out boldly, feels guilt-ridden, and then tortures herself. Hence, all the empty wine bottles."

"Hmm. That's an interesting read. Are you worried?"

Tom shook his head to answer while he chewed. "She manages to look respectable when necessary. She had me completely fooled between her collar and the saccharine smile."

"Could her behavior damage Lucy's reputation?" Liz asked, feeling herself tense.

Tom stared at the ceiling as he thought about the question. "I doubt it. Lucy is well-established here. People love her. She is one of the most sensible people I've met in the Church. For all her kindness and compassion, she's shrewd when it comes to people. She'll know how to handle Susan if it comes to that."

"Have you noticed how much Susan looks like Erika?" Liz said. "I found it weird when I first saw her. Then I remembered how many of my partners after Maggie had bottle-blond hair and hazel eyes. I guess I thought I could replace her with someone who looked like her. Didn't work, of course."

"The first relationship can be a powerful influence on those that come after it. And if Susan was Lucy's first, she could have a blind spot where's she's concerned." Tom glanced at her. "It's strictly a hypothetical, of course. I'm just speculating."

"Oh, God. I hope not. That's how I got involved with Maggie again. I couldn't see how mismatched we were because I so desperately wanted to get back together with her. The cancer made it more complicated, of course. I just couldn't leave her after that."

"So, you were trapped by your need to save her?"

"And because of my professional interests, I was in a special position to think I could."

"Did Lucy help you see that connection?" asked Tom curiously.

"No, I figured it out myself during those lonely nights when I had nothing better to do than mull over my past sins."

"Being loyal and kind is not a sin." Tom said, helping himself to more peanuts.

"No, but enabling people isn't good. That's what I'm worried about with Lucy. I hope she's not giving Susan money. Erika left her very well off."

"I doubt it. Lucy is supportive, but she's too smart to be an enabler."

"She is smart, isn't she? I stepped in shit today when she asked me to read her book. It's actually pretty good, just disorganized. I told her so. She didn't like it."

"Well, Liz, would you like it?"

"No, I guess not." Liz drained her glass. "Fortunately, she forgives easily. She doesn't save up her resentments like Maggie."

"Sounds like you're still holding a grudge against Maggie."

"She slept with a man out of spite. That's unforgiveable."

Tom gave her a hard look. "Forgive her, Liz. You'll live longer. Let it go and move on."

"Is that your advice as a priest? Turn the other cheek?"

"No, it's my advice as your friend and someone who's known you a long time. Being angry with her just hurts you. You have better things to do."

"Thank you, Father Simmons. I'll take it under advisement. And now, regarding my bill for the house call…"

"You're going to charge me?" he asked with mock horror.

"No, I'll donate the fifteen bucks I spent on plumbing supplies to St. Margaret's. I was thinking of taking it out in trade. Invite me and Lucy down to Jeff's. It's always nice to have another view of the ocean."

"Only if you take us out on the boat so we can see the fireworks on the Fourth."

"I was planning on that, but I never got around to calling everyone." Liz's cellphone vibrated in her pocket. "That's probably my girlfriend," said Liz, digging into her shorts for the phone. "Isn't that an absurd term? Lucy hasn't been a girl for decades, but she told me that calling her my lover is old school, and it dates me."

Tom chuckled. "We're all stuck in our time."

Liz tapped open the call. "Yes, Mother Lucy, I am here with Thomas, having a glass of very nice…" Liz turned the wine bottle to see the label. "… pinot grigio."

"Let me speak to her, please," said Tom.

Liz tapped on the speaker and set the phone on the table.

"Lucy, I want to thank you for lending me your *girlfriend* for a few hours. She fixed the plumbing problem efficiently and assured me the bill will be minimal."

"That's good to hear, Tom, but thanks to Olivia we have a fund for repairs," said the voice out of the phone. "You could have called a plumber."

Liz and Tom exchanged a look. Liz muted the phone. "Don't tell her about the mess in her office. It will just get her upset." Tom nodded, and Liz tapped on the sound.

"Yes, I know, Lucy, but I couldn't get a plumber to come out on a Sunday. I'm ever so grateful that our mutual friend came to rescue me."

"Now that everything is under control there, can you send her back? She promised to cook dinner tonight, and my daughter says she's fainting with hunger." There was a brief pause. "Would you like to join us?"

Liz rolled her eyes. Tom saw it and asked, "Lucy, is this a sincere invitation? Your girlfriend is making faces."

"Liz, do we have enough for Tom?"

"Now, you ask?"

"Well, do we?"

"Yes, but no leftovers for your lunch tomorrow."

"I'd rather have Tom's company."

"Your wish is my command," said Liz, bowing. "We'll be there soon." She tapped off the call. "I guess we should escape before Susan notices we're gone."

"Probably a good idea. Let me change into something more formal than shorts and flip flops."

"Why? That's what I'm wearing," said Liz, looking down at her outfit.

"So it is," said Tom with a smile.

30

Susan glanced around the dining room of the Gypsy Queen. She and Lucy had just come from their weekly hospital visit, so they were wearing their clerical collars. Susan was sure people were staring at them, but all the other diners were occupied with their meals or conversations.

She'd felt self-conscious about her clothes since arriving in Maine. Webhanet attracted a cosmopolitan gay crowd that was especially design-conscious. The tourists wore the latest fashions. Susan's wide-legged pants drew the most stares. In her opinion, tight jeans looked ridiculous and should be reserved for teenagers. She preferred pants with elastic waistbands that she could cover with loose tops.

With her trim figure, Lucy could wear any fashion. Today, she had on a pale-gray, form-fitted clerical blouse, which looked much more comfortable in the heat than the traditional black Susan wore. While Lucy watched the people passing on the sidewalk, Susan allowed her eyes to linger on her assets. She was still so lovely, despite the passage of time—as beautiful as when they'd made love for the last time on the night before Susan's ordination.

Although the Episcopal Church had relaxed its stance on homosexuality, the broader Anglican communion still believed that same-sex couples should remain celibate. Lucy believed it was a matter of conscience. "God is love. It would be unimaginably cruel of God to create people to love one another and not allow them to express it physically."

Lucy had looked baffled when Susan tried to articulate why they could no longer have sex. Lucy never took her seriously, and why would she? No matter how Susan prayed for chastity, she was a backslider. Secretly, she set her ordination day as the incontrovertible end of their sexual relationship. Tears streamed down Lucy's face while Susan packed her car with everything she owned to head for a curacy in the Midwest. The sight of Lucy's image growing ever smaller in the rear-view mirror nearly broke Susan's heart.

Susan looked up and noticed Lucy studying her over the rim of her wine glass. After hearing her mention the empty bottles in the recycling bin, Susan hadn't dared to order wine.

"You're very quiet today, Susan," Lucy said, her therapist's eyes subtly making assessments. "Is everything all right?"

"Of course." Susan forced a smile. "I'm sorry I'm not better company."

"That's not it. You seem very self-absorbed. What are you thinking about?"

"I was remembering the last time we made love. How beautiful it was. How you haven't changed."

Lucy's smile was bittersweet. "But I have changed." She rubbed the frown lines between her brows with her fingertips. "Last winter really aged me."

"I can't even imagine. First, you have the joy of meeting a woman you love enough to marry, and then you lose her such a short time later."

Lucy swallowed audibly. "It was painful."

"I'm trying to respect your grief. That's why I've kept my distance."

Lucy's green eyes widened. "Kept your distance? What do you mean?"

"Well, I thought…now that you're free…"

Other than blinking several times, Lucy maintained her carefully controlled expression. Susan recognized that look. She often used it herself in pastoral counseling. "Susan, what are you trying to say?"

"I thought maybe, after you've finished mourning your wife, there might be a chance for us."

Lucy gazed out the window at the people passing on the street. Finally, she turned back and gave Susan a long, hard look. "Are you saying you want to rekindle our relationship? Is that why you came to Maine?"

"No, I came to comfort you in your bereavement. To pray with you, like we did when you were recovering. I know how much praying together helped you heal."

Lucy let out a long sigh and stared at her wine glass. "Yes, prayer can be a great comfort during grief. Susan, I appreciate your thinking of me and wanting to comfort me, but–"

"I know it's a surprise after I left like that. You probably thought it was over, and I didn't care. It nearly broke my heart to leave you. I still love you." Susan saw Lucy's eyes grow even wider. "Now that you're free, we have a second chance. Don't you want to explore a relationship?"

Lucy opened her mouth and shut it again. She was obviously struggling to find the right words. Finally, she said, "I'm sorry, Susan, but I'm not available right now."

"Lucy, I understand. You need to mourn. Grief takes time, and everyone deals with their grief on their own timetable."

Lucy's expression was intense. "Susan, you left. I often thought about you, wondering where you were and how you were doing, but after I got over the pain, I went on with my life."

"I expected that, but I still love you."

"I love you too, but we're not going to be together again."

"We were so good together, Lucy. Remember how it was?"

"In your memory, we were good together. I can't go back to your guilt trips and vacillation. I can't watch you punish yourself for your sexuality."

"I've changed."

Lucy shook her head. "Maybe you have, but I can't go back there with you. I watched you suffer and torture yourself with your Catholic guilt. I'm past that now." Her tone was gentle but firm. "You helped me, so I want to help you, but you can forget about getting back together."

"I can't. I still love you," said Susan, feeling increasingly anxious. She realized she'd spoken too loudly and looked around. Fortunately, it was noisy in the restaurant, and no one was paying attention.

Lucy looked directly into her eyes. "Susan, I'm already in a relationship."

"With Dr. Stolz? Oh, that won't last. That's just sex. You've always needed so much sex."

Susan recognized the little spark in Lucy's eyes as controlled anger. "It's not just sex. Liz and I have been friends since I came to Maine."

"You got involved before you healed from losing your wife. It won't last."

"How do you know? And who are you to decide when I'm finished mourning my wife?" Lucy's carefully modulated tone only emphasized how angry she was. She finished the wine in her glass and set it down decisively. "Susan, you can forget this charade of comforting me, and we are *not* getting back together."

Susan suddenly felt desperate. She wanted to get up and run, but they had taken Lucy's car, and they were far from home. "Lucy, I'm not feeling well."

Lucy signaled to the waiter. When he came to the table, she handed him her credit card, explaining, "We're in a hurry. Please run it through with a twenty percent tip. Thank you." She reached out for Susan's hand. "Are you all right?"

"Yes. I just need to get out of here," Susan said, gulping air.

"We can go to the park across the street and talk. For obvious reasons, I don't want to have this conversation in the rectory."

The waiter hurried back with her credit card. "All done," he said. "No need to sign the receipt."

They walked to the park in silence and sat down on a bench under a tree. "How are you feeling?" Lucy asked.

"Much better, but I needed to get out of there. Everyone was staring at us because of our collars."

Lucy's eyes looked concerned. "No one was looking at us."

"You know how people are. When you notice they're staring, they look away."

Lucy looked perplexed, but she nodded. "Susan, where did you get the idea I'd want to get back together?"

"You were so happy to see me."

"Of course, I was happy to see you! You could have died for all I knew. I was so worried. You have no idea! I do care about you."

"I know you do," replied Susan meekly. "I'm sorry if I offended you."

Lucy's expression hardened. "Enough of this subterfuge. I need you to tell me the truth. You didn't just come all the way to Maine because you missed me. What's really going on?"

Susan's heart began to pound. "Please don't send me away. I have nowhere else to go."

"Of course, I'm not going to send you away. You can stay in the rectory for now, but you do need to look for a job, a real job. Have you applied to the clergy openings on the diocesan website?"

Susan shook her head.

"Why not?"

"Because the bishop revoked my license."

Lucy's eyes noticeably widened. "Why?"

"I was caught by the police…for driving while intoxicated."

Lucy's face flooded with sympathy. "Oh, Susan, why didn't you tell me? We can get you help. In fact, there's a wonderful AA group for lesbians in Portland. Our bishop is a kind and compassionate man. We can speak to him to see—"

"Lucy, I'll consider going to AA, but as far as your bishop goes…" Susan shook her head.

"Don't you want to have your license as a priest reinstated?"

Susan stared at the ground. "I'm not worthy to be a priest."

Lucy sat back, looking frustrated and worried. "That's why participating in the liturgy upsets you so much," she said, drawing the obvious conclusion.

"Until I get myself sorted out, I wouldn't dare approach your bishop, no matter how wonderful you think he is."

"I think you should go to him and explain your situation. If you want, I'll go with you."

"No," said Susan, "I'm too ashamed. And I don't want him to contact my bishop."

"Why not?"

"I'm sure he would have lots to say. He offered me rehab before I left."

"That's very compassionate. Why didn't you take him up on it?"

"I left before I could. I should tell you, I left rather abruptly. The DUI is on my license. That's why it's so hard for me to get a job. It seems every place wants a drug test and a background check. You must have a lot of drugs here."

"We do. Opiate abuse has been a big problem. Oh, Susan, can't you stop drinking long enough to pass a drug test?"

"I don't know. I haven't really tried."

Lucy breathed out a sigh and gazed at the couple holding hands on the park bench across the path. Susan could see her mind was working. "Okay," she finally said. "We're going to find an AA meeting, and you're going to join it *today*."

"I don't know if AA would work for me."

Lucy gave her stern look. "Go to a meeting or leave the apartment in the rectory."

"Lucy! Please, no."

"Tough love. Just do it, Susan. I'll give you a list when we get back to the office, and you find a meeting. Okay?"

"Yes, okay. Obviously, I have no other choice, or I'll be sleeping in my car again."

Lucy's green eyes grew large. "You were living in your car?" she asked in an incredulous voice.

"Yes, before your kind Father Tom allowed me to move into the curate's studio. It was the first time I'd slept in a real bed in weeks. Not since I left South Dakota. You think I had the money to stay in motels?"

"I don't know what to think. This is the first time you've been honest with me, Susan. And that breaks my heart because I thought you knew you could trust me."

"I do trust you. Why do you think I headed here? I knew you would help me."

"You took a big risk, Susan. What if I hadn't forgiven you for abandoning me when you left? It's probably a good thing you came to Tom first. He's so soft-hearted."

"I think he was trying to please you…his boss."

"Maybe, but I'm not sure I would have offered you the curate's studio."

"You wouldn't?"

"No, I would have expected you to be able to look after yourself and to pay for your own accommodations."

"I only had so much money saved, not a lot. I need to make it last. If you think priests are paid poorly in Maine, you should see what they get in South Dakota. And I've never been a good saver."

"Were you spending your money on alcohol?"

"No. Well, some of it, of course."

Lucy got up. "Let's go," she said. "When we get back, I'll print out a list of AA meetings. You find one that meets today."

Susan nodded.

Lucy sighed and headed toward the path. Susan followed, knowing that when Lucy was on a mission, there was no stopping her.

31

Melissa watched her mother water the houseplants in the sunroom. She was humming softly, which was a good sign. Ruth loved music. She was delighted to learn that Jack was a fellow member of the Metropolitan Opera Guild. They had many other common interests. So far, so good.

"You're certainly in a good mood, Mom," said Melissa, announcing her presence to avoid startling her.

"What's not to be in a good mood about?" Ruth's Queens accent was still as strong as the day she moved out of the city. "The sun is shining. The salt marsh is so lush with all its many shades of green, and I saw a blue heron this morning."

"Next time you see one, tell me, so I can take a photo."

"So you can post it on Facebook or whatever you do? No, you should look at nature with your own eyes. Beauty is meant to be experienced, not to get likes on Facebook."

"But if I share it with people who aren't lucky enough to live in such a beautiful place, is that a bad thing?"

"If it makes other people feel better, it's not wrong," said Ruth, gazing out at the bright-green sea grass.

"Is this a good time to talk, Mom?"

Ruth searched her daughter's face. "Is it something serious?"

"Maybe. Let me tell you what I'm thinking, and you be the judge."

Ruth put down her long-spouted watering can and gestured toward a wicker settee. "You look worried, Lissa. Is something wrong?" she asked, sitting down beside her.

"I have a big ask, Mom. Really big."

The wicker creaked as Ruth sat back. "Go on. I'm listening."

"Courtney Barnes needs to move. Her landlord is replacing her trailer with a newer model, and he's doubling the rent because in this market he can get it. If she doesn't sign a lease at the higher rate, she has to be out by the end of the month. Courtney has looked everywhere, but everything is so expensive."

"What does this have to do with me?" asked Ruth, narrowing her eyes.

"Mom, you have this enormous house. The bedrooms in the guest wing are empty most of the time."

"Your father wanted a big place so our friends and family would come up during the summer."

"And they did…in the beginning. The only people who still come up are Becca and her family. Last year, during the pandemic, they didn't come up at all."

"That's because they didn't want me to get sick." While Melissa had been talking, Ruth's face went from open and pleasant to stony. She'd already drawn the obvious conclusion. "You want to move your girlfriend in here."

"Yes, but I want you to know she is willing to pay rent and contribute to the expenses."

"Your father left me in good shape. I don't need any help with the expenses."

"I know you don't, but fuel costs are going up now that the demand for oil is increasing."

"I can pay for the oil. I don't need help." Ruth frowned. "I don't think it's a good idea."

That was the response Melissa had feared. "Why not, Mom? You have all this space in your house. Someone needs a place to live. I think it's a great match."

"No, I don't think it's a good idea," Ruth repeated.

"Why not?"

"I just don't."

"But, Mom…"

"I like my privacy. I don't want strangers in my house, using my things."

"Courtney's not a stranger. You know her."

"You know her, Melissa. I don't know her. It's my house, and I decide who lives here."

"Obviously."

"And you would live here with her?"

"Yes, we're exploring a relationship."

"Exploring? That sounds very iffy. What if after you 'explore,' you find out it's not working? Then I have someone living in my house, someone who has a child. I can't just throw her out on the street if you break up. No, Melissa. It's not a good idea."

"Mom, I really care for this woman."

"Maybe you do, but I'm done with getting involved with your friends. It never lasts. By the time I warm up to someone, you break up. I can't take it emotionally, especially not with a child involved. You know how much I like children. No. It's no good."

"It's different this time. I think I love her."

"You think? You're not sure?" Ruth shook her head. "You've been sleeping with her for two months, and it's love? You don't know what love is. Love is what I had for your father. Love is when you stand by someone when they lose their job. Love is when you're old and sick, and your spouse takes care of you, like I took care of your father. That's love."

"Mom, I admire how you stood by Dad. You were a good wife."

"Damn right I was, and he wasn't always easy to be with. There were years when he was building up the firm and I hardly saw him. And that's what you should be doing—working on your career. This is the time, in your forties, when it's really important. Does this Courtney know you have to go back to the office?"

"Yes, we've talked about it."

Ruth took a long, deep breath and gazed at the salt marsh. "So, it is serious."

"Please, Mom, I wouldn't ask if there were other options, but everything is so expensive now. I can only afford so much and still keep my condo in Boston. I'll need it because I don't think I can commute every single day."

"Maybe that's a sacrifice you'll have to make."

Ruth got up, effectively ending the discussion.

"Mom, please say you'll think about it."

"I don't have to think about it. The answer is no. And don't beg me, Melissa. My mind is made up. You always have a place in my house, but don't try to move your girlfriends in here."

Melissa sensed that continuing the conversation would only aggravate her mother, so she let it go. "Thanks for listening, Mom."

"You're welcome." Ruth picked up her watering can and went back to tending her plants. Discouraged, Melissa decided she needed to get out of the house. Fortunately, it was Saturday, so she wasn't chained to her computer to prove she was working. "Mom, I'm going into town for a while. Do you need anything?"

"We could use some cream for coffee. And if you see something for dinner, pick it up. Otherwise, we'll have leftovers." Melissa noted that Ruth's tone was pleasant, as if she'd already forgotten the discussion because it wasn't important to her.

In the driveway, Melissa admired the shiny, almost-new Subaru. Having her own car was so much better than depending on her mother's or needing Courtney to transport her. She hated to wake either of them early to drive her to the train station.

The commute was the worst part of living in Maine. The fact that she was even willing to do it was testament to her feelings for Courtney. Ironically, she had told her mother she was in love, yet she hadn't even told Courtney. She'd been saving those words for a romantic dinner, something that occurred more often now that Courtney's ex lived nearby and took his daughter out for the evening.

Before she went into the grocery store to get the cream, Melissa decided to look for shorts in Reny's. Her city wardrobe had included some summer wear, but in Maine, people wore casual clothes everywhere. As she browsed the racks, she bumped into a small redhead wearing a pretty sundress and sandals that revealed her bright red toenails. She almost didn't recognize the rector without her collar.

"Lucy! How are you?"

"Melissa! How nice to see you!" Lucy's brilliant smile made Melissa feel she meant every word.

"I see all of Hobbs shops here."

"Why not? You can find everything you need, from fishhooks to curry sauce." Lucy proudly held up a jar of Tikka Masala. "Goes great with left-over chicken. I'm learning to cook," she confided behind her hand. "Sometimes, I cheat."

Melissa chuckled. "I'm so happy to see you. I was thinking about stopping by to say hello." In fact, the idea had occurred to her on the spot.

Lucy's smile grew warmer. "My door is always open. Hey, I was going to stop at Awakened Brews for some coffee. Would you like to join me?"

"Sure. Great idea."

"I need to pay for the curry. Can you wait a minute? The line in the front looks pretty long."

"This is the busiest time of the summer. That's not surprising."

The line, snaking back into the store aisles, was barely moving. "You know what? I have plenty of this at home," Lucy said. "Let me put it back, and we can go."

Melissa felt guilty for taking Lucy away from what she'd been doing. It was the sort of thing her sister, the rabbi, would do—drop everything to listen to someone. People like Becca and Lucy seemed to have an instinctive ability to sense when someone needed to talk. Their kindness meant sacrificing their time, yet they always seemed willing to give it. To someone who billed for her time, that seemed strange.

Lucy returned from putting the merchandise back on the shelf. "It's crazy in here today, I can't wait to get to a quieter place and an iced coffee." Gazing into the woman's green eyes, Melissa understood why everyone fell in love with her.

Although it was a short drive to the coffee shack on Route 1, the traffic was backed up for miles. Awakened Brews was packed when they arrived. To Melissa's amazement, tiny Lucy effectively elbowed her way to the desk to put in their names on the list. "Sometimes, my collar will get me a seat faster, but I hate to take advantage of it."

Melissa was glad Lucy wasn't wearing a collar. She couldn't say that without it, she looked like any other woman. Even in her fifties, she was drop-dead gorgeous. A bit of opera glamour still remained in the way she moved and put herself together. Jack had raved about Lucy's voice, so Melissa had downloaded some of her recordings. When she listened to them, she couldn't understand why someone so talented would give up her career, especially because few ever made it to the top in classical music.

"Thank you for taking the time to have coffee with me," Melissa said after they finally sat down at a table on the back terrace.

"I never refuse a cup of coffee, and I really have been wondering how you're doing. What's new with you?"

"They decided everyone has to go back to the office, which screws up my plans to move to Maine. Now, I need to figure out how to manage the commute and not kill myself."

"So, you've definitely decided to move?"

"Yes, if Courtney and I can figure out where to live."

Lucy's brows puckered slightly, but otherwise, her face remained impassive. Melissa reminded herself that she was a trained couples counselor. "I know what you're thinking. Lesbian U-haulers."

Lucy laughed. "I haven't heard that one before, but I admit I'm new to lesbian culture. It sounds like you think things might be moving too fast. Can you tell me more?" Melissa tried to get her thoughts together, but she was distracted by watching Lucy's bright red lips close around her straw. "Go on. I'm listening," Lucy urged with a smile.

"Courtney needs a new place to live. Where she's living is a dump. The landlord is replacing it with a new trailer. Unfortunately, he also wants to double the rent, which he can do in this overheated market." Melissa paused to see how Lucy was taking this information, but she was listening with a pleasant expression. "Courtney has been looking everywhere for a place, but the rents are so expensive. I figured if I chipped in, she could afford it."

"So, you're letting her practical need to find a place to live drive your relationship?"

"It's not really my choice. Courtney needs to move, and doesn't have many options. I asked my mother if she can move in with us. She has all that unused space in her house."

"What did your mother say?"

"No, and she was very clear that she meant it."

"Clarity is good. Are you disappointed?"

"Yes, and hurt. It wasn't her refusal that hurt. It was telling me my love for Courtney isn't good enough. Despite her liberal attitudes, I've always suspected that my mother has issues with me and Becca being gay."

"That's sad. Is your mother religious?"

"Not especially, but she's very much a cultural Jew."

Lucy nodded as she absorbed the information.

"I'm sure you've considered other options."

"I have. I even considered selling my condo in Boston, but that would be crazy, especially because I still need it on the days I don't commute."

"Could you both move to Boston?"

"If Courtney can get a job there. Yes, I suppose we could. But administrative jobs aren't that easy to get unless you're in a school in a really bad neighborhood."

Lucy sipped her coffee and looked thoughtful. "I'll ask around to see if anyone knows of a reasonable rental. Sometimes, people in my church offer places to rent. They aren't always advertised in the newspapers or on websites, so Courtney would have no way of knowing about them."

"I'd appreciate it."

Lucy's expression suddenly brightened. "Liz Stolz has a very nice one-bedroom apartment over her garage. She built it for her mother, but it was barely used. My wife and I lived there during the lockdown. I could ask her about it."

"I don't know. A one-bedroom is small for three people."

"It's pretty big, and it has a cozy sleeping alcove with a daybed. A pocket door slides out to make it a separate room. At least, Courtney and her daughter would have a clean, pleasant place to live while you figure things out."

"Courtney wants something more permanent. Moving is expensive."

"It is, but she could put things in storage. Did you consider moving in with your mother to be a permanent arrangement?"

"No. It was a stop-gap. And I only moved in with Mom to keep her company during the pandemic. She has a new friend, so she doesn't really need me around." Melissa responded to Lucy's curious look by saying, "Thanks for asking Liz to introduce my mother and Dr. Dreyfus. That seems to be working out."

"Good. And you should probably thank your mother for turning you down. Try not to focus on the rejection."

"Why not? That's what it was."

"Be grateful she was honest with you. You know that moving in with your mother probably wasn't the best solution."

Reluctantly, Melissa nodded.

"Finding a workable living arrangement for Courtney is more important. Do you want me to mention it to Liz?"

"Thanks, but I can ask her myself. You don't mind if I say you told me about it?"

"Not at all."

"I'm really glad I met up with you today, Lucy. Maybe we should go back and get your curry."

Lucy smiled. "I'll go during the week, when it's less crowded, but you could buy me another iced coffee. They're one of my *many* weaknesses."

<h1 style="text-align:center">32</h1>

Rev. Bartlett came into the pilot house bringing a beer for the skipper, who wore an Acadia ball cap perched jauntily on her head. Courtney observed the tenderness of their interaction, the little smiles, the soulful looks. They stood close, hips touching. Yes, they were a couple.

"You want to stay, Luce? There's a bench seat there that folds down. See there?" said Dr. Stolz.

"I want to talk to Brenda and Cherie for a bit. I haven't seen them in a while." She smiled warmly at Courtney and Melissa. "Keep an eye on the skipper, girls. She's a cowboy."

"Thanks for taking us out today, Liz," said Melissa. "It's wonderful being out here on the water."

"I would have invited your mother and her new friend, but after Tom and Jeff backed out, that would have left Jack as the only guy."

"Don't worry. Mom and Jack went to New Hampshire to climb Mt. Washington. In a car, of course. Mom's not in shape for mountain climbing."

"Good for them. It's beautiful up there." Dr. Stolz carefully navigated away from an approaching boat. "Where's Kaylee today?"

"She's spending the Fourth with a friend. The family has a cabin on Sebago," Courtney explained. She missed having her daughter on a holiday weekend, but she was glad that she was finally making some friends. It was always harder for a student arriving late in the term.

"Why don't we have fireworks in Hobbs?" Melissa asked.

"Fireworks are banned in Hobbs," Dr. Stolz explained. "Of course, that doesn't stop people from having them. There are no fireworks on our beach to protect the nesting plovers. Our beaches are part of a federal conservation program." Liz cut the motor. "I'm going to drop anchor here, so we can have dinner. Wait until you taste Cherie's Southern Fried Chicken and slaw. Oh, my God."

"I saw that potato salad you made. That looks pretty good too," Melissa said.

"I love Fourth of July. It's an excuse to make great salads and watch fireworks." Dr. Stolz craned her neck to look down to the deck, where her other guests were obviously engaged in conversation. Even so, she spoke in a soft voice. "While I have you two alone, I heard that someone is looking for an apartment." Courtney glanced at Melissa, knowing the exact source of that rumor. "If there's any interest, I have an unoccupied one-bedroom apartment over my garage. It would be snug for the three of you, but the place has a sleeping alcove with a French door."

"I'm on a tight budget," said Courtney.

"Oh, I think you'll find the rent very affordable. It's on a separate gas and electric meter. Pay the utilities, and you have a deal."

Courtney exchanged a look with Melissa. This was too good to be true. "I'm not that desperate. I can pay rent."

"I know, but no one's living there, and it's just wasted space. I built it for my mother. She died last year, so she won't be using it any time soon."

"That's really too generous, Dr. Stolz."

"Please, Courtney. Call me Liz. And I decide what's too generous. If you feel you have to pay me something, I'll take a hundred dollars a month to help pay the guy who cuts the grass. It's not a legal apartment, so I can't really charge you rent."

"Are you sure about this?" Courtney asked incredulously.

"It's only temporary. I'm sure it will be too small to live there long term, but it's a place to hang your hat until you find something better. It's furnished. Do you have a lot of furniture?"

"No. The place I rented is furnished."

"If you need storage space, there's some room in the loft over my shop. Otherwise, the self-storage in town is pretty reasonable."

"That's so kind," said Courtney grasping Liz's hand.

"Check out the place before you thank me. It's pretty small."

"The sleeping alcove sounds tight for my daughter."

"Don't worry. I promise it's bigger than solitary confinement. You'll see when you take a look at it."

Courtney watched Liz head down to the main deck to lower the anchor line. She stepped back and let it spin to depth before tying it off. Sam McKinnon got up to help her. They playfully punched one another and laughed. The conversation of the women on the deck was also punctuated with laughter. Courtney looked at their happy, engaged faces and realized how lucky she'd been to land in Hobbs.

"That was very generous of her to offer you an apartment for literally nothing," said Melissa, putting her arm around her.

"Did you tell Dr. Stolz I need a place to live?" Courtney said, trying to modulate the disapproval in her voice.

"No, I meant to call her, but I didn't get a chance. I mentioned that you were looking for a place to Lucy. I guess she told her. The place is supposed to be small, but very nice. I think you should look at it."

"Oh, I will, if for no other reason than courtesy. Dr. Stolz has a lot of influence in this town. I want to stay on her good side. Was it your idea that you'd live there with us?"

"That would be fun, but I'm guessing it will be too cramped for the three of us. Let's say, I'll visit often. Meanwhile, we can both save up to get a house."

"Why do you need to save? I thought you made a big salary."

"I do, but I have a lot of expenses. I'm paying a mortgage on the condo in Boston. Commuting is expensive…I just bought a car. I have to dress up at my job, so a lot of money goes on my back…"

"Okay, I get the idea." Courtney found it hard to commiserate with Melissa's financial problems, when her grocery bill kept getting bigger, especially in the summer when they raised the prices for the tourists.

Melissa leaned over and kissed her cheek while no one was looking. "Mom and Jack are away for the weekend. You and Kaylee want to come over tomorrow? I can make pizza on the grill."

"Did I hear someone say pizza on the grill?" asked Liz, stepping back into the pilot house. "Come over tomorrow, and you can taste mine and see the apartment. Bring Kaylee."

"Won't we be intruding?"

"Not at all. Lucy will be there and Emily, her daughter. She loves kids. A few other people. Nothing fancy, a low-key holiday weekend cookout. In fact, that's something I should warn you about. There are always people at my house, especially in the summer. We're not generally noisy, but when Lucy sings, she can be pretty loud."

"Lucy sings for you?" Melissa asked. "I've wanted to hear her sing."

"She only sings by special request, but some wine helps get her going."

"A tipsy opera singer. Now, you've got me really curious," said Melissa. "I accept."

"Wait a minute," said Courtney. "Don't I have anything to say about it?"

Liz clucked her tongue. "Ladies, I don't want to create discord. Why don't you talk it over and get back to me? Now, come down and have something to eat."

Liz hopped down to the deck. Watching her, Courtney spoke her thoughts aloud. "It's hard to believe she's almost the same age as your mother."

"I know. Proves age is just a number."

Courtney drew Melissa back into the cabin. "I wish you'd given me a heads-up before you started telling everyone I need a place to live. Now, I look desperate."

"No! They already know the situation. How rentals and houses have been snapped up by people trying to escape the pandemic. They know schools don't pay enough."

"I hope you didn't tell them about Doug not paying child support."

"No, of course not. That's no one's business."

"Melissa, I appreciate what you're trying to do, but I really need to do this myself. This is part of finding out if I can manage. I haven't been on my own since I got married."

"What's wrong with saying you need a place to live? Networking is a great way to find real estate. I wouldn't have found my condo in Boston without help from a woman I work with."

"But I'm not you, Melissa. I can't accept charity from the town doctor. It doesn't look good, especially because she's an advisor to the school board."

"It's not charity, and it's a simple transaction. She has the space. No one is using it. She's certainly not going to talk about it because the apartment's not legal."

"But what does she get out of it?"

Melissa raised her shoulders. "If you get a nice apartment, what do you care?"

"I care because I'm a public figure in this town. I can't afford even the hint of impropriety. I need this job. Melissa, I don't mean to sound ungrateful. But, please, in the future, let me handle these things. If I need your help, I'll ask for it."

Liz called up from the deck. "Hey! You two better get down here, or all the food will be gone!"

Melissa reached out her hand. "I'm sorry. Still friends?"

Courtney took her hand. "Next time, ask first."

33

Lucy's daughter and the trans woman seemed to gravitate toward one another. Now that she was mostly recovered, Denise was more personable. She wore a form-fitting dress that was a little too dressy for a casual gathering on the doctor's deck. Susan wondered if transsexuals usually overdressed, like drag queens. Most women wouldn't go to all that trouble.

Lucy's daughter was a little awkward, but sweetly innocent, almost naive. Lucy had explained that her strict adoptive parents had kept Emily away from things they considered sinful like TV and the Internet, so she'd been forced to learn to navigate the modern world on her own. When Lucy had said that her daughter was on the spectrum, Susan had no idea what to expect. Unless someone studied the girl carefully, it wasn't obvious that her reactions were occasionally slightly "off." Someone had taken the time to train her to react, even when the emotional response wasn't there.

Denise was going out of her way to draw out Emily. Susan wondered if their oddness created a kind of solidarity, but as the conversation went on, it was clear the common denominator was music.

"Aunt Liz has a Steinway grand in her media room," said Emily. "Want to see it?"

"Do you play the piano, Dr. Stolz?" asked Denise, turning in her direction.

"I do, but not as well as Emily."

"Emily, don't you think you should ask before you show things in someone else's house?" Lucy asked in a firm, but kind voice.

"I lived here during the lockdown," Emily explained to Denise. "I feel like it's my house too."

"Of course, it's your house too, Emily," Dr. Stolz said warmly. "Go ahead. Show Denise how well you play. Maybe you'll get her to sing for you."

"Would you?" asked Emily, showing flickers of genuine enthusiasm. Yes, she had emotional responses. They were muted, but definitely present. Denise nodded, looking pleased to be asked.

After the two young people went into the house, Dr. Stolz stood up. "I have homemade blueberry pie and local ice cream for dessert. Any takers?"

"Oh," said Melissa. "Thank you, but I ate too much of that delicious pizza. I need a breather."

Their host engaged the eyes of each person at the table, but they all shook their heads. Susan liked the doctor's affability. She hadn't expected to like her, but she also hadn't expected that level of informality from a retired surgeon. Sometimes, it seemed a bit forced, as if she were overcompensating to get it right.

Susan had been watching the doctor and Lucy closely. It was clear from their body language that they were already in a sexual relationship. She wouldn't dare ask Lucy to confirm it, mostly because she didn't want to know, but every time their eyes engaged, Susan felt a little flash of jealousy.

"Okay. Dessert can wait," said the doctor, settling back into her chair. "If we give the kids some time to warm up, maybe we can have a little concert. Lucy, I promised Melissa you'd sing for her."

Lucy glared in her direction, but it was totally fake. She really didn't mind. "Liz sets me up like this all the time," she explained to Melissa. "I wish she'd give me some warning."

"I just did. Consider yourself warned."

Lucy turned to Susan and spoke in a confidential voice. "I forgot to tell you that you're about to have company in the rectory. Denise's friend in Webhanet is going back to New York, now that the theaters are opening again. I told her she could move into the other curate's studio until she finds another place."

The idea of having the trans woman living right next door unsettled Susan, but she smiled and said, "You're so kind, Lucy."

Dr. Stolz tapped the assistant principal's hand. "See? I'm not the only one who takes in strays. Except there's more room over my garage than in those little curate's studios at the rectory. They really are like solitary confinement." Susan noticed the doctor waiting for Lucy's reaction to the little dig. Lucy finally looked at her from under her brows. Susan had to turn away. She couldn't watch them anymore.

"Courtney, when you're ready to move, I have a pickup and so do Sam and Brenda. If you want, we can help." Courtney's look of surprise drew a smile from Dr. Stolz, who added, "What's the matter? You don't think old ladies like us are up for it? Ask Lucy. We helped her move. Right, Lucy?"

"Yes, and I recommend them. They are very good movers, despite their advanced age," replied Lucy, obviously playing along. "But you do need to pay them…in beer. Feeding them is also advised. They like to eat."

Susan marveled at how easily Lucy, the sophisticated former opera star, had adapted to this semi-rural community. With her natural warmth she fit right in. *Because she doesn't judge people,* Susan thought. *Why can't I be more like her?*

Lucy suddenly looked up. Susan followed the direction of her gaze and saw that Emily was approaching. Seeing Lucy as a mother added a whole new dimension. Her loving expression when she looked at her daughter was precious.

"Mom, Denise wants to know if you'll sing with her. She's been practicing her half of a duet, the one you assigned."

"Sweetie, we're with Liz's guests now. Can't it wait?"

"No, she really wants you to hear this."

"Will you excuse me?" Lucy asked, rising.

"Hell, no," Dr. Stolz said, getting up. "We're coming with you. Right?" She looked at each of her guests for a vote of approval.

"You better believe it," Melissa said, jumping up.

On the way to the media room, Susan got a better look at the interior of the house. The furnishings and decorations suggested a North Woods camp without the shabbiness. Everything was high-end and clearly expensive. The media room was shockingly large. It could hold a substantial audience. It did, indeed, have a Steinway grand piano and a small stage.

"Sit anywhere you like," Dr. Stolz said, waving at the rows of leather home theater seats. "I'll turn on the stage lights." She disappeared into an alcove and brilliant lights came on.

"Liz! This is between Denise and me," Lucy protested. "Don't turn it into a performance."

"I promised Melissa you'd sing for her if I gave you some wine." Dr. Stolz took a seat on the sofa at the front and folded her arms on her chest. "Obviously, Denise figured out how to stream to the speakers."

"Yes, thank you, Dr. Stolz. Emily showed me."

Emily looked pleased to be acknowledged. Shaking her head, Lucy climbed the low stairs to the stage. Denise pointed her phone to some unknown source, and music began to play.

Lucy's voice was as wonderful as ever as they began to sing a duet from Monteverdi's opera, *L'incoronazione di Poppea*, but the sound coming from Denise's throat was incredibly pure, almost like a choir boy's. When they finished singing, the small audience applauded enthusiastically, but Denise looked disappointed. "See? I still can't find the notes without singing in my head voice."

Dr. Stolz approached the stage. She spoke quietly, but her voice carried. "I told you, Denise. Your vocal cords are still the same length. All the hormones in the world can't make them shorter." Denise's face fell. "None of my business," the doctor continued, "but your voice is superb. Why would you want to change it?" She looked toward Lucy for support. Lucy came over and put her arm around Denise's shoulder.

"I agree with Liz. You already have such good technique as a countertenor, and such a powerful, unique sound. Why frustrate yourself?"

Denise looked up at the audience. "Excuse me. I didn't mean to have this conversation in front of all of you."

Melissa stood. "Not that my opinion means anything, Denise, but that was absolutely amazing. Will you sing something else for us?"

Lucy made a quick exit from the stage, leaving Denise to stare after her.

She sat down on the sofa in the front where Dr. Stolz had been sitting. "Go on, Denise," Lucy encouraged. "Your audience wants an encore."

"Only if you promise to sing later."

"All right," Lucy agreed, sitting back, "but now, it's your turn to shine. Sing us something from your regular repertoire."

Denise started the recorded music to an aria from Handel's opera *Rodelinda.* Susan looked around at the other faces. Everyone was listening with amazement to the otherworldly voice that was neither male nor female. At the end, the small audience applauded enthusiastically. Denise made a little curtsy and hurried off the stage as fast as her high heels would allow. Lucy ascended the stairs and assumed her perfect stage manner.

"Since Liz is our host, she gets first choice. She's asked me to sing 'Ebben' from *La Wally.*"

Susan sat forward. This was one of her favorite arias too. She closed her eyes and allowed Lucy's voice to sweep her away. It brought back memories of their first year together, before she'd dared to confess her love. They had spent hours listening to music before they'd found their way into bed together. They'd talked incessantly, sharing their deepest secrets and reading poetry to one another. When Lucy had finally gotten over her allergy to religion, they'd prayed together. If only they could have stayed celibate, maybe they would still be together, but Lucy, with her passionate nature, would never have been satisfied with a sexless relationship.

The impromptu concert continued. Lucy induced her daughter to show off her amazing keyboard skills. "She learns everything by ear," she explained as Emily took a seat at the piano.

"But Mom taught me to read music too."

"You're developing quite a reputation as a teacher, Lucy," said Denise. "Maybe a second career for you?"

Lucy laughed. "I think it will count as my third, but it's something to think about for my retirement."

After the brief piano recital, Susan noticed that the young couple looked anxious to leave. From the way they looked into one another's eyes, it was obvious they had plans for the evening.

"Thank you, Liz, for having us," said Melissa. "The pizza was wonderful, but the concert was absolutely superb."

"Thank you for singing for us, Lucy. And you too, Denise." Courtney reached out her hand to the trans woman with a genuine smile. "I learned more about music tonight than I did the whole time I was in school. You are truly gifted."

"Thank you," said Denise graciously. "I love to perform."

As much as Susan would have liked to prolong the time with Lucy, she realized she would be expected to leave along with the others, and it was probably a good idea. Her shift at McDonald's started at six. Those Egg McMuffins didn't make themselves.

After Denise and the young couple left, Susan approached her host to offer her thanks. "You've made me so welcome," she said. "Your home is beautiful, and I really enjoyed the pizza."

Dr. Stolz walked her to the front door and stood with Lucy and Emily to wave from the porch. Susan wondered if they planned to stay the night. The thought fanned the little flame of jealousy burning inside her. It grew in intensity as she drove back to the rectory.

Susan only noticed that she was being followed when she slowed down to turn into the church parking lot. The white SUV behind her turned with her and then blue lights started to flash. Susan stopped instantly, and the car behind her almost slammed into her rear bumper. Susan's heart began to pound as she watched a shadow approach behind a flashlight.

"Good evening, Ma'am," said the young woman. "Do you know why I stopped you?"

"No, officer," Susan admitted, gripping the steering wheel to keep her hands from shaking.

"You were exceeding the speed limit. May I see your driver's license, registration, and insurance card?" Susan searched in her purse for her wallet and opened it to show the license, but the policewoman said, "Could you take it out for me, please?" Susan struggled to get it out of the tight-fitting sleeve. "I see you have South Dakota tags. You're a long way from home. Are you visiting for the summer?"

"Yes, but I'm thinking about staying, if I can."

"Can't find a better place than Hobbs," replied the young officer affably. Susan wasn't used to such friendliness from the police. In South Dakota, they were mostly humorless. "Do you have your registration and insurance card?" Susan found the documents in the glove compartment and handed them to her. She held her breath while the woman looked them over. "Your insurance card is expired."

"I have the new one at home. I just forgot to put it in the car." It was a lie. Susan hadn't been able to afford the insurance, so she'd ignored the bill that arrived in the mail before she'd left. She held her breath.

"We can't check out-of-state insurance. Please make sure you put it in your vehicle as soon as possible," the officer said politely.

"I will, officer. I promise."

"I clocked you at six miles over the speed limit. You were weaving a little, so I thought I'd check that everything's all right."

She shined her light into Susan's eyes, which made her blink and flinch away. Did she suspect she was drunk? She hadn't had a drop of alcohol all night. "Yes, I'm fine, thank you," she managed to say. Finally, the light moved away, and Susan breathed a sigh of relief.

"Where are you heading?"

"Here. I live here, at the rectory."

"Oh!" said the young woman as if she'd been pinched. No doubt, she was disturbed to learn she had stopped a member of the clergy. "Ma'am, I won't write you up this time. Please observe the speed limits in the future. Have a good evening." She touched the brim of her hat and handed back the documents before heading to her car.

Susan drove at a crawl through the church parking lot toward the rectory. Shaking, she hurried inside and locked the door. From the window in the stairwell, she could see the police car still parked in the same place.

The blue flashers were off, but the interior lights were on. Susan crept down the hall. Everything was quiet. She guessed that Tom was probably out with his friends.

Inside her apartment, Susan went to the window to draw the shade.

The police car hadn't moved an inch.

34

Lucy looked up to rest her eyes. She'd only expected to approve the church bulletin, not edit it. Susan was supposed to be overseeing the student intern who'd been putting it together, but the text was riddled with typos and grammatical errors. Lucy would have expected a former English teacher to do a better job. When they met again, she would let Susan know her work on the bulletin was unacceptable.

"Mother Lucy, Chief Harrison is here to see you," said Jodi, standing in the doorway. "She says it's important. A police matter."

Lucy was instantly anxious. It wasn't unusual for Brenda to stop in say hello, but she almost never came on official business. "Send her in," said Lucy, closing her laptop.

"Good morning, Lucy." Brenda took off her campaign hat and bent to accept a kiss on the cheek. Lucy could instantly see from her grave expression that something was very wrong.

"What's the matter, Brenda? You don't look happy."

"I thought I should come in person to discuss this issue." Brenda handed her a manila envelope.

"What's this?"

"The documentation. I thought you might like to read it."

"Brenda, please sit down and tell me what's going on."

Brenda took a seat in one of the visitors' chairs. Lucy sat down beside her. "Your friend, Susan Gedney, was stopped last night by one of my patrol officers."

Lucy tried to make sense of what Brenda was saying. She had been with Susan the entire evening and hadn't seen her drink a drop of alcohol. "You didn't stop her for intoxication? I was with her the whole evening. She wasn't drinking."

Brenda shook her head. "No, Vachon didn't report intoxication, but she noted slight weaving, more like Ms. Gedney might be looking at her phone and driving distracted."

Lucy sat back and breathed a sigh of relief.

"In fact, she was barely speeding. Another officer probably would have let it go, but Vachon is new. Unfortunately, in doing her job so conscientiously, she overlooked the most important part."

The detailed introduction was making Lucy impatient. "Brenda, I hate to rush you, but please, get to the point."

"When we stop someone for speeding, we search the database for other moving violations or criminal activity. The officer is supposed to wait for the results of the search before releasing the suspect, but the data was coming from South Dakota, where the record system isn't the fastest. I think Vachon was thrown by the fact that Ms. Gedney is living in your rectory." Brenda turned in her chair. "Lucy, did you know your friend has two DUIs on her record? Her license was temporarily suspended. While she was driving illegally, she fled the scene of an accident. Fortunately, no one was seriously hurt." Brenda exhaled a deep sigh. "I'm sorry to have to tell you this, Lucy, but your friend is a fugitive from justice."

Brenda paused and Lucy was grateful. She was stunned, and it took longer than usual for her mind to absorb the information. How could the woman she'd had on a pedestal for years have fallen so low?

"I'm sorry, Lucy," Brenda repeated. "I thought you'd want to hear this directly from me rather than in a text or a phone call."

"Thank you, Brenda. I appreciate that you came in person."

"I came because I want to know how you'd like me to handle it."

Lucy was surprised to be consulted, but she wasn't sure what to say. She hedged by asking, "How would you usually handle it?"

Brenda looked thoughtful. "Well, we don't have reciprocity with South Dakota's DMV. That means I'm not obligated to report her to the local authorities. Ms. Gedney hasn't been charged in the hit-and-run. They only identified her car because the license plate came up on a video feed. They can't even confirm that she was the driver, only that it was her vehicle. If they want her extradited, they can request it. She's broken no laws in Maine, so I can't arrest her. But I think we need to do something, don't you?" Brenda gazed at Lucy expectantly.

"Yes, of course," Lucy agreed.

Brenda's voice was gentle when she asked, "Did you know she had a drinking problem?"

"She told me about one DUI."

"There could be more violations in other states, but I didn't do a thorough search."

"What happens if you tell the authorities in South Dakota?"

"They may request extradition. In minor cases, where there are no serious injuries or damage, they might decide it's not worth it to send someone out here to bring her in."

"What would be the best outcome?"

"Ideally, she returns to South Dakota and surrenders to the local authorities. She'd lose her license, but if she agrees to go to rehab, they might be lenient."

"She couldn't do her job as a curate in a rural community without being able to drive."

Brenda sighed. "I know. These cases are never easy, but think of all the people who are killed by drunk drivers."

"Believe me. I am thinking about them, but I'm also thinking of the most compassionate way to deal with Susan. Once I found out about her drinking, I insisted she go to AA. She's been attending the meetings as far as I know."

"That's good." Brenda leaned forward and spoke quietly. "Lucy, you and I both know we deal with things differently up here. There is no such thing as 'by the book.' That said, this has the potential to become a serious situation. I think we need to do something about it."

"I know, and I agree. Give me some time to figure it out."

"I will follow your lead on this, Lucy. She's your friend. Meanwhile, I'll identify where to report finding the suspect."

"You won't do anything before telling me?" asked Lucy anxiously.

"Absolutely not." Lucy was never more grateful for Brenda's calm professionalism. "I have to go. Thanks for listening. I'll wait to hear from you."

She put on her hat and nodded to the envelope in Lucy's lap. "Those are the copies of the police reports on the DUIs and the hit and run."

"I'll take a look at them. Thanks for coming over, Brenda."

"Lucy, I came because I trust you to handle it."

As Lucy watched Brenda walk out, she wished she felt worthy of her confidence. She gazed out the window as she considered what to do. Overlooking the fact that Susan was wanted by the police in another state was out of the question. She agreed with Brenda. Susan should return to South Dakota and give herself up to the local authorities. Now, she needed to determine the best way to persuade her.

Lucy tried to go back to editing the church bulletin, but she was too distracted to focus. She thought about how Susan had wisely and compassionately shepherded her through her recovery. She had known exactly which support group Lucy should join. She had cleverly come up with the idea of Lucy taking self-defense lessons so she could master her fear. Now that the roles were reversed, Lucy was confused.

Concentrating on the bulletin was impossible. Lucy got up and went into the hall where her admin sat. "Jodi, I have some things to do. Would you mind checking the bulletin for me?"

Jodi brightened, looking proud to be tasked with something so important. "Sure, Mother Lucy. I'd be happy to."

"You can take it home with you and work on it there. I'll email it to you. Can you have it done by tomorrow afternoon?

"Absolutely!" said Jodi, packing up her desk.

On the way back to her office, Lucy looked out the window. Susan's beat-up Chevy was in the parking lot. The Mt. Rushmore plates stuck out even among all the summer visitors' plates. Lucy wondered if the South Dakota police would treat Susan kindly. She wished she'd asked Brenda the penalty for fleeing the scene of an accident. She dearly hoped jail time wasn't involved. Maybe they'd be more lenient because she was clergy. Lucy hated to think that way, but Susan needed compassion, not punishment.

Lucy trudged up the stairs to the residential floor above the rectory offices. She passed an open window where a warm breeze wafted in from outside. It was such a nice day, yet Susan was sitting alone in her room.

Lucy knocked softly on the door. She listened carefully, but she couldn't hear any sounds from inside. She waited a moment and knocked again. Still no response. She got halfway down the stairs when she decided that this was a problem that couldn't wait. She went back and knocked harder. This time, the door opened a crack.

"Lucy," said Susan, looking out from a completely dark room. "I'm sorry. I guess I fell asleep." Susan brushed her blond hair out of her face. She looked pale without makeup and old.

"I'm sorry to disturb you, Susan, but we need to talk. Please come down to my office after you get yourself together."

"Sure, Lucy," she said, but she looked reluctant. "I'll be down in a few minutes."

As Lucy walked downstairs, she wished that Susan had invited her in. She'd rather not discuss this subject in the coldness of her office. Another setting might invoke the warm feelings of their friendship to help convey her concern and compassion for Susan's situation.

Lucy was watching the bumper-to-bumper traffic on Route 1 when Susan finally appeared, wearing cropped pants and an attractive top. She'd styled her hair and put on a little makeup. It heartened Lucy to see that she cared enough about her appearance to make the effort.

"What's the matter, Lucy?" asked Susan as she sat down.

"The police chief was here today."

Susan's face instantly stiffened. "I wasn't drinking."

"I know you weren't. I was with you," said Lucy in a kind tone. "Of course, I don't know if you have a secret stash, but I trust you."

Susan's anguish was obvious. "I don't know why you would trust me. I don't really seem like I deserve it, do I?"

"Why didn't you tell me you were in so much trouble? Why didn't you trust *me*?"

"I was afraid you'd report me. You have big responsibilities here in Hobbs. You need to do the right thing."

"I do, but you need to do the right thing too."

Susan sighed and nodded. "I know, but I can't."

"Oh, Susan, what happened to you? How did you become an alcoholic?"

"I always drank too much, but I was better at keeping it under control in the beginning. After I left you, I knew it was a mistake, but I couldn't keep sinning with you. You didn't believe we needed to be celibate, but I did. I couldn't ask that of you. I had to be away from you because I didn't trust myself not to fall into bed with you. I wanted you so much. I still want you even though it's a sin."

"That's your old Catholic guilt talking. God made us this way. God doesn't make mistakes."

"You know how long it took me to stand for ordination. Part of me believes, a deep part of me from my Catholic past, that women shouldn't be ordained. Did you read about that woman who renounced her priesthood because she believed it was invalid?"

"Yes, I remember reading something about that."

"Well, I thought of doing it too."

"Susan, if you feel that strongly, maybe you should. But when I first met you, all you wanted was to be ordained."

"Why did I ever believe that's what I wanted?" asked Susan, staring at a point over Lucy's head. "Why did I ever think it was all right to make love to another woman? I did it in the convent too, but then I could go to confession, and the sin would be gone. Just like that." Susan sliced the air with her hand.

"Susan, have you been drinking?"

Susan nodded. "I had a bottle of wine left, so I drank it. It went right to my head."

"You should call your sponsor."

"I know, but I don't want to." Susan gazed listlessly at the floor.

"You desperately need counseling, but first, you need to deal with your drinking problem, so you can think straight."

"Whatever you say, Lucy. I'll do whatever you say."

Lucy wrestled with her frustration. She needed Susan to be invested in her recovery, not go along because it was the path of least resistance. "We could try to get you into a rehab facility."

"I was fired by my church. I have no insurance."

"We could do an emergency request to get you on Medicaid."

"Lucy, why do you care?"

"Because I love you, Susan."

"If you loved me, you'd take me back. I can change, Lucy. I really can."

"I don't love you in that way, Susan, but I do love you as a friend." Lucy wanted to add that she also loved her as one of God's children who had lost her way, but this wasn't the moment for a sermon.

Susan gave her a mournful look. "So, there's no hope for us?"

Lucy shook her head. "We had our time, but it's over. I'm grateful for all you did for me, for showing me the profound love God has for me and helping me heal. You were my friend when I really needed a friend. Now, please let me do the same for you."

"Whatever you say, Lucy."

Lucy recognized the belligerence that came from the alcohol talking instead of Susan. "You know it doesn't work that way. You need to want help. If you do, I'll do whatever I can to support you."

"Okay," said Susan and covered her face with her hands.

"I'm going to call Liz Stolz for a referral to rehab. She has connections I don't."

Raking her fingers through her hair, Susan nodded her agreement.

35

In the silence of the car, the ring of a phone startled Liz. Lucy searched in her bag, and Liz couldn't help but see its interior, which was barely controlled chaos. "How do you find anything in there?" she asked, drawing an impatient look from her passenger.

"Pay attention to the road," Lucy ordered with a firm look. She finally located the phone and answered the call. "Hello, sweetie. Did you enjoy Cherie's gumbo?" Obviously, the caller was her daughter. When Liz had told her PA that they'd gotten a placement for Susan and were heading upstate, Cherie had invited Emily for dinner.

Out of respect for Lucy's privacy, Liz tuned out the conversation with her daughter. She stifled the impulse to yawn because she didn't want Lucy to know how tired she was. She'd been up since five as usual. Lucy, who liked to walk on the beach before sunrise, had probably been awake even earlier. After such a long day, Liz was glad to be heading home.

They'd been extremely lucky to find a bed for Lucy's friend at the Rise Again rehab facility. Usually, there was a long waiting list, but since the pandemic, people were fearful of being in residential facilities. When Liz had called, the director's assistant had agreed to take Susan that day, if they could arrive by five.

Liz glanced into the empty backseat, relieved not to see Susan glaring back at her. On the way up to Augusta, she had been mostly silent. When she wasn't shooting hate darts into the back of Liz's head, she stared out the window at the pine trees along the highway. Liz could understand her hostility. Being exposed in front of a rival was humiliating, but Liz couldn't understand her coldness toward Lucy, who had never been anything but kind to her. Kindness was evidently not what the woman had been looking for.

"Liz, how much longer before we get home?" Lucy asked.

"We're not far now. Less than an hour."

"Yes, sweetie, go to bed if you're tired," Lucy gently instructed Emily. "I'm glad you're home. I love you." She tapped off the phone and returned it to her bag. "Love to Aunt Liz and thank her for driving me," Lucy repeated, conveying her daughter's message.

"Those adoptive parents certainly taught her to be polite."

"For all their faults, I thank God for them. I don't know if I could have done such a good job raising an autistic kid. It must have been quite a challenge."

"She does very well. She processes everything intellectually rather than emotionally. But she's very smart and observant. Give her credit, too." Liz noted the sign showing the distance to Portland, which jived with her estimate of when they would get back to Hobbs.

Lucy reached across the console and patted Liz's thigh. "Thank you for being there for me, my faithful knight."

"You're welcome, my lady," said Liz, glancing over to give her a quick smile.

Lucy's smile in return was weary. "Susan drove all the way from South Dakota, so I guess she thought I'd be there for her too."

"No disrespect, Lucy, but I think she had another agenda. But why would she think you'd still be interested after she dumped you? After you'd just lost your wife?"

"I don't know what she was thinking," Lucy said with a sigh. "I wish I knew."

"I was a little worried you'd fall for her again. She's your type."

"My type? What do you mean?" Liz could feel Lucy's eyes on the side of her face studying her curiously.

"You know. Lanky blondes with blue eyes. Like Erika."

"I never even think of physical types," Lucy said impatiently, "They might resemble one another, but otherwise, Erika and Susan couldn't be more different. Erika could be intense, but she had a wonderful sense of humor...once I figured it out."

"Yeah, Susan is kind of humorless."

"She is not!" said Lucy defensively. "She's in bad shape right now. You'd be sad too if you'd gone through what she has."

She made her own mess, Liz thought. "I'll give you a pass for lacking objectivity because of your past, but I can't figure out how you would be attracted to such a loser."

"Liz, please try to be kind. Sometimes, people show up in our lives for a reason, and Susan was there for me at exactly the right time. If not for her, *I* might be the one heading for detox."

"You're too strong for that."

"You should have seen me. I was a mess when I sang for that ordination. Susan cared enough to stand by me and help me recover."

"She was your fan when you were an opera star. She probably already had the hots for you."

"I'm not sure about that. She was so conflicted about her sexuality. All that Catholic guilt really messed up her head. But her faith was so strong. She was so sure she had a vocation to the priesthood. I was jealous, in a way, of her certainty. I think I adopted it as my own to get through my crisis."

"Are you saying your vocation wasn't a call from God?"

"I'm saying those were the circumstances. When God calls, she usually doesn't ring your cell phone or send you a text message."

"Lucy, I'm sorry for your sake that Susan ended up this way. The person who brings you out always has a special place in your heart. I never forgot Maggie. After forty years, I still wanted her as much as the day she left. Too bad our second shot was a misfire."

Lucy patted Liz's shoulder in sympathy. "You tried."

"Before you knew Susan was an alcoholic, were you tempted to get back together?"

"Not even for a minute," Lucy answered instantly. "I'm with you now. I love you, and I'm in love with you. I'm not looking for other options."

Liz was pleased to hear Lucy's confident declaration. She felt she owed her the same. "I'm not looking for other options either. Despite what everyone thinks, I'm not a player."

Lucy turned and gave her a long hard look. "I knew that, but you like to think you are."

"Is that so? I bet you think you have me all figured out."

"No, not completely. Some things though."

Liz wasn't entirely sure she wanted to hear what Lucy had to say on this subject, but she was curious enough to ask, "Such as?"

"Hmm. Let's see. I think you became a player to protect yourself. Your experience with Maggie really hurt you. You went on the offensive so you could do the leaving instead of the other way around. At first, vengeance made you seduce women and leave them. After a while, it stopped being about punishing Maggie and became a game." Liz didn't want to admit Lucy was right, but she was. "That's why I wouldn't give in to you on the boat last year. I knew you weren't serious."

"My lust was serious."

"So was mine, but that wasn't enough, and I wasn't going to hurt my wife or my best friend that way."

"Some best friend. Now, she can't even be bothered with you."

"She might come around…eventually."

"Okay. You're on to me. What else have you figured out?" Liz was actually reluctant to hear more, but she was flattered that Lucy had given her psyche so much thought.

"I know why you're naughty."

"Naughty? You mean my teasing and lewd jokes?"

"Yes, your bad boy behavior. The obvious reason you were naughty was to get attention. It must have been hard to get your mother's attention with all those noisy brothers. Punishment became a kind of reward. Ironically, the more you used that tactic, the more you felt rejected, so it was an endless loop of rejection and bad behavior." Lucy paused and looked at her curiously. "Liz, you're smart. I'm surprised you haven't figured this out by now."

"Oh, I have. I just don't know how to stop it."

"Yes, you do. You have stopped it…at least with me. You've stopped the lewd remarks and sexual teasing because you realized I want to be involved with an adult woman, not a bad, little boy."

Liz's skin began to crawl. Everything Lucy had said was uncomfortably true. Liz wanted to sink into her seat and disappear.

"You want to hear more?"

"No, I think that's enough. It's pretty humiliating to find out you know all those things about me."

"One more thing, and then I'll leave you alone. I know why you can stop your bad behaviors with me."

"You do?"

"Yes. It's because you trust me to love and accept you, the real you under all the layers you've grown to protect yourself. The competent doctor, the butch player, the skeptical philosopher, and the bad, little boy are just some of them. You trust that I'm not going to reject you the way your mother did. You know I'm not going to throw you away."

"Okay, Lucy, I think I've heard enough now." Liz felt like someone had just ripped off all her clothes and left her naked.

Lucy reached out and touched her shoulder. "It can be painful to hear how accurately someone else can read you."

"How long have you known these things about me?"

"I figured you out pretty fast."

"And you still liked me?"

Lucy's merry laugh was musical. "Liz, I love you! The truth is, I've loved you since the moment you came to my church and invited me to dinner."

"You love everyone."

"I do, but not like I love you."

After that stunning conversation, Liz was grateful for the extended silence. A part of her felt invaded by Lucy's perceptions. Another part was grateful that someone could articulate the things she couldn't even tell herself.

She was startled when Lucy patted her thigh. "Thank you for coming with me. I don't know if I could have made this long trip by myself."

Liz admired how easily Lucy acknowledged her weaknesses, as a statement of fact without apology or self-recrimination. Liz would have stood on her head to prove that she was able to drive to Augusta and back, despite her fatigue. She'd never admit that she wasn't fit for duty. It was how she'd been raised, to get the job done, no matter what. The lesson had been reinforced many times over in her medical training. Unlearning it wasn't going to be easy.

"I'm glad you could find Susan a bed so quickly," Lucy said. "I hope they approve her emergency application for Medicaid. If not, I'll ask the bishop if we can add her to our insurance temporarily as supply clergy."

"What the hell is that?" Liz's mind produced the image of a water spigot dripping people wearing collars.

"They're priests who fill in as needed where local churches are between vicars or rectors," Lucy explained.

"I'm pretty confident she'll get Medicaid," Liz said. "She has no income to speak of. Otherwise, we can sign her up for emergency Obamacare. Between the two of us, I'm sure we can come up with the money to pay the premiums."

"Why would you help her?" Lucy asked. "You were afraid she might take me away from you."

Liz patted Lucy's hand on her thigh. "I'm doing it because you care about her, and I love you."

When Lucy spoke, her voice was thick, and Liz saw she was wiping away tears. "You keep doing that, I'll have to love you even more than I do. I don't know if I can, because I already love you so much!" Lucy searched in her bag. Liz realized she was looking for a tissue.

"In the glove box," she said, pointing. "It's full of napkins from Awakened Brews." Lucy found the napkins and blew her nose loudly.

"Allergies," she murmured.

"Uh-huh."

<h1 style="text-align:center">36</h1>

Lucy leaned against the counter as the slices of cinnamon raisin bread browned in the toaster. She watched Liz lazily scrolling her phone screen while she silently drank her first cup of coffee. Lucy combed through Liz's wild, gray curls affectionately with her fingers, attempting the impossible task of smoothing them down. "You have more cowlicks than anyone I ever met."

"Including two hair whorls. It's supposed to be a sign of genius…or insanity."

"I vote for genius." Lucy kissed the top of Liz's head. "Thank you for staying last night."

"You're welcome." Liz raised her face, and Lucy planted a soft kiss on her lips. "Little did I know that you'd keep me up half the night."

"Making love always relaxes me. Better than sleeping pills," said Lucy. "Don't you sleep better after sex?"

"Yes, but you need so much of it."

"I don't *need it*, Liz," Lucy protested indignantly. "I enjoy it. Having regular sex is good for your health…good for your brain. By the way, you're the one who told me that." Lucy reached around her and gently tweaked her nipple. Liz flinched dramatically. "You love it. Stop complaining."

"I thought we were going for a walk."

"We are going for a walk. I need to say my morning prayers. I always say them as the sun rises. I thank God for the gift of a new day, for my life, for the lives of my daughter and all my friends. I especially thank Her for you."

Liz frowned and took a sip of coffee, her way of saying she'd had enough religion for the moment. "It's hard to believe your friend's been up in that rehab place for a month already. Do you think it took?"

Lucy raised her shoulders. "I guess we'll know soon. I've talked to her a couple of times on the phone, and she sounded more like the Susan I used to know."

"The best statistics put success at only seventy percent."

"Depends on which studies you believe. Some show rehab success as high as eighty percent. It's all about the motivation of the client. Right?" Lucy kissed the top of Liz's head. "You're so grumpy sometimes. Try being optimistic for a change!"

"Why? That's what I have you for."

The toast popped up with a sharp, mechanical noise. Lucy spread it with soft butter and cut it on the diagonal into triangles. "Thanks," Liz murmured when Lucy put the plate in front of her. "My grandmother used to cut my toast that way."

"So did mine," Lucy smiled at the memory of her grandmother, who'd introduced Lucy to this guilty pleasure. It had become Lucy's go-to quick breakfast, but Liz had been feeding her so well that she was developing a little tummy. Now, she kept the bread in the freezer and reserved it for special occasions. Liz seldom stayed the night at the beach house, so having her at the breakfast table qualified as an occasion.

"I wish you'd stay here more often," Lucy said, putting two slices of bread into the toaster.

"I don't like sleeping in a queen-sized bed."

"You built that bed."

"I know. That's what Erika wanted."

"She liked to snuggle. Unlike you, but you're getting better at it."

Liz grunted an acknowledgement of the compliment.

Lucy leaned against the counter while she waited for her toast. "I'm glad the judge in South Dakota sentenced Susan to more rehab instead of throwing her in jail." It had been worth spending all those hours on the phone. Lucy had spoken to Susan's bishop. After listening to Lucy explain the situation, he did the right thing and reinstated Susan's health insurance. Susan's rector didn't want her back at first, but he had to agree that she'd been a diligent, hardworking priest. He promised to consider taking her back.

"I wish I could go with you today," Liz said. "I know how anxious you are. I'm glad Brenda is taking you up there."

"We don't really have much choice," said Lucy. "The state police in South Dakota insisted on a chain of custody. They're meeting Susan in Sioux Falls to take her to the rehab facility. But Brenda could have sent her up with one of her officers. She's a good friend."

"I hope Susan is nicer to you than when we brought her up there. She had some puss on her."

"Liz, I haven't heard that word in forever."

"Showing my age, I guess."

"You worry too much about your age. Eight years isn't that much difference." Lucy's toast popped up. She snatched it out and buttered it. She savored the sweetness as she bit into it. How could something so simple give so much pleasure? She said a little prayer of thanksgiving for the gift of cinnamon-raisin toast.

"Luce, I have a question for you…"

Lucy chewed and gestured with her toast for Liz to continue.

"Do you still have my grandmother's diamond ring?"

Lucy tried not to look surprised at the question. "Of course, I do. I'd never sell it or give it away. I know it's a family heirloom. In fact, I wanted to give it back after Erika had that new engagement ring made, the one with the stone from her mother's ring. I said I thought we ought to return your grandmother's ring, but Erika thought you might be offended."

"While she was alive, I would have been. I'm not an Indian giver."

"There's another old expression I haven't heard in years. And it's racist too. Shame on you, Liz."

"You know what I mean," said Liz, looking contrite. "How am I supposed to keep up with all the political correctness? It changes every day."

"You just pretend you don't know. I bet you're very careful in the office."

"How can I help it? Ginny and Cherie are always on my case."

"Good. I'm glad someone keeps an eye on you. And yes, I still have your grandmother's ring in my jewelry box. Someone in your family getting engaged?"

"Maybe," Liz said with a vague shrug.

Lucy fought the impulse to smile. Even when Liz thought she was being sly, she was so obvious. As Lucy continued to watch her, she realized Liz actually thought she was getting away with it by feigning nonchalance. Who did she think she was kidding?

Lucy popped the last piece of toast into her mouth. "I'll give you the ring when we go upstairs."

When Lucy handed Liz the faded, velvet-covered box, she murmured, "Thank you." She opened it and sighed, probably picturing the same scene Lucy was remembering—poor Erika practically stuttering as she proposed to Lucy in the basement of the Webhanet Playhouse in front of half the town.

The sound of the lid being snapped shut startled Lucy back to the present. Liz tossed the box into her duffle bag with her clothes.

"You should be careful with that ring," warned Lucy. "I'm sure it's valuable."

"Damn right it is. You don't get diamonds of such clarity of that size anymore. My grandfather couldn't afford an engagement ring when he proposed to my grandmother. After he made it big, he gave her that ring. She never wore it. She was a simple woman. She never understood what she was supposed to do with such a fancy ring."

"But it means a lot to you."

"It does. It was hard to give it to Erika to propose to you. All the best gifts hurt a little to give."

"Like the O. Henry story," said Lucy.

"Not quite as ironic."

"No?"

Liz frowned, evidently not understanding. Sometimes, the simplest things went over her head. "We should go for our walk," she said glancing at the time on her phone. "I need to get to the office."

The day was slightly overcast, and they were the only ones on the beach. They headed to the water's edge because it was easier to walk on the packed, damp sand. Usually, Liz's long-legged strides left Lucy breathless, but today, her walking companion moderated her pace. She reached out for Lucy's hand and put it into her pocket with hers. "Tell me when you start praying," she said, "and I'll leave you alone."

"I can pray with you holding my hand. It will make it even more special."

"Doesn't it bother you that I'm not religious?"

"No. I know you are an honest seeker of truth. I can respect that."

"Good," Liz pronounced, "because I can't promise more."

"God loves you. Let Her in. It's not hard."

"I'm not really interested, Lucy, but thank God for me."

"You can thank Her yourself. You don't need me for that."

"I thought it was your job to be an intermediary."

"My job is to preach the Gospel and celebrate the Eucharist but talking to God is something anyone can do. Even you. But first you have to let Her in. I know how hard it was to let down your guard and let me in, to let me love you, the real you, the beautiful, loving, sexy you."

Liz stopped and looked at her. "Keep up this kind of talk, Lucy, and I might have to throw you down in the sand and have my wicked way with you." Lucy could see the exact moment when Liz remembered the rape. "Sorry. I forgot," she murmured.

Lucy squeezed her hand to reassure her. "It's okay, but no sex on the beach. We don't know who might show up."

After Liz left for the office, the house seemed so quiet. Her energy always made the air crackle with excitement. She was an active person, someone who did things, who fixed things, and made things. Even when she was asleep, the atmosphere felt different. When Liz was awake in the dark, Lucy could tell right away. She could hear her mind thinking and planning.

Emily was still asleep upstairs. Her presence never made as much racket as Liz's. Now that Emily had finished her summer papers and symposia, she liked to sleep in. Often, she didn't wake up until ten or later. Lucy reminded herself that young people need more sleep.

Lucy showered and dressed. The weather service had predicted a warm day. The collar would be annoying in the heat, but Lucy put it on to make a statement. She hoped that seeing this visible symbol of their shared priesthood would remind Susan that she had a duty beyond herself. For the same reason, when they'd checked Susan into rehab, Lucy had made sure to tell the clerk that the person she was admitting was the Rev. Susan Gedney, not some broken-down, alcoholic nobody. Lucy scolded herself for the prideful thought. A broken-down alcoholic was as loved by God as any priest. No one was more or less important in God's eyes.

When Lucy came downstairs, Brenda was waiting outside her squad car. She went around to open the passenger door. Like Liz, Brenda was always chivalrous.

"Thanks for driving, Brenda."

"My pleasure. Plus, I get to spend the morning with one of my favorite people."

"Oh, Brenda, you're such a charmer. I love you," said Lucy, standing on tiptoes to kiss her on the cheek before getting into the car.

The police chief tossed her hat on the backseat. "I want to tell you how much I appreciate the way you handled this, Lucy," she said, buckling her seat belt. "You allowed Rev. Gedney to preserve her dignity but also face the consequences of her actions. I hope she appreciates what a good friend you are."

"Susan was there for me when I was going through a hard time. It's the least I can do."

"Not everyone remembers to give back," said Brenda, backing out of the driveway. "Good for you, Lucy, but I wouldn't expect anything less of you."

For most of the ride, Brenda talked about the new deck she and Sam were building at her house. They were planning a big Labor Day party to celebrate its completion.

"I might be in New York that weekend. I have to turn in the next installment of my dissertation."

"Everyone gets Labor Day off, Lucy. Even priests."

Lucy laughed. "Priests are like doctors. We're always on duty. But I think Liz has something special planned for that weekend. There's a Met Opera gala in the park."

"Well, that's different. Maybe we'll change the date."

"Don't do it on my account."

"I was thinking of Liz, but you're important too." Brenda winked in Lucy's direction. Yes, she was a charmer.

While they waited in the lobby for Susan to come down from her room, Lucy clasped her hands together tightly. She wasn't actively praying. It was an old trick from her opera days she'd used before going on stage.

Finally, Susan arrived, pulling her black suitcase behind her. As if in protest, the little wheels squealed as she approached. She gave Lucy's collar a quick glance and touched her own throat. "Lucy," she said shyly. "Thank you for coming to pick me up." She eyed Brenda cautiously. "I see you've brought reinforcements."

"Don't worry. Chief Harrison is a good friend. She's here to support me."

"She's here to make sure I get on that plane to Sioux Falls."

"Yes, that too," Lucy admitted.

"Hello," said Susan, offering her hand. "Thank you for giving me a ride to the airport."

"Glad to be of help to any friend of Lucy's," Brenda said amiably, "but we should go if we're going to make your plane on time. The roads are jammed. The summer people, you know."

When they reached the car, Brenda stowed Susan's luggage in the rear compartment. She opened the back door. "You both can sit in the back if you want. Lucy, I'm sure you would like some time with your friend. It will be a while before you see her again." Brenda's sensitivity made Lucy want to hug her, so she did.

After they settled into the backseat, Lucy reached for Susan's hand. "I'm so proud of you for getting through your rehab."

Susan released her hand and stared at her lap. "I'm so sorry I put you in this awful position. I embarrassed you in front of your friends. They must think I'm horrible."

"They've all had their struggles. They're not judging you."

"I've made a real mess of things. How can you ever forgive me?"

"I forgive you, but you need to forgive yourself. You have a long road back, Susan, but I have faith in you."

"Thank you for everything you did…with the bishop…the judge…my rector."

"I only talked to your rector and the bishop. They did the rest. Your bishop may be too conservative for my tastes, but he seems like a good man."

"I had a long talk with my rector. He's willing to give me another chance."

"What about the vestry?"

"Apparently, they don't know anything about this. The rector was embarrassed, so he explained my absence as family leave for a sick relative."

Lucy raised her brows.

"I know. It's not the best situation. If they find out, I might have to find another church. Either way, I have to find a new job. The school's not taking me back. They have a zero-tolerance policy for substance abuse."

"I'm sure you'll find something. Or you could get a fresh start elsewhere. Maybe you can come back to Maine. We have two priests at St. Margaret's, so we can't hire you, but there are always churches looking for priests."

"But you said there's no hope for us," Susan said with a pained look.

Lucy took a deep breath before she spoke. "Susan, we had our time, and it was beautiful, but it was over a long time ago."

Susan's face fell.

"I'd be happy to welcome you back as my friend. Can't that be enough?"

"I guess it will have to be," said Susan, turning to look out the window.

37

Courtney sat on the balcony deck overlooking the pine forest and savored the quiet. Usually, she couldn't wait for a moment alone. Kaylee was always at her elbow, or someone at school needed her attention. Being completely alone was refreshing but strange.

Kaylee was spending her first weekend with her father in his new apartment. He'd finally gotten a coaching and phys ed job at a high school in Waldo County. Coaching for the football season had already begun, so he was finally drawing a salary. He'd worked out an arrangement to pay the back child support, which meant Courtney could continue looking for a new place to live. For now, the apartment over the doctor's garage was working.

She wished Doug had stayed on the West Coast. The idea that her ex was nearby still made Courtney anxious. He acted so proprietary, especially when Melissa was around. Courtney imagined him extracting information from Kaylee when she spent time with him. Maybe he did, but so what? They were divorced. She wasn't doing anything illegal. She knew it was all in her head, but she felt like he was watching her. When she'd mentioned it to Melissa, she was kind enough not to laugh. "I think you're projecting your feelings of guilt onto him. You're still not comfortable being with a woman, are you?"

It was shocking to hear, but Melissa's assessment was probably right. Courtney still worried that someone at school might find out and cause problems at school. She nudged Melissa away whenever she tried to show affection in public, even something as innocent as a kiss on the cheek. She certainly didn't want any repercussions impacting her daughter, although Kaylee seemed to be adjusting to life in Hobbs better than she was.

From the little deck, Courtney watched Liz Stolz come into the backyard with a beat-up drywall bucket. She pulled on some gloves and began weeding a garden bed. The classical music streaming through a small speaker was pleasant rather than intrusive. A few minutes later, Lucy Bartlett came out of the house with her laptop. She was barefoot, but she wore a large, floppy hat. A redhead that fair would certainly need to be careful of the sun. Courtney couldn't hear what they were saying as they sat together on a bench, but they were obviously deep in conversation about whatever was on the screen. Liz took the laptop and typed rapidly before returning it. Lucy kissed her sweetly on the lips and headed into the house.

When her landlord returned to her weeding, Courtney saw an opportunity to talk to her. She hadn't expected to enjoy the company of a woman old enough to be her mother, but she did. When they talked, Courtney wasn't even aware of an age difference, although she still wanted to call her Dr. Stolz.

Courtney headed out through the back door of the garage into the garden. Liz noticed her approach and sat back on her haunches. "Hey, Courtney. What brings you? Everything all right over there?"

"Yes, it's great."

"That's good. Being a landlord can be a real pain in the ass. That's one reason I never pushed to make that apartment legal. I get enough emergency calls from my friends to fix leaks and fried appliances. I don't need them from a tenant too."

"I appreciate you making an exception for me and Kaylee. I've heard from some of the teachers that I'm not the first stray you've taken in."

Liz laughed. "That's true. I'm glad to help when I can." Liz gestured to a nearby bench. "You're welcome to keep me company as long as you don't mind if I work. I want to get this bed done before dinner."

"No, please, go ahead. I interrupted you."

"You and the redhead." Liz took out her phone and lowered the volume of the music. "You by yourself today?"

"Yes, and I'm not used to so much quiet. Melissa is visiting her sister in New York. Kaylee is with her father."

"It's a shock to be completely alone when you're used to having people around. I had to get used to it again. Fortunately, I enjoy my own company."

"I think I used to like mine. Since I became a mother, I'm almost never alone, so I don't know if I like it or not."

"Yes, that comes with the territory. Then they go to college, and you're stuck with yourself again. Lucy's going through a little empty-nest syndrome now that her daughter went back to school."

"Why doesn't Lucy come out and enjoy this beautiful day?"

"She's a vampire," said Liz with a completely straight face. Courtney couldn't stop herself from bursting into laughter. Liz smiled until she regained her composure. "Really, Lucy needs to stay out of the sun. That's why she walks on the beach before sunrise. Redheads are especially susceptible to skin cancer." Liz gazed in the direction of the house. "And she's on a tight deadline. The first half of her doctoral dissertation is due at the end of the month."

"I admire her for going back to school at her age."

Courtney realized Liz's grunt was actually a chuckle. "I do too. Who goes back for a doctorate in their fifties? It's not like she'll get a raise at her job, but she's been wanting to write this book for a while. She thinks those extra letters after her name will give it more authority."

"It was really hard for me to go back to school as an adult."

"I know what you mean. After I became chief of surgery, I went back for a master's in administration so I could talk to the suits at Yale. At a certain point in your career, you think you know everything. Nothing like being back in school to put you in your place."

"What's Lucy's book about?"

"Sex."

Courtney tried to hide her surprise but just couldn't. "Not really."

Liz put her hand up. "I swear. Ask her. You can bet she'll be out here soon. She's in a real panic today."

"I hate writing," Courtney admitted. "It was the worst part of going back to school."

Courtney watched Liz yanking out the crabgrass. "I'm not distracting you from your work?"

"Not at all," said Liz. "I'm happy to see you outside, enjoying the good weather. Are you comfortable in that little apartment?"

"It's perfect. When Melissa stays, it's a little tight, but it's perfect for now."

The door of the house opened, and Lucy came out into the garden. "Courtney! How wonderful to see you!"

"Hello, Mother Lucy."

"Oh, please. Just call me Lucy. No collar on today," said Lucy, pointing to her throat. "I'm off-duty."

"I bet you're never really off-duty," said Courtney.

Lucy sighed. "Not really. Neither is Liz, but we like to pretend, right?"

"That's right." Liz got up. "I bet you have a question."

"It can wait. Let me visit with Courtney. I hardly ever see her." Lucy took the seat beside her on the bench.

"I've been meaning to bring Kaylee to church more. I think it's important for children to grow up with religion."

"Why?" asked Lucy, her green eyes curious.

Courtney hadn't expected that question. She had to think for a moment. "That's what I was always told, that it's important to give children a moral foundation."

"I never discourage anyone from coming to church," said Lucy, "but a moral foundation should come from the parents. The Church should only reinforce it."

Liz shot Courtney a warning look. "Don't get her started. Lucy has unconventional views about everything."

Lucy moved a little closer to Courtney. "Where's Kaylee today?" Her tone sounded warm and interested rather than intrusive, so Courtney felt compelled to answer her question.

"With her father. Melissa's in New York visiting her sister. The twins are celebrating their birthday."

"So, you're by yourself?" Lucy asked. "Why don't you join us for dinner?" She turned to Liz. "We have enough, don't we?"

Liz rolled her eyes. "Yes, we have plenty. Lucy is cooking, which is always an adventure." Liz's expression told Courtney this was an inside joke that she shouldn't touch.

"Thank you, Lucy. I'd love to."

Liz and Lucy conferred for a moment about her question. Courtney watched her walk back into the house, her bare feet gingerly avoiding the debris on the stone walkway.

"You two are so cute together," Courtney said, inadvertently speaking her thoughts aloud.

"Cute," Liz repeated disdainfully. "Shocking, isn't it? Older women fall in love." Liz made big eyes. "They even have...gasp!...SEX!" She laughed. "I guess that's hard for someone your age to imagine."

Courtney tensed, anxious that she might have offended her landlord and someone so important in town. "I didn't mean it that way."

"Sure, you did. When I was your age, I couldn't imagine it either. But I don't think of myself as old. In my mind, I'm probably younger than you are."

"Really?" asked Courtney, intrigued. "How old do you think you are?"

"Late twenties. Early thirties. Don't ask Lucy how old she thinks I am. She'd probably say, twelve."

Courtney laughed.

"How old do you think you are?" Liz asked, yanking out more crabgrass. She shook the dirt off the roots before she tossed it in the bucket.

"Early thirties," said Courtney after a moment of thought.

"See? We're all cases of arrested development." Liz threw the last batch of weeds she'd dug up into the drywall bucket. "I think I'll call it a day. I'll never get any work done between you and Lucy."

"I should go and let you work. I'm sorry."

"Don't apologize all the time. Women apologize too much. I invited you to stay." Liz picked up the pail. "Well, come on. Let me get you something to drink, and let's see what Lucy is up to."

On the way to the house Liz dumped the weed pail in a compost bin at the corner of the garden. "See those two beds by the fence? If you're still here next year, they're available if you want to plant a garden."

"Thank you. The truth is, I have no idea where I'll be next year. Melissa keeps talking about saving up money to buy a house."

"Is that what you want?" Liz asked, rinsing her hands under the outdoor spigot.

"I don't know. I just went through a divorce. I'm not sure I'm ready to jump into another commitment."

Liz nodded. "I get it. I swore I'd never get married again. But never say never, right? Things change." She glanced in the direction of the house.

"Melissa seems more interested in living together than me. She brought it up. But she seems pretty entrenched over at her mother's. I just don't know if I'm ready to live with someone again. It's enough living with Kaylee."

"Listen to your instincts. You don't have to rush into anything. It's not like I'll pressure you into signing a lease." Liz dried her hands on her shorts, leaving damp handprints running up each leg.

"I really like it here, but I'd feel better if you let me pay you rent."

Liz waved dismissively. "Save your money. I don't need it, and you do. But now, let's go see what my friend is up to. She can wreck my kitchen faster than a nor'easter."

38

August was winding down, and the sun rose a little later each day. It was still dark outside when Melissa stumbled into the sunroom with her coffee. She was surprised to see her mother already sitting there. "Mom! What are you doing up?"

"You've been getting home so late I hardly ever see you," Ruth said, pointing to the chair opposite hers. "Sit down. I want to talk to you."

"Mom, I don't have much time." Melissa glanced at her phone.

"I know, and I don't want you to miss your train, but I want to tell you this before I change my mind."

"Tell me what?" Melissa asked uneasily. She took a sip of coffee to wake herself up enough to listen.

"Jack is retiring next month, and we've decided to take a cruise around the world."

Melissa sat up straight. "Wow! That's a surprise."

Her mother gazed reflectively into the marsh. A thin band of pink light had appeared on the horizon.

"I thought so too, but when you find love at this age, you don't ask too many questions."

"I do. I did a background check on Jack."

"You didn't!" exclaimed her mother indignantly.

"Yes, I did. I don't want my mother hanging out with shady characters."

Ruth rolled her eyes. "Melissa, you worry me sometimes."

Melissa tapped open her phone to see the time. "Mom, I've got to go soon. Is that all you wanted to say?"

"No, I want you to know I'll be gone at least six months, maybe more, if we decide to explore the ports of call. In fact, I'm not really sure when we'll come back."

"Oh," was all Melissa could muster in response.

"I've been thinking about your request to move your friend in here.

You're right, of course, there's so much unused space in the house. If you want her to move in with you while I'm gone, I'm fine with that."

Melissa studied her mother's face. Two months ago, she would have jumped up and kissed her. Now, she didn't know what to say. "Thanks, Mom, that's generous of you, but Courtney moved into an apartment over Dr. Stolz's garage."

Now, it was her mother's turn to look surprised. "Is that what you want?"

"If it's working for her, yes. I only asked you if she could move in because she was desperate. I was only trying to help."

"Watch out for that, Melissa. It's good to look out for your own, but you can't help everyone."

Melissa gulped down the remainder of her coffee. "Mom, I'd really like to stay and talk, but I can't miss this train. Otherwise, I'll have to drive into Boston. Once the summer people leave, I wouldn't mind so much, but this time of year, the traffic is horrific."

"After this weekend, it will calm down a little. The seniors will come for the good deals on rentals and then the leaf peepers will arrive, but there's nothing worse than late August."

Melissa bent to kiss her mother on the cheek. "Thanks for your generosity, Mom. I really do appreciate it."

Melissa flew into the kitchen, where she made another cup of coffee in her travel mug. She grabbed her briefcase from the bench outside the door and raced out to her car. If she hurried, she would just make it. She might have to run from the parking lot to catch the train. She was glad she always wore running shoes for the commute and carried her high heels in a canvas bag in case she was running late.

The light at the end of Gull Island Road was red. "Come on. Come on," Melissa urged. When it changed, she roared into traffic.

Melissa finally relaxed when she saw the crowd on the platform. Fortunately, someone was pulling out of a parking spot near the front. As Melissa hurried up the stairs, she heard a familiar voice call to her, "Don't worry, Melissa. We won't let the train leave without you."

Melissa waved to the redhead standing on the platform. "I'll hold the doors open, if I have to," called Lucy. "Don't worry. I'm stronger than I look!" She raised her arms in a body-builder pose.

"My favorite train companion," Melissa said, trying to catch her breath before bending to give Lucy a hug. "Back to New York?"

"Yes, the second installment of my dissertation is due today. I should have left yesterday, but I was…uh…busy." Her green eyes smiled in a way that indicated the reason was extremely personal.

"How's your book going?"

"I think it's going well, but I'll tell you more after I hear what my advisor has to say."

"Becca says she thinks it's brilliant."

Lucy looked delighted. "Did she really?"

"She told me you're very brave, but you should expect lots of pushback."

"Yes, I'm girding my loins for the fight." Lucy laughed merrily when Melissa glanced at her crotch. "It's invisible armor…not like Mormons wear, and it's not a chastity belt either."

Melissa loved the amazing things that came out of this woman's mouth. You never knew what to expect. Today, her colorful mask warned, "Don't make me use my opera voice."

The train rattled into the station, five minutes late. Melissa breathed a sigh of relief, realizing how close she'd come to missing it. Now that she saw Lucy standing there in her collar, she wondered if the delay had been divine intervention.

They managed to find facing seats. "Our usual spot," Melissa said, reaching down to help Lucy put her bag into the overhead rack.

"I can do it," Lucy protested, lowering the handle into the bag.

"I'm taller," said Melissa. "It's easier for me."

"I'll buy that argument. Thank you." Lucy sat down. "When I traveled, I left it to others to handle my luggage. Sometimes, things disappeared."

"I don't think your clothes will fit me, Lucy."

Lucy laughed. "I didn't mean you'd make off with my bag." She sighed.

"I'm so out of practice. I travel so seldom now. There was a time when I could be ready to go out the door on a minute's notice. Well, not quite. An hour, for sure."

"It must have been exciting to travel all over the world as an opera singer."

"In the beginning, but then the novelty wore off. I loved singing but getting to the venues was exhausting."

"I used to travel a lot for my job. I suppose that since things are opening up again, I'll be doing more of it. My apartment in Boston is so small, I never minded traveling. Now, I'm not so anxious to get away."

"Are you still thinking about moving in with Courtney?"

Melissa shrugged. "Since Courtney moved into the garage apartment, she can manage. The urgency isn't quite the same."

"We had dinner with her the other night. She seems to like it there."

"And that's fine. We get together often enough. I'm glad she found a place. It takes the pressure off me and gives us more time to figure things out."

"Taking the time to figure it out is a good thing."

"Oh, it is, especially because I don't have a good track record with relationships."

Lucy tilted her head as if it would help her hear better. "Why is that?"

"Oh, Lucy, please don't play therapist with me."

"I'm not!" Lucy protested in a righteous voice. "Melissa, I get paid for counseling. We're talking as friends."

This woman had an answer for everything. Melissa eyed her cautiously. "Maybe because I always felt so much pressure to get married, I resist the idea of being tied down to one person."

"When you say pressure to marry, I assume you mean to a man?"

Melissa nodded. "I think my mother has finally accepted it's not going to happen. I am forty-one years old, after all. That's a long time to hold out hope for someone to change."

Lucy shrugged. "I didn't come out until I was in my forties. I dated men until then. People change. Look at Courtney."

"Yes, that bi thing really worries me. I still think bi people can't make up their minds."

"Does she know you feel this way?"

"Yes, I've told her. She's very defensive about it. Why can't she just say she loves women now?"

"Because that's not her truth, or she would say it."

Melissa looked out the window. "You're right, of course. And it's my prejudice. Nothing she's doing." She inhaled deeply and released her breath in a long stream. "I don't think I'm ready for this relationship."

Lucy smiled. "Maybe you're not. And that's okay. The good news is you have time to figure it out."

"Yes, I guess I do. There are so many moving parts to this, and the logistics aren't in our favor. This commute is killing me. Sometimes, I think I should just move back to Boston."

"Do you want to move back to Boston?"

"Not really. I want to see how this turns out."

"Maybe you should be open to other people while you do."

Melissa shook her head. "I'm not really interested, and if I were, I don't have the time." Melissa looked up and saw that Lucy wasn't really buying that reason. "I really care for Courtney. I might even love her. I just don't know yet."

"It's okay not to know. Sometimes uncertainty is the right thing at the right time."

Melissa studied Lucy's kind eyes. "Please don't take offense, but I want to tell you something."

Lucy's auburn brows rose, but she said, "I don't take offense easily. Go ahead."

"I feel really lucky to have older women like you and Liz and the other Hobbs ladies as role models. When I look at you, it makes me think there might be hope for me."

"Of course, there's hope for you, Melissa. You'll find your way. Look at all the wrong turns and about-faces we've made. None of us is where we expected to be when we were your age."

"That's why it's so helpful to talk to you."

"Thank you, and I'm not offended. It's a gift to get old. Not everyone gets the chance." Lucy looked reflective. Melissa wondered if she was thinking of her wife. "It's probably good that we can't see the future."

"You're probably right. But if you could give your younger self advice, what would it be?"

"Buckle up and enjoy the ride," Lucy said without a moment's hesitation.

39

Riding the uptown subway, Lucy tightly gripped the handle of her suitcase as the train lurched out of the station. She'd been anxiously counting down the stops between Penn Station to her destination. At this rate, she'd have to bring her luggage to her 4 PM meeting with Spangler. She'd been foolish to schedule so tightly. What if the delay in New Haven had been longer?

She should have left yesterday. Delaying her departure for another night with her lover had sounded romantic, but now she wondered where her head had been. She thought of the chapter she'd started writing on the brain fog that accompanies falling in love. One of the characteristics was risky behavior. Now, she was proving its real-life effects by racing against time. She wasn't an adolescent who couldn't bear to spend a single night apart from her lover. There had been other nights when she and Liz had slept in their own beds—Liz in her forest retreat, Lucy in the beach house. For some reason, the idea of being separated by hundreds of miles made it different.

Lucy gauged the progress of the train against the time on her phone. She knew exactly how long it took to walk from the station to Spangler's office. If there were no delays, she'd only be about five minutes late, but she decided to call to warn him.

"Don't worry, Lucy. I know you're coming a long way. I have nothing else scheduled today. I'm looking forward to seeing you." He sounded casual, which Lucy hoped meant he was satisfied with the latest submission of her dissertation. That made her a little calmer, especially since he'd only acknowledged her email submission with "Thanks."

She was relieved to see they'd finally repaired the sidewalk on campus as she dragged her bag toward the theology building. Fortunately, most of the time she was on campus, she wore clericals, so the bag wasn't as heavy as it could be. She sighed. She'd be doing this many times over the next couple of years, so she'd better get used to it.

Spangler looked relaxed in a navy polo shirt when she came in. Usually, professors who were ordained wore collars on campus, but it was a Friday before the last official weekend of summer, so why shouldn't he be dressed casually? He was wearing a mask, as they all were now that the delta variant was surging. Liz had given her a stern lecture about it before she left.

Lucy took the printed copy of her chapters out of her bag and put it on the desk.

"Thank you," said Spangler, "but you didn't need to drag all that paper down in your luggage. I could have printed it out if I needed a hard copy."

"I want the submission to be official."

He laughed heartily. "It was official when I got the copy by email. You worry too much, Lucy."

Lucy struck an attentive pose, waiting for feedback. It was still hard to hear criticism of her work. Working with Liz made it a little easier. In the process, Liz also seemed to be learning some tact.

"I'm impressed, Lucy. You're developing your arguments beautifully. So much of practical theology is descriptive and personal, so it often meanders. You've been focusing in on your key ideas like a laser. Your writing has gotten much tighter."

"Thank you. I've had some help with that."

"Oh?" Spangler's eyes instantly clouded with concern. "I'm sure you know, Lucy, that this dissertation has to be your own work. You can't allow others to have too much input."

"Every word of what I've submitted is my own. The help I'm getting is with organization. Here let me show you." Lucy turned on her laptop, navigated to her working files, and turned on "track changes." She handed the laptop across the desk. "This is my original file showing the comments and the suggestions my friend made."

"Is your friend a theologian?" asked Spangler, putting on his glasses.

"No, but I also had my associate rector, Tom Simmons, who has a doctorate in theology read the final version. He gave me some positive feedback. My editor—I guess you'd call her—is a medical doctor."

Spangler leaned on his hand and looked through the file. "This is the consequent, move it down," he said, reading Liz's suggestions aloud: "Needs a citation…Too wordy, condense…You already made this point. Is there really more to say?" He chuckled. "Your friend knows how to mark up papers. Is she a teacher?"

"She was professor of surgery at Yale and visiting professor at NYU for a few years."

Spangler closed Lucy's laptop. "It's not often you find a medical doctor interested in theology."

"She minored in it and philosophy. It was one of the many things she shared with my wife."

"For someone who hated theoretical subjects when you were in divinity school, you certainly gravitate toward intellectual types."

"Yes, I do," said Lucy, frowning. "I don't know what that says about me."

"It probably means you're very smart and need a lot of intellectual stimulation."

"It's funny you would say that. I'm surrounded by geniuses. My father-in-law almost won the Fields Medal in Math. My daughter will probably get her PhD before I do. Erika was a genius and so is Liz Stolz. She's my secret editor, by the way."

"All right, Lucy. I'm satisfied you're not cheating." Spangler handed back her laptop. "I also know you to be an ethical person, but make sure the comments and feedback you get don't substantially change your original work. Editing is fine, but it needs to be your thinking. *You* need to write this paper."

"I understand."

"I don't have much else to say except keep up the good work. You get a gold star on this round." He leaned back in his chair and regarded her with a little frown. "How have you been, Lucy? You look so much happier. I was worried about you. I kept wondering how I could help you with your grief."

Spangler had always been kind whenever they got together, but this was the first time he'd taken an overtly pastoral role. Lucy wondered if she seemed like she needed ministering.

"I was fortunate to have the support of my community. Not only my congregation. All my friends pitched in to help me."

"One in particular?" Spangler asked. "I've noticed your writing has become more optimistic. I know you're writing a book about sex, but somehow, it's become sexier." He laughed a bit nervously. "I don't know how else to put it. I don't want you to think I'm prying, but I noticed you worked really hard on that chapter called, 'Sex and the Single Christian.'"

"I did work harder on that chapter, and I hope you don't think it's self-serving. The event of marriage doesn't guarantee or even measure the depth of commitment. For people in same-sex relationships, marriage wasn't even an option until the church changed its thinking."

"I agree with you, Lucy, but many people won't. Be prepared for a slew of objections in your thesis defense. I recommend focusing on the 'commitment' aspect and not the 'single' part. You could start shoring up that point now and make it a recurring theme. Perhaps a chapter solely devoted to that subject would be good."

"That's a good idea," said Lucy. She was already thinking of how to weave it into what she'd already written, even if it meant a departure from the logic Liz was trying to teach her. "I've recently been accused of being a lateral thinker." Lucy pushed her hands back and forth from her ears.

Spangler laughed. "I've been accused of that myself. In the life of creation and in our own lives, we weave a complex fabric of experience. Straight lines can only be drawn after the fact."

"I remember your lectures on that subject," said Lucy. "They really stuck with me."

"Have you heard anything from the publisher?"

"Yes! I meant to tell you. They're definitely interested and want to see more."

"That's wonderful news. Keep me posted." He got up, signalling he was ready to end the meeting. "I'm sure you have better things to do on this holiday weekend than sit around talking to me. Keep up the good work, Lucy. You're doing great."

As Lucy dragged her bag across the campus to the student residence, she thought about Spangler's concerns. It had never occurred to her that Liz's editing or Tom's comments could be a problem, but so many public figures and top-tier university students had been caught plagiarizing. She was lucky that Spangler had known her since divinity school and trusted her.

After she checked into the dorm, she finally took a long-awaited bathroom break. Just as she sat down, her phone rang. She remembered she'd promised to send Liz a text when she arrived. As much as she loved being in a relationship again, she didn't always appreciate having to account for her whereabouts.

Her caller turned out to be Rebecca Morgenstern, asking to move their dinner date to seven thirty. Exhausted by the long train ride, Lucy didn't relish the idea of eating later, but she called her right back.

"I have a new widow here, who needs my attention," Rebecca explained. "Do you mind?"

"Works for me. Same place?"

"Yes. See you later. Thanks for your understanding."

There was never any question. Lucy understood the obligation to give time to someone who desperately needed to talk. She only wished it wasn't today, but that's how it was for clergy or doctors. Maybe that's why she and Liz made a good pair.

Lucy checked her messages. Yes, there was one from Liz: *Well, did you get there?* Liz would be home from work by now or on the boat, so Lucy called instead of texting.

"About time," Liz growled when she answered.

"I'm sorry, sweetie. There was a delay in New Haven, and I was ten minutes late for my appointment with Spangler. I even had to drag my luggage to the meeting." Lucy sat down on the bed and slipped off her shoes.

"You overscheduled, and I let you get away with it because I was selfish. Next time, don't box yourself in like this. Are you being careful? COVID cases are rising in New York."

"Don't worry. I'm always careful."

"Good. Now, get some rest, so we can have phone sex after your dinner date."

Lucy made a loud kissing sound into the phone before ending the call. She pulled out her tab collar, relieved that she wouldn't need it again on this trip.

40

"Food! Thank God! My stomach was growling during the whole per-formance," said Liz, arranging her napkin on her lap as she eyed the salad the waiter had brought. "I was afraid they would throw me out for making so much noise."

"Good thing the concert was outside," said Lucy, "and the chairs were spaced apart."

"Was I really that loud?"

Lucy laughed and shook her head. "Liz, I'm only teasing you. I couldn't hear a thing. Besides, I was listening to the singing."

Liz gazed across the table, trying not to focus on the low neckline of Lucy's new dinner dress, which showed enough cleavage to be suggestive without being immodest. She wore her red hair in a sophisticated upsweep. Her faux diamond earrings and necklace looked real. She could have been one of the glamorous opera stars on the stage. In fact, she'd worried that she'd be recognized in a venue so close to what had once been her artistic home, but in that crowd of Met Opera super-fans, it was inevitable. Some people had turned and pointed in their direction. In response, Lucy had smiled graciously.

"Have I told you how beautiful you are tonight?" Liz asked.

"At least, five times. No, six, I think. But I don't mind hearing it from you. Other people, eh. 'You look beautiful.' So what?"

"Only a beautiful woman can say that."

"You look pretty good yourself. Thanks for getting dressed up for me. Even a skirt!" Lucy patted her chest. "Be still, my heart!"

"It's a special occasion. Finally. Our big date! I hope you don't mind eating so late."

"Liz, please stop worrying. This evening keeps getting more won-derful. I'm used to eating late. When I sang, I could never eat before a performance."

"Neither could Maggie." After Liz realized what she'd said, she raised her eyes from her plate with a guilty look.

Lucy smiled warmly. "It's all right to talk about her, Liz. She was a big part of your life...and mine. I talk about Erika."

"That's different. Erika was my friend, and it wasn't her idea to leave you." Liz stabbed a tomato with her fork. "Maggie fucked a man to get back at me."

Lucy gave her a stern look. "You complain about Maggie holding a grudge. Listen to yourself. Don't drag that emotional baggage into our relationship. It's in the past. I'd much rather talk about the future."

"Uh, oh. Are we going to have 'the talk'...like you had with Erika?"

Lucy made a face. "You two shared way too much. Did she even tell you how I was in bed?"

Liz shook her head. "I asked all the time, but one thing about Erika, she was always discreet about her sexual partners."

"Unlike you, I bet."

Liz raised her shoulders. "I'm reformed now. Remember?"

"Sometimes, I wonder," said Lucy with a skeptical look. "No, we don't need to have that talk. I think you and I understand one another...and my views have changed."

"I guessed that from your chapter on sex before marriage. Did you write it to justify our relationship?"

"Not exactly. Let's just say it nudged my thinking forward. It's lunacy to think people can wait until marriage. It's part of that wrong-headed purity culture that encourages self-loathing and recriminations. Look what a mess it made in Susan's life." Lucy looked up from her plate. "I heard from her yesterday. She's doing well in rehab."

Liz's grunt sounded like she didn't care. In fact, she did, so she expanded on it. "That's good news. I'm glad for her sake it's turning out well."

"Me too," said Lucy. "What else do you have planned for this evening?"

"You have to ask?"

Lucy rolled her eyes. "I mean besides *that*."

"I thought we'd have a romantic after-dinner drink in the lounge of the Plaza."

"You're really going all out tonight."

"I'm trying to recreate the special evening we missed in June."

"It still surprises me that you're such a romantic."

"Oh, come on, Lucy. We've been playing knight and lady for years. You knew."

"Of course, I knew. I see you, Liz." Lucy put down her fork and leaned on her hand. "Does it still bother you that I can read you so well?"

Liz shook her head. "Not anymore. Now, I find it sexy."

"Sexy? Really?" Liz's eyes widened as she felt Lucy's bare foot running up her leg. "How about having my priest's hands on you?"

"I don't know about your hands, but your foot is really turning me on."

The waiters removed their salad plates and the plates of the tasting menu arrived in quick succession. The tiny food sculptures were imaginatively constructed. Some of the exotic ingredients were perched so strategically they seemed to be held up by air. Their bright colors delighted the eye. The combination of unusual tastes confounded all expectations.

"I hope there are more of these tiny plates," Liz grumbled. "Or we're going out for pizza after this."

"You're kidding, I hope," said Lucy, looking up from her plate. "This is a wonderful adventure. I've been wanting to eat here since forever!"

Liz smiled. "Of course, I'm kidding. Sometimes, I miss a more sophisticated lifestyle, but given the choice, I'd choose Hobbs any day."

"But can we come to New York sometimes?" asked Lucy with an endearing pout. "I really miss it too."

"Maybe we can come here for our..." Liz caught herself just in time, but she saw Lucy's brow arch slightly.

"All right, Liz. You look like you're ready to explode. What are you up to?"

"Can you wait until we get back to the Plaza? Please."

The foot caressed her leg. "I guess so. I don't want to spoil anything you planned."

"Oh, shit, Lucy! Now, I have to tell you."

"No, you don't. I can wait." Lucy's eyes were at odds with her words. "I love you." The warmth in her smile made Liz melt like candle wax.

"All right, that's it! I have to tell you." Liz unzipped her bag and put the ring box in the middle of the table. The waiter approached, but she waved him away. "I'm giving it back. I had it cleaned and resized to fit you better. As you can see, I also got a new box." She looked up and saw that Lucy's eyes had filled.

"But I liked the old box because it was your grandmother's."

"You can have it back if it means that much to you," Liz said. "I didn't throw it away…for sentimental reasons."

Lucy stared at the box. "Liz, are you sure about this?"

Liz took out the ring. She reached across the table for Lucy's hand and slipped the ring on her finger.

"Perfect fit." Lucy leaned her chin on her clasped hands. "Well?"

"Well, what?"

"Well, say something!" Lucy released an exasperated sigh. "Since you're tongue-tied, I'll do the asking. Will you marry me?"

"Every day for the rest of my life," Liz declared with great enthusiasm.

"And you promise to give back the old box?"

"I do."

"Save that for the ceremony," said Lucy. "I think we should have Tom marry us, don't you?"

"I agree."

Liz didn't see or taste the plates that came after that or the amazing desserts that followed. Her eyes were busy watching Lucy's red lips as she ate. They exchanged tender looks. Words were unnecessary.

Lucy leaned into Liz's body as they took the taxi up to Central Park. Liz gazed up at the city lights from the taxi window. Everything here was so bright compared to Maine at night.

"Liz?" asked Lucy with a pleading look as they walked into the hotel. "I don't want to deviate from your script, but do you mind if we skip that after-dinner drink?"

Liz took her arm and pulled her close. "Sure, Luce. Are you tired?"

"A little, but you know that's not why."

In the elevator, Lucy took Liz's hand. "I'm blessing you," she whispered. "You don't mind?"

Liz shook her head.

Finally, the elevator stopped on their floor. Liz opened the door to their room, delighted to see it was exactly what she'd planned—a suite overlooking Central Park with a perfect view of the New York skyline.

She kissed the nape of Lucy's neck before unzipping her dress. She took off her jacket and carefully hung it in the closet. "We're so neat," she observed as Lucy hung up her dress.

"I really like this dress, and I know you. You're like Erika, obsessively neat."

Lucy slipped off her lace bra and panties and slid under the sheets. Liz could feel her eyes watching as she took off her blouse and hung it next to the jacket. She searched through the closet for a skirt hanger.

"I love premium hotels. They always have skirt hangers."

Lucy leaned up on her elbow. "Keep going. I'm enjoying this."

Finally, Liz slid into bed beside her.

"Hold me," said Lucy. "Hold me tight!"

When Liz took her in her arms, she realized she was trembling. "Oh, Lucy, what's the matter?"

"Don't leave me!"

"I'm not going anywhere."

"You can't promise that. You're a doctor. You know there are no guarantees."

"There are never guarantees, but Lucy, you've got to have faith!"

"Oh, what irony! The lost sheep tells the pastor to have faith!" Lucy gathered her closer. "Let's make love. We'll both feel better."

Their lovemaking was not the cataclysmic reunion that Liz had imagined. It was a gentle dance, so tender and sweet that after her climax, Liz found herself weeping into Lucy's breasts.

"Shh," Lucy soothed, stroking her hair. "I've got you." Liz felt her warm hand resting gently on the back of her neck. The slight pressure was comforting.

When Liz felt calmer, she sat up. She nudged the tears off her face with her shoulders. "The view of the city is amazing, isn't it?"

"Yes, it is, but the stars are brighter in Acadia."

"There's nothing like the stars in Maine."

Lucy lifted herself over Liz's thigh and sat between her legs. Liz held her in her arms, inhaling her scent and enjoying the feel of her bare skin against her naked chest. "Can we come back to New York for our honeymoon?"

"If you like," Lucy said. "Maybe we need to establish some new traditions."

"But not forget the old ones."

"We won't." Lucy gently stroked Liz's forearm, making the hair rise. "They're part of us now."

Also by Elena Graf

The Hobbs Series

HIGH OCTOBER

Liz Stolz and Maggie Fitzgerald were college roommates until Maggie confessed their affair to her parents. When Maggie breaks her leg in a summer stock stage accident, she lands in Dr. Stolz's office. Is forty years too long to wait for the one you love?

THE MORE THE MERRIER

Maggie and Liz's plans of sitting by the fire, drinking mulled wine, and watching old Christmas movies get scuttled by surprise visits from friends and family.

THIS IS MY BODY

Professor Erika Bultmann, a confirmed agnostic, is fascinated by Mother Lucy, the new rector of the Episcopal Church, especially when she discovers Lucille Bartlett was a rising opera star before mysteriously disappearing from the stage.

LOVE IN THE TIME OF CORONA

Police Chief Brenda Harrison shows an interest in Liz's biracial PA, but first Cherie needs to get past her loathing for all law enforcement since a state trooper shot and killed her sister.

THIRSTY THURSDAYS

Liz Stolz initiates Thirsty Thursdays, a weekly cocktail party on her deck, so her friends can socialize safely during the pandemic. Pretentious, overbearing Olivia Enright pursues Liz's friend, architect Sam McKinnon, and tries to push her way into the tight-knit group.

THE DARK WINTER

Erika hires Sam to build a sound-proof practice room for Lucy. Fortunately, the early Christmas gift is ready before tragedy strikes. As the women of Hobbs pull together to help a beloved friend deal with her loss, the dark winter brings tension and realignment in their small community.

SUMMER PEOPLE

Melissa Morgenstern, a high-profile lawyer from Boston, is spending the summer with her widowed mother. She's doing some trust work for Liz who introduces her to the attractive Courtney Barnes, Hobbs Elementary's new assistant principal. The arrival of Susan, Lucy's ex, complicates her deepening relationship with Liz.

STRANDS

Cherie hears her biological clock ticking and would like to start a family. When a shocking tragedy creates an opportunity for her and Brenda to become parents, their friends need to step up to make it happen.

THE RECTOR'S WEDDING

The sudden opportunity for Lucy to return to her singing career throws everything in her life into doubt—her vocation as a priest, her settled life in Hobbs, even her upcoming marriage to the woman she loves.

THE VANISHING BRIDGE

Rev. Susan Gedney tries to rebuild trust after her humiliating exit from Hobbs. Bobbie Lantry always needs to rush away to take care of mysterious elderly woman. They need to share their secrets, but do they dare?

Passing Rites Series

THE IMPERATIVE OF DESIRE

A coming-of-age story that takes a brilliant aristocratic woman from La Belle Époque through a world war, a revolution that outlawed the German nobility, and the roaring twenties to the decadent demimonde of Weimar Berlin.

OCCASIONS OF SIN

For seven centuries, the German convent of Obberoth has been hiding the nuns' secrets—forbidden passions, scandalous manuscripts locked away, a ruined medical career, and perhaps even a murder.

LIES OF OMISSION

In 1938, the Nazis are imposing their doctrine of "racial hygiene" on hospitals and universities. Margarethe von Stahle has always avoided politics, but now she must decide whether to remain on the sidelines or act on her convictions.

ACTS OF CONTRITION

After the fall of Berlin, Margarethe is brutally assaulted by occupying Russian soldiers. Her former protégée, Sarah Weber, returns to Berlin with the American Army and tries to heal her mentor's physical and psychological wounds.

About the Author

Elena Graf has published four historical novels set in twentieth-century Europe. Two of the titles in the Passing Rites series have won Golden Crown Literary Society and Rainbow awards for best historical fiction. In addition to her historical series, the author has written a series of contemporary novels set in Maine. She pursued a Ph.D. in philosophy but ended up in the "accidental profession" of publishing, where she worked for almost four decades. She lives in coastal Maine.

Find out about events and new books at her website, elenagraf.com. You can write to Elena at elena.m.graf@gmail.com. Or find her on Facebook.

Elena is a member of iReadIndies, a collective of self-published independent authors of Sapphic literature. Please visit our website at iReadIndies.com for more information and to find links to the books published by our authors.